Phillipa

Robert Hilliard

ISBN: 0984248919
IBSN-13: 9780984248919

Pubished by
PARLANCE
P.O Box 391114
Cambridge, MA 02139

For my son, Mark, who brings history and its meanings
accurately to life
&
For my daughter, Mara, who finds a voice for those who
oppressors would keep silent

As nightfall does not all come at once, neither does oppression. In both instances there is a twilight when everything remains seemingly unchanged. And it is in such twilight that we all must be most aware of change in the air—however slight— lest we become unwitting victims of the darkness.

–U.S. Supreme Court Justice William O. Douglas

Chapter I

Phillipa Kohn was born in Munich, Germany, in 1910. She was born of a cultured, well to-do family. Her grandfather Philip, on her mother's side, had been a Rabbi and this was often noted at the dinner table when she was a young girl to compensate for the fact that her father was a stockbroker and occasionally, as stockbrokers sometimes do, did not fully display the ethics toward other people that one might expect in a family that boasted a Rabbi among its past generation.

Phillipa, to maintain the tradition of culture (actually, there was no evidence that there had ever been a writer, an artist, an educator or a statesman in the immediate Kohn lineage—or even more than one Rabbi) was sent to the best private schools to study and learn what some called the important cultural things in life. Dance, music, art, drama, literature and, later, how to choose and wear the best clothes, how to entertain at social gatherings, how to attract and, in the course of logical events (providing she had learned her lessons well), how to rebuff young men.

When she was quite young she learned what was meant by poise and character. This attribute was acquired, in part, through a growing awareness of things other than those learned in a book or in her immediate physical surroundings. Her house was a large one, to the south of Munich proper on the road to Landsberg, surrounded by similar homes with flowing lawns, white concrete driveways and tall green hedges. Later, when she was a woman, she would especially remember the hedges. Within their sanctity she had grown up under her mother's expert tutelage.

"You must remember, my dear," Anna Kohn would say, "the great difference between the cultured class and . . ." hesitating, not daring to touch the word fully with her lips ". . . the rabble." Phillipa felt a warmth from the immaculate cleanliness (her mother often used the word Godliness) of the green-bushed temple that was distinct from the ugly common outside.

Until she reached the age of five her mother alone taught her. Not that her mother was formally well-educated or informally well-learned. But she aspired to be, and by virtue of her standing in the social community as the wife of a successful and well-do-do stockbroker, she sometimes felt she was. She imparted to Phillipa her knowledge, knowledge primarily based on pride: "Always hold your head high, always proud. You are my daughter and you are better than all other daughters. You must never let yourself be like the others, but you must be above them."

Phillipa accepted the words, though she did not quite know what they meant. "How, Mommy? I will do what you say, Mommy. How do I do it?" Anna Kohn was not quite sure, herself. In her own mind it had to do with an aloofness, a bearing that kept her apart, a feeling that put her above others. It was an avoidance of the commonplace, it was an avoidance of the emotions of the commonplace. She tried to put it into words for her daughter.

"When you see other people do something, you must not necessarily do what they do, but you must stand apart

and do differently, do better; when other people say something, you must not repeat their words, but have words of
your own, more important words, different words; when
other people feel something, when they laugh or they
cry, you must not laugh or cry just because they do." She
thought a moment, trying to find the sum of advice: "above
all, you must not be common or ordinary, you must not
show weakness."

"I can't fight like Aaron across the street does. I tried but
I can't. Does that mean I'm weak, Mommy?"

Anna laughed, then put the laugh aside. It was a serious
matter. It was not a time for childish truth. "Not that kind
of weakness. You are better than anyone else, and you must
always show you are better. You must never let people see you
do anything that seems like weakness. For example, you must
never be sad over what happens to other people."

"Like when Kurt broke his arm jumping over the
hedge?"

It seemed a bit cruel, even to Anna, but the point was
clear and waiting to be made. "Yes, like when Kurt broke his
arm. You must be polite and tell him you are sorry, but you
must not be sad. It is not your trouble, it is his."

"I was sad when he cried. He hurt himself. I wanted to
cry. Can I not even cry, Mommy?"

"No, Phillipa. Never. Never cry. That is the greatest
weakness of all. No matter what happens to other people—or
even to yourself—never cry. It is the greatest show of
weakness."

And so, at this early age, Phillipa learned the meaning
of sympathy; rather, she learned what it meant not to have
sympathy. Sympathy was a weakness, her mother taught her.
"This is a hard life, Phillipa. There are too many people who
take away your joy because they need you. Other people are
not important. Only you."

Phillipa could not, at the age of five, fully understand, and this became the core of her training: Precisely, the lack of understanding. Phillipa turned six and Anna was faced with a decision, to send Phillipa to the common school or to the best private school. It was a matter of pride to rule out the first alternative immediately. It was unthinkable. Yet, to send Phillipa away to a private school would remove her at too early an age from maternal influence. A private tutor, officially licensed, was hired. Actually, Anna did not care too much whether Phillipa learned either the things of knowledge or the knowledge of things. But, first, a tutor was fashionable, and, second, a tutor was important to correlate the learning that inevitably must be taught, with an independence and a poise dictated by Anna Kohn that would not come from a school of public learning. It did not matter that, in these years of World War I, Germany had perhaps the finest school system in the world. It did not matter that there was a great and profound independence of culture—perhaps not the culture that much of the rest of the world appreciated ("Verfluchte English," Anna often commented), but a strong one, nevertheless.

The tutor, Heinrich Lippo, was a Frenchman turned German. (His given name had been Henri.) He was, of course, Jewish. Anna considered this a required filial obligation. Lippo was sensitive about his French background and training; soft, indolent, decadent, filthy, he called France. "It is surprising that a man of my strength and capability could have remained in that place"—he avoided the word "France" whenever he could—"as long as I did. This is the country in which I belong."

His lessons were authoritarian, dealing with authoritarian subjects. Phillipa learned the dates of 'Karl der Grosse" (tutor Lippo rejected the appellation Charlemagne as much too Gaelic), Henry the Third, Frederick Barbarossa, Friedrich der Grosse, the Russian czars of the 18th and 19th centuries, the confederation of Metternich (Lippo admired his imperious organization), the Franco-Prussian War (Lippo, a boy of five at the time, embellished with each telling his stories of the invasion of Parts, of the weakness and fear of the cowardly French and the bravery and strength of the Prussians), Bismarck and, especially, of the brave German fight in the war of 1914 in the continuing battle against the forces of evil and subjugation.

Most of all, Phillipa learned about the great figures themselves. Lippo delighted in the strength and cruelty of Henry III, and told time and again of the rage Metternich felt at the organizations for "democracy" that called upon Lafayette for inspiration. "A strong man, Metternich. Did he feel sorry for these sniveling little people? Did he compromise? Did he degrade himself by even bothering to speak with them? Of course not. He ignored them. He simply passed a law making illegal any recognition of the peoples' petitions. A smart man. A strong man. A wise man. The people—he laughed at them. He was above the people." Then, a little tenderly, not out of love, but out of respect for the aptitude of his pupil, he would say: "Like we are above the people, my dear Phillipa. Like the great Frederick, so we must be great." Truth to tell, he would look about the room first, reluctant for anyone but Phillipa to hear his words. Not that he didn't believe his words, but it was, after all, a bit embarrassing. He was still only a schoolmaster. His life-long ambition to be a politician or a military man had not yet seen fruition. At the age of 50 he began to feel an acute need for his voice to resound, even in the empty rooms of the Kohn house.

In the closing days of the war, in 1918, he got his chance. He had been tutor to Phillipa for two years when, seeing the war going unhappily, he felt it his duty and his opportunity to do his part.

"There are not many more years left to me," he said. "I must make them worthwhile. I must make my mark before life ends." Because of his age he had not been permitted to take an active part before; indeed, he had not made a great effort to do so. But now, because of the shortage of manpower and his knowledge of French and of France he applied for, received and accepted a commission as Oberst—a Lieutenant in the information services of the German army. He did not delude himself: The war could not last much longer anyway.

He went off proudly, stepping briskly away from the house, through the garden, up the walk, past the gate opening between the large green hedges surrounding the house and yard. Phillipa watched him from the front door, waved to him. He did not turn, did not look back, but continued to march, his head high and proud, as though he were already commanding all the unseen people in front of him. For a moment Phillipa was sad that he did not turn and wave goodbye. Then there was no regret. She remembered his teaching. It did not matter. He was, after all, unimportant. She felt a little annoyed with herself but, knowing why, quickly forgot the feeling. Her head high and proud, she turned on her heel as Lippo had done and walked briskly back into the house. She did not forget him, her teacher for two years; but she did not remember him, either. He remained in the back of her mind like the memory of a useful household appliance. It was to be many years before she would see him again. Had she known how, she might have remembered more of him and thought more about him. As it was, his teaching was accepted, refined, and polished to its highest degree of utilitarianism.

Her education continued during the next few years with several and varied tutors. Those with whom she agreed— and her personality had become, even in these early years, both flexible and independent—she learned from. Those

with whom she disagreed did not remain long in the Kohn
household. Phillipa's friends were few and well-chosen from
the neighborhood, now grown into an enlarged and exclusive suburb of Munich. The families of some of the wealthi-
est manufacturers and businessmen in Bavaria lived there.
Phillipa became one of a little clique, of which she was never
really part. She went to parties, spoke with other children,
occasionally even played with them, though not, of course, in
the street, not gutter games of the poorer children who lived
further in toward the city. She shared no secrets, no problems,
accepted no help from her peers in any childhood difficulties, nor did she offer any, no matter how difficult might be
the situation of any of the other children. The mothers in the
neighborhood admired her and complimented Anna Kohn on
her daughter's fine upbringing. Anna was flattered. Phillipa
was not. She cared neither for praise nor condemnation. She
paid no attention to either. She was independent. The words
that came from other people meant nothing to her. She did
have one close friend, a little girl whose father had begun his
career in the same brokerage office as her father. Herr Perling
had not made as much money, nor had made it as quickly
as had Herr Kohn. However, he had plodded steadily and
had reached a financial status where his savings, a mortgage;
and sufficient borrowing enabled him to obtain a house in
the same street as the Kohns, which he did at the insistence
of his wife. He might have gotten along in fair manner, but
his scale of living, due primarily to the many and expensive
parties Frau Perling felt she had to offer to maintain social
position, put his cost of living high above his income.

His daughter Carol came often to the Kohn house, to sit
and talk with Phillipa. Phillipa mostly listened. Carol had
dreams, of princes and emperors and white horses. She read
many books of fairy tales, and Phillipa, having been taught
to disdain the stories of sentimental fantasy, found Carol's

recitations of these stories both childishly ridiculous and strangely interesting and beckoning. She would not suffer her mother to find a book of fairy tales in the house and, with a seeming disinterested approach, encouraged little Carol to tell her about them. She began to like Carol, against her rationalized judgment. Through the ages of ten and eleven they were inseparable, Carol constantly talking and telling of her thoughts and plans, Phillipa silent, listening, interested, but seemingly unmoved.

Artur Perling, pressed by the inflation that beset Germany in 1921, by the unceasing spending of his wife, and by the vagaries of the stock market found it necessary to recoup his own overspent budget and began to invest in a number of stocks. Unfortunately, having no capital, he used some of his customers' money. It took little time before his dealings were discovered and less time after that for his brokerage firm to be dissolved into bankruptcy. He was forced to give up his home and move his family to the city, where cheap apartments were available. Phillipa had not heard of the reasons for Carol's moving. On the day the moving van pulled up to the Perling's house, she walked over to find out what was happening.

"We're moving," Carol said.

"To a bigger house?," Phillipa suggested. Perhaps the Perlings would be much wealthier now, much more important. She would not mind visiting a richer home than her own, richer people than herself.

"No."

"Oh, to one the same size?" Phillipa didn't care. The hierarchy of relationship would remain the same.

"No."

"Where?"

Carol hesitated. 'To the city. To an apartment. Papa lost his business and we have to move to a smaller place now."

Phillipa heard the words, thought for a moment, but nothing that mattered came to her mind. There was nothing to say. She looked at Carol for another moment. "Oh," she said, turned and walked away.

She had no more close friends after that. During the following years, until she was fourteen, she continued deep into her studies and training. She had grown immeasurably, in dignity and poise. Her dark eyes were large, always sharp and glowing, yet cold and distant, like forbidden gems in the head of a worshipped and feared idol. At fourteen her private tutoring ended and she was entered into an exclusive preparatory school in Munich. Anna worried at first, hoping that Phillipa's adjustment would be satisfactory and annoyed that any adjustment should have to be made. Phillipa liked it. Her adjustment was perfect. So she felt. They were all so young and immature and childish, the other students. She was much more advanced, so far above them, she thought. Even as she walked through the halls from class to class, she walked with her head higher, tilted up more sharply than that of anyone else. It was a good feeling, the obviousness of her superiority. Best of all, she did not have to associate with the other students any longer than she cared to. Anna drove her to school every morning and picked her up every afternoon.

Years afterward Phillipa would think back to her fourteenth summer, when she was given her first real opportunity to apply the lessons of her childhood. Her parents had acquainted her with Munich: with the Opera House, with the front rows of the orchestras at the theatres, with the better movie houses, with the food at the swank restaurants and hotel dining rooms. Of course, she had visited the Rathaus, had studied the paintings at the Old Pinakothek and New Pinakothek museums, had seen the complete collection of the Glyptothek museum, had touched the Propylaen gate on the palace square, had met many artists at the Academy of Fine

Arts and many scholars at the Bavarian Academy of Arts and
Sciences, had attended concerts at the Conservatory of Music,
and had once even visited the Nymphenburg Chateau. But
she had not yet seen the people of the city.

One afternoon in June, as the school semester was ending, her history teacher intrigued the class with stories of
early Munich, of the influx of farmers from Wurtenburg, of
woodsmen from Baden, of technicians from Westphalen,
of miners from Hesse, of merchants from Brandenburg. A
"melting-pot" the teacher called the city. The term amused
the class. To Phillipa it meant a large vat of boiling steel
into which small statues representing people were thrown,
to disappear into a molten state out of which rose the
Bahnhof and the buildings and the stylish hotels. She was
not quite certain what the teacher meant by tenements and
slums. The other students didn't quite understand, either.
These things had never been made part of their visual experience. It might be an enjoyable affair to see some, several
of them thought, like visiting a new museum. Phillipa
and some of her classmates who also lived in fine houses
circled by tall green hedges decided to visit this heretofore
unknown part of Munich. The next afternoon, after classes,
two chauffeured cars drove Phillipa and a dozen of her
schoolmates to the center of Munich. At their insistence
they were permitted to go off on their tour without chaper-
ones. In a holiday mood, they walked into the poorer section
of the city to see for themselves what and who the "rabble"
were.

It was an excitement for them, for what they saw was
indeed new. They passed through streets where there were
no trees and no gardens. No yards and no hedges. Only row
upon row of red brick, packed more and more tightly into
another row of red brick, block upon block. They came finally
to the houses made out of wood and cement, grey, yellow

and black, one against the other, squeezed tightly, bulging as
if each was trying to reach out for a breath of air. Garbaged
streets, once white sidewalks yellowed with neglect, doorways
dark and forbidding even in mid-afternoon, peeling paint,
rusted metal, splintered glass.

Phillipa and her companions studied what they saw as
if it were a motion picture, not reality. Children with dirty
hands and unwashed faces; boys and girls of their own age
with old clothes, ragged and torn, thin faces and bodies,
cheeks hollow and hungry;. men with deep eyes and hard
mouths, careless, slovenly, the world angry with them and
they, in turn, having no vent to their anger but upon each
other and upon themselves; women with unkempt hair and
hanging bosoms and bulging bellies, old, tired, the world
giving them no reason to hold on to youth.

Phillipa looked closely and studied what her mother
called the "rabble."

"Why," Phillipa asked herself, "do these people live in
such filth and unpleasantness when there were nice homes
in the suburbs and pretty clothes in the shops?" She felt a
refinement in her own culture, a strength, a superiority. Her
companions looked at the same things she did. Some of them
saw, some of them didn't. A few paid no attention. Others
pointed fingers and made small jokes. A few hung their heads
and looked the other way, pretending not to see.

Two boys and two girls came down the street. Their
clothes hung loosely. Their thin bodies laughed. Maybe
they had just come from a hidden and dark hallway, someone thought. Or maybe from an apartment with the shades
drawn? Children of fourteen and fifteen who have no play-
grounds and no money and no back yards have to turn to
themselves for amusement. They held hands, walked closely
together, their bodies brushing against each other. Phillipa's
companions stopped and looked at them, some guessing at

what they would have liked to be true, transferring a hidden freedom to their own minds and bodies. The children of the streets stopped.

"What are you looking at?," one called. "Why don't you go back to your nice beds and silk sheets and look at something else?" They laughed.

Phillipa's friends turned, started to walk away. The caller, a tall, thin boy of perhaps fifteen, followed them.

"She looks pretty in that fancy (he made it come out the equivalent of "fawncy") dress," he said, pointing to one of the girls walking near Phillipa. Then, to one of the boys, "But I bet she looks much prettier without it."

Now the laughter was louder as the caller was joined by his friends. What other amusement was there for them? What other way of proving some kind of equality? The visitors from the suburbs hurried on, ashamed for themselves to hear this kind of talk in the streets in the afternoon. They might think such things, even speak of them at a party, or in a house with the doors bolted, or at night. But not on the street in the afternoon.

The taunts of the two boys and two girls continued.

"Rich kids, rich kids. Papa's got a million." They laughed uproariously. Their language turned to the vulgar. They followed the visitors, who tried to make their way hurriedly back to the center of town and to the waiting automobiles.

"You may be rich, we may be poor, but we'd rather have nothing than be silver manure." Then the variation: "We're poor, you're rich, but we know who *our* father is, you sonofabitch." And without pausing, another: "We've got nothing, and we look like our clothes don't fit; you've got money, but you look like a pile of. . . ."

"Shuttup!" One of Phillipa's companions, a good-looking, well-dressed blonde boy of fifteen, stopped, turned and shouted to the tormentors. In an instant a stone flew, hit him in the

face, his nose began to bleed. The others stood dumbfounded
by something they had not experienced before: Violence. They
watched him as he took a clean white handkerchief from his
pocket, wiped the blood. Another stone came on the wings
of laughter and hit him on the shoulder. He looked at his
friends, anguished. They stood helplessly, not knowing how
to help. He was alone. He started to cry. The tormentors
laughed even louder. The insults became stronger. Finally,
one of the boys in Phillipa's group, a husky fellow of sixteen,
stepped forward, asked the antagonists to stop. They laughed
at him. He grabbed one of the tormentors, smaller than himself, began to punch and slap at him. The other boy of the
streets, without hesitation, came to his friend's aid, together
they forced the interloper to the ground, pummeling him. He
looked toward his group. No one made a move to come to his
rescue. He broke loose, ran as more stones began to fly. His
sleeve was torn, his pants and jacket bruised, and he made
an angry effort to keep the slowly forming tears from his
eyes as the torrent of stones and language and laughter grew
heavier. Phillipa's group looked around for sanctuary. There
were no tall green hedges to find safety behind, only dirty
red brick and garbaged gutters. They all began to run, the
boys shouting, the girls crying. All, that is, but Phillipa. She
wanted to run with them, but she couldn't. She was frightened. Her stomach began to tighten into knots. She was hurt,
confused, ready to cry. Only once before in her life did she
remember actually feeling tears. When she was eight years
old, in 1918, her uncle had been killed fighting the English
in France. She hadn't really known her uncle. She felt no
reason to cry. But she unwittingly walked into her mother's
room, saw her mother crying, was confused by the sight, and
tears began to well up in sympathy as she went to her. Her
mother stopped immediately, as though she were ashamed,
and without a word left the room. As soon as her mother had

gone, Phillipa felt abandoned. She felt she had been chastised. It must be, she thought, because she had dared show tears in her eyes. She felt sick to her stomach. At the time she really didn't know why.

Now, at fourteen, as the knots began to tighten and the tears were ready to come, she was consciously aware of the fear of giving in to this feeling. She searched for words to replace emotion. It didn't matter, she decided, if it were the rabble who were laughing and the cultured whose heels and tears scampered quickly down the street. She would not cry; not for one and not for the other: If she ever allowed herself to cry, it would be only for herself. And this, she assured herself, would not happen, for crying was an acknowledgment of weakness, of sickness, of inferiority. Slowly, her head high, her eyes steady and dry, she began to walk after the others. There was still a token of fear, but she forcefully, deliberately held it back. The taunts followed her and a stone struck her in the small of her back. Fear welled up with the hurt and then they both were pushed back. Then they disappeared. They did not reach her face. I'm too strong, too superior, she repeated to herself, over and over, as she studiously took measured and slow steps away from her antagonists. She was overcome with a great calm, a lightness, a relaxation. She smiled. She knew then that never in her life would she be forced to allow herself the weakness of tears.

By the time she was twenty the tall green hedges were no longer a symbol. She didn't need a symbol. "Mama," she would say, "you don't have to tell me any more. I'm grown up now." And she was. She went out often with young men. She had completed normal school in Munich and had spent three years in Vienna at the Academy of Art. She returned neither a painter, a musician, a writer, or an artist. But at a picture gallery she was able to remark, "Only Rembrandt found such delicate values in the reflection of light"; at a concert she could say, "For Tannhauser he is all right, but for the Walkure I would prefer a conductor with more personal depth and feeling"; at a play, "The director did not provide the actors with a sufficient number of personal antagonisms"; at a literary tea, "The plot is good, but the characters are too one-dimensional. The author should read Lessing"; at any place where people gathered, "Thank you, I do enjoy and appreciate the finer things of life."

Phillipa never lacked for companions; in fact, she was in constant demand. On occasion, she found an afternoon or evening in the company of a young man—or woman— enjoyable and exciting. But most of the time she was bored. Most of the time, seeking something more, something else—she wasn't really sure what—she was forced to remove a young gentleman's arm or hand with a blunt and disdainful "no." This in itself did not bore her. She was physically attractive and the contemplation of this was no less pleasing to her than to most young women of twenty. She had developed into physical maturity, one she considered well-met with her emotional and intellectual growth. She was five-feet-six-inches tall, black velvety hair hanging loose, emphasizing within its borders a smooth, clear skin, and waving softly above large dark eyes, full silken cheeks, barely and tactfully rouged lips. Her body tended toward plumpness, but with a roundness that filled clothes without exaggerating them. Her breasts were firm, unshakable even as she walked, and her back curved haughtily upward from well-defined hips. As she contemplated herself and evaluated the mental capacities and emotional strengths to go with her physical attributes, she was bored—and yet in one sense, pleasured—by the thought that she could not find a man (and later she began to think and finally to be certain that she would never find a man) to complement and to serve this perfection.

The hangman of Europe, war; the cat-o-nine tails, hunger
and disease, have impressed upon the people a culture of
short life. When a girl reached the age of twenty-one she was
considered, and understandably so, an old-maid. Philipa's
mother often urged her, sometimes with subtlety, at other
times with argument, toward marriage.

"You're twenty-one," Anna told her. When I was twenty-
one I was already married and had a baby.'"

"I'm not ready to be married, Mama," Phillipa answered.
"I'll marry, perhaps, when I find someone worthwhile. There's
no rush."

"It's not pretty for a girl of twenty-one not to be married," her mother insisted. "People will think there is something wrong with you. Then no one will ever ask you."

Phillipa would jerk her head up straight and her eyes
would flash at the familiar argument. "People are not so important as to worry about what they think. There is only one
person who is important. Myself."

Her mother could not, would not cope with this argument. It was, after all, the desired product of her own
teaching. But teaching and practice were not always easy to
reconcile. She would try again.

"But you go out with so many boys," she continued. "So
many nice boys, clever boys, rich boys. Certainly you can pick
one and get married. At twenty-one you should be married.
You should know one eligible boy, certainly.'"

"One," Phillipa answered deliberately. "I know one. Karl
Remmler. Shall I marry Karl Remmler?," she asked, and her
mouth would curl into a smile and her eyes would relax into
a haughty sparkle.

"He's a Gentile," her mother would reply. "You cannot marry a Gentile, Phillipa." Anna would be upset now,
shouting. "You always mention a Gentile. You cannot marry
a Gentile."

Her point won, Phillipa always found special satisfaction
in following up her advantage over her mother. It made her
maturity more complete. "But you want me to get married,
Mama. And he is the only one I would marry."

The first few times they had this argument Anna would
be near tears; after that she became reconciled to a moment
of shouting, then slowly would turn away, hoping to retain
some measure of grace, knowing she had lost.

"All right, Phillipa, I won't talk to you about it now.
Then don't get married now. Later. We'll talk later."

Phillipa was raised in a partial atmosphere of Judaism.
Not that the Kohn family practiced (or, in fact, had even
read) the tenets of the Torah or could recite the Ten Com-
mandments; but her grandfather *had* been a Rabbi, and this
much they could not forget. The observance of the Holy
Days (if it were convenient) and the adherence to some of the
larger and easier to practice principles of the Hebrew religion
served as a balm to a family conscience that might otherwise
suffer from self-imposed (and self-judged) hypocrisy. Until
Phillipa went to Vienna to study, her friends (particularly her
boy-friends, chosen or approved judiciously by her mother)
were Jewish. In Vienna, and afterwards, her choice of friends
became a part of her own moral decisiveness. At first she felt
that there must be something different about Gentile boys
and this prompted her to meet and go out with them. Perhaps because for the first time the preferences of dating were
her own, she felt there must be a difference.

She had developed a strong self-interpretation of her
own superiority. She began to think that if she were to marry,
she would marry a Gentile. "If nothing else," she insisted to
herself, "they are different."

Chapter II

In 1933, when she was 23 years of age, Phillipa had already decided what the taste of life would be. The few girl friends she had had—she preferred to think of them not really as friends, but as acquaintances—were married. Phillipa looked upon them with none of the envy that was expected from the unmarried European young woman of the early 20th century. She felt too independent to marry, too self-assured, too strong to permit herself to be legally bound over to another—though she had absolutely no fear that there could be any physical or moral restriction for her no matter how tight any legal covenant. She did not dismiss the possibility of marriage; rather, she subordinated it. Twenty-three years was an age of youth, she told herself, and she resolved not to lose any of it. Freedom gave her choice, choice gave her decision, and decision without extenuating circumstances could always be resolved in the best interests of Phillipa.

She liked to amuse herself at parties—not the record-playing, informal, love-making parties of the early Thirties, but the sober, serious, society parties where one went to meet important people, to discuss important things, to drink many cocktails and to resolve the evening with a mixture

of blankness and false competence, knowing that the stamp
of maturity had been there somewhere, but feeling that the
content had, in effect, been equivalent to that received by the
theatre-goer who takes pride in the intention to view art and
then chooses the most insipid musical or awkward farce that
might be enclosed within the potential majesty of the theat-
rical form. Phillipa half-consciously admitted this to herself.

It was with this unspoken expectation of superior sophistication that she went to a party one evening in the summer
of 1933. The hostess had been one of her classmates in Vienna, a girl whom Phillipa had little special feeling for, except
that the frequent parties of Eloena Gloeter enabled Phillipa to
publicly affect a formidable pose of superiority in comparison
to her friend. As she rode in a taxi toward the manor house
built resplendently within the city limits of Munich, Phillipa
compared the positions of Eloena and herself, finding satisfaction that although Eloena had achieved all the things that the
standards of society had designated as desirable for a young
woman—marriage, wealth and prestige—it was Phillipa who
was most envied. Phillipa reasoned: Her training was now
being applied to her own freely sought enjoyment of life;
Eloena's learning was now put to best advantage almost solely
as a hostess to academic personalities. Her husband, Burkhardt Gloeter, was a publisher of textbooks. He had never
attended university; indeed, had never, if the gossips were
correct; even finished gymnasium, his high-school studies.
But he was a clever businessman and by virtue of offering immediate publication to volumes written by young university
teachers who had not yet made the reputations or proper contacts to obtain more prestigious publishers for their works, no
matter how fine they might be, Burkhardt Gloeter had managed in the space of five years to get his name inscribed as co-
author of some twenty of these books. Phillipa did not deny
the value of this wealth and prestige, but she felt that virtue

was far overbalanced by the gross, fat oldness of this man who was much older than Eloena Gloeter. It was this fact, Phillipa believed, that was the cause of Eloena's passion for constant party-giving, and Phillipa often told her as much, that the parties were more excuses to relieve the unromantic boredom of her husband than anything else.

It satisfied Phillipa that Eloena did not disagree with her. Eloena envied Phillipa her independence. Often she despised her for the same reason. Phillipa laughed when she learned this, for she was nevertheless always invited to Eloena's parties. It gave Eloena a feeling of pride to show off Phillipa. Eloena knew that Phillipa was, without doubt, the most attractive of all the women who came to her parties. Not the prettiest, perhaps, nor the most intelligent. But she was more than adequate in both respects and those others who might have once outshone her were married; and, after all, what man attending a party can look as hopefully at a married woman as he could at one who was unmarried?

Phillipa's status was established and assured the moment she entered the book-lined drawing room that served as the central gathering place at these parties. The men brought her cocktails, the women engaged her in conversation in an attempt to keep their escorts away from her, and by virtue of her ability to remain unruffled, unmoved, and by herself, when necessary, Phillipa formed the one gravitational center of the room around which all else rotated. This was not plan as much as habit; this was Phillipa. Ordinarily, after a few hours Phillipa was ready to leave, having achieved all the amusement of pride that she felt she could for that evening. But strangely, this one April evening, she found herself alone. As usual, many of the planetoids she had wrapped about her had, after fruitless attempt, settled for liquid refreshment or a walk in the garden with their original companion of the evening. Some of the women were gathered together in one corner lightening their loneliness with conversation. As she looked about the room she was unwillingly annoyed because of the fairly large group of men and women, many of whom had previously been centered about her, who were now at the far end of the room, in front of the wall bookcases, forming a circle around a man who was speaking. As she made preparations to leave and no one broke from that group to see her to the door, she hesitated.

It is unimportant, she insisted to herself, and yet she could not let it pass. Then, as disinterested as she could make herself, she asked a man sitting morosely with a drink on the edge of his chair, staring into a half-empty whiskey glass, the name of the young speaker who so held the attention of the others.

"Walter Penmann," the man said. She knew no more than she had known a moment before.

"I do not know him," she said and began to walk away.

The drinker looked up, called her back. "You should. He's a young professor at Heidelberg University. A brilliant man. A teacher of ethics. A philosopher. Chairman of the Philosophy Department, I think."

The drinker, one of the satellites unknown to Phillipa except by name, but who, nevertheless, had known the warmth of her smile and the cold of her rejection, twinkled in anticipation of someday seeing her experience the inquietude that he had felt.

"You ought to meet him, Phillipa. A very brilliant man. He'll go far."

Phillipa nodded, began to walk toward the group now engaged in animated discussion.

"An independent man, a strong man," the drinker whispered after her, satisfied that she did not hear this last and smiling in anticipation of hoped-for consequences, that for once he was more prepared for than was she.

As she walked toward the group, Phillipa felt an interest in this man she had never met. Not because he was a teacher or thinker, but because he could apparently hold a group with words alone. Too many others Phillipa had met she categorized as card-trick performers or lurid-story tellers; this man appeared to be, in a way, something like herself. He was himself. She let the words of his name repeat themselves; Walter Penmann. She rationalized her gravitation toward the group.

I'm really not interested,"she told herself, "it is really not important to me, it is just something to do." And yet, as she reached the edge of the crowd, she felt she wanted to know about this man who had momentarily replaced her as the usual center of attention at Eloena Gloeter's parties.

She smiled as she stopped and looked at Walter Penmann. She reflected upon what she felt was a superiority of objective reflection. "Just like a Walter Penmann is supposed to look," she said to herself.

She saw a thin man, not too tall, but whose slenderness gave the effect of added height. She saw his eyes only as two dark spots, hiding—or perhaps only hidden—behind his glasses. His nose was slight, fitting well into his narrow dark face. He had a thin mustache and as Phillipa studied his fasce she could see the beginnings of a black goatee. She estimated his age at about 35. He was no more attractive than many of the men she had known and, she speculated, perhaps a good deal less so. When he spoke his words came slowly, heavily, as if he weighed his verbal thoughts carefully through philosophical analysis into logical solutions. Phillipa thought of the word "cautious" and held on to it for prospective use. Phillipa watched Walter Penmann slowly turn the eyeglasses in his hand and listened to the same rhythmic turning of his words.

"As Croce has put it, it is not only that man has an intuitive grasp of feelings and images, but he must as well have a knowledge of the unique. To have this knowledge—to know what is unique—he must be well-versed in all else in the world."

His ponderousness both attracted and repelled Phillipa. At first she thought to equate these impressions with the word "sloth," but she knew that the use of the word was a rationalization, to assuage her outer misgiving of having walked over to listen to him at all. He was not slothful. He was slow, yet definite. There was no laziness in his ideas. He knew what he wanted to say, and although it took a moment for the words to be conceived and arranged and projected, he said what he wanted to, without equivocation. Although this was not something that she felt she ought to be impressed with, she did acknowledge it as a point in his favor. What she did feel impressive was the attitude of the group toward him. It accepted his words as though they were a gospel of philosophical faith. They questioned, but did not argue. He clarified and reinforced his ideas. He was, Phillipa determined, the molder of the group, the leader, the strong one. She admired this.

She knew that it was her will of personality that had given her her own strength. Although she had no doubts about her superiority of mind, she had never, it seemed, had occasion to use it on the highest level. She had always conquered the inner with the outer. She had never had to go beyond her personality alone. As she listened she found herself, too, caught up in the speaker's words. She, too, seemed to be held by what he was saying. The situation—and she let the thought cross her mind fleetingly that maybe it was Walter Penmann himself—presented a challenge to her. She decided to mold the situation—including the man—as she wished them to be.

Walter Penmann was concluding: ". . . therefore, to be an artist, one must have a sound philosophical and, I insist, a political background."

Almost before he had finished, Phillipa softly but firmly interposed.

"You suggest something universal. Art is made by the individual. That is poor thinking. You contradict yourself."

Walter looked at her, his attention taken from momentary surprise at the challenge to fix itself upon her sharply outlined face, her lips, her dark eyes and hair. Some in the group looked at Phillipa and smiled to themselves, knowingly. They knew what she was about. Others wondered at the rebuking of the presumably incontrovertible. Walter opened his mouth, slowly gathering his words to answer her as a professor corrects a student. Phillipa watched. Then, confidently, at the moment before he spoke: "As Nietzsche tells us," she said, "art is achieved when the will of the strong individual masters its environment and exerts the fullest power."

Walter hurriedly formulated his thoughts to answer this. Ordinarily, he would have had little difficulty, but the unswerving eyes, the almost doll-like unmoving face of the girl stopped him. It dared him, and he saw in her face a challenge that suggested more than an academic discussion. This time he deliberately waited until the girl spoke again.

"A universal art suggests a universal mediocrity. The artist is the most prolific of individuals. Therefore, she"—Phillipa emphasized the word *she*—"must be the most independent and the strongest, within her own personality framework."

Eloena Gloeter, from another part of the room, had seen Phillipa approach the group and had arrived to hear most of her words. She laughed slightly, aloud, as she silently verbalized to herself Phillipa's purpose. She felt sorry for Walter, yet diffused her envy of Phillipa into a personal osmotic inheritance. She accepted the stares of those who turned to censure her laugh, felt a moment of haughty strength with Phillipa, then turned slowly and left.

The balance of interest of the group began to shift from Walter to Phillipa, leaving Walter without the assurance of acceptance. This disturbed him, almost frightened him, for it was now clear to him that this was not a matter of academic argument, but clearly a clash of personalities. He was no longer on his own safe ground. Aware of his own hesitancy, he looked upon the group as potentially hostile observers, waiting for him to prove himself. He could not operate under pressure and, knowing this, searched for a way out. The faster he tried to think, the more difficult it was for his thoughts to coordinate themselves as he wished. He was a thinker, not a man of action. He was a fighter, but with thoughts, not actions.

He waited for the woman—clearly she did not appear as a girl any longer—to speak again, to let her take the lead, to take the attention away from his dilemma. But she remained still, looking at him, directing all eyes to him. He waited, and waited too long as he realized that he had become dependent on her action, that the resolution of his embarrassment was to be decided by her.

"I see, perhaps," he said, "that you are not clear as to the foundations of aesthetic criticism." These were words borrowed from a classroom when he wished to avoid open argument with a student. They were pretentious words and he knew that they were not the right ones for that situation. He tried to turn them into humor. "Perhaps," he said, lowering his voice suggestively, "if you would speak with me alone, I can clarify matters for you." He avoided condescension in his tone, nodded toward the French doors leading into the garden. There was an appropriate amount of laughter and he felt relieved, yet certain that he had handled the situation quite unsatisfactorily.

Phillipa merely smiled, without other visible change
of expression. Several in the group—colleagues of his who
were acquainted with Phillipa—understood his dilemma
and turned away, disappointed. A few, putting themselves in
his position, mumbled that it would indeed be worthwhile
for Fraulein Kohn to have a private audience with him, told
him they would see him later, and casually turned away. The
others broke up into small groups, most trying unobtrusively
to put themselves into a position where they could follow
Walter's and Phillipa's next moves.

Walter and Phillipa were alone. She wished to continue
her advantage, although she wasn't sure why. She suddenly
felt a loathing for this man who gave in so quickly. She had
been certain there would be a struggle. Her success was too
easily won. Yet, he was a man of importance, and she could
not bear to dismiss further possibilities of triumph.

He remained silent.

"Well, let us go into the garden," she said, loudly enough
for all who were deliberately listening to hear. He hesitated,
looked about the room for a moment, then awkwardly put his
hand under her elbow and escorted her through the French
doors. They walked along the edge of the high green hedges.
Eloena, fascinated with the hedges that surrounded Phillipa's
home, had made certain that her husband would provide the
same for her home. It permitted her to compare, in this deco-
rative instance at least, her security with that of Phillipa.

Walter at first tried to talk about art, about philosophy.
Phillipa, by keeping silent, turned the conversation into the
channels of things that meant nothing and took a long time
to say. Phillipa delighted in the small talk because it put
Walter at a further disadvantage. He could not find words
and often substituted ideas for trivia, felt embarrassed, then
had to wait for Phillipa to determine the next line of conversation. He silently chastised himself for depending on her

and at the same time found that it gave him a kind of secure
feeling that he liked. In his youth he had had relatively little
experience with women. Rarely had he gone out with girls.
The girls he had known he considered light, foolish and dull.
From the age of eighteen on he had paid serious, full-time attention to his studies and had decided that he had no time for
women. Only at parties such as the one of that evening did
he meet and talk with women, and he had not yet met any to
make him change his attitude.

As they walked he began to watch Phillipa more closely.
He forgave her now her challenges earlier in the evening.
After all, he told himself, even though her observations on
philosophy were invalid they had been well-chosen and pronounced with certainty. He was struck—no, overwhelmed—
by her force of personality. She was obviously respected by
others for her strength, he thought. He looked at her face and
it appeared to him beautiful—not so much as a human face,
he observed to himself, but as a perfect painting.

By allowing himself to be dependent on Phillipa's choice
of conversation topics, he was able to gradually free himself
to talk of things of unimportance. He found that he could
make some small talk, the banter between people that sometimes passes for thinking that had heretofore eluded him. It
was the presence of this woman that had made the achievement possible. Just as when, as a child, by letting his mother
decide what they would talk about, he had been able to just
talk. Phillipa began to seem to him like an abstract of perfect
beauty, like a concept of his philosophical love of aesthetics
that had achieved the ultimate: human form. He said none
of this to her. He remained as dignified as he could, self-
sufficient even without the overwhelming silence that was
his usual way.

Phillipa was not altogether sure that her victory had been
complete. Because of his reserve, she wondered from time to

time whether indeed he might not all the while simply be
condescending to her, especially in his gradual acceptance of
her deliberately unimportant subjects of conversation. Yet,
she silently insisted, she was sure enough of her own strength
to be convinced it was otherwise. She, of course, gave no hint
to him of her doubts.

When they returned to the house, they found almost
everyone gone. Walter was hesitant, yet almost demanding
in his insistence that he take her home. This pleased Phillipa and she graciously told him that she would be pleased
if he did so. In the taxi he fidgeted, more of his reserve and
deliberateness returning. There was no more small talk. Ner-
vousness, uncertainty with himself, Phillipa thought. Yet, he
seemed preoccupied. She wondered.

Phillipa was annoyed that Walter didn't attempt to kiss
her good night. This was unlike all the other men whom she
had captured for an evening, whom she had used to reinforce
her strength. She had anticipated a request for—and her refusal of—a kiss, a date. She was annoyed and at the same time
vaguely pleased. This gave him an advantage, in this one
thing alone, an equality with her. He did not come begging
as the others often did; that made the challenge greater and
she determined, then, that someday she would make him do.

Walter put his hand tentatively—or was it casually?—on
hers before she closed the door of her house.

"I would like to ask you to go out with me . . . ." He
hesitated.

She felt self-satisfied. She contemplated her refusal. But
before she could answer, he continued.

"But perhaps I shall not." He removed his hand.

Phillipa felt herself beginning to flare inside. Not? Not?
She calmed her inner anger. She took hold of the door, about
to close it. It is not important, she told herself. He was not
important enough to get upset about. Yet, she felt that she

had been insulted. It disturbed her and she knew it. She was now on the defensive. She would have to wait until he spoke.

"This is why I say that," he explained with obvious effort. "Your name is Kohn." He stopped, measuring his words. "That is Jewish? "Your family is Jewish?"

"Why do you ask that?" She had never before let herself be put into such a position. She had rejected any religious affiliation. A minority designation contradicted her feeling of superiority. Now it had been openly proposed to her and she was angered. She waited.

"I know the prejudices . . . let us say habits . . . of many Jewish families. I should like to ask you whether you are very religious."

Phillipa understood now and contained a smile of self-vindication.

"Why?," she asked again.

"It might save some embarrassment, for you or your family, before I ask you to go out with me. You see, I am a Gentile."

In that moment, Phillipa made up her mind. She had been attracted to him as an object of conquest partly because he had seemed different. The reason for the attraction was now justified. She smiled, her head a bit higher, her voice a bit more commanding.

"I shall be very pleased to go out with you," she said.

Chapter III

Walter spent that summer in Munich. He had come to do some research into Bavarian political philosophy, especially into the history of what had been a small self-proclaimed patriotic society that grew into the newly elected ruling group of Germany, the National Socialists. Although after six weeks he had obtained the material he needed, he decided to remain the entire summer, until the beginning of the fall semester at Heidelberg in September. He was a diligent worker, and in the weeks of research he managed to get his work done even though he saw Phillipa almost every afternoon as well as every evening.

What had begun as a game for Phillipa developed into an uncertainty that forced her to continue to see Walter, although at times she was certain that she already had spent too much time with him. The more she saw of him, the more she was disturbed by his own peculiar manifestation of independence and strength—an intellectual kind of strength. His frequent periods of silence interested her because she not only wanted to know what he thought, but she felt, more and more, the need to control that thought. She developed a respect for him, then an admiration, and finally, an attraction.

She could tell herself all this dispassionately because she knew
that emotionally she was more powerful than he. Walter
sensed this and did not object to it and he let what was before
a purposeful coldness toward women morph into an idolatry
for her. Both had found in their relationship, ostensibly one
without obvious common ground, something neither had
known before.

Frau Kohn learned about Walter, though not from her
daughter, for Phillipa no more thought about telling her
mother about Walter than she would about any other personal feeling or event in her life. Her own uncertainty about
Walter, her failure thus far to know that she had complete
control over this man, as she had been able to achieve over
all others, made her especially unwilling to talk about him.
One day her mother asked about him and was told that it was
none of her business.

"If you marry him, it is my business," Anna Kohn insisted.

"If I marry him, it is solely my business," Phillipa corrected. And then, deliberately: "And I very well might. You
have been badgering me for years to get married. Now perhaps you'll have your wish."

"I forbid it!" There was no mention made of Walter not
being Jewish. It did not have to be stated aloud that this
alone was Anna Kohn's objection.

Phillipa needed no further challenge. If she had to prove
once more who was the stronger, well, she would do so. This,
plus the "difference" she had found in Walter, was enough to
make her think, for the first time, of the possibility of marriage to Walter.

There was another factor. For the first twenty-three years
of her life Phillipa had been on the fringes of society. She
dominated the middle-class gatherings wherever she had
gone, but often she thought about moving upward in the

social scale—into the area of political and artistic figures of
the highest note. Walter could very well provide her with
such an opportunity. He was a full professor, a doctor of
philosophy, and through his books and articles had achieved
a status of importance in the intellectual, artistic and political circles of Germany. He had a firm acquaintance with what
Phillipa considered the finest cultural element in the country.
Actually, she cared little and consequently knew little about
the politics of the country. It made little difference to her, she
felt, who was in control, for by her very non-political behavior she was not involved in anything that she believed could
cause her any problems. The newspapers were full of the successes of the new Chancellor, Adolf Hitler, but neither he nor
his triumphs meant anything to her. The practicalities were
not important to Phillipa; only the position was.

Walter felt, in a more academic sense, much the same
way. The practicalities were sometimes elusive to him. He
did not approve, philosophically, of many of the ideals of
the National Socialist Party. But he was an academician, a
researcher and writer, not a politician, he reasoned, and in
the overall pattern those things that he did not agree with
would, as everything else, soon pass. He was reinforced in
these beliefs by many of his colleagues who also believed that
practical politics were for the politicians. In their estimation
the philosopher, the academician was concerned with the
world to understand and interpret it, not to change it. Like
most teachers in most ages, Walter was secure in his academic
ivory tower. And, like most teachers, he did not accept so
trite a statement that when the Ostrich is killed, it is the
Ostrich's own fault.

Through the summer Phillipa went with Walter to many
gatherings and met many important people. Her triumphs on
one level of society were transferred to a higher level of society. Although Walter was always close, she did not hesitate to

attract men nor did she take pains to avoid making enemies
of jealous women. Indeed, she felt a satisfaction in the latter
and even encouraged this form of pseudo-masochism. In her
ability to withstand the enmity, to find satisfaction rather
than disturbance with it, she felt that she was testing and
proving her emotional strength.

In September Walter returned to Heidelberg. For a
while Phillipa toyed with the idea of forgetting him. But she
missed the parties or, rather, the importance among important people that she had established for herself. And, in a way,
she also missed Walter. She was still attracted to him, though
no longer by mystery. She searched for the right word. For his
comfortableness, she told herself. No, that was not sufficient
for her ego, she thought. For his intellectual strength—and
her ability to control it. That was more like it. She began to
visit him at Heidelberg often.

In November the German people gave a 90 percent vote
of approval for the policies and government of Adolf Hitler,
and in early December she was invited by Walter to attend
a social affair at the university given in honor of one of the
ranking officers of the new government, Dr. Hans C. Gurtner,
who, as Minister of Justice, had agreed to lecture to the law
students at Heidelberg on the concepts of ethics in justice.
Walter was well qualified in the field by virtue of several
important articles on ethical justice and, as chairman of his
department, served as head of a committee to greet and entertain Dr. Gurtner and to be moderator of the lecture forum.

Phillipa had not yet met so highly placed an official and
with Walter's own role in the proceeding so important, she
eagerly accepted his invitation to be hostess for the affair. Her
expectations were not unfulfilled. Where Walter was content
to limit himself to academic protocol, she was not. Hers was
the social role. Dr. Gurtner was a heavily built man who carried himself with a deportment befitting his position: proud,

aloof, appropriately stern. He wore a heavily starched wing-collar, his tie blending with the grey of his suit. He wore thin-framed glasses, held lightly on the bridge of his nose, giving him the appearance of scholarliness and authority at one and the same time. He divorced himself from most of the gathering that attended the party in the evening following his afternoon lecture. He sat stiffly in a small Louis the XIV gold-trimmed armchair, lightly padded, with a stiff back. It gave him the appearance of extreme height and the dignity of straight posture.

"We must go and talk to Dr. Gurtner," Phillipa insisted to Walter. "I have met him only formally thus far."

"I don't think it's possible," Walter said, half-apologetically. "No one seems able to get near him. Several of my colleagues tried this afternoon. Either he dismisses them quickly after a first greeting or, if they want to converse, he begins to lecture them on the benefits of national socialism. I don't want to get involved. Because I don't quite agree with his theories of justice, as an official of the university I don't want to put myself in a position where I may get into disagreement with him."

"Then agree with him."

"My conscience won't let me do that."

Phillipa didn't argue. A few minutes later Walter was called over to a group of colleagues at one end of the room. Phillipa had come explicitly to meet Gurtner and she resolved to do so. She walked to the serving table, took a drink, then held it without drinking it until she saw that Gurtner was alone. Without hesitation she walked easily, with deliberate slowness to a chair near him, purposely paying no attention to him. He looked at her idly as she approached, then with surprise as she passed him without a glance and sat down, seemingly not knowing that it was he, a now very important person, sitting next to her. He was somewhat intrigued that she did not come toward him, like all the others, to begin belaboring him with petty talk and inconsequential knowledge about legal affairs in order to make his acquaintance. He was unimpressed with such people. In fact, his own acknowledged and self-taught superiority demanded that he ignore such people. Indeed, he had not wanted to come to Heidelberg in the first place, except that he was convinced that presenting his ideas at this important university, where he retained his scholarly reputation, would do much toward furthering the purposes of his party.

"Good," Gurtner then decided as he glanced at Phillipa, "I shall not be disturbed by her." But he could not prevent himself from glancing again. "An attractive woman," he thought.

He looked around the room. His brusque manner clearly had been communicated and succeeded in keeping others away. 'I should not mind her company for a time," he told himself, his thoughts turning away from politics and recalling a liaison at an inn near Garmisch that was small and discreet. But the woman made no move. 'Surely she knows who I am," he thought. "If I am not mistaken," he mused, "perhaps I have already met her." He could not recall where. He looked again at Phillipa. She saw him, he was sure, but she gave no sign of acknowledgment. He began to feel a personal slight. Was this woman so brash as to consider herself so important as not to make an overture to him, a man in his position in the government? Suddenly, without thinking that he would do so, he turned and spoke to her.

"You, too, are bored with the proceedings?"

She sat still, deliberately taking her time. Then slowly she turned toward him. She had guessed correctly. He was, after all, simply another man. She had had her way.

"Should I not be?," she asked, without expression.

He stopped himself from smiling, then adjusted his glasses with seriousness. "You are an intelligent woman," he said, without inflection, casually, taking care not to confuse flattery with a complimentary statement of fact.

Phillipa said nothing, not even the expected "thank you." For a moment Dr. Gurtner felt confusion. He was the most important figure at this gathering. Yet this woman deigned to act as if she were more important than he. He sat back, stiffly, coldly. He could not dismiss his interest in her. He turned to her again.

"Are you a teacher?"

"No."

"The wife of a professor?"

"No."

The curtness of her answers was too much for him and he was about to turn back, this time to ignore her. Phillipa sensed his reaction, determined that she had reached the proper moment to follow up her advantage. Before he had a chance to settle back in his chair, she looked directly at him.

"You are Dr. Gurtner?," she asked casually.

Although he was surprised that she could not know, he was pleased that her cold behavior had not been directed toward him and his position, but was apparently due to her not knowing for certain who he was. His ego was satisfied and he nodded to her.

"I commend your intelligence," Phillipa began. Gurtner was disappointed. His interest had been wasted. She was simply another woman to annoy him with flattery, as had all the others before and after his speech and for most of the evening thus far. "For your intelligence in relation to this gathering," Phillipa quickly continued. "These discussions here this evening are so pedestrian. Not very important when one considers what is really important."

It was not a question or a statement asking for approval. She said it matter-of-factly, as though it were incontrovertible fact.

"An intelligent person can do little else than separate himself from such an environment as best as possible," she said, nodding to the relatively long distance between where they were seated and the main body of the gathering.

This was a kind of flattery he had not expected. Indeed, he did not consider it flattery, but obvious truth. He was pleased that someone understood his real relationship to these people. He appreciated this woman's observation.

'Then I must commend you on your intelligence, as well," he told her.

Now he did not expect a thank you and he did not get one. This was a woman of the same mold as he, he thought. He wished for a moment that he were twenty years younger. He looked at Phillipa and mentally compared her with his wife. It was an unhappy comparison and he reflected upon his own indiscretion in making it and quickly took the thought from his mind.

"It is good to speak to someone who understands such things," he said. "Who are you?"

She hesitated. "My escort is Professor Penmann."

"Professor Penmann. An old colleague. An able man."

He had not thought twice about Walter, his host for the event. Walter had now become part of the mass of faceless persons who had been hosts in his busy speaking schedule of the past few months. This woman's escort? Well, there must be more to the man than he first thought. A quiet man, a learned man. But obviously a man who was not able to use his abilities to their best advantage in the political service, as he was. Yet, perhaps a more able man than he appeared to be. After all, a man who had such a companion as this woman . . . .

Walter had left his colleagues and was looking for Phillipa, then saw her in conversation with Gurtner. He was surprised, then admiring. No one else had been able to exchange much more than a formal greeting with the Minister of Justice during his entire visit thus far unless it was to listen to an extemporaneous lecture on national socialism. But Phillipa was not being lectured at and, indeed, appeared to be engaged in calm, pleasant conversation. He walked slowly to that part of the room. When Gurtner saw Walter approach, he invited him to move up a chair and join them. Walter hesitated for a moment, then did so.

Gurtner, finding himself for the first time that day in what he felt was adequate company, discussed the new government with them. Rather, he told them about the new government, delivering his words as though they were judicial opinion, leaving neither room for questioning nor the possibility that they could be other than absolutely correct. His delivery was weighed and his words were emphatic. He believed that these were ideas of unmatched importance and he wanted to impress them upon his listeners.

"I do not speak with the intensity of Herr Hitler"—he hesitated—"or even Herr Goebbels"—there was a slight implication of sarcasm as he mentioned Goebbels' name—"but my meanings are nevertheless as sincere." Then without the slightest hesitation of self-consciousness: "Der Fuhrer is the law, while I am justice."

Phillipa nodded with a knowing smile. Gurtner acknowledged this as not only agreement but understanding and appreciated it. Walter tried to stifle a frown, could not. Gurtner noticed it.

"You do not agree, Dr. Penmann?"

Walter tried to avoid being questioned. "Oh, I am afraid that my ethical conceptions are probably just a bit different from yours." He tried to dismiss the matter lightly.

But Gurtner had gone too far, especially by permitting Walter to socialize with him as an equal, to permit even the possibility of his ideas being questioned without the questioner being put in the right.

"What disturbs you? I shall explain," he offered with clear condescension.

Walter tried to think of a way out. But Phillipa pushed him. It was an advantage for her and at the same time, she thought, the only way to avoid a serious situation for him.

"Tell him, Walter. I'm sure Dr. Gurtner will explain any problems to you satisfactorily."

This pleased Gurtner as much as it displeased Walter. Walter could not negate Phillipa's suggestion without obviously insulting both her and Gurtner. The thought crossed his mind that she was really trying to help him, to give him the chance to ask a simple, unimportant question, get an answer, and permit the matter to dissipate. Yet, he could not do so because the very nature of the demand was a frustration of his own free will. It was difficult for him to organize his words.

"I do not believe any man can be justice." He stopped; realizing the implication of the tone of what under other circumstances would be merely a theoretical statement. He added quickly: "In terms of abstract thinking, of course. I am certain you yourself are well qualified for your position."

"You contradict yourself, Herr Professor," Gurtner said sharply.

"I believe in distributive justice," Walter said. "Not the punishment of a man because he has done something bad in the eyes of his society, but punishment in terms of the overall harm he has done with the deed according to how, in its overt form, it has affected the majority of mankind." He did not say it as clearly as he wished. He felt pressed. But he had gotten it out, nevertheless.

"Ah, and you believe then that I am of the school of retributive justice," Gurtner said.

Walter nodded.

"And you are correct," Gurtner added. "Retributive justice alone can assure a stable and strong society. If a man commits a crime against the state or, indeed, threatens the state without having committed an overt action, then he must be punished. Directly. To wait upon philosophical determination means to wait until, perhaps, it is too late for effective punishment—for preventive punishment." He stressed the word preventive. "I will clarify this even further for you. If society—the state—needs a certain kind of man and a certain kind of behavior from that man for the benefit of the state, then all who deviate from that standard, willfully or otherwise, have in effect committed a crime against the state and must be meted proper justice."

"Remember what Nietzsche said, Walter," Phillipa interposed. "The weak in a society where only the strong can create are criminals."

Her intrusion stopped Walter as he was about to answer Gurtner. He did not want to argue now against Phillipa as well, just as he wished he did not have to argue with Gurtner. Yet, he felt a moral obligation to disagree with Gurtner's stated concept of justice. As he once more tried to gather the proper thoughts and words, Gurtner spoke.

"The young fraulein is quite right. And in the strong state the strong man must be judge. Therefore, I, in this state, am justice."

It was clear to Walter that Gurtner would permit no further argument. It was also clear that to object further would also embarrass Phillipa. "I understand your point completely," he told Gurtner. He retained the satisfaction that he at least had not said that he agreed. He hoped Gurtner would accept what he said without further questioning.

Having put Walter into a difficult position, Phillipa now extricated him, deliberately and well aware that her entire action had strengthened her ability to control Walter and indebt him to her at the same time. She suddenly rose, without apology.

"I must reluctantly leave now, Dr. Gurtner. Your company has been a great pleasure."

Walter did not immediately understand and did not stand. Gurtner rose sharply to his feet.

Phillipa looked at Walter.

"Are you ready, Walter?"

Walter hurriedly stood.

Gurtner clicked his heels, bowed from the waist, bent forward and kissed Phillipa's hand. Phillipa looked about the room, satisfied that enough of the guests had seen and were properly envious.

"A most fortunate pleasure for me," Gurtner said, "Fraulein . . . ?"

"I would be pleased if you would call me Phillipa," she smiled. Inside she suddenly felt insecure.

"Then Phillipa it is." Gurtner bowed again. "I would be pleased if at any time you were to be in Berlin, you would pay me the honor of a visit." He was suddenly charming, the stiffness melted. Then he straightened up, the sternness back, his dignity paramount as he turned to Walter. He halted only a moment, but just long enough so that though it did not necessarily appear so, what he said might be taken for an afterthought. "And you, too, Dr. Penmann, if you should be in Berlin. I shall be happy to continue our discussion and clarify further for you."

Walter thanked him. He and Phillipa bade Gurtner good night. Phillipa accepted, without appearing to notice, the stares of the people as she walked briskly, purposively through the room to the door. Gurtner sat back in his chair and watched Phillipa as she left. He half hoped that she would stop at the door and smile a parting goodbye. She continued without turning or giving the slightest hint of a backward glance.

"Quite a woman," Gurtner muttered to himself, pleased that she hadn't.

Phillipa was quiet in the taxi on the way back to her hotel. It was pleasant to contemplate, calmly on the outside, with excitement on the inside, her triumph of the evening. She was especially satisfied with how effectively she had controlled Walter—and with the knowledge that it would be easier to do again and again. Her satisfaction with what she had accomplished with Gurtner was marred by her memory of the last few moments with him. His asking of her name. She had read and heard enough about the new regime to be wary of her name, Kohn. Not that there was any danger to her, she reasoned. Jews of her father's wealth and position were cooperating wholeheartedly in the economic policy of the government. It was only the other—the ghetto-type Jews, the ones that didn't really matter—that needed to be concerned. Yet, the situation was a delicate one. The sentiments of the new government were clear, and if one knew her name before they knew who she really was. . . . She cursed her father for her name. If her name were not Kohn, how far she could go now, in situations such as these, with the important people such as Gurtner she could meet through Walter. If her name were not Kohn, she thought, if it were something like . . . for instance . . . Penmann . . . .

Chapter IV

For a while Walter was more disturbed over the incident with Gurtner than he thought he would be. He did not mention it to Phillipa because it upset him that she had so easily put him into a position where he could be embarrassed—and then just as easily given him an opportunity to step out of that position—an advantage he had not taken. He did not mention it because he did not want to disturb her or, rather, disturb the equilibrium of their relationship. He was dependent upon her moods, elated when she was bright, gracious and tender toward him, despondent when she was tense, sharp or angry with him. He felt an emotional need for her that he told himself was too strong, was not logical, was too demanding of him for his own good. Yet, at the same time, he found that he was unable to be happy in his thinking and working when she was not there. He felt an incompleteness those weekends when she did not come up from Munich. He felt an inability to function at gatherings that Phillipa did not attend with him. He was aware that Phillipa's sharing with him was largely limited to gatherings, meetings, parties, official functions. His life was much more than that: his students, his classes, his reading, his research, his writing.

Yet, in the image he had created of Phillipa, he told
himself that she would become part of this life, too, as she
was part of the other. When he was with her and when he
thought about her, he looked for incidents to justify this
belief: he made special note of the discussions where Phillipa would contribute an important point; of the time she
took to speak with a student of his who might stop him on
the street when they were together to ask him a question;
of her questions, no matter how idle, on what he had been
studying in the library or whether his most recent article had
been accepted yet for publication. He did not undervalue her
ability to move forward in creating new relationships and to
help him while doing so. It had been she who had eventually
relieved him of the worry over Gurtner.

One week after Gurtner's visit, the Chancellor of Heidelberg University received a note from the Minister of Justice
commenting on the "helpful service rendered him by
Dr. Walter Penmann and the beautiful young lady who ac-
companied him." The chancellor personally thanked Walter
for his contribution to the standing of the university in the
eyes of this important government official. Walter elaborated
on such things in his thoughts, and with each new consideration found himself more and more in love with Phillipa.
He found it increasingly difficult to follow his usual pattern
of working and studying long into the night. He could not
concentrate. His mind was always on Phillipa. Especially
when she was not there and when there was no event in the
forthcoming days that would bring her there. Especially in
her absence he longed for her, and as he built in his mind
the perfect picture of a woman he loved, the love turned into
worship. One evening he came to a decision.

That day had been a trying one for Walter. His academic
well-being had been shattered by an experience that he did
not wish to acknowledge. At the time of Gurtner's visit, one

of Walters colleagues in the Philosophy Department, Herbert
Kamm, an extraordinarily bright young man of not more
than twenty-five of age, had opposed many of Gurtner's ideas
by questioning the Minister of Justice during the forum that
followed Gurtner's lecture. Walter remembered being grateful for Kamm's remarks because they embodied much of his
own criticism, criticism which, under the circumstances, he
decided to keep silent and to save for the pages of a manuscript. At first Gurtner had been nettled by Kamm's questions, then had answered him briskly and commandingly, and
ultimately simply ignored him. In actuality the questions
and the incipient argument had been a quiet one, not unlike
the countless philosophical arguments that always accom-
panied such a forum. Some weeks afterward a message from
one of Joseph Goebbels' assistants reached Kamm, requesting his presence in Berlin. At first Kamm was ready to go,
but with no indication of why he was being summoned, he
phoned Berlin to find out. He was told that it was necessary
to determine whether his philosophical ideas and his methods
of teaching were in the best interests of education. As Kamm
later said, he believed that this was a legitimate request. But
as he also said and wrote to Goebbel's assistant, he questioned
a political office's prerogative to inquire into non-political
matters and he suggested that he make such a report to the
proper authority, the Academic Dean of the University. He
enclosed with this letter a memo he had received the year
before from the chancellor of the university commenting on
good reports the chancellor had heard of his fine scholarship
and congratulating him on his efforts as a teacher.

For more than a week he heard nothing and assumed—
hoped, rather—that his letter had been effective and the
matter had been dropped. Then came another letter from
Berlin, demanding his appearance. The harshness of the letter
prompted Kamm to take a stand as a matter of principle.

"I shall not be intimidated," he asserted. "It's neither
their business nor their right to question me." And, then, as
if to find theoretical justification for his action, and understanding clearly—perhaps for the first time—the reason
for the situation: "Because I disagreed with the Minister of
Justice, because my ideas may be in conflict with some of
the ideas of the government? We are, after all, a democratic
Germany. The present government was elected by the people.
Why should I be a party to the subversion of Germany?"

He was emphatic. Exactly one week later he received a
short, formal note from the office of the Chancellor of the
University, informing him that his contract would not be
renewed for the following academic year. The note gave no
reason, no explanation. He went to the president's office to
determine why, and after several hours finally had a brief interview with the chancellor's assistant. He was told that "the
chancellor left word, if you should call, to inform you that, re-
grettably, you have been dropped from the faculty—for purely
administrative reasons of budget and course realignment."

Herbert Kamm could not argue with these reasons, but
for confirmation went immediately to Walter who, as head
of his department, certainly would not only know of such
an action, but would have initially recommended it. For a
moment, wanting to believe that this was indeed the reason
for his dismissal, he was angry that Walter did not have the
integrity to inform him of these plans and of his, Kamm's,
status. Then, realizing that this was not the reason at all, he
composed himself before reaching Walter's office. Walter had
been completely unaware of Kamm's dismissal. As Walter
read Kamm's note of dismissal, he felt a sudden fear, an unin-
tentional realization that if it had not been for Phillipa he too
might have been in Kamm's position. Even here, in privacy,
he suddenly felt a reluctance to speak frankly. He was relieved

when told the reason given Kamm and pushed the other thoughts completely from his mind.

"They certainly should have let me know first, Herbert. But, of course, I don't determine university policy."

"Do you know about any course changes, about any budget cuts?" Kamm asked.

Walter hesitated. "I did not ask for any. But, of course, decisions on a higher level . . ." He paused, not knowing how to end it.

Kamm stared at him, waiting for him to say something more.

After what seemed like a long while: "I'm damned sorry, Herbert. Damned sorry."

Kamm waited, without a word, then finally: "Then you will do nothing for me?"

"What can I do? I have been sitting here thinking. What can I do? A note from the president . . . I can call the chancellor's office to confirm it, if you wish."

"That's not what I mean. You know that's not what I mean."

Walter knew something more could and should be done. But he didn't know what. He did not really know what Kamm wanted him to do.

"What can I do?," he repeated.

Kamm studied him. Now he was angry with him.

"If you don't know, then I can't tell you."

"I'm damned sorry," Walter said again. "I'll give you a good recommendation. You should be able to get another position in another school."

"You really think so!" Kamm tried to hold back the bitterness. "Don't search for an answer, Herr Professor. Words mean nothing. Find the answer in your beliefs. In your conscience."

"I'll talk to the chancellor this afternoon," Walter said. "I'll find out what it's all about." He tried to find some encouragement for Herbert, but had none to give.

"I'll be off for France in the morning, Herr Professor," Kamm said. "I need not wait until January. You can, I'm sure, get someone from Dr. Goebbels' office to take my place until the semester is over."

Walter rose. He did not know whether to offer a handshake. He held back. "I'm sorry," he said.

"I suspect really more than you now know," Kamm suggested.

Walter did not want to acknowledge his meaning.

"Why France?," he asked.

"Why not?" Kamm turned to the door. He stopped, the door half open. "Maybe I'll see you there someday, Herr Professor? I hope not, but maybe I will." His anger had subsided. His statement was one of sad conviction. He closed the door slowly, leaving Walter staring after him.

Walter knew the philosophy of Socrates, had studied the lives of Joan of Arc and Thomas More, and was an admirer of Bernard Shaw. But that was all in the abstract, in an impersonal cogitation of the brain regarding important matters that need not ever be applied in a world outside of the academic classroom or the library stacks. He had no doubt of the implications of what had happened to Kamm, but he refused to make the implications real for himself. He would not relate the philosophical theory to the actuality of being out of a job, of being unable to work at all, or of many things worse into whose immediacy he had not yet been thrown, but which remained still only on the unprinted pages of history. The meaning didn't puzzle him; the reality did. He could not cope with the reality. He did not know what to do about it— just as he had not known what to do about Kamm. Indeed, he was not sure he should do anything about it except think

about it. Perhaps some further reading into the concepts of
free opinion, into the variant, into the philosophies of the
non-conformist would help? He chose the dialogues of Plato
for rereading, seated himself that evening in the easy chair in
the library of his small house near the university. The library
was almost the only room for him. It combined, for him, a
living-room, den, dining room, and bedroom. He worked
there frequently far into the night, venturing rarely into
the kitchen at the rear of the house except to prepare a meal
when he felt that hunger was distracting him from his study.
Often he worked so late that he did not bother to climb the
short flight of stairs to one of the two bedrooms on the second
floor. Now he prepared for such a night of study. But it didn't
come. He found himself unable to think in the abstract as
he read the dialogues. They pushed themselves into reality.
Kamm had been fired. This was reality. He laid Plato gently back on his desk, chose a newly acquired volume of the
collected *Back to Methuselah* plays of Shaw. He liked to read
them again and again, for within the depth of Shaw's philosophy was the excitement of dramatic action and the relaxation
of entertaining humor. But here, again, the abstractions
forced themselves into realities, for the words he read came
from people who seemed real, people who he could not avoid
identifying with Kamm. He could not study. The more he
pushed himself into thought, the more the entire sequence
earlier that day with Kamm came back to him. The more
he thought about it, the more embarrassed he became. He
should have taken action, he told himself, at the same time
admitting that he had no concept of what kind of action he
should have taken. He felt, for some reason, that he must still
do something. Yet, he was not a man of action. He would
not even know where to begin. He rationalized that his own
best efforts, his own best contributions and self-realization
dictated a course of thinking and writing. Someone should do

something for Kamm, he argued; and then, thinking again, convinced himself that he was not the one; that no matter how good his intentions, he would not be able to do anything that would be effective.

It angered him, this inability. If only he were the type of person who could mold the outward world. If only he could make a decision in relation to life itself and carry it out. This is what he had lacked all his life, he admitted to himself. This was an old musing, but now it seemed to have more pertinence than it ever had in the past. Even as a child, he had been quiet, alone, not sharing his thoughts or deeds even with his parents. Normal aggression had been subverted into reading and studying. Normal action had been oriented into academic pondering. He did not minimize the importance of his studying, writing, philosophizing. But he regretted that because it could be done away from the world at large, he had permitted himself to do it that way. Now that the philosophical problem had been thrust upon him as a practical political one, he realized that he needed help. He desired help.

Phillipa was not like him in this respect, he knew. She would know what to do. One way or the other, she would do it. She was confident of her strength in the world and he knew that she would take whatever action she wished when she wished. How she could help him now! Even her presence would give him assurance. How he needed her now, he thought. His awareness of his need for Phillipa had been a long time in coming, yet he had known all along that it would come. It had needed only the one incident, the special realization, to make it definite in his mind. He thought about his hesitation, his ineptitude in this situation and he thought about how he would act if Phillipa were there. No more procrastination, he thought. She would help him decide, she would reinforce his decision, she would guide him and encourage him in his action. And in some things, he thought, if he could not act, why she herself would take the action for him.

He repeated these thoughts over and over. He left the library, continuing the thoughts as he walked slowly up the stairs, prepared himself for bed. The cold of the late autumn cut through a crack in the window frame and the sheets of the bed were starched and cold. Almost hostile. He lay himself flat upon the length of the bed, tried to imagine what it would be to have warmth at that moment, to have the full warmth of Phillipa. Before his eyes closed, he had made his decision.

Chapter V

Phillipa only momentarily hesitated. Life had become an extremely boring occupation. Munich was now merely a place to spend time between visits to Heidelberg. She wanted to get away from her family. Not because of petty quarrels, of the usual family disputes about the daughter-growing-up end the daughter-coming-of-age. Phillipa had reached her womanhood many years before; indeed, she often delighted telling herself that she had achieved her spiritual, mental and emotional womanhood long before she had attained the physical one.

At the dinner table one evening she made known her intention to marry Walter. She said it casually, as if she placed the same importance upon it as the buying of a new book.

"I'm going to Heidelberg Saturday to marry Walter Penmann," she said. Simply. With no inflection, no emotion.

Her mother stopped eating, put down her fork and stared. Her father made certain to finish the piece of meat on his fork, chewed it down quickly, then held his fork half-way between his mouth and the plate, more in suspension waiting to see what Anna Kohn would do than from any intention of his own. Anna tried to talk, got half of the word "Phillipa"

through her throat, then got up quickly, scraping the chair
back from the table, and hurried to her room. Bernard Kohn
stared after her, glancing then at the empty chair, then
hesitatingly at Phillipa, who continued eating calmly as if
nothing at all had happened that did not always happen at a
dinner table.

"You know your mother takes things badly," Phillipa's
father said. He felt embarrassed to talk about it, pretending
as if the talking about an emotional thing was beneath his on
business-like attitude and behavior. He wanted to say that
it hurt him, too, but he didn't know how. "You should have
told us a little easier"—he paused—"for your mother's sake,"
he added eagerly. The eagerness suggested that he wanted to
say more about his feelings.

"I can't change your mind?," he began, begging the
words because he knew they were useless. Phillipa didn't
bother to answer. It wasn't necessary. Bernard Kohn felt fifty
years of life weighted upon him. He sat and stared at his
daughter, wanting to talk. He, like Anna, had been opposed
to earlier talk of marriage with Walter Penmann. Not that
Walter wasn't a well-educated well-respected man. But, first,
he was a philosopher and a philosopher was not, in the best
sense of the doctor-lawyer-businessman tradition, a professional man; and, second—and outside of the rationalization,
it really was first—he was not Jewish.

Bernard stared with far-away eyes for perhaps five minutes, watching Phillipa's hand move rhythmically, stepping
her fork back and forth from her plate to her mouth. Things
in his mind that he wanted to say came only as shadows to his
lips. He could not hold them firmly or long enough to make
them into words. She was his flesh and blood, he wanted to
say, his only child, his inheritance, his love. All parents loved
their children, he thought to himself, though all children
didn't love their parents. Love without love. The feelings of

hurt and incapacity, transferred now into pain as he thought
of his wife in her room, probably crying bitterly in her loneliness of a newly proscribed future, made him uneasy. Phillipa
saw his mouth begin to tremble and his eye sockets contract
into themselves. She felt sorry for him. She knew he wanted
to talk with her and to feel from her a sympathy for his problem. But he didn't know how. For so long, for twenty-and-
more years he had been able to detach himself; to act as with
unconcern, to escape the duties that a closeness of fatherhood
proclaims upon a man that now, when he wanted to show
concern, he didn't know how.

"I'm sorry" he said simply, without bitterness, only sadness, and left the table to join his wife.

Phillipa didn't see her mother or father for several weeks
after that.

She finished eating, called to the cook to clear the table,
slowly, deliberately went to her roam, packed the most important of her belongings, phoned for a taxi, and took a train
to Heidelberg. It wasn't that she was unconcerned about her
parents: It was simply that she was not concerned.

The wedding was a simple one. Just Phillipa, Walter and
two witnesses and, of course, the Burgermeister of Heidelberg, a youngish, thin man with heavy-rimmed glasses who
read the terms of the marriage law with measured meaning
as though he waited philosophical approval from Walter
for every word. Dr. Guido Termini, one of Walter's closest
friends at the university, was a witness. He was a big man,
almost six and a half feet tall, well over 250 pounds, with a
large, round, warm face, jovially smiling, appearing one moment like the Sherwood Forest description of an affable Friar
and the next moment like a once heroic and famous football
player. He might have been either. His youth had been spent
divided between football and studying for the priesthood.
Fortunately, he so proclaimed later, he learned to do neither

one well enough to satisfy himself and in self-discipline took
a path opposite to both, he said—that of a scholar. He was a
professor of Italian language and literature at the university
and second only to Walter as intellectual leader of the more
or less select group of professional and amateur philosophers
from all departments of the university who met in an informal discussion from time to time.

The other witness was Mathilde Berrun, an oldish
looking woman who was no younger than her appearance.
Of French descent, she had never developed the sometimes
healthy look sometimes absorbed from the French countryside and at the age of sixty-five was thin as a needle, hollow as
a flute and brittle as a comb. She was Walter's combination
cook and maid in his small house near the campus. Now that
he was marrying she considered her five-year duty to him at
an end and she performed this one final official act to Walter's
service before returning to northern France to live out her life
with two sisters in similar old-maidish circumstances. Physically, she was healthy enough to live to be a hundred; mentally, she was preparing herself for an all-too-soon grave.

In other circumstances Phillipa would have preferred
a large wedding. But since it was out of the question—a
large wedding would, of necessity, have involved her parents
as a show of family solidarity and interest and pride—the
smaller, the better. In fact, she saw little need for a ceremony
at all. The officially stamped piece of paper issued by the
Heidelberg city authorities did not guarantee love or honor
or obedience—and even if they did, there would be no way
of enforcing the edicts. Marriage was a matter to Phillipa of
Phillipa's will. She would make as much or as little of it as
she wished, legal deed or no legal deed. With Miss Berrun
leaving Germany and Dr. Termini understanding that the
details of the wedding would be mentioned only discreetly,
if at all, Phillipa intended simply to move into the two-story,

five-room house of Walter's and become a regular, rather than
the heretofore intermittent part of Heidelberg's intellectual
and social life.

She had already conditioned herself to accept Walter's
small home. He apologized for it, knowing he should not
and yet, not yet really knowing Phillipa, unfavorably and
guiltily comparing it with the large house in Munich. Before
Miss Berrun left she cleaned it immaculately—although in
the library she still did not deign to touch any of Walter's
books. The library was sacred, the large desk an inviolate
temple upon which lay in scattered disorder all sorts of sheets
of paper, some printed, same typewritten, others penciled.
Notes, lectures, articles and books in process, letters and,
falling victim to no discrimination of any sort, utility and
tailor bills. The utility bills were high. Walter's penchant
for staying up reading, studying and writing until all hours
of the morning with as many bright lights as were needed
to comfort him and light his intellectual way were a boon to
the electric company. The tailor bills were another thing. He
liked his clothes clean, sometimes even pressed if the occasion
warranted. But he had no eye for style, indeed, no interest at
all in the subject. A blue pair of pants, if they were comfortable, were perfectly satisfactory with a green jacket, provided
it was also comfortable. He always felt it an academic duty
to wear a white shirt and tie, sometimes, if the weather were
chilled, covering them with a light pullover sweater. But
clothes were, in Walter's estimation, made to protect the
body, not compensate for it. It wasn't an intellectual snobbery
of style; he just was simply too busy with what to him were
important things to bother about clothes.

His interests converged primarily on the books that
lined the shelves of the room, completely covering one wall,
from ceiling to floor. His large wooden desk stood in front of
this wall. To the left of the desk, at the far end of the room,

forming a right angle to the library, a large window looked
out onto the miniature lawn and lean shrubs that constituted
the embryo of a hedge leading from the street sidewalk up to
the front door of the house. There were no curtains, although
two drapes nailed clumsily onto the window sidepieces gave
the interior a moment of wine-red decoration. A paper shade
served both as the protector of privacy and as the doorman
of sunlight and air. The other side of the room, opposite the
book shelves, was lined in too orderly order with antique-
looking pieces of furniture that were too obviously not
antiques. First, an unsightly desk-secretary, the desk part
locked and the key long since lost. Walter thought about it
occasionally, wondering if there were any things of importance in the desk. A few books, a few papers lined the glass
enclosed shelves above. A high-boy inappropriately stood
next to the first piece, more pleasantly filled with a set of
Dresden dishes and some Venetian-made glassware. A low
fireplace pushed into the wall next to it. It had no tools,
no fire-screen. The bottom concrete, however, was scarred
with black, giving evidence that it was, on occasion, used.
Straddling the mantle above the fireplace was an elongated
clock that ticked very loud and looked even louder, a piece   •
of highly polished wood with gold hands that chimed every
quarter of an hour. Miss Berrun often had complained about
it and stuffed a piece of paper into the face to stop the hands
because the chimes annoyed her. Walter didn't mind their
loudness because when he became occupied with his work he
heard nothing, no matter how disturbing it might be at any
other time.

The placement of the furniture gave the room a long,
narrow look. The library joined the entrance hall, which
continued the narrow passage past the open arch of the living
room. It cut to the right around the stairway that led to the
two bedrooms and the bathroom on the second floor of the

house and it ended a few feet in back of the stairway at the
kitchen door. The stairway was visible from all of the living
room-turned-den (Walter's living was done in the library,
and the living room became an adjunctive extension of that
room), especially from the large flowered-slip-covered easy
chair that sat immediately inside of the arch. It was Walter's
favorite resting place, giving him, unconsciously, a feeling of
command over his castle.

The castle shook the first night of their marriage.

Walter had made certain that Miss Berrum would be
gone. He thought it would help ease his growing self-
consciousness to make sure that the other bedroom, sometimes occupied by Miss Berrun when she worked late, would
be empty that evening. For days Walter had thought of what
he would do that first night. Not specifically, not exactly, but
in vague terms of eroticism, of feelings of his senses of taste,
of touch. He sensually visualized Phillipa's body, the dark
hair hanging loose and long like black velvet, the clothes
stripped away revealing perfect roundness and hardness and
softness all at once. As he tried to hold on to these feelings
and make of them concrete and lasting pictures that he could
physically touch, they pulled and darted away into fuzziness.

Phillipa smiled indulgently as he lifted her at the beginning of the stone walk and carried her past the slight shrubs
to the front door and over the threshold. Yet, even with her
awareness of her condescension to romanticism, she shivered a
bit. The feeling was good.

"Put me down, Walter," she laughed as they stepped
inside. "What will the neighbors think!"

For a moment he thought of this seriously, then smiled
broadly. "Damn the neighbors!" He tried to throw the words
softly through his teeth, to create with the hint of vulgarity
the impression of strength. He attempted to lift her higher,
to start with her up the stairs.

"No, Walter. No. I say no." She smiled all the while, but the words were adamant.

He felt he should feel brave and the best impression of bravery, he thought, is not to give in to compromise.

"Now, Phillipa, it's our wedding night."

He grasped her tighter, one hand curling around her thigh, holding fully into the flesh, giving him strength through physical pressure and physical expectation. He walked several steps up the staircase.

"Your husband shall conduct you to your bridal bed." He flipped the words purposefully carelessly, as though they and he should both be enjoyed in anticipation.

Phillipa squirmed.

"I do not wish to be handled like a servant or like a toy. I said to let me down."

The smile had gone. The body stiffened, making the weight uncomfortably heavy for Walter. It must be a game, he thought. He was being strong and she was teasing him by being independent. He must win, of course, he reasoned. But it must not become too serious, he determined. Yet the struggle itself was of importance. He continued up another few steps.

"The bride struggled . . .," he tried to laugh through gasps of breath, for the suddenly heavy body made going difficult. "The bride struggled to keep intact the virginity that . . . "

He was interrupted by Phillipa's open hand slapping him hard across the side of his face. He was more surprised than hurt, more at a loss to understand what had happened than angry. He put her down slowly. She didn't move, but just stared at him. As she stood looking at him squarely, without expression, her eyes unwavering, he began to feel heat inside. Now he was angry. She had no right to do that, he thought. He wanted to slap her hard across her face, pick her up, struggling or no, throw her across the bed upstairs, release his

anger inside of her, then triumphantly tell her he had made
a woman of a girl-at-games. His eyes met hers, gathering
strength for his conviction, working up inside of him the moment to take the action. He waited just long enough to give
himself verbal assurance, to rationalize what he intended to
do. "I can play games, too," he muttered silently to himself.
"I will show her who is stronger." He waited too long.

The waiting—a second, a moment, a twinkling—was
long enough to make an eternity. At that instant, when emotion freely given might have spared him a lifetime of similar
instants when he wished he could have that one to do over, he
stood outside of himself, removed from his own feelings and
intellectually chastised himself. "A flash of life, unused, untouched, can be more important than an eternity," he said to
himself. And in the same breath of thought he knew he had
hesitated too long. He watched Phillipa's eyes steady upon
him, her body directly in front of his, daring, yet unmoving.
With a barely understood and barely felt involuntary resignation he let whatever emotions remaining in him dissolve to
thoughts, the feelings and urge to action supplanted by the
philosopher's consideration of the effects of action.

"She might resent what I would do," he told himself, half
in his mind, half in his throat to emphasize the reality of the
thoughts. "It might destroy the basis of our relationship."
And then, "but if I give in to her, the man-woman relationship might be destroyed and be put on too formal a plane."
The puzzlement came to his face and his not knowing what
to do twisted out the smile that he had fixed upon his lips
from the moment of the slap. His eyes wavered. Phillipa saw,
let a thin wisp of satisfaction creep across her mouth, quickly
turned and walked alone up the stairs to the bedroom.

She spent the next two weeks crumpling entirely the
walls of Walter's castle. The old-fashioned furniture that had
decorated one side of the living room was sold. A modern

cabinet for the china and glassware took one corner. The fireplace was repainted and bright new tools and a silvered fire-screen took an important place in front of it. The other side of the fireplace, toward the front window, was divided by a new, latest-style, armless couch, angling out from the fireplace wall. Directly is front of where there would no longer be a fire—a fire might dirty the bright new fire tools—was a cocktail table of light mahogany, low, with sharp corners. At the back of the couch squatted a small table and magazine rack with a lamp and a straight-backed uncomfortable chair that was labeled—Walter frequently and unsuccessfully speculated on the reason—an "easy" chair.

Walter's own easy chair and desk were the subject of serious consideration one afternoon when he returned from teaching a class.

"I have decided to make this side of the room mare presentable for company," Phillipa told him. He stared at her a moment. If he were going to be hesitant on some things, he was not going to be on others.

"It is as presentable as I want it to be," he told her quickly, somewhat surprised at the force of his voice. He almost had to consciously restrain himself before be finished the sentence to keep the pitch from rising.

Phillipa looked at him with surprise.

"A smaller desk, a file for your papers . . . ," she began, calmly.

He didn't let her finish.

"Neither my desk nor my papers shall be touched."

He waited for her next words, ready to interrupt them, too.

"My desk and my papers shall remain as they are, as I want them to be," he repeated.

For emphasis he half-dropped, half-slammed his small briefcase onto the desk.

Phillipa was about to became angry with him, to chas-
tise him, to make him regret his outburst. Then she decided
against it. This was only a little thing. The desk could be
made neater, the easy chair could be moved back from the
arch and almost hidden behind it so that it was not visible
from the hall, and the bookshelves could be straightened.
Walter would appear to have a victory and she would have
lost nothing. She would have gained his gratitude, permitting her the easy prerogative of decision without trouble
regarding something else at some future time.

"You are right, Walter," she said slowly, as if it had been
obvious all along and there had been no need for his loud and
impatient proclamation of his privilege. "You must have your
books and papers in your own order to work with. I would
not think of disturbing them. I only intend to help you fix
them so that their use may be easier for you." There was no
emotion in her voice. The statement was calm, ending on
a note of incompleteness, beckoning to him to finish what
could be finished only awkwardly now.

"I'm sorry," he sputtered. "I didn't mean . . . ." He
stopped.

"That's all right, Walter. I understand." There was no
condescension in her voice. Yet, it could not be more condescending.

"Thank you," he said apologetically, as a child who had
just been reprieved from a whipping.

It was almost a month after her marriage before Phillipa
heard from her parents. A phone call came from her father's
office in Munich.

"I should have called before," Bernard Kohn said, "but
I was busy." He did not ask how she felt, did not ask if she
were happy, did not mention Walter. She didn't expect him

to and it satisfied her justification for her rejection of Bernard
Kohn that he didn't.

"Your mother didn't want me to call," he continued,
"that's why I didn't."

His contradiction explained itself. There is more sentiment underneath than he himself believes, she thought.

"Your mother is very ill," he said slowly. "She has been in
the hospital since you've been away."

Phillipa smiled sardonically at the deliberate ease and
speed with which her father said "since you've been away"
instead of "since you've been married."

"Will you came to see her, Phillipa?"

It was the first tine her father had ever asked her for anything outright. She didn't answer. She wanted him to
beg her.

"Please, Phillipa, will you come to see your mother? Even
for one day."

She was satisfied. "Yes, I will."

She wanted to ask how Anna Kohn was, how seriously
ill she was. Yet, they still refused to show acceptance or even
acknowledgment of her marriage. She said only, "I will come
tomorrow morning."

"Thank you." Her father's voice was thin now, not so
sharp, not so big. After a moment it was businesslike again.
"Come directly to my office and we'll go to the hospital from
there."

Phillipa found a tired woman, a woman whose bitterness
had turned into the greater debilitation of regret and hopelessness. Anna's feeling of having lost a daughter irretriev-
ably was genuine. She was not organically ill, although the
hospital room, white and starched in a corner of the building
away from the other rooms, the prim efficient nurse, and the
hourly visits by the doctor gave the impression that she must
be. What had been a wonderful adventure for Anna in the

raising of her child had suddenly turned out not to be a game any longer. The dependent child had grown into the independent woman and the obviousness of the development that she herself was most responsible for achieving was something that she had somehow never thought about actually facing. Now her hope and will were gone.

Phillipa visited her mother several times during the next two mouths. Finally, Anna Kohn was able to leave the hospital and go hone. The suffering had dulled. With the resignation of those who resolve their problems through self-pity, she accepted what had happened as inevitable. Neither she nor Bernard ever really forgave Phillipa, but since she was, after all, their only child, they were forced, at last, to accept what was done as done.

Within a year Phillipa's mother died. Not from lamentation, for that had passed. The mental suffering had long since ceased as an active ingredient of life. It had been set deeper, underneath the consciousness. Phillipa's marriage was not mentioned between Anna and Bernard. In way of compensation or guilt the name of Rabbi Phillip also disappeared from family conversation. The disappointment was a component part of Anna's death. It might have been the most important part, but in medical terms the cause of death was listed as pneumonia.

Phillipa went to Munich for the funeral. There were no tears from her. There were from her father. She learned something, watching her father cry at the cemetery. She found here one more bit of evidence that he was not solely a one-dimensional image that went to an office in the morning and returned in the evening to sit and read a newspaper, and provided in an abstract, bookkeeping manner for the upkeep of a home and family. He had some human feeling. Relatives and friends crowded the small plot of ground in the Jewish cemetery north of Munich. Already, in that winter of

1933, there were signs of the attitudes of the German people. Several tombstones were overturned. Others had been defiled with vulgar words in black charcoal lettering. The peculiar American Indian symbol she had seen in art books, the recently-become Swastika, shone darkly on white tombstones.

Her mother was buried in a plain wooden casket. A Rabbi read some prayers and the body was solemnly lowered into the ground. It was a silent moment and Phillipa felt and conformed to the silence. The moment was important to her because she intellectually knew that a part of her was of necessity being buried. Emotionally, she tried to repulse the feeling. She was not entirely successful. A small knot of regret gathered in her stomach. She found it necessary to look up at the other people, their faces sad, their tears unbroken. She saw the black veils and black hats and the dark, fashionable dresses, new and pretty and freshly bought for the occasion, incongruous with the supposed mournfulness of the occasion. The knot lightened. The knot disappeared entirely with the Rabbi's eulogy to her mother, telling of her virtues, eternal qualities, and beauties of soul. She wanted to laugh now, watching the faces intent on the Rabbi's words, heads nodding agreement from one end to the other of the deep circle of people. The Rabbi had never even met her mother!

Suddenly she saw her father again. Standing next to her, he had blended in with the others. For a moment he had ceased to exist for her. Now, as the eulogy continued and the sadness was drenched onto the mourners in its full potential, he moved slowly away from the crowd, not waiting for the end. No one noticed. They were all too intent on their empathy with the pity in the Rabbi's words. Phillipa followed her father. She saw him walk to a small cluster of trees, stop behind one away from the sight of the crowd, pull out a handkerchief, blow his nose once, wipe his eyes, then cry deeply and fully into the protection of the white linen.

Phillipa did not want to embarrass him and returned to the ceremony. She was embarrassed. Death was done; only the living remain and they cannot be helped by tears, she felt. The living must help themselves, not grieve over that which is ended. Yet, she could not help but feel that she had learned something special. Her father must have loved her mother very much.

Chapter VI

After that one afternoon in Munich she returned to Heidelberg. She told Walter nothing about the funeral. She rarely spoke to Walter, except when he initiated conversation, and then only about things that were either completely unimportant or of the utmost importance. The everyday matters of living between husband and wife somehow eluded them—no, not eluded, but carefully misplaced by Phillipa, who rejected the sentimentality that such matters suggested. The marriage continued without serious incident. If it weren't satisfying, it was apparently, for each of them, not completely unsatisfactory.

Phillipa began to share, more and more, Walter's status as a center of intellectual attention. Almost every evening they went together to parties, concerts, recitals, lectures, performances, discussions. She met the socially prominent, the intellectuals, the artists, the wealthy. Her knowledge broadened. Her repartee quickened. Her charm captivated. Her beauty increased.

Walter received more and more compliments and more and more envy.

"Walter, old boy," a colleague told him, "that wife of yours is remarkable. Not only did we have a fine discussion after the opening of the play last night, but she is lovely to look at."

And from another colleague: "That was a very fine party at your home yesterday, Walter. Phillipa without a doubt is the most bewitching hostess I've had the pleasure of meeting. And I wasn't the only one who thought so."

And still another: "I envy you, Walter. You must be indeed proud to be seen with such a lovely woman as Phillipa. When I really envy you, though—if you don't mind my saying so—is after you return home at night!"

Walter had led an academic life. The release from the academic often results in an overly-compensated emotionalism. He sought a reprieve from the chains of strength and self-reliance on conviction and belief. For a while he sought their counterpart in the freedom of a sexual bed. But only for a while. The freedom became painful debility when he began to realize Phillipa's resentment. What to him was tenderness was to her weakness. He felt no reason to hide the tears of life or the passion of virility or the enervated body of relaxed fulfillment. Yet, when she would remove his hand from her breast, tie back the long black hair that he had spread on the pillow as an artist would arrange the details of a model he was painting and, without a word, turn to the side of the bed, there was no protest. Instead, his stomach would fill with the pain of annoyance—not with her, but with himself. He would feel that he had done something wrong, that his was the fault, that he was incapable of pleasing her with his love-making. In a philosophical argument with another professor he would protest forcefully until he would will his point; in a discussion with a student he would be potent until the student understood his principle; with Phillips he did not find this kind of strength. His love was a worship and in his worship there was no challenge or blame.

In compensation he turned more strongly toward his scholarly studies. He gorged himself with work. He read and wrote almost to excess. He worked far into the night, sometimes till early morning, energizing what now seemed clear to him to be his only real area of strength. He began to look forward, as the high point of his week, to the weekly meetings at his home of a number of his prominent colleagues who had organized a discussion group to analyze matters of common intellectual interest. He began to spend more and more evenings at home, preparing an extra-good lecture, compiling research for an article, translating a paper from another language. He took Phillipa less and less to parties and discussions, artistic and social events. Phillipa didn't mind too greatly. She had by this time gotten to know most of the people that she felt she should know. She went by herself.

The coldness that grew between them was less indifference than it was disdain on Phillipa's part. She had never loved anyone but herself and her love for Walter was consequently no more and no less. It was nothing. There was the closeness that comes out of sleeping in the same bed, her concession to the convention of marriage. But it was not an intimacy; it was only a nearness. They talked sometimes: at the breakfast table of the party or concert she had been to the evening before; at lunch of his classes and students and events at the university; at dinner of necessity. Often he would try to interest her in the political discussions of the time. In this year of 1933, as the rebirth of Germany dramatically leaped forward, his interest as a philosopher and a political thinker gradually was forced to become more than provisional. He sought a basis in his thinking for an understanding of what was happening and he wanted his wife to find the same kind of understanding. If he could not share—in fulfillment—her bed, he wanted to share—on a plane in which he would find himself equal—a community of thought.

"But politics is about people," she told him. "The ordinary, crude people. I don't deny them and I don't abuse them. I just don't concern myself with them. I would rather concern myself with the finer things."

Walter often thought that he would like to concern himself with "the finer things" of life, too. But he could not. The coarser things, the things that intrude into a man's conscious life and so dominate it that he reverts to the escape of the subconscious; the things that continue to follow him, into the subconscious—the daydreams, the nightdreams poured themselves over Germany and into Heidelberg and into Walter. These were matters to think about and Walter, whatever else he was, was a thinker.

It came shortly after Herbert Kamm's dismissal, long enough after it for Walter to have been able to sleep nights again without worrying about Kamm's present occupation and not long enough after it for him not to see the clear connection. Early 1934 in Germany began peacefully enough. The new National Socialist regime had awakened the country to the needs for German unity and nationalism. A good thing, generally, for education, Walter thought, for he was interested in the growth of the schools and the system. But—and his fears held back the verbalization—he was also aware that nationalism and unity carry with them conformity. The nonconformists began to go. The orders were subtle at first. All teachers were to take an oath of loyalty to the state. First in the elementary and secondary schools. There was same comment, but not much. One or two teachers in every school refused to take the oath on principle and, Germany ostensibly being democratic, they were allowed to take their refusal to the courts. Due process disposed of the cases quickly. They were summarily fired. They were given the opportunity to seek other jobs, outside of education. They were considered poor risks for student minds. When the loyalty oath reached the universities, the public began to be more aware of its significance. Many intellectuals protested, suggesting that all professors stand in a body against the "invasion of academic freedom." At one university, in Berlin, many of the professors did. They were suspended. New, less qualified teachers were given their posts. Many courses were dropped from the curriculum.

"Education suffers," Guido Termini told Walter one day as they talked of the incident. "It was once a good university. Now its level of education is less than that of a good secondary school."

"I agree," Walter admitted. "But what can I do about it?"

"You and I and everyone else. We must fight against it."

Walter smiled. "Give me my slingshot, Guido. I'll go to battle against the Phillistines!"

They were seated in a small cafe near the college, drinking a beer after classes. Guido, ordinarily loud and carefree, now leaned forward across the table, almost scowling.

"It is not something to laugh about." He pushed a paper toward Walter. "A petition. Look. The entire German Department, most of the Italian and French Departments, the Music and Art Divisions, the Political Science Department . . . almost all of the important faculty have signed. You get the Philosophy Department to so the same."

Walter studied the typewritten sheet: "We, the undersigned, loyal German citizens and faculty members of Heidelberg University, protest the dismissals of fellow educators in other institutions of learning solely on the grounds that they have refused to sign the loyalty oath . . . ."

Walter looked up. "This is dangerous, Guido. Should the authorities see it . . . ."

Guido laughed now. "You're pulling my leg, Walter. Eh?"

Walter realized the stupidity of his remark. He continued to read: "We further protest the judgment of a professor's educational contribution on the basis of external political evaluation. A professor's contribution to the educational advancement of the university and country should be judged solely on the basis of classroom teaching, research, and writing . . . ."

Walter did not have to read any further. "It's admirable. I agree with it." He hesitated a moment. "If I post it on our faculty bulletin board, what might happen?"

"Before or after it is signed?"

Walter shrugged. He had asked another foolish question, he admitted to himself. He put the paper in his briefcase, as if he were simply being courteous to Guido in so doing. He took a full draught from the beer stein in front of him, let the liquid settle and warm him before he stood, reached out to shake Guido's hand, ready to go. Guido reached out a large, hairy hand and restrained him.

"Not yet, Walter. One thing more. We are afraid this is not the end, but only part of the beginning. Several of us in our discussion group feel that we ought to make this item a particular point at our next meeting, at your home."

Walter ordered another beer. Now he was being thrust into the situation personally as well as professionally.

"This is only the first step," Guido said. "If we allow the National Socialists to impose one measure restricting freedom in even the slightest degree, then we open the floodgates. We must organize our group to spearhead a fight against this terrible thing."

Walter thought a moment, deliberately taking care in his choice of words.

"Frankly, Guido, I do not believe I can worry yet. We are a democratic country and we have elected our heads of state and our governing bodies. If the Chancellor and the Reichstag veer away from democratic practice, then we shall simply vote them out of office."

He wanted to believe what he said, but as a philosopher he knew the impracticality of what he had said. He smiled as he realized that his own intellectual rationalization demanded a different answer, even one that he might not personally like. "Unless, of course," he added, "the people do not understand what is happening."

Guido smiled with him, nodding his head.

Walter sat for several moments more, looking upon his own thoughts as he might analyze the thinking of one of his students in the classroom. He knew what he should think and say and he damned himself for not being true to his own intellectual process.

"Let me have a few days with the petition, Guido. I'll see what I can do." He wished he could be energetic about it. He was grateful that Guido understood and did not press him. And then, to assure Guido and, perhaps even more, himself, "And we'll make this the topic at our discussion group next week."

When the discussion group met the following week, it was already an old topic. The morning following Guido's and Walter's meeting a special meeting was called by the Chancellor of the University. The assembled faculty was informed that, that very afternoon, every one of them would be requested to sign an oath of loyalty to the German state. Those who did not sign would be dismissed from their positions. The chancellor's statement was brief, to the point and no sooner did he finish with the final word than he turned on his heel and walked hurriedly from the auditorium. There was no opportunity for protest or even questions.

The moment the chancellor left, the auditorium became a bedlam. A few cheers, a few muttered curses, then a roar of "no . . . no . . . no" resounded through the room. In a moment Guido was at Walter's side, and in another moment they were joined by their friends and colleagues, the members

of their discussion group who had suddenly been thrust into
a situation that they could not prepare for in the theoretical
solitude of abstract discussion. Alex Schardheim, the political scientist, was there, Erich Dresser, the mathematician,
Max Gruenberg, the teacher of literature, Maria Anneman,
the former actress who taught drama, Gilbert Guerdon, the
half-French, half-Spanish artist who divided his time between
the art department and the teaching of aesthetics in Walter's
department.

They resembled other spontaneous groups of friends and
departmental colleagues who quickly formed is various parts
of the auditorium, rushing to each other, at first talking excitedly, then more quietly, trying to bring some order to their
talk. The groups formed and reformed in the auditorium,
small gatherings of men and women cohesing, breaking up,
individuals speaking their individual sentiments to other
individuals and groups, and reordering again. Guido went
to the front of auditorium, shouted down the hubbub, and
proposed the first course of action.

"If we all stick together, if none of us sign, they will not
be able to replace us all. They cannot. They found it impossible to replace all of those who refused to sign in Berlin.
They would have to close the university, which I am sure they
will not do. If we all stick together our fight is won. They're
stopped right here."

Erich Dresser disagreed.

"It is not important enough, to lose a job. Let us sign,"
he argued. "All they want is assurance of loyalty. Then we can
go on teaching just as we did before."

"Do you really believe that, Erich?," Maria Anneman
asked.

Erich didn't answer.

"And the rest of you?," Guido demanded.

"I am not sure."

"I think so."

"I would want time to think."

"I will have to discuss it with my wife."

"That is the only way."

"We must stand together,"

Then, with bitter casualness, from Max Portnoy, a professor of American history: "Hang together or hang separately!"

Most of the faculty had formed groups dictated by departmental assignments or, as with Walter's group, philosophical and political interests. Some faculty left the auditorium, either ready to go the way of the majority, whether for or against the loyalty oath, or buried in academic neutrality and unwilling to participate at all in anything controversial.

"What difference all our arguing?," Erich Dresser decided, as part of Walter's group. "We're only a small part of the faculty. What influence can we have?"

"A great deal," Maria Anneman insisted.

"Give me a cigarette," Guido said to no one in particular. One was pushed into his open hand. He talked as he lit it. "We're the leaders of a good part of this faculty whether we like it or not."

"If we choose to be. Often we don't choose to be." Richard Kazorin, a tall, good-looking man in his middle forties who taught Russian history, joined them. He was one of the early members of the Communist Party in the Heidelberg area and made no secret of his affiliations or beliefs.

"We can talk a lot of our colleagues into refusing to sign, "he said.

"Enough refusals and . . .," Maria Anneman began but was interrupted by Dresser.

". . . and that many more fired," Dresser said. "It's not worth the fight now." He found it necessary to explain his position. "Believe me, I'm a liberal thinker. You all know that. But I'm also practical. And now is the time to be practical."

"And take a stand," Maria added heatedly.

"I don't think so," said Dresser quietly. He did not want to create unnecessary antagonisms among these people, his friends. He let the matter pass for the moment.

"Philosophers are like second grade schoolchildren," Kazorin offered.

The others looked at him, caught unaware by the seeming non-sequiter. Walter bade him explain himself.

"Just because we do not approve of some of the government's ideals does not mean that everything they do may be wrong," Kazorin said. "There can be elements of good mixed with evil."

Alex Schardheim protested. He didn't fully understand what Kazorin was trying to say, but in his politically academic way felt uncomfortable.

Kazorin did not permit himself to be stopped. "I'll finish in a moment," he said. "What I feel is that Germany is building towards something. It may be an eventual death. Or, if properly handled, it may mean an eventual rebirth."

"There is no guarantee that the forces of good will overthrow this Hitler government," Gilbert Guerdon insisted. "And you can't tell me there may be any good in Hitler." He was adamant.

"You're ahead of me," Kazorin said. "I think there is certainly a possibility that the forces of good, as you call them, may gain the political victory."

"I hope for it, too," Guerdon said, emphasizing the word hope. "I think communism may well come to power here. And I would like to see it do so," He was intellectually a Marxist. But he was not given to vacillations of allegiance or to quick acceptance of new political philosophies or practices. Communism, barely fifteen years old in practice, was not yet the instrument Guerdon believed it could be, and although he agreed with Kazorin in principle, he took no active part in its development.

Dresser could not keep silent. "I protest such an attitude from one of our group. In discussion, it is one thing, but when a crisis threatens, it is another. You may think what you will, but when one advocates revolution . . . ."

Guido patted Dresser on the shoulder. He didn't attempt to placate him, for he felt there was no need to do so or to justify Guerdon. He tried only to calm him. "I don't think there's a possibility of that for a while, do you Erich?"

Dresser slowed his anger for a moment and agreed with Guido. Then, strongly: "But the more we talk, the more I wonder at the purpose of further talk. All this loyalty oath does is make better the chances of a unified and stable Germany."

Guido looked at him as if he had heard the rattle of a snake, knowing that he was at the moment out of reach, but nevertheless heeding the warning with a little extra care. Kazorin was speaking again.

"Dresser's point is exactly correct," Kazorin said. "We're undertaking a socialist experiment. In order for it to succeed, we need unity. Granted that Der Fuhrer had other ideas in mind when he offered the oath—perhaps I should say when Herr Goebbels offered the oath"—he corrected himself as the sudden knowing smiles challenged his first statement—"it will nevertheless be an opportunity to see how effective a unity we can create. It is only a small thing anyway," he shrugged.

"I'm just as interested in a socialistic experiment as you are," Guerdon fairly shouted, "but not at the expense of first destroying socialistic freedom."

"And you think, after this," Walter asked Kazorin, "there will be no further oaths?" His question was sincere, for although he knew the answer, he was beginning to lead himself to his own conclusions, using as a dialectic the mouthing of opposing ideas.

"No one can object to an oath proclaiming loyalty to the German state," Max Gruenberg said quickly, the sounds becoming mechanical certainties, black and white. "No one can be hurt. Everyone is loyal to the state."

"Suppose there is someone who is not?" It was Walter's question again.

"Explain yourself," said Kazorin.

"A little while ago I wasn't sure I would have wanted to," Walter said. "It has been a slow process for me to bring into verbalized convictions those ideas that I knew intuitively to be true." He gave a slight laugh. "It isn't always easy to be an honest pragmatist; we don't know what we have to admit." Walter's face now was serious. "Yes, Richard, let us tie it up," he said. "If we permit one oath and thus accept the principle of oaths as being acceptable, then what is to prevent the government from instituting at any time more oaths pertinent to various and sundry kinds of loyalty or to any activity or thought?" He continued before Dresser could interrupt. "I know. What kind of oath can they devise?" He waved away Kazorin's intended interruption. "That is not the point. The point is that they have established a precedent."

Walter was in the center of the group now, as he had been in the past. Guido smiled in satisfaction and Walter was warmed by his own satisfaction of importance.

"That is something to think about in the future," Walter planted in their minds. "Now, the second point. Suppose there is—just suppose—a Luxembourger or a Lichtensteiner or an American who is teaching here and who is loyal to his own country and who cannot in good conscience sign an oath of loyalty to Germany. And suppose, too, that he is a good teacher, a fine teacher, who contributes importantly to the learning and thinking of our students. Should he then be a hypocrite and sign or should he then refuse to sign and have the state deprive our students of an excellent part of their education? Now that is another dilemma."

Dresser winkled his nose as though any argument was spurious now. The more he thought, the more convinced he became of the righteousness of the government policy and the more he was certain that discussion was inappropriate.

Kazorin watched the others. "Intellectually, that is a good point," he admitted. He was relegating the argument to a plane of ideas when, in fact, action was required. "I have a plan," Kazorin said, "to solve the entire problem." He sat on the edge of a row of chairs and lit a cigarette, posing a calmness that helped ease his words and make them more adaptable in performance than they might have been in content. "The oath is an experiment. It may be a noble experiment. Actually, none of us here can get hurt. You, Maria, an actress, you cannot be hurt. You, Walter, a philosopher, you may have qualms of principle, but in actuality you cannot be hurt. You, Erich, you cannot be hurt, not you Max, a Jew, nor you Guido, or myself, a communist."

Max Gruenberg agreed. "Richard is right. What is there really to fear from a loyalty oath? We are all safe."

"And the few who are not?," Guido asked,

"But that is my plan," Kazorin answered. "Everyone can be safe. Anyone can sign the petition. Clearly, it only implies a loyalty to the state. A reasonable request. Other implications are not pertinent here."

"Man lives by bread alone, Richard?," Guerdon posed, the sarcasm biting in his voice.

Kazorin ignored him. "If there are any who, for good reason, refuse to sign and are fired, then we shall take action. Then, in such a case, we shall all resign or threaten to if the wronged ones are not reinstated. That takes care of your second objection, Walter."

Walter nodded. "For the moment it could. But later?"

"We'll discuss later when later occurs," Gruenberg said. "We must decide one point at a time. We must be logical, Walter—and excuse my using that term to a philosopher."

"But you mathematicians know whose logic is really the best logic," Walter replied with a friendly smile. The others laughed.

For the moment there was no more argument. The compromise seemed satisfactory. They spread out, then, to any others still holding forth in the auditorium, one by one indicating the plan they had developed, one by one meeting with similar decisions by others and with relieved acceptance of a compromise that would not subject any one person either to the threat of individual reprisal or punishment or to the ostracizing by colleagues.

"Do you really think we can pretend that we will solve the problem by locking the barn after the horse is stolen?," Guido said to Walter as they left the auditorium along with the rest of the quickly dispersing crowd.

"No," Walter admitted. "I don't. But I think further argument would have been fruitless. You saw the attitudes of the others." Then, after a moment: "Perhaps it is best to wait and see." They walked into the unexpected, unusual freshness of the street. "We have enough promises from departments and individuals agreeing with our compromise to assure sufficient protest if it comes to that. All we have to do is initiate it."

Guido let his head hang in solemn thought, the fat of his chin curling up into two and three layers of incongruity. "I'll go along and see," he muttered, "I'll go along and see."

That afternoon tight silent groups of men and the few women on the faculty gathered in departmental offices. Occasionally a loud voice signified protest, a moment or so of verbal argument that indicated non-acceptance. But as the hurriedly mimeographed slips of paper just large enough to contain a statement of loyalty and a signature were brought into the offices by slowly moving administrators looking as small and apologetic as they could, the groups dissolved as one after another affixed a name, then walked from the room to a classroom or to a home or apartment or to the other-directed stimulation of a Bierstube. For those who felt strongly against the oath, the ceremony was bitter and their own actions unjustifiable and deprecating. For those who were unconcerned with the political, implications of the oath and who cared little one way or another, their signing was simply another formality in a bureaucratic society that required constant formalities of memos, statements and signatures. For those who believed that the oath was important and necessary, their signing was a flourish of affirmation in their country and in the ego enthusiasm of nationalistic patriotism. But many did not appear in their departmental offices that early afternoon. Some because they had made a decision not to sign. Others because they wanted to think more about it.

Walter hurried to his house after leaving Guido. Although he knew what her response would be, he wanted to talk to Phillipa about it. In the recess of his hope, there was the anticipation that he would get from her the understanding and interest that would make his decision their mutual one.

"We were given a loyalty oath to sign for the university," he said.

She looked at him, now with a solemnity of her own. "Loyalty to what?," she questioned.

He told her.

"That doesn't sound so terrible," she said. "You have nothing to be afraid of in signing it."

"That isn't the point. Once you give up freedom of thought for one reason, then you give it up for any reason."

Phillipa tried to indicate a slight amusement. "You talk foolishly, Walter. You become so somber over these things and use phrases that mean nothing except to philosophers."

"I am a philosopher," he said with quiet anger.

She tried a new tack, sat down, shifted deep into the easy chair. "If you wish, think like a radical, but please don't talk like one," she told him disdainfully. She paused a moment. "Foolish," she said bluntly. "Foolish to even think of it. Why place yourself in danger? Why put your neck out? Why go against rightful authority?"

"You have flouted authority, Phillipa," he answered. "You have acted independently when you thought it was necessary."

Logic was a useful tool for her only when it reached the conclusion that she already held. She ignored his analogy.

"Strength is important," she said. "The strength of our country necessitates an undivided Germany, an undivided loyalty. The independence and strength of all of us requires the signing of such an oath. On moral grounds. You don't have to have made clear to you the practical considerations. We must live on something. I must live on something."

It was not necessary, Walter thought, for her to have emphasized the "I."

The impulse for self-preservation decided the issue. The compromise plan of Walter's group provided the rationalization, the way out, for many of the rebellious. Even Guido signed. Most simply stated that the issue was not important enough, not impressive enough to fight about at that time. In his heart Guido sadly told himself that at any given moment from that time on there would probably never be an issue that would any longer be considered important or impressive enough to take a stand on at a specific time. Walter felt this, too. When they met later that afternoon, after having lent their names to the pledge of loyalty, they exchanged soft glances, a warmth of friendship in understanding each other's and their own embarrassment, and yet each felt and saw at that moment a sudden fear of their comradeship having been defiled and being drawn part through no willingness on their part.Some did not sign. Gilbert Guerdan refused. Others, on political grounds, on nationality bases, or for religious reasons did not feel they could contract their loyalty away from the moral commitment of where their real loyalty lay. Others, citing ethical objections, declared that loyalty could not be legislated, that conformity could be and that, as teachers who had the obligation of creating independent minds, they could not succumb to conformity which, in turn, meant mediocrity. Dismissals and suspensions came quickly.

For many of those who did sign, the dismissals of colleagues were not unexpected; but it was still an eventuality that they had not wanted to face. It was as if those who had been dismissed had deliberately created a difficult situation for those who signed. Now the latter had to face the problem of their own integrity, for it was their acceptance of Kazorin's compromise plan that assured them of their own moral righteousness and justified their signing. Now, with the dismissals, they were faced with the commitment to action they had accepted with the compromise.

A few days later Walter's group, at its weekly meeting, was faced with the problem. Without hesitation Guido proposed the immediate fulfillment of their commitment to the plan. Now, suddenly, to several of the group, the plan became unworkable.

"Why unworkable? Why impossible?," Guido demanded. "Because it means we may put ourselves in jeopardy? That is not only possible but the only honest thing to do."

"There's nothing we can do," Dresser said. It was past and done with. "With those dissenters gone, we shall have a more unified faculty, a closer-knit group of professors."

"Better professors?," Walter interposed.

"More loyal," Dresser responded sharply, "means better." He paused, then concluded: "It is impossible to have a good teacher whose mind is filled with foreign or disloyal ideologies."

"Mathematics is universal, Erich," Walter said to him. "Because you think the same formulas as do other mathematicians across the earth, that does not make you subversive."

"But ideas are not universal," Dresser countered. "Some ideas are good, some bad. Mathematics are pure."

Walter knew Dresser was correct. This had not been the point he wanted to make. "But hypotheses are not pure," Walter said. "They must be proven. And before they can be proven, they must be stated and understood and tried. Then, if they are proved false, they can be discarded. Professor Einstein's theories should not be thrown away without analysis and testing simply because they are not yet all accredited into the pure body of knowledge, that body of knowledge which has been proven loyal to truth."

Guido joined the discussion. "And ideas are in the same category, only more so because ideas are rarely proven as coldly as is fact. They vary and are adapted to all cultures, all civilizations. They are moving, as is the world. They are not static. Therefore, in order to have a progressing world, we need many and varied ideas. Otherwise we stagnate and die."

"And if the ideas are bad?," Dresser suggested. "Afterwards it may be too late." He smiled, feeling there could be no answer to this argument.

Guido smiled back. "And at their worst, they can only result in the kind of stricture that you would impose from the beginning. Like through a loyalty oath. So at least testing the ideas gives us a chance for advancement. Your way, it is stifled from the start."

Dresser lit a cigarette, trying to retain a smile of superiority, trying to affect a pose of disdain for words, poor counters for the pure logic of mathematics.

They spoke, one by one, as a classroom of students following the formality of recitation. Maria Anneman thought they had a moral obligation to take group and individual action according to Kazorin's plan that they had accepted. And just as they had urged it upon their colleagues and were thus responsible for many of them signing the oath, they were now equally responsible to attempt to get these same colleagues to take immediate protest action against the dismissals in accordance with the provisions of the compromise.

Max Gruenberg was vehemently against such a course. "They are finished, the others. It's over and done with. Now we can live in peace. Let us forget it. May I remind you that this, too, shall pass. We shall be troubled no longer now." Gruenberg slouched forward in his chair, a man appealing to his friends, hopeful, needful, for their understanding. "I have been a member of this college for forty years. I am seventy. I can retire. But I don't want to because I could not live without my students and my books. That is my entire life to me, my classes and my teaching." His thinned, wisped white hair, slender, stoop-shouldered body looked even older as he said this. "This, too, shall pass. We shall live in peace now."

The others fidgeted is silence. There seemed to be nothing more to say. Walter felt no need to speak any longer. He knew, inwardly, at one moment what his decision would be and knew the next moment what he wanted it to be. He had his own problem to resolve. Kazorin sat in a straight-backed chair at the far corner of the bookcase, at the rear of the group. He had remained silent throughout the entire meeting. Now the others, almost as if in accusation for their dilemma, looked at him. He, too, was caught between commitment and fear.

"Nothing from you, Richard?," Guido said. "You, who have as much to lose as anyone." It was not his intention to make Kazorin a scapegoat. He wanted him to take a stand on a personal basis. "Look at Guerdon. Gilbert was dismissed. Even if he had signed, he probably would have been dismissed. Remember, he is a communist. Don't you think the same thing will happen to you?"

Kazorin did not protest. He didn't deny the truth of Guido's statement. He tried half-heartedly to justify himself. "I don't think any idea necessary to university life is being destroyed," he said. But he didn't believe it and didn't expect any of the others to believe he did. He spread his legs wide and slid down low against the back of his chair and brooded.

Alex Schardheim hesitatingly suggested that the plan should he forgotten, if only because few of their colleagues would go along with it. "It was a mistake to begin with," he said. "We're educators," he continued. "We're thinkers. It's one thing to sit and discuss and analyze on a high plane. But it's not proper for us to run about like a bunch of anarchists provoking action. It's degrading to our dignity."

"Only a small group needs to take the lead," Guido said. "The rest will follow. Only the leaders are needed. When the others see they are not alone, they will join us."

"What I am saying," Schardheim answered, "is that this is, after all, only a small thing. It is in reality only a small issue, not big enough or threatening to fight about. Why risk losing everything when we really have so little to gain!"

Walter wanted to answer. He thought through the ideas and words. He thought about the histories of civilizations of the past, of the early beginnings of intolerance and dictatorships. He knew that the pattern would be the same—many small issues, none big enough or threatening to fight about, until one day . . . .

Guido interrupted his thought pattern and provided the words. "Issue piled upon issue," Guido said. "Oath upon oath, stricture upon stricture, little by little, until all vestige of democracy will disappear." Guido had stood up, at the verge of anger, to say this. Now he resumed his surface joviality and sat again. "So think about that!," he said. It was more of a command than a suggestion.

Conscience suggested that they meet that afternoon. Instead, they decided to adjourn and bring their individual decisions the following morning. If enough of them decided to fight the problem through, then, as a group, they would. If not, then it would simply become a small issue molded into the pattern of forgotten history.

Walter's stomach quivered. He wanted to discuss it with Phillipa, openly and fully. Yet, he was afraid to, for he knew what her response would be. He had to speak with someone and, as his wife, she was by right closest to him. He resolved to do so. Before she could stop him, before she could trample the words in his throat, he told her how he felt, that he wanted to fight, that he believed he must make formal protest against the dismissals.

"It is my duty. It is my word of honor," he insisted. It was said almost as a plea for her to allow him to follow the dictates of his conscience. "What happens in the rest of the university may very well be greatly affected by the decision of our group."

"And you ask me for advice? Or permission?"

Walter was embarrassed, as he knew she would somehow make him be. He did not intend to ask advice or ask permission. He wanted confirmation. And yet his attitude seemed nothing so much as a request for yes or no, for the liberty to act as *she* best saw fit. He was unable to face both the decision and her rising opposition. He tried to minimize his own determination. Now he wanted to get out of it.

"I just mention it. I don't know how many of the others will stand together."

"Not you. Not you, Walter. You are too intelligent."

"I don't know," he muttered. He had hoped, somewhere in his mind, that there might have been an understanding, that there might have been the recognition this one time that his need for moral integrity required action. "I don't know." He lapsed into the safe solitude of his intellectual rationalization.

"There is a logical comparison," he said weakly, "to the beginnings of the Spanish inquisition, to the trials of Cromwell, when they began with just this kind of incident that was allowed to grow."

"The same old stuff. The same old comparison," she said wearily. She was prepared to become very angry with Walter if he held to his insistence. "Hogwash!" Then she held her anger. Now she was calm again and purred.

"We have been all through this, Walter, just a few weeks ago. You will not go through with such foolishness, Walter, will you?" She came close to him, caressed his head with her hands, pushed her body against his. She let him know silently but firmly what he would be alienating.

It was no use, he thought. He felt her power. It was too strong for him. He could not fight Phillipa.

"No," he sighed, the heaviness that hung over and surrounded him disappearing and at the same time creeping into him and weighing him down with interminable resignation. "No. I won't go along with them."

"Good," Phillipa laughed gently. Inside she laughed a long time.

But the laughing began to pall in Hitler Germany. Even as Walter's group and the university faculty decided to take no action, the State did. The restrictions got worse. Those who had not signed the first oaths were not seen again on the campus. New oaths and new affidavits appeared. Government inspectors from Berlin visited the schools and universities, questioned heads of departments, questioned individual teachers. A silence of fear descended when these visits were announced. Teachers and professors peremptorily were informed their services were no longer needed. They were not told why. They were not permitted appeals, they were not confronted with accusations or accusers, if any. The forces for the protection and growth of the society of the State assumed full control. When the State began to feel the need for the strengthening of national loyalties, a new menace was introduced and a new restriction or oath prescribed.

Walter's group had not met for several months, not since the abortion of the plan to protest the previous "small" issue. A new wave of dismissals hit the university and, along with a number of other faculty members, one of their members was to be dismissed. With reluctance, they met again.

"I was mistaken before," Kazorin said. "It was not just another small issue. It was part of a pattern that we now see all too clearly."

Dresser had become more outspoken in the passing months. A man who never spoke quite as clearly as his scientific brain should have permitted him to, he now felt a newfound strength of power and did not hesitate to articulate.

"Just because you are to be dismissed," he told Kazarin, "does not mean that the pattern is bad. Perhaps the pattern is good." He did not hide his disdain for Kazorin.

Even Maria Anneman was frightened. "If you resign from the Communist Party and denounce all of its tenets, then perhaps they will permit you to stay on."

"You think so?," Kazorin said. "I thought that might be so three months ago when Gilbert Guerdon was fired. But I don't think so now. Last time it was an oath of loyalty. Today it is an oath that one is not a communist. Tomorrow it will be an oath that one never was a communist." He suddenly smiled, then laughed loudly.

Guido asked him why he was laughing. Guido was solemn now. The past few months had robbed him of the innate brightness and happiness of his every moment.

"Because it's funny," Kazorin answered. "And you know why it's funny? Because someday soon there will be an oath that pertains to any one who ever associated with communists or had a communist as a friend. And . . ."—he could not stop laughing long enough to get all of the words out—"that will mean each and every one of you . . . because you know me!"

Max Gruenberg laughed too, but only in derision. "You talk like a fool, Kazorin. Why don't you renounce the communists and stay on?"

"Because I believe in free ideas and it is my privilege to have my ideas freely."

"But communist ideas are not free ones," Gruenberg replied.

"I shall not argue that. They may not be, they may be. But whatever they are, unless I have the privilege to have them, then I am not free." They did not argue with that. He continued: "The entire idea of giving in is foolish. We gave in last time. I felt safe. Now you see how safe I am." He spoke slowly, looking from each to the other.

"Think, my friends," Kazorin said, "whether you are a liberal or a monarchist or a Moslem or a Jew, like you, Max Gruenberg, or a Catholic, like you, Maria Anneman, or anything that might smack of an independent, different belief and you will see that you are not safe, either. Perhaps you can still defeat this if you fight it now? Perhaps not? Maybe we have permitted ourselves to be led past the point of no return." There was no laughter, no bitterness now, only seriousness in his voice and manner. "I am leaving now," he said. "I have a country to go to. But when it happens to you, where will you go? What will you do? Where will you hide? Or will it be too late for you to hide?" He shook hands carefully with each one. "Three months ago I cut my own throat. I hope you will think more of yours." He walked quickly and confidently out.

There was silence for a long time. Finally, Guido made a proposition, with bravado, yet tentativeness. "Let us try one more time. Let us see if we can still organize a protest and stop this whole thing right here and now." He looked at Walter. Walter did not permit his eyes to meet Guido's, lowered his head and remained silent.

No one spoke. Finally, Max Gruenberg stood up. He said what the others had hoped they would not have to say. They were relieved to let him speak for them. "It is only a small issue," he said. "Let us protect ourselves. We have done nothing. They shall not bother us. This, too, shall pass."

Chapter VII

The communist was fired. Anyone suspected of having been a communist was fired. Some were imprisoned. It did no good to refuse to participate in the probes and the questioning. It made no difference if one invoked the Weimar constitution and the privilege of freedom of speech and, presumably, freedom *from* speech, if desired. Silence was guilt. Evidence and rules of law disappeared from the German legal system.

Walter attended one of the hearings.

A large, wolf-like man with a round, full bristly face punctuated by sharp jagged teeth in his smile had begun to make a reputation in German political circles as the conductor of loyalty hearings. His was a popular role—the conscience of the people, of the state, of the law, ferreting out those who were suspected or were accused of being disloyal to the State or who, at some future date, might conceivably consider being disloyal to the State. This young man, Karl von Fort, then only 35, was a protege of Gurtner, a little too harsh and crude for Gurtner's suavity and sophistication, but nevertheless capable of doing the job so although Gurtner did not accept von Fort socially, he did not reject him publicly and, indeed, accepted him politically, thus granting the man and his methods his approval. Actually, the Minister of Justice had only one concern: That von Fort might replace him someday, riding into power on the slogan, "I am Justice!"

Peter Lewald, a young teacher of philosophy who had come to Heidelberg just the year before from the University of Vienna, had been informed that he was to appear in Mannheim before the von Fort tribunal for questioning about un-German activities. The notification shocked and frightened him. He searched his past activities, he searched his mind for something he had done, something he might have said or thought that prompted the hearing. He could find nothing. Lewald phoned von Fort's Mannheim office and attempted to speak with him.

"The Baron has not yet arrived from Berlin," he was told.

Lewald thanked the secretary and hung up the phone. Later that afternoon he heard a radio news broadcast that stated that von Fort had arrived in Mannheim the previous day and was setting up his tribunal for hearings the following day. The radio broadcasts did not use the title, "Baron." There was too much crudity for Goebbels, as well as for Gurtner, in von Fort's behavior, and the former chose to believe that the "von" had not been a legitimate part of his name, but had been added for political and social prestige. Without Goebbels' approval, the "Baron" was never officially recognized—at least not in public pronouncements.

Lewald called Mannheim again. He spoke with the same secretary.

"I have mentioned earlier, Herr Lewald, that the Baron is not here."

"But I heard on a radio broadcast . . ."

The secretary, annoyed, interrupted: "He is too busy to speak on the phone."

"I only want to find out what he wishes to question me about." There was no answer. After a moment, as if in apology for asking such a question: "So I may be better prepared to help"—and here he paused just long enough to decide that he would use the term—"the Baron obtain the information he desires." Again, silence. Finally, after a long pause: "Perhaps you will tell me what he wishes to question me about?"

He could feel a mocking smile in the answer: "But, of course, you know!"'

"No, I am sorry, I do not know."

There was a sarcastic titter. "Of course you do!"

"No, I am sorry, I really don't." Another pause. "Perhaps you can postpone my hearing until you can send me particulars about what I am accused of so I can be better prepared."

The answer came quickly. The voice now harsh and commanding. "The hearing cannot be postponed. You will be here at ten o'clock tomorrow morning."

"But what is my crime? How can I defend myself if . . ."

"Ten tomorrow morning!"

The phone receiver clicked down hard at the other end. Lewald stood helpless, the phone in his hand, waiting for the ringing in his ear to die down. He made no attempt to call again. He sat down and smoked a cigarette. He told himself not to be frightened or worried. But he was confused. He had watched the process of loyalty strengthened in the year past, had seen friends and acquaintances leave their jobs, had felt sorry for those who were summoned to hearings, but concluded that there was a sound reason for any action that might have been taken against them, and let it go at that. He had completed his university education only a few years before, this was only his second teaching position, and he was interested only in doing his best as a teacher and in impressing Walter Penmann, the head of his department, and in eventually progressing from the status of instructor to assistant professor.

The project facing him the next day was a complete unknown. He moved toward it—or rather the hours moved him toward it—as if he were in a hollow darkness, unable to help himself or know exactly where he was going, albeit inexorably going. He wanted to shrug off his increasing concern, but could not help but go back to thoughts about himself.

"Why would I be summoned?" He pondered the possibilities. "As a teacher I could unknowingly be teaching my students un-German ideas. The State would not want that, of course." He brightened now. "Of course, someone suspects me of teaching irresponsibly. That must be why they want to see me." This explanation satisfied him. He was certain that his teaching was beyond reproach and that no one could prove otherwise. He pondered this. "There could be no other reason," he assured himself. "And I am not afraid of anything I have done in the classroom." A plan formed in his mind and he went immediately to the Philosophy Department office.

"Professor Penmann"—he addressed Walter respectfully, not having yet become one of the inner circle and not daring to violate protocol by assuming a first name basis without being bid to do so—"I have been called to Mannheim tomorrow morning."

"Von Fort?," Walter questioned. The question was routine. By now the occurrence had become commonplace.

"Yes." He tried to erase any hint of worry in his face. "The only thing they would want of me, of course, is to be certain that my work in the classroom has been above board. Now, if you were to come with me, as my superior, to verify, if you will, that my work has been loyal and that I have not used the classroom for subversive indoctrination, then the matter undoubtedly will be cleared up quickly."

"You have been told that is why they want you?," Walter asked. "To question you about your classroom work?"

Lewald's face narrowed. "Why else would they want me?"

Suddenly Walter felt on the defensive, as if he had been put in the position of accusing not only Lewald, but the State

itself. He felt a shiver of revulsion in his stomach at the fact
that he should feel fright so quickly, so easily.

"I don't know," Walter answered. "Is there any other possible reason?"

"I cannot think of any. I am confident of my own loyalty.
It can only be that they are interested in making certain that
there is no subversion in the universities, a most laudatory
endeavor. You can testify in my behalf. You have come to my
classes and noted my work."

"And you think, if they have called you, that they will
now be satisfied to let you go?" Walter knew he should
not have said that the moment the words blurted from his
mouth.

"I do not understand, Herr Professor," Lewald said with
deliberate, respectful, yet condescending challenge. "You
surely do not question the motives of the State?"

Walter wanted to stand up, take the young man by the
shoulders, sit him down hard and pump what he believed was
the truth into his head.

"Have they ever checked solely on classroom behavior?,"
he wanted to ask. "Have they ever really been concerned
with how a person teaches? Have they ever based a decision on a professor's academic record?" But he swallowed the
words, felt them choke inside, then felt a little better as the
thoughts, at least, were completed, the sentences expressed,
even inwardly. There was no choice for him but to smile indulgently as though one or both of them had misunderstood
that moment of conversation.

Walter picked up the phone, called his secretary in an adjoining office. "Gertrude, have Herr Lewald's and my classes
informed that there will be no meetings tomorrow." The
departmental secretary made note.

"I will go to Mannheim with you tomorrow," Walter told
the young teacher.

At eight-thirty in the morning they boarded a bus for
Mannheim, twenty kilometers away. Walter had not told
Phillipa where he was going. By ten o'clock they were seated
in the courtroom of the Rathaus, a low, long building set
off by a lawn reaching to the street. It was a building of
fairly new design, suggesting cold, hurried performance,
somber and spare in its lines. It was highly functional. Von
Fort entered shortly after they arrived. He moved without
hesitation to the judge's bench, walking heavily and almost
clumsily. There was the slightest trace of a limp in his right
leg. Walter looked especially for it. He had read about that
limp in the newspapers. Von Fort, 18 at the time, had been
a member of the German Army in the Great War and had
been assigned to an infantry battalion in 1918. His battalion
had participated in the unsuccessful attempt of Ludendorff
to cross the Marne in early August in the fight against the
American forces, and von Fort had often spoken glowingly
of the battle, of German heroism, and of his own part in the
battle. Once, in a speech, he announced that he was carrying
10 pounds of shrapnel in his leg, the result of wounds received in that battle. It was believed that privately Goebbels
had snickered when he heard of von Fort's claim, but there
had, nevertheless, never been an official counterclaim. It had
leaked out unofficially to the public—through Goebbels' own
discretion, some believed—that von Fort's only injury in the
war had been a break in his right leg suffered from a fall during a drunken beer party shortly before the Second Battle of
the Marne. In either case, Walter reasoned, as he watched von
Fort climb the few steps to the raised platform at the front
of the roam, the limp was legitimate. Sometimes, attributed
by some of von Fort's followers to an apparently gritty and
Herculean effort, the limp disappeared.

Von Fort spread same papers out on the desk in front of
him. It was a very high desk, high enough for von Fort's head

to barely come over the top of it, higher than the level of the man standing on the floor in front of it and facing it, of sufficient height for sufficient prestige.

It was a day for reporters and photographers and the room was crowded with them. There were ordinary citizens, interested in the proceedings designed to keep their country free, as they saw it. The crowd was strangely excited and expectant, Walter mused, somewhat like the ancient Romans must have been, he thought, when the Christian dissenters were brought to the bar to be thrown to the lions. The air carried a tenseness that belied the formality of legal procedure expected in a courtroom.

Lewald was calm now. He was self-assured. This is an interesting experience, he thought, although he continued to wonder why he was there. He would answer whatever questions were asked. Certainly no concrete evidence could be directed against him or his classroom deportment in any way, shape, or form. There were two hearings that morning. Lewald saw the other witness, at a separate small table several yards in front of him, an older man of some sixty-plus years, almost completely bald with white wisps of hair. He wore a dark blue suit, perfectly cut, a rounded collar and a dark tie with a diamond stickpin prominently displayed in its center. He looked vaguely familiar.

"Theodor Harz," a court secretary called. The secretary was a young man in a light grey suit, looking like a university student and affecting the manner of one who had just vanquished the college president in a public game of chess. Superiority was all on his side.

Theodor Harz walked briskly to the stand. The name and manner were easily identifiable now. Harz was a cinema star of great note. He had vied for a time, in Germany, with the antics of the young English-American performer, Charles Chaplin, but he was no match for "Charlie," "Karl der

Grosse," "Charlemagne," "Charlot," as the latter was sometimes variously called. Several years before, with the advent
of talking pictures, Harz had seen his popularity drop as one
of the leading film stars in Germany. However, he was still
known for his occasional picture appearances and, with the
recent barring of many foreign films and the concentration on
German-made cinema, his popularity had begun to rise again.
He was confident and sure of step as the questioning began.

Walter watched with special interest. This was the first
hearing he had attended personally, although the newspaper
and radio accounts had provided full accounts of the procedures. He was especially aware, through the media reports, of
the apparent arrogance and lack of cooperation on the part of
many witnesses in refusing to answer questions quickly and
directly. Harz proved to be such a witness. Walter followed
the question and answer exchange carefully.

Von Fort: You are Theodor Harz, motion picture actor?
Harz: Yes, sir.
Von Fort: You know why you are here?
Harz: No, sir.
Von Fort: (looking through some papers on his desk)
You, Harz, have been accused of actions detrimental to the
welfare of the State. That is why you are here.
Harz: (sitting silently a moment, attempting to retain
his composure, debating whether to become angry) Oh?
Von Fort: (his voice droning without emotion) You are
accused of un-German activity.
Harz: Who has accused me, sir?
Von Fort: That is secret information. It belongs in the
secret files of the Ministry of Justice. I cannot give you that
information.
Harz: Then what am I accused of, sir?

Von Fort: That is confidential. We cannot reveal our evidence at this time. For purposes of State security.

Harz: Then, if there is no charge, sir, I cannot be put on trial. Good day, sir. (rising to leave)

Von Fort: Sit, Herr Harz, before you are in contempt of this body.

Harz: (a faint flicker of smile across his lips) I mean no contempt, sir. Of the court. Will the court please inform the accused what he is accused of, so the accused can offer his defense?

Von Fort: (angrily, his voice rising) Harz, I will not hesitate to hold you in contempt. Guards!

(Two men with little patches depicting bolts of lightning sewn onto their shirtsleeves stand on either side of the witness chair.)

Von Fort: Now, Harz, understand this. (pausing to turn his profile to the photographers who have moved forward to take a picture of Harz flanked by the guards) This is not a trial. This is a hearing. We only wish to ascertain your loyalty to the State.

Harz: Yes, sir.

Von Fort: All we ask you to do, Harz, is to demonstrate your loyalty as a German citizen. (then, as if talking to a not too bright child) Now, is that too difficult for you to understand, Harz?

Harz: I am loyal to the ideals of the German people and government.

Von Fort: Very good, Harz. Now you seem to understand. Let us go on. We have evidence to the contrary.

Harz: What evidence sir? From where? From whom, sir?

Von Fort: (his voice racing with anger again) Harz, I have tried to explain to you. This is a serious business. The security of the State is threatened. We cannot make public secret and confidential information. (relaxing and almost smiling) All I need, Herr Harz, is proof of your loyalty.

Harz: But how am I to prove it, sir, besides saying that . . .

Von Fort: (interrupting) Then you are disloyal!

Harz: I assume I am innocent until proven guilty. I am loyal. Show me where I am disloyal and I shall prove it is not so. Show me . . ."

Von Fort: (jumping up, shouting) We will have no more of that. I hold you in contempt. I'll have you thrown in prison.

Harz: (jumping up, shouting at the same time as von Fort) I'm willing to answer any charges you have. Just make your charges. What kind of law and justice is this? Make your charges and I'll answer them.

Von Fort: (trying to out-shout him, banging his gavel down on the table unceasingly) Guards, shut that man up. We're not going to make this a platform for a personal speech against the government. Guards, shut that man up.

Harz: I only ask for what's fair. I only . . .

(The guards roughly grab him and push him down into the witness chair. He sits camly now, upset at having let himself become so upset. His heart pounds, but his face is stolid. At first there had been the smile of an anticipated virtuoso performance. Now there is only complete seriousness.)

(Von Fort sits down again, wipes his face and neck carefully with a handkerchief, reaches for the papers on his desk, looks at them cursorily, and begins again, his voice droning, as if nothing had happened.)

Von Fort: Because this is a just a hearing, I shall give you another chance.

(Harz sits silently, not saying a word, not moving a facial muscle. Von Fort glowers down on him.)

Von Fort: Are you ready, Harz?

(Harz stiffens as if he awaits the impossible, the improbable, the unsolvable, the riddle of the sphinx.)

Von Fort: (softly and slowly) Are you now, Harz, or have you ever been a communist?

Harz: (looking up, without emotion) Is that what I am accused of? (the words are slithered through his lips, acting out a surprise that was not really there)

Von Fort: Just answer the question, Herr Harz.

Harz: May I ask you a question, sir?

Von Fort: No. I ask the questions.

Harz: I only wanted to ask . . .

Von Fort: (interrupting) I said I ask the questions. You answer them.

Harz: : . . if some accuser said I was a communist, because if I . . .

Von Fort: (interrupting again) I shall have to hold you in contempt once more if you continue.

Harz: . . . if I answer yes, I shall be thrown . . .

Von Fort: (shouting) Do you hear me, Harz? Guards!

(Each guard grabs one of Harz's arms. He stops his words for a moment, then continues as if the guards were not even there.)

Harz: . . . into jail. And if I . . .

Von Fort: (shouting, losing all control) Harz, shall I take more drastic measures? More drastic measures, Harz?

Harz: . . . answer no . . .

Von Fort: (standing, suddenly holding hack his shouting and attempting to give his voice authority and maturity, resigned to what he has to do) All right, guards, remove that man.

Harz: . . . then on the word of my accuser . . . who I do not know and who does not even appear and who for all I know may not even exist, I . . .

Von Fort: (his attempt at dignified authority having failed, beginning to shout again, like a child who has been unable to make a complicated toy work properly) Quickly, guards. Quickly, guards. Remove him quickly. Disrupting the court. Making a mockery of justice. Quickly, guards.

Harz: (even as the guards pull him roughly from the courtroom and out through a door at the side) . . . then I'll be put in prison anyway. (now shouting to make himself heard as he is pulled outside the courtroom and the guards try to shut the door behind him) How can I answer the question? How can any honest man answer the question? This is not fairness. This is not justice. This is not . . .

Von Fort: (rapping his gavel louder and louder, his voice almost in a scream, but not quite drowning out Harz's) Order in the court. Order in the court.

Harz: . . . humanity! (his voice is abruptly stopped as the outer door is slammed shut behind him)

Walter's reaction was one of unbelievability. He should laugh and be prepared to applaud, he thought. Harz would come back from the outer room and he and von Fort would stand together at the front of the room and take bows. He had to believe that this was true. A dramatic performance. A charade. Anything else was too frightful to consider. Even the great Chaplin had not, in his memory, given such a performance as had Harz. He imagined how hilarious and pointedly tragic it would be—in keeping with the "little tramp's" style—to see a Chaplin movie in which the little man was carried off by two husky guards, his elbows spreadeagled at his sides, his feet furiously kicking at empty ground beneath him, to a fate that only von Fort and Gurtner knew, proclaiming in his naïve way his civil and political rights as strongly as had done the little Theodor. It must be a scene from a Chaplin movie, he thought. But he sat in quiet horror, reluctantly accepting that what he had seen was only all too real. As the confusion of fear subsided within him he wondered how clear Harz's proclamation had been to the observers in the court. The noise of the gavel, the movement of the guards, the shouts of von Fort had disrupted Harz's speech so fully that it had taken all he could do, in his deliberate concentration, to keep the separated parts in one intelligible whole. Perhaps that was why the newspapers had never printed the comments of those accused, he thought. The newspapers told only the names and occupations of those being held in contempt for not cooperating. Or was it, he thought, because Harz had been the first one ever to speak up in such a manner? He would wait for tomorrow's newspapers to read Harz's comments in full. But he didn't really believe that he would find them there.

Lewald was visibly shaken. He was no longer calm and confident. Walter stared at the young man next to him, not now a teacher aspiring to the rank of assistant professor of philosophy, but a perplexed boy. Lewald desperately searched his memory now, trying to find something in his past that would link him with subversion, with disloyalty, with bolshevism, with anything that would help him understand the nature of what he would be called upon to deal with in a very few moments. But try as he might, he could find nothing. Why, he had never even talked very much about current political things, even in private, informal discussions with friends. Of course, in philosophy classes different political theories were discussed from time to time. As a student he had to study some of the things objected to by the Ministry of Justice. The books had been assigned by his professors. He couldn't help it if his professors were foolish enough to recommend books about the Russian Revolution and the French Revolution and the American Revolution. He, himself, would not use them in the classes he taught. The philosophies of Voltaire and Marx and Lenin and Thomas

Jefferson were dangerous philosophies, he insisted to himself. He would mention them to his students only in passing from now on, he vowed. As he looked up at the bristly face of von Fort looking down upon him, he decided he wouldn't even mention them at all.

He began to sweat now as the secretary called his name. He remembered some of his professors and mentally cursed them. Professor von Stubbendorff, Professor Hendrick, Professor Cramer—these three he remembered especially. They had promoted discussion of ideas of this kind. They had talked about communism and socialism and democracy. He hated them now, for it was they who were at fault, not he. He could not keep his thoughts straight. Of course they were not at fault for anything, he permitted himself to think. They were merely teaching facts. Some he accepted, some he rejected, but they were simply facts. And of course they also taught ideas. The aim of the teacher is to teach young people how to think. Ideas are necessary for thinking. He had to have ideas. They were good teachers. They were not to blame for his present situation. It made him feel better—feel stronger—to think of their innocence, thus proclaiming his own, until he looked up from his thoughts and found himself at the testifying chair. There were no guards there. He was all alone, the man, von Fort, towering above him and the people, too many people, big people, important people, frightening people, not at all like the accepting faces of the students in his classrooms, in front of him and all around him, surrounding him and converging on him.

He felt very small and very alone. He tried to gather the past to provide himself with comfort or, if not with comfort, with justification and understanding. He remembered his roommate at the University of Vienna. Nils Viklund, a Swedish boy who had come to study art. Viklund's father had been socialist mayor of his town and Nils had not only accepted his father's beliefs, but had taken them a political step further. Until this moment Peter Lewald had dismissed Viklund's talk as simply the political bohemianism expected of all artists. He had paid little serious attention to it. He had remained friendly with Nils and they still exchanged letters—after all, it had been only little more than a year that they had last seen each other. Perhaps it was his relationship with Nils that was the cause of his summons. Nils had returned to Sweden as a dedicated—he hardly dared even think the word in that courtroom—communist. Well, it was not his fault, his acquaintance with Nils. It was the Dean at the University who had found them an apartment together. Dean—he searched for the name—Dortman. Dortman's fault, it was.

The room was suddenly quiet. Von Fort was speaking.

". . . and we must remember that we are Germans, with intelligence and, above all, dignity. We must not demean ourselves as did the previous witness. We must act with dignity. Each of us must act like a man. We must not stoop and shout and scream and crawl as did the previous witness. If a man is innocent, then he has nothing to fear from this tribunal."

Lewald realized that von Fort was directing these words specifically to him. He nodded his head.

"Yes, sir." He said it proudly, deliberately. Von Fort's words reassured him of his own loyalty and he forgot the rushed thoughts of a moment before. Foolish trepidations, he assured himself. What had he to fear? He had been silly and childish. "With dignity, like a man" he assured von Fort.

Von Fort smiled. Lewald was further assured. It was a friendly smile. If a witness were friendly, then von Fort could be friendly. Why did some people vilify the man? He did not blame von Fort for being hard and stern with those who were unfriendly. If he had a similar responsibility to defend his country, wouldn't he feel the same way?

Walter set himself to listen and watch carefully once
again, this time prepared not to be surprised at anything.
He watched von Fort repeat the procedure of idly shuffling
through some papers in front of him, heard the same, almost
bored droning of his voice.

Von Fort: Name?

Lewald: Peter Lewald.

Von Fort: Occupation?

Lewald: Instructor in Philosophy at the University of
Heidelberg. (this said proudly; it was a position to be proud of)

Von Fort: (putting the papers aside, talking softly and
fatherly to Lewald while making certain that the father-
figure image permeated the room as a whole) Now, Herr
Lewald (then with gentle deliberation) . . . Peter. As you
know, the teaching profession is one of the most important
to the State . . . (waiting for Lewald's nod). It is a sensitive
area, that of teaching our youth. Their minds must not be
poisoned with foreign ideology, with tenets contrary to those
of the State and of the people.

Lewald: (nodding as vigorously as he is able in hearty
agreement) Yes, sir.

Von Fort: Therefore, within the due judicial procedure
accorded me by the Federal Government of Germany, I have
called you to question you and obtain your cooperation in
investigating certain areas. We can never be too careful, you
know.

Lewald: Of course. (smiling now, wondering why he had
been fearful earlier; von Fort was really a pleasant, friendly
person)

Von Fort: We have information, Herr Lewald, concerning
you.

Lewald: Yes, sir?

Von Fort: We wish to determine to what extent you are
guilty of what this information accuses you of.

Lewald: What is . .? (stopping himself just in time, confused for a moment, not knowing what to say except to ask what seems like a logical question, and then remembering what happened to the previous witness who asked such a question) I . . . uh . . ."

Von Fort: (appreciating Lewald's predicament and his obvious attempt to be cooperative) Of course (smiling indulgently), this information is secret.

Lewald: (smiling back) Of course.

Von Fort: We must be careful with our youth. You understand that, Lewald?

Lewald: Yes, sir. And I think it is an excellent job you are doing in protecting the ideals of the German youth. I am not much past a youth myself.

(He begins to laugh, then sucks his cheeks together embarrassed as he sees the surrounding arc of unsmiling faces in the room. He sees von Fort's steady, unchanging half-deigned smile and drops his mouth completely.)

Lewald: I mean to say, sir, that I want to cooperate with you.

Von Fort: Good.

Lewald: (certain now that he was doing the right thing, that this was the proper approach) I am prepared to testify fully about my teaching. In fact, to cooperate completely with you, sir, I have asked to come with me here today the head of my department, who can testify to my teaching and whether or not I have done anything untoward in my work with my students. I am fully prepared to open my complete conduct toward German youth to this inquiry.

Von Fort: (in the same tone and manner as if he had not heard a single word Lewald had just said) Tell us about your relationships with Bolsheviks, Lewald.

Lewald: (dumbfounded, unable to fathom an answer) The head of my department is here with me, Herr von Fort.

I brought . . . (stopping, unable to comprehend what had happened to the logical progression of a few moments before)

Von Fort: Your relationships with the Bolsheviks, Lewald?

Lewald: None, sir. I . . . I have had none. (very slowly, trying to adapt to this unexpected question) None, Gnadige Herr.

Von Fort: This is contrary to our information. Are you now or have you ever been a communist?

Lewald: (quickly and more strongly.) No, sir.

Von Fort: I will repeat the question. Are you now or have you ever been a communist?

Lewald: No, sir.

Von Fort: That is not in line with our information. Let me put it another way. (his voice has no anger, but is still patient and calm, moving along without inflection) Have you ever spoken uncritically about communism?

Lewald: (quickly) No, sir.

(As he sees von Fort's unmoving stare, he thinks again about his courses at the university and in particular about a discussion once of *Das Kapital*. But certainly, he tells himself, that was not "speaking" communism.)

Lewald: (hesitating, slowly) No, sir.

Von Fort: (his voice rising for the first time) You hesitate, Lewald. We want the truth. Why do you hesitate?

Lewald: Well, sir, in university classes we . . .

Von Fort: (interrupting) Once more, Lewald, I ask you to answer the question. You are a teacher of philosophy, are you not?

Lewald: I am, sir.

Von Fort: Have you studied communism? Do you know about communism? Have you spoken communism?

Lewald: (more and more frightened and confused, afraid to state anything but innocence) No, sir.

Von Fort: (like the cat who has swallowed the canary)
Then tell me, Herr Lewald, if you are a teacher of philosophy,
including all philosophies, including even the evil of communism, how can you teach its evil if you know nothing about
it, if you have not studied it, if you have not spoken about it.
I would call that an incompetent teacher.

Lewald: (caught in the trap, without a choice of answer)
Yes, sir. In that sense, sir, I have studied communism.
In university classes. I meant to say so before, sir. I was
going to . . .

Von Fort: (interrupting, with a fixed smile and droning
voice, a slight, hoarse laugh, almost a giggle, directed at the
spectators) Well, we got that answer finally, didn't we! Let's
see if the other answers will be easier to get, Lewald, shall
we? (then, not waiting for a response) Now, Lewald, have you
ever discussed communism?

Lewald: (resigned) Yes, sir.

Von Fort: (the rasping giggle again, nodding his head
in satisfaction, then turning to the papers on his desk as if to
gain factual reinforcement for the next question) Have you
ever possessed communist literature?

Lewald: (certain of his answer and remembering von
Fort's opening remarks on dignity) No, sir. No, sir, I have not.

Von Fort: (suggestively) You are perfectly sure of that,
Lewald? You would not want to perjure yourself, would you?
Would you like to think over your answer?

Lewald: (frightened by von Fort's apparent certainty of
his premise, but unable to find justification for it) I'm trying
to think, sir, but I . . .

Von Fort: (interrupting again) Think carefully. Never
possessed any revolutionary, any subversive literature?

Lewald: Well, sir, I . . .

(He thinks back to a class he had had in American
philosophy and a copy of a book containing the writings of

Thomas Jefferson. He shudders as he remembered it. At this
very moment it was in his room, in his bookcase! He gulped.
Maybe they had searched his rooms while he was in the
courthouse? The book had been ordered barred from universities by the authorities just a few months before and he had
removed it from his office but had forgotten to remove it
from his apartment bookshelves and confine it to the furnace.
He was trapped. He was guilty. Now he shouted it, as if to
assuage his guilt.)

Lewald: Guilty, Mein Herr. Yes, Mein Herr. A book . . .
from school . . . not on purpose . . . I did not mean . . .

Von Fort: (voice raised again in interruption.) The question: Have you possessed subversive literature? Yes or no.

Lewald: Yes, sir.

Von Fort: And now, a final question. Have you ever associated with communists?

Lewald: (not thinking twice now, feeling any explanation or protest would be useless, he had, in fact, anticipated
the question and immediately remembered his friend—he
detested the name now—Nils Viklund) Yes, sir. But it was
not my fault, sir. I didn't know that . . . (looking up, seeing
von Fort's smug face, stopping of his own accord)

Von Fort: So, you admit it. You have talked communism.
You have possessed communist literature. You have associated
with communists. And yet you deny being a communist.
(The coarse laugh gurgled through his throat as he said this
last)

Lewald: I can explain it, sir. It was . . .

Von Fort: The court has been lenient with you, Lewald.
Now, I want the whole truth. Don't pretend to set yourself
up against the State.

Lewald: No, sir, I do not. I do not, sir.

Von Fort: Good. (then, more to the spectators than to
the witness) We are not here to harass you, Lewald. You

understand that. We are here only to protect the security of our country. Subversion is sinister, clever, hidden. Why, I suspect you yourself might not have even been fully aware of how you were being used as a tool by communism, by communists. You can help the State by clearing the air. If we find that you have turned from your former ways and are indeed loyal, there is no reason why you cannot continue in your present position. If you do not clear the air, if you do not tell us the complete truth, then, of course, I would not wish to believe that any university would want you to train the minds of our youth.

Lewald: What do you want me to say, sir?

Von Fort: The truth.

Lewald: (not knowing how to say what he knows von Fort wants, and what he knows he must say) I don't know where to begin, sir.

Von Fort: Let us get back to the first question. Are you now or have you ever been a communist?

Lewald: (wanting to get it over with) Yes, sir, I suppose so, sir. In a way, sir, I suppose I must have been, according to the evidence brought out in court. (then, with affirmation and a new kind of courage, almost proudly) But no more, sir. I hate communism. I hate revolution. I hate subversion. I hate radicalism. (gathering momentum, feeling that now he is on the right track) I have turned from any relationship with it I might once have had. I was a foolish youth to have permitted it to come so close to me. But I disown it now, fully, completely.

Von Fort: (leaning back, pulling the papers with him, as though he would study them again, waiting a moment for Lewald to feel satisfied with himself, then leaning forward again, pushing the papers ahead of him, not looking at them) Good. I had no doubt that you were now a loyal German. In fact (pointing at the papers), our information tells us that.

But we must always be certain. (after a long pause) Now that we have ascertained your loyalty, let us have the names of the people whom you knew previously to be subversive or communistic. This would be, then, clear proof of your continuing loyalty. The names of those persons dangerous to the State.

(Lewald is completely surprised. He felt that it was easy enough to tell them what they wanted to know about himself, but how how could affirm for a fact anything of that nature about others?)

Lewald: But . . . I recanted, sir. I don't know any . . . (the words fade off softly, almost as if ready to melt into a sob)

Von Fort: Don't spoil your chances now, Lewald.

Lewald: (straightening up, in one final effort) But you told me to behave with dignity, sir. To behave like a man. I have tried to. I am trying to. But you don't let me. I want to tell the truth. But it gets twisted. I tell the truth now. I . . .

Von Fort: (standing now and shouting) Guards, guards!

(The guards surround Lewald, who sinks back in his chair.)

Lewald: (feebly) Please don't take my manhood. I have lost my dignity. Please, sir. (Lewald bends forward in the witness chair, starts off toward von Fort, insupplication, almost on his knees before the investigator. He does not see Walter closing his eyes, sorry and sick and not able to endure the sight of the young man's degradation.)

Lewald: Please, sir, don't make me crawl.

Von Fort: Do your duty as a loyal German.

Lewald: Please, sir. Please sir. (on his knees, tears freely staining his face) Please, sir.

Von Fort: (standing high over Lewald) Names!

Lewald: Please . . .

Von Fort: Names!

Lewald: Please.

Von Fort: Names!

Lewald: (rising to his feet, half bowed, sinking back into the witness chair Professors . . . (very slowly, barely audible; the secretary leans forward to catch every syllable and write them on a new virgin white sheet of paper) . . . Hendrick . . . Cramer . . . von Stubbendorf.

Von Fort: Who else?

Lewald: Nils Viklund. Swedish.

Von Fort: More!

Lewald: (morally and ethically exhausted) That's all, sir.

Von Fort: Certain?

Lewald: Dean . . . (the words become stuck in his throat and barely reach the open air)

Von Fort: What's that?!

Lewald: (as a last gasp) Dortman . . . Dean Dortman. That's all, sir. On my honor, on my honor, that's all.

(Lewald takes a handkerchief awkwardly from his pocket and wipes the tears from his face.)

Von Fort: (sitting back in his chair, his face bristling with a suppressed smile) You have done yourself proud, Herr Lewald. As an honest and loyal citizen of this nation. It was difficult for you, I know. On that account the people of Germany must admire you that much more. Your hands are clean. (after a moment, the boredom back in his voice, his eyes turned to the papers is front of him, without a glance at Lewald) You are dismissed, Herr Lewald.

Lewald moved slowly from the witness chair, walking painfully, shrinking from contact with the physical world that seemed to also want to avoid contact with him as through he were covered with burns that were too sensitive to be touched. He repeated over and over, half to himself, half to whomever or whatever was willing to grant absolution at the hearing of the words: "Don't make me crawl. Don't make me crawl." The words were no longer meaningfully clear to him. He felt only their retching and tearing hurt.

Walter walked to the exit of the courtroom and waited far the young man. He felt that he should look after him and yet he could not bring himself to do so, as he heard Lewald's words repeating themselves . . . "don't make me crawl," and saw him crawl to save himself. Walter knew some of the people whose names Lewald had given and wondered what would happen to them now.

Chapter VIII

Peter Lewald continued in his position at Heidelberg. No one would dare challenge him now. Walter thought about suggesting that he be transferred to a different department or that a post be created for him at another institution, but he did not seriously consider proposing it. It was small satisfaction that Lewald kept away from him. Whenever they approached each other, Lewald avoided him. Whenever they spoke, Lewald never looked him straight in the eyes.

When the suspected communists and subversives and disloyal citizens had all been purged and the central authorities were satisfied that they effectively controlled the university, the issue of conformity became dormant for a while. The desire to believe that the crisis had passed provided the university community with a rationalization for academic business as usual, for a plunging into the bureaucratic committee duties of education that took their energies from truly significant thought . . . and significant teaching. But at Heidelberg, as all over Germany, the educators, the artists, the intellectuals, the working men and women could not remain in perpetual lethargy as much as they might have desired to do so, and a restlessness of mind and spirit returned.

They looked about them and wondered if a subversive menace really did exist. Same even went so far as to suspect that
perhaps a menace had never even existed at all. Many Germans thirsted for a freedom of expression and thought, even
though they could not and would not put their longings into
overt terms. But the dissatisfaction was there, under the surface, slowly fermenting, and in the year 1934 the government
became aware that new scapegoats were needed.

Nationalism was growing furiously, feverishly. Human
fuel had to sustain the propagandistic and militaristic fires.
The Jews were next into the German furnace. As it turned
out, literally as well as figuratively. Guido Termini had met
Walter during an intermission between classes one afternoon
in early autumn, shortly after the beginning of the academic
year. They walked dawn the hall together, silently, side by
side, but not too close together, not speaking. They passed
Maria Anneman, exchanged a perfunctory but friendly greeting. Maria smiled as she passed them. Guido's voice was
cheery and booming. They passed Max Kanner. They nodded
curtly. Max stopped them.

"Any more this week?," he whispered. He looked around
the hall before he spoke, checked again after he asked the
question.

Guido lowered his voice, but asked the question openly,
naively. "Any more what?" He was deliberately wary of Max.

"Any more?," Max repeated, as if there should be no
question as to his reference.

Guido played the game. "If you didn't hear of any, I
guess there were none." Guido patted Max on the shoulder.
"See you again, Max," he said more loudly, and continued on.

"I don't trust that one," he told Walter after they had
turned the corner of the hallway. His voice was low. The hails
were quiet. No more of the loud, boisterous laughter that
Heidelberg had known. No more of the animated discussions

and arguments among the students as they left the classrooms after studying issues of controversy. The university thought in whispers. Ideas that were spoken too loudly could be heard all the way to the Ministry of Justice in Berlin.

Walter and Guido went into the faculty washroom. Walter breathed a sigh as they pulled the door closed behind them. Guido motioned his fingers to his lips, walked quickly over to the enclosed toilets, peeked over the partition of each one. "It's all right," he said. "No hidden ears in the toilet bowls."

"Six students yesterday," Walter said.

"Reasons given?"

"No."

Even in the privacy of the bathroom the words were low and quick, as if the softer and faster they were, the less chance there was for them to have any meaning to an outside listener.

"Communists?," Guido asked.

"That was a long time ago."

Guido nodded. "Jews?"

"The quota was strict. No surplus," Walter said,

Guido nodded again.

"One of them came to me last week," Walter continued. Wanted me to come to a meeting they were holding. They wanted to form a discussion group. A philosophical organization with administration sanction. All open and above board."

"You didn't go?"

"No.".

"Wise," Guido said. If anything, he had become even more careful now than Walter. He kept repeating to himself a slogan: A principle isn't worth anything unless it accomplishes something. He often wondered how much he really believed this and how much was platitudinous rationalization.

"Yes, I think it was wise," Walter nodded. "They were getting together as prospective members students who were neither members of the Nazi youth group nor of the military training program here."

"And the administration found this out?" The question was rhetorical. "Someone in the organization?" Guido knew he didn't have to ask this, either.

Walter nodded.

"Well, at least some of the students are trying," Guido said. "At least there is a nucleus."

"For what?" Walter's question was more of an ironic challenge.

"For the day when they really will be needed. They sacrificed their university careers for that."

"What more can they be needed for?," Walter asked. He fearfully already knew the answer. "University careers are important," he added, as if to avoid getting an answer to his question.

"Lives are more important," Guido said.

A rattling of the bathroom door stopped their talk abruptly. Guido stepped quickly to the washbasin, began to run water over his hands. Walter flushed a urinal, then went to the basins. Guido began drying his hands. The trespasser was a member of the economics department, a new faculty person who had been hired the previous spring following a personal recommendation by Deputy Minister of Education Krosick, it was whispered around the campus.

"A warm day," the economist observed.

"Very warm for fall," Guido said pleasantly, threw the crumpled paper towel into the wastebasket and started out without a word or glance to Walter. The economist stood at the urinal, threw the words to Walter, who was now drying his hands and beginning to crumple his paper towel.

"But it will be a cold winter, as always."

"As always," Walter said and left.

Walter caught up with Guido, who was deliberately walking slowly, around the corner of the hallway,

"According to the novels, more plots are hatched and discovered in bathroom stalls than any other place," Guido laughed. "So I thought we'd better play it safe."

Walter smiled an acknowledgment. They walked down the hall toward the chancellor's office and the faculty bulletin board.

"Only a few minutes until my lecture," Guido said, looking at his watch.

"Let's see what the news is for today," Walter suggested, motioning toward the bulletin board.

Max Gruenberg, a bit out of breath, fell into a rhythmic pace at their sides. "Haven't see you two for a long time," he said.

"No, not since . . . ." Guido didn't finish.

"I sometimes miss those old meetings," Gruenberg said.

"They were interesting." Walter spoke agreeably, noncommittally. He missed the meetings very much. There had been none since Kazorin's dismissal. The future had telegraphed itself clearly. Some welcomed it. Others feared it. Most simply accepted it. By silent agreement no more meetings were called. Mutual talk implied mutual trust. Guido had observed to Walter at the time: "I wouldn't trust my own mother today, and she's a remarkably trustworthy old lady."

"I really didn't think they had to end." Gruenberg pursued the subject. "Just because we disagreed about Kazorin. After all, it was only one issue. It passed quickly. Like everything else."

Walter and Guido remained silent. They reached the bulletin board, scanned it idly. A fresh, white piece of paper, a new notice, caught their eyes.

Guido glanced over it quickly, capturing its meaning.

Walter read it more slowly, speaking each word, barely audibly, under his breath: "For the greater strengthening of our country, our ideals and our mission, for greater solidarity among the people of Germany, for the greater glory and protection of the German Aryan race, faculty members of Semitic origin of fifty (50) percent or more blood line are hereby notified that their services will no longer be required by the University of Heidelberg, effective as of the above date."

It was dated that very day and signed by Reichminister Frick himself.

Walter and Guido turned together and looked at Max Gruenberg, whose face fixed on the notice as he reread it and then reread it again.

His seventy years, previously held alert and youthful by his service to his country and to his people, the German people, as an educator, suddenly became seventy years of heaviness, of hopelessness, devoid of meaning or accomplishment. In that moment he became an old man. He bowed his head, stood with his eyes closed in front of the bulletin board. It had now reached him and he knew he himself had permitted it to. The other two men turned away. There were no words for Gruenberg that could help. They expected none from him. He had given his final words a long time before reality, and now reality had shown them to be false. There was nothing left. Even now, as he tried to say them, he knew there was no truth to them. They welled inside of him and were not even worth the energy of a whisper. They choked him and lied to him. They had betrayed him. In his own sorrow he vaguely began to transfer his unhappiness to faceless others and wondered how many more had been content to say, "This, too, shall pass."

The other men walked away and left him there, alone with his thoughts.

The pogrom extended into the student body, into the clerical and custodial services. Soon all educational institutions in Germany were void of Jews. The Catholic was united with the Jew in the role of victim when Herr Goebbels proclaimed that their religious belief also conflicted with the political and national loyalties of the State. Each group thrown into the refuse pile by the German overlords brought cheers from the German populace, much as the American lynch mob cheered as the noose snaps shut and breaks the neck and stops the breath of the living human body. When one cheer began to fade, another victim was found, another poplar tree lined with rope, another issue of hate fired to fever pitch, another trap sprung.

People create ideas, so people went first. But people leave ideas behind in tangible form—in books, art, music, plays. All carriers of ideas were, of course, dangerous to the German State. Books by any person convicted or accused were banned from libraries and schools. Books with ideas that were objected to officially or by rumor were barred. Day after day list after list issued from the chancellor's office at the university: "The following titles shall not be used in classes."; "The following titles shall not be made available any longer in the library."; "The following titles shall not be referred to in class by an instructor under any circumstance." ; "The following titles may not be kept in any faculty office and, by extension, are not expected to be part of a faculty member's home library."

Walter felt like an animal trapped in a cage. Never an extrovert, always a man of thought rather than action, he had been able to adapt himself, though forcibly and with regret, to the previous edicts effectively enough to keep his position without more than the usual fear which had become endemic to most positions at the university. But the destruction of books that had become sacred to him imposed a more difficult burden. He felt the bars of ignorance coming closer and closer and he felt himself pacing back and forth, from one bar to another, with each turn of his back permitting the steel trap to creep up a little more on him. Little by little, he wondered how long it would be until it would crush him.

He did not speak of his feelings to Phillipa, although he very much wanted to. In the evenings he would sit at his desk, going over his papers, preparing his lectures, carefully pruning and censoring the words and ideas that had become so much a part of his thought and teaching over the years, and resentment and guilt welled up inside of him and he longed for someone to share it with, to relieve him, even momentarily, of even a miniscule bit of his burden. But Phillipa, flesh and blood in front of him, was not there for the sharing. She seemed to know when he felt this way and seemed to studiously turn the conversation to something else when it began to move toward these matters. When he did say the words that told of his fears and his hurt, she dismissed them easily as if she, too, might perhaps feel as badly as he did if she let herself—and it was quite clear that she would not let herself. One time he tried to make her understand the danger from a personal standpoint.

"They shall not stop with Jews in universities and in other official or influential positions. They shall get down to the man in the street, to the housewife," Walter warned.

But Phillipa tossed it off. "Perhaps. But even if they do, it is not my affair. It is theirs." Then, before Walter could say more: "I don't go to the synagogue."

"Do you suppose that matters?"

"No. Not really. I am rationalizing. But only because I don't think it's important enough to bother thinking out a real answer."

"You should be frightened, Phillipa. I am afraid."

"For me?" She smiled patronizingly.

Walter almost expected her to add, facetiously, "now isn't that sweet?" He was glad she hadn't. "For both of us," he said soberly.

"That's so sweet of you," she replied softly. "I have done nothing to the State," Phillipa said, "why should the State try to do anything to me" She tried to dismiss the matter in its entirety. "Besides," she insisted, "it doesn't matter that I'm Jewish. You'll protect me."

"Me? How?"

"You're Gentile." She stood up and walked lightly toward the staircase. "Good night, Walter," she said sweetly.

A few days later Walter was confronted with the problem again, only this time it required an immediate decision, possibly a dangerous one, one which he was not prepared to make and which he hoped he never would have to make. At lunch one afternoon he was approached by one of his students, Ernst Puzinger, an extremely bright young man who had interested him on many occasions by his willingness to ask questions and initiate disagreements in class on issues that otherwise would be controversial enough for Walter to feel the necessity to avoid bringing up himself because of the possibility of being led into unwise—or its equivalent, nonconformist—comments.

"May I speak with you for a moment, Herr Professor?" Ernst was very tall and very thin. His body was angular, casting lights and shadows that gave the impression of a dark sadness. He had a face with sharp features, a prominent nose and jutting cheekbones. His thick black hair was trimmed evenly around his head as though it had been shaped by a bowl. A black mustache was being cultivated on his upper lip. He was only 18 and came from a relatively poor family. His thirst for knowledge was great. In looks he was not at all the stated ideal of the Aryan type—in fact, quite the opposite. Indeed, he looked a lot like a young Adolf Hitler.

"It is extremely important," Ernst said, overtly noting
Walter's initial hesitation. Walter was stung by this notice.
He had never refused to see a student and the hesitation had
been unconscious, a motor response, reflecting the fear that
permeated everything. Had his fear gone as far as to deny him
the independence of a spontaneous talk with a student?

Walter followed Ernst to the street, the latter opening
a book on philosophy as they walked, pointing to a page,
innocently asking a question on Hegel, the transparency of
all of this obvious to Walter. When they were out of sight of
the restaurant, walking down one of the main streets of the
city near the universit, in the bustle and noise of hurrying
passersby, Ernst abruptly closed the book.

"It is not philosophy I wish to speak with you about,
Professor." Walter nodded acceptance of his willingness to
listen. "I will be brief," Ernst said. "A number of we students
have contacted a number of professors we believe we can
trust. We have scheduled a meeting of those professors and
ourselves. We think it can be an important meeting. I am
certain you know what I mean."

Walter looked around automatically. He spoke almost in
a whisper, knowing how foolish and melodramatic he must
sound, yet somehow not able to act otherwise.

"Perhaps I do not know what you mean," he said. "And,
even if I did, how do you know you can trust me?"

"I already have," Ernst replied, "by speaking to you about
this at all."

Walter remained silent.

"I suppose one can tell," Ernst added. "We discussed all
the teachers first and compared notes from our observations
in the classroom."

"That proves nothing."

"Can ideas and opinions ever really be proved?," Ernst
suggested. "We can only observe and conclude. In your class,

for instance, I noted that in your discussion of Hegel you seemed enthusiastic when teaching about his dialectic, but not so much so when teaching about his nationalistic ideas."

Walter smiled, impressed. "How do you know which are good and which are bad?"

"I read as much as I can. I know which I believe to be good and which bad. Apparently in much the same proportion as you do. That is why I came to you."

Walter was silent again, deliberately leaving it up to the young man to take the initiative. The important concern in Walter's mind was still not mentioned. Ernst understood this.

"It could be a trap, of course," Ernst told him. "I can only ask you to trust me . . . us. Just as we trust you."

Walter realized that there was nothing more that Ernst could do or say on this matter. It had to be done on trust. Anyone else in that particular class he would have had doubts about. But this student he trusted.

"Where is the meeting?," he asked.

"You will come?," Ernst inquired eagerly.

"Perhaps." Then, in a low volume of voice. "I always come to student-faculty parties if my time permits."

"I must know for certain. There are a number of other professors who have agreed. All those we asked, in fact. You are the only other one we feel sure enough of." He hesitated. "I know what a risk it is for you. For everybody. I think you are safe."

Walter smiled indulgently. "Where is it?" His tone was definite. He would commit himself no further.

Ernst understood. "I will let you know tomorrow. After class. He looked across the street, then turned away from Walter. "I will leave you now." Then, in a clear voice, as he walked away: "Don't worry, Herr Professor, I will do my lesson to please you well."

Walter smiled, then narrowed his face, troubled by the unknown that the situation presented. Yet, in the very unknown there was hope. Perhaps there were those willing and capable of effective thought and action that he did not now suspect existed. Perhaps a nucleus of teachers and students working together might be a constructive force? He continued walking, turned down a side street that would take him back to his office at the university. Was Guido involved, he wondered? Dare he speak to Guido about it? He knew he could not. Even with the best of intentions, any break of the trust could lead to disaster for all. Yet, Guido should have been invited. Guido should be there. He wished he knew.

As if they were seeking each other, yet consciously trying not to let the other know, Guido and Walter met in a corridor after their final classes at five o'clock. As if purposefully on both their parts they walked with deliberate casualness and one block out of the way on their way home stopped in front of a small cafe.

"One beer before supper?," Guido suggested.

"For appetite," Walter agreed.

They both sat silently, studied the steins of beer as the waiter set them out on the table.

"Shall you begin or shall I say it first?," Guido broke the silence.

Walter laughed, then tightened his lips. He didn't know how to begin. Without the need for words they each knew what the other was thinking. They both knew that neither could use the words necessary to bring the thoughts into the open.

"It is a strange feeling, not being able to talk to one's best and closest friend," Guido said.

"Very strange," Walter nodded.

"Talk is a delicious thing. Discussions. Conversations." Guido spoke slowly and evenly. He planned in his mind what he was going to say. "Discussions like our little group used to have. I miss them. Don't you, Walter?"

"Very much." Walter picked up the verbal marker. "It would be nice to have discussions and meetings again." He moved it to the next square. "Perhaps even with some students? Don't you think so, Guido?"

Guido smiled broadly. It was no seccret now. But they both were beginning to enjoy their little game and continued to play it, warm in their understanding of each other.

"Definitely," Guido proclaimed. "I was thinking of it only this morning. Perhaps we can have something like it very soon?"

"Perhaps! Would you like that, Guido?"

"I think I would." He patted Walter's arm across the table. "Would you, Walter?"

"Yes, I would."

"Ah, then it seems we are agreed. We both would." Then, softly and seriously: "When?"

"I'll know tomorrow."

"So will I."

Together they picked up their steins, the foam still white on top, clinked the glasses across the table, smiled to each other, and drank a toast. Though neither proposed one, they both knew it was to the future.

The meeting was held in a small apartment in the center of the city, in a busy neighborhood. It was in what had become one of the poorer parts of town, inhabited mainly by laboring families and students, neither of whom could afford the luxury of more than the decaying brick walls, the peeling plaster ceilings, the gouged wooden floors, the hall bathrooms shared with the one or two other apartments on the floor. The section had, in one sense, become known as a segment of Bohemia. The wealthier students at the university, those from business or nobility homes, lived in private houses or in new apartments either close to the university or on the outskirts of the city. The poorer students budgeted the little money they had, primarily for books, art, theatre, music, which left virtually nothing for rent, food and, sometimes, even for beer. They lived in that section and, like the students in the song, were always on hand for a song or a game, not so healthy, not so wealthy, but certainly, in their own beliefs at least, rising to fame. Walter smiled as he walked up the two flights of steps, holding on to the banister to keep his balance on the narrow stairs and trying not to hug the loose, tottering stiles of the stairway too closely for fear that they might come loose and topple the staircase on him. The words of "Estudiantina" hummed themselves to him and he noticed the sudden congruity of their meaning. For some reason that he could not quite understand, he was not worried now. He had been worried the entire night before. He had been given the address and time the previous afternoon and didn't sleep much of the night. Disappointment as much as worry had troubled him. The meeting was potentially something of importance, partly because of its hope, partly because of its danger, and he wanted to share his participation in it with someone. He was disappointed because he wanted to tell Phillipa about it and he knew he could not.

He had arrived at the apartment alone, at the precise time given him. Though it was not said, he suspected the arrival times had been staggered so that no two people would come at the same moment. He knocked on a door that had tacked to it a typewritten slip of paper marked "Werner." A blonde boy of some twenty-two years, strong, tall and lanky, opened it.

"Good afternoon, Herr Professor, welcome to our party."

Walter recognized the young man. He was a senior student, due to graduate that coning June. Walter remembered him from the football fields. Heinrich Werner was

Heidelberg's outstanding soccer football player and one of
Germany's finest collegiate athletes. His appearance there,
indeed, the use of his apartment, unexpectedly shattered one
of Walter's ideological sets. He had never expected an athlete
to be a thinker, particularly one of liberal inclination. He
smiled at this little prejudice of his, never admitted so openly
before, now so flagrant before his objective mind. He realized with amusement that his initial fear had apparently so
subsided that even at his moment of entrance into what was
an unknown and potentially dangerous situation he could
mentally pause and analyze his relatively unimportant reaction in this manner.

Even though there were not many persons there, every
seating place was occupied and the small room, crowded and
cramped, looked even smaller than it was. Walter sensed
a relaxed stirring as he entered the room and concluded
that he probably was the final person expected. Werner did
not introduce him, but let each person, instead, introduce
himself to Walter as if he, Walter, were already known to the
others—as, in fact, he was. On the only couch in the room, a
low, long, narrow, red-covered sagging piece, sat a large boy,
fat and full-faced, blonde-haired, the hair hanging loosely and
pulling down over his forehead.

"Willy Baier," he said, offering his band. As he stood,
Walter could see that he was younger than he looked. His
face was baby-faced, huge dimples in the cheeks. The double
chin and prematurely round belly made him look older than
his nineteen years. Baier was only in his second year of studies
and Walter had not yet had him as a student. But he had
heard of him and knew that the flab of the body was more
than compensated for by a solidity and quickness of mind.
Baier had, the year before as an entering university student,
founded a political debating group and had begun to gather
a reputation in rhetorical dexterity. The events of the past

year had made inadvisable, from the administration's point
of view, the continuance of the group. Next to Baler sat
Guido. Walter, without purposely thinking it, mused at the
seating arrangement. In twenty years Willy might well look
as Guido did now. Guido nodded to Walter, a broad assur-
ing smile. The man next to Guido stood, shook hands with
Walter firmly.

"Good to see you, Walter," Erich Da Sola said. He had
been born in Germany of a German mother and a Portuguese
father and had always considered himself more German than
Portuguese. He had learned his father's language as a child,
growing up with complete bi-lingual proficiency, and now
taught in the Spanish-Portuguese Department of the university. He was tall, thin and sandy-haired, about fifty-five
or sixty years of age. He looked younger. He was a big man,
over six feet and, though thin, solidly built. His face was
good looking, still retaining traces of a younger handsome-
ness. He might have passed for a movie personality except
for the thick, horn-rimmed glasses. Walter had not included
him in his speculation of who might be there. He had never
been close to Da Sola, had never spoken much with him,
although he had met him frequently at informal parties and
at official functions. Da Sola was an outspoken man, but
practical enough never to speak in public of anything self-
incriminating.

Next to Da Sola, sitting on the floor at the other end of
the couch, was a student Walter knew.

"It is good to see you here, Professor," Felix Lindner said,
his voice tentative. Felix was a shy lad, about 20, of medium
height, medium complexion, without any distinguishing
feature about him. He melted into the sea of heads in the
classroom, disappeared into the large, diffused groups at parties, won no special distinction academically, was not known

in campus affairs, played no sports. The only reason Walter remembered him was because of his occasional examination essays, often sharp, often brilliant, always incisive. His writing was imaginative, combining creative ideas and form with sound basic thought. Sufficient reason to remember him, Walter thought, and a good young man to have in such a group.

On the only easy chair in the room, sunk deep into the middle of its sagging springs, was Maria Anneman. Walter was surprised to see her. Maria noticed his look.

"I finally made up my mind," she said to him, without his requesting an explanation. "As an artist—and an actress is an artist," she smiled, "I find that art cannot grow, nor can culture, nor can people in an atmosphere of conformity and fear. So . . . ," she smiled again, this time as if the decision were obviously the only one she could have made, ". . .I am here!" The uncalled for and unneeded explanation nevertheless reassured Walter.

On the window seat, from which a row of books had been cleared and placed on the floor, sat Ernst Puzinger. Walter nodded and smiled to him. Puzinger stood and nodded, his smile indicating a common expression of appreciation.

They were all. Just eight of them. Four teachers and four students. Not a very large group to counter five million soldiers and sixty million people, Walter thought. Not a very extensive force to face the combined power of all the ministries in Berlin.

The right side of the room opened through a large irregularly grey-plastered alcove into a flat, narrow kitchen. The kitchen table had no chairs and Walter was aware that the rickety uncomfortable wooden chair on which he now sat—its back to the door through which he had just entered and facing most of the other people there grouped along the back wall and the

side wall containing the only window in the apartment—was
one of those from the kitchen. Heinrich Werner sat next to him
on the other equally decrepit kitchen chair.

Willy Baier began. He spoke firmly and decisively.
"This is all of us. No more are coming. Not to this first
meeting, at any rate. I think I ought to make it clear quickly
what our idea is. We have planned this for some weeks.
This is only the start, the beginning. We don't intend to
form an underground organization to fight all of the Nazi
party. I have heard talk that some students and professors at
the University of Munich may do so. Yet, in a sane practical, effective way, it is nevertheless the Nazi party that we
must fight. I think it is agreed by all here that it is the Nazi
party and what it stands for that is the cause of Germany's
trouble."

Walter permitted his own thoughts to come to a verbal level and realized from this short and simple statement
that although he had not consciously made such a choice or
purposely led such a course, by virtue of his own feelings and
of the circumstances that had half-carried, half-invited him
here, he was now willing and ready to plan a fight against the
Nazi party.

"We can't attempt to counter the entire party," Baier
continued, "but we can do the little we are able in our own
sphere, in the university."

"Is that agreed upon? Is that what everyone here thinks
is the starting point?," demanded Ernst Puzinger. He had
gotten up and was standing by the door now as if it had to be
guarded against some certain but unknown thing. "If so, let
us be agreed, and if not, let us thrash it out."

"Very wise," Erich Da Sola said. "Let us limit ourselves to
our limitations. Each one according to his own capabilities.
Our province is the university."

There was no dissent and each one nodded in acceptance.

"Is there a particular plan of action?," Guido asked, deferring to Werner.

"No," Puzinger jumped in sharply. "No plan."

"That's why we got together," Werner said more slowly. "To think of something."

"Well, let us begin with some ideas, then," Maria suggested. "Let us hear some and then settle on some approach."

"May I suggest something?" It was Felix Lindner, the quiet young man. He waited for approval before continuing, although the informality of the discussion made such a procedure unnecessary. "It is wonderful for all of us to be here," he went on, "but it is also dangerous. Instead of taking extensive time to discuss ideas for agreement that are really not solutions, but assurances to ourselves of our broad aims, perhaps we can assume from the beginning that our aims are mutually agreeable and perhaps we can get immediately to the point. We want to remain here just as little time as possible. I don't think anybody would suspect Werner—his being an athlete gives us a useful stereotype, if Heinrich doesn't mind my saying so—but one cannot be too careful."

Walter agreed. "What will our main, immediate action be?," he asked.

Werner thought that some plan of sabotage would be most effective. "Direct action," he insisted. "I don't know what kind, but something to show them that there is an opposition."

There was quick disapproval. Some of it was rather blunt, calling the demand for sabotage at this point a measure of juvenile impatience. Guido would not let either the suggestion or Werner's competence be passed off so hastily.

"Sometimes direct action is the only thing that will work," Guido said. "But," he added, "only when nothing else will. Let us try same other means first. But let's not pass off Werner's idea until we are certain that we have a better one."

"A rumor campaign? A whispering, disruptive campaign," offered Ernst Puzinger.

"Handbills. Books. Leaflets," said Maria Anneman.

"Perhaps an immediate enlargement of this group is first necessary," suggested Erich Da Sola. "To build it up until we have enough strength to think of concerted work in any area we choose."

Walter felt this was the first suggestion with a solid keystone. "Erich's plan is good," he said. "We can only be a thorn and not a very big one, at that. But with more, many more, we can be a sharp needle. At least sharp enough to bother them."

For an hour they threw ideas back and forth, determining the advisability of Walter's approach, agreeing on it in principle, attempting to find a valid rationale for its implementation. It was Felix Lindner, quiet since his previous contribution, who coordinated their thoughts once again.

"There are many more like us on the campus," he said. "They, like us, are afraid. Other professors, other students. They have been intimidated . . ." and he added hastily, humbly, "just as we have been intimidated."

The others smiled, acknowledging the bitterness of the truth. "What I propose we do," Felix continued, "is plan to show the others that they are not alone. Just as we, here, have gained some strength in learning that we are not alone, so will all the others. Even just eight of us, at first, if we spread ourselves thin, we can seem like many, and the others, thinking there are many, will jump at the opportunity to do what they believe in and would be afraid to do if they felt they were isolated and alone. Just as we would be afraid—as we have been afraid—to act alone."

"There are many who feel the way we do," Walter said. He looked at Guido. "We know many of them—rather, we knew many of them. Some might come back into the fold if the opportunity presented itself. But," and he said this slowly, as if in warning, "we cannot expect to accomplish miracles. We cannot expect to change Heidelberg University or to undo anything that has been done."

"But we can prevent a further wrong, perhaps," Da Sola added. "We can influence the university. Enough students and professors, enough of us working together, can influence the university." Then, as an afterthought: "I hope."

"I think so. I think people still feel within them a certain longing for independence and freedom," Maria said.

Guido stood up, walked back and forth in the narrow space a few times. He had been unusually quiet. Now he was apprehensive. "There is one important factor that we must be aware of. The Nazi youth and the Nazi party itself have become exceptionally strong. The old Junkers and military and nobility classes have adapted to it like Heidelbergers to beer. We may be completely overwhelmed in numbers. Whatever we may do may be completely aborted."

"But we must take the chance," Maria insisted.

"I think we can be a match for any of them," Werner said.

"I would make you my champion any day," Guido told him, "against any single representative they might choose for a clash of arms. But I don't think they would fight that way." He didn't mean to be sarcastic and urged his tone toward gentleness as he reached the end of the sentence.

"We must chance it," Puzinger said.

"Of course we must," Guido assured him. "Only we must not rush in with our feet, but with our heads."

Felix Lindner reminded them that time was moving quickly. Walter attempted to sum up.

"Then we are agreed that there are many who would be in sympathy with us. We are agreed, too, that our plan must be to reach these people. To have them help us. To have

them help themselves. To try to influence the university in a
way we think most beneficial and proper. And what is there
to gain by that?" He paused a moment, then before anyone
could answer, finished the thought himself: "The knowledge that there is a flame of freedom left, that others at the
university will know, that other universities and schools and
other students and teachers in Germany will know. What
happens here may be an example for them to follow." Walter
was speaking quickly now, faster than he had ever spoken in
a lecture room. He was excited by the idea, caught up in the
drive toward its fruition. He wanted to move ahead quickly,
to put into operation with all possible speed whatever the
plan would be.

"But exactly what is it that we shall do?," Walter concluded. "That is our next and most important problem."

"It cannot be something unimportant. It cannot come
down out of the clear sky, nor can it be artificial or manu-
factured," Guido said, still standing. He thought a moment
longer. "What will stir the others we think are there, whose
support we want? What will unite them? What unites
people?"

The others watched him, waiting for the answer, as if
he were asking a rhetorical question. But, indeed, he didn't
know, himself. "What unites people?," Guido asked. He
paused. "Walter, what unites people?"

"A common goal. Or, if a goal cannot be stated, a common suffering, a common fear, a common need."

Felix Lindner spoke slowly and carefully. "The next
time there is a threat to the university—or what we feel is a
threat—those others who think like us will also feel it is a
threat. Unknowing, they will be united in spirit."

Da Sola jumped in now. "That is our method. We must
have an issue. And if we can judge by past performances, the

ministry in Berlin will create one for us. When that time occurs, we can go ahead."

"Go ahead with what?," Willy Baier asked. "I do not
mean to be supercilious, professor, but what do we do?"

"You are correct, Willy," Da Sola answered. "Not only
what, but how?"

"When people are divided, they can be conquered. When
they are unified, it is difficult to defeat them. Does that
suggest something?" Walter said the words and knew the
answer, but partly out of habit, partly out of the still continuing trepidation over what he was doing and concerned about
a too-active participation in the group, he left the answer for
the others to form.

"Solidarity. In union there is strength." Puzinger stood,
his face aglow. "And how does a union win its battles? By
striking, of course. By mass protest. Look at the success in
America."

"Exactly," Walter said simply.

They were all excited now. The meeting was nearing its
end. The solution seemed to be near.

"When an issue occurs that is strong enough," Guido
said, "we shall call a general strike of the university. If
enough of us participate, although our fuhrers may be
angry, they will be attentive, as well, to our show of
strength. If we are successful, we have a chance of forcing
that specific issue in our favor. If that happens, then it may
not yet be too late. For everything." He waited a moment,
and then, reluctantly, added what he and they knew he had
left out. "If we fail, it means only that that day will have
arrived for us that will come in the not too distant future,
anyway."

Maria agreed. "We circulate leaflets, telling of the protest. We name time and place and the way it is to be done."

"Like pretending to be sick. All professors and students will be requested to stay out on a particular day because of illness. And if enough stay out . . . ," Puzinger fairly shouted the idea.

"Maybe even picketing," Werner added, "If we get enough, perhaps even picketing."

"I'm not so certain a strike would have the greatest chance of success," Walter said. "That means that each person who does not attend class, who does not show up at his office can be individually labeled. This makes difficult our goal of achieving effective mass action because it puts each individual on the spot."

Guido supported Walter. "There is great merit in that. If I may have the privilege of exchanging my enthusiasm of a few moments ago for a strike to something else. Perhaps the most effective way to get enough people to participate would be to get students and teachers gathered in a huge body, anonymously, in front of the university or in front of the chancellor's house, maybe in silent protest, maybe shouting or chanting. With enough, there will be too many to be able to identify the ringleaders. Too many to do anything to."

Da Sola was not so certain. "Even so, some could be caught. Some could be expelled or dismissed. But more important, this kind of approach can very well result in physical violence. Wherever you get a mob together, even in the best of intentions, you cannot guarantee the results."

"Of course," Guido said. "I know there is, in one sense, a greater risk. Yet, for the individual who may wish to participate, there may be a smaller risk. Think of it in terms of our long-range purpose. In terms of building morale. We don't know how many will stay out ill in a strike. Because they will be acting individually, they will not see the action of the others. But if we appoint a certain time for all to gather at a certain place, then many can come as onlookers, to see, to judge the strength, and if they see enough others who came to see, then they will join in the mass protest."

Da Sola reluctantly agreed. "If it is successful it would be the most effective plan in terms of results. I will go along."

The others supported the idea. They tried to judge the merits logically, found that the risk, though in some ways greater than an "illness" strike, could be compensated for by the potentially greater benefits. Only Felix Lindner made a further objection.

"It is a fine idea," Felix said. "Perhaps it is because I am not a person of direct action, myself, but I would prefer to see the effect of the pen first before we try the sword."

"It might be too late," Werner said. "Time is growing short. It might very well be our last chance."

"That is what convinces me," Maria told them. "It may be our last chance, as Werner says. Before the brown-shirts have taken over everything. We have to take the risk."

"I think this is a principle of action that can accomplish something," Guido offered.

Willy Baier stood. "Then we wait for the issue, call a quick meeting of this group and get out leaflets, word of mouth, posters, handbills calling a protest rally."

The meeting had come to its conclusion, and the others stood now, too. They began talking simultaneously and the little living room was filled with the excitement of action and hope.

Does anyone have a mimeograph machine?," Heinrich Werner asked.

"I have one," said Puzinger. "At my apartment. I've used it before . . . before 1933," he smiled.

"Then we are all agreed?"

"Agreed."

"And complete confidence, complete silence about this meeting?"

"Not a word to anyone!"

"Let us leave it up to Guido Termini to decide when a meeting is warranted," Walter suggested.

"All right with me," Guido said.

"Agreed!"

"And I shall contact Puzinger, who shall contact all of you as he did this time," Guido said. He looked at Puzinger, who nodded satisfaction with this role.

They walked to the door together, ready to leave together, as though they had just ended a happy, bubbling party, elated with the success of time well spent. Walter stopped them.

"This is a good way to begin to attract attention," he said. "Are we to have our demonstration right now on the front sidewalk?"

"Let us leave a few minutes apart, one or two at a time," Lindner said.

"Care in this whole affair is of utmost importance," Walter reminded them. "As we said, it may be our last chance."

Chapter IX

For several months there was comparative calm on the campus. The outside world did not fare so well. In upper Bavaria, where the climate was pleasing and the open country plentiful, barbed wire fences began to enclose wide areas of land, filled gradually with wooden barracks, eventually to be stuffed with people. Since German "lebensraum" was by national policy a precious thing, as the population of the enclosures would grow, plans would be needed to prevent the inhabitants from bursting the bounds of the limited space available. German ingenuity ultimately went to work. Malthus' principle of depopulation was put into scientific application: Gas chambers, furnaces, nooses, starvation, disease, work until exhaustion and death and, among more refined measures, the utilitarian use of human skin for lampshades and other exotic products—necessitating, only as a by-product, of course, the elimination of the human being.

The German people apparently did not mind. The decrease in the civilian population resulted in confiscated wealth for the state and, in the process of overflow—and, in some instances, through more efficient direct transfer of property—more wealth for the German people, too. Morally,

the people chose not to hear what they heard. The newspapers
said little. It wasn't a pretty thing to talk about. When anyone did bring it into the open, the people shut their ears and
branded the story-teller as un-German. This was sufficient to
dispose of truth and permit the populace to sleep at night.
Although, at times, not too soundly, and in some cities, such
as Dachau, after a while not too comfortably because of the
continuing stench of burning bodies that permeated the
atmosphere for miles around.

The university life settled down to a mechanistic movement. Social gatherings virtually ceased. One could not tell
who was still a friend and who had become the enemy. There
could be no talk at gatherings; even an innocent remark
could carry unhealthy innuendo. For Walter, his books, the
radio, and films became the center of life. There were occasional parties: in honor of a visiting minister from Berlin,
in honor of a new book sanctioned by Dr. Geobbels' office.
Walter and Phillipa would invariably be invited, but Walter
disappeared from the center of conversation. He sat in corners
now, listening, glancing earnestly at his watch, waiting for it
to be time to go home. Phillipa, however, enjoyed the talk,
large or small. She was always, somehow, on the right side of
the conversation. No matter what she said, everyone seemed
to be pleased. On the rare occasion that Dr. Gurtner visited
Heidelberg, Phillipa was the minister's guest of honor. A flat-
tering and flattered guest she made, too, escorted to dinner
on Gurtner's arm, asked by Gurtner to the first dance, seated
by Gurtner in the most comfortable chair. Walter found his
evenings taken toward the amusement of Frau Gurtner, a tall
distinguished looking woman of about 50. She must have
been an actress or a showgirl in her youth, Walter judged.
But youth soon leaves, and if beauty has been the only attraction for the man, then the drabness of life begins to settle too
quickly upon the woman. She walked slowly, spoke slowly,

when at all, and if she could have would have faded into the
nearest piece of furniture, to disappear for the evening until
the time came to dutifully arise to accompany her husband
home. She made, however, an impressive entrance. That was
all Gurtner used her for.

For Phillipa, the parties were not frequent enough. Occasionally, Phillipa would go by herself. Walter did not mind.
There was always a valid excuse for him to remain at home:
preparation for his classes. What he did mind was the type
of party she attended now and then: the loud, beer-brawling
Junkers-Nazi gatherings. The jubilant, exuberant nationalistic orgy of ideas. The often lascivious, often sadistic early
morning endings to these parties. Walter was pleased that
Phillipa did not stay long at these affairs and that, after attending several, did not go to any more. She did not object
to the ideas. But she did disdain the brutish, naked actions
and manners. They were much below her, much too undigni-
fied. She treated them with disgust. Yet, on those evenings
when she sat home with a book, Walter reading close by, and
not a word exchanged between them for hours, she regretted that she did have a more accepting attitude toward the
parties.

The winter of 1934 was a cold one. The winds had come
early, sweeping down the usually more temperate Rhine
River, hammering an icy November and December into the
university town of Heidelberg. The winds continued into the
spring semester, into the second week of February. And then
suddenly, as if the city had submitted and could no longer
resist, the winds ceased. A passiveness settled over the city's
buildings, its offices, its people.

By the beginning of the spring semester, independence
and protest had disappeared. All those who might have
proven a security risk to the German state (except some, like
Walter Penmann, who had successfully managed to conceal

their beliefs) were gone. Many who by life-long profession had been teachers were now in Austria, Belgium, France and Eastern Europe. Some, fearful of the worst, emigrated as far as England and America. A few who wished to remain in Germany tried to find jobs in other fields. Fewer, scattered throughout the country, tried to rally back against what they felt was injustice, but thus far had no success. The strong hand of authority was not to be shaken or budged. If anything, it closed its grip more rigidly around the country.

Walter worried more about the youth than about anything else. The spirit of Prussian militarism had revived. The sabre-fights became commonplace. The inevitable rash of scars suddenly appearing on hands, faces and arms became the mark of distinction for youth, just as in America, for instance, the winning of a "letter" on a college athletic team was a mark of distinction. Even in classes Walter could begin to see stony, leering faces, not interested in learning but in reinforcing. Reinforcing what? The extra-curricular schooling. The schooling that had become the new acme of knowledge. The Hitler youth organization meetings. The Nazi clubs where, in addition to speechmaking, dueling, wrestling and all the necessary elements of "toughening up" and "propagandistic" training, the youth were taught fully and—strangely enough, to Walter—with an excited eagerness on their own part, the elements of Nazi philosophy and its goals. All other philosophies and ideas, they were taught, were subversive.

The university faculty had no special problems in the classrooms. By this time the courses had been closely proscribed. Undesirable books and subjects had been eliminated. The syllabi were closely checked by the chancellor's office. No longer was their makeup left to the authority of the department concerned with the course. Walter received a syllabus for each course offered by his department. He was not to question it or revise it, but to teach it. Schopenhauer, Nietzsche,

Hitler. These were subjects which he knew. It was not a question of distortion. He would not distort. He taught them honestly, straightforwardly. His teaching pattern differed in only two ways. He offered no opinions and be stressed no element more than another, except where he felt it would not be noticeable. As long as he taught the philosophies of Nazism, there could be no trouble. The young men in the class who clung to being students first and militarists and nationalists second or not at all became uneasy. They read banned books whenever they could find any available in the city. They occasionally proposed questions about other philosophies. But they, too, were careful. The young dedicated Nazis were, on the other hand, entirely pleased with the system of teaching. They enjoyed it. It further heightened their intellectual self-satisfaction. Whenever they encountered other facets of thinking it became their duty to report the divergence to the central authorities. They liked this. It became a game with them. In the classroom they waited for their Nazi-induced ideas to be reinforced, at the same time challenging either the teacher or a fellow student to make a counter-claim, to even suggest an alien idea. The more names they could turn over to the authorities, the quicker their rise in rank in the Nazi youth movement.

It became a race. Students who studied their assignment the day before class and were able to discuss it intelligently were immediately suspect. Names were listed in the Nazi youth office. Young men who by choice or circumstance were not members of the Nazi youth group were listed. The Nazi youth became the elite, everyone else a potential subversive, a member of an incipient subservient class. The Nazi youth, spurred on by their own beliefs and reassurances of superiority, began to express their power in physical action. A student would be found brutally beaten. Another student would be wakened in the night and the swastika burned onto his chest.

Another would have his clothes torn from him, taken into the
street, whipped, and driven nude and bleeding into the center of the town. At first the local police investigated. When
they discovered who was behind the outrages, they pressed
their investigation no further. The students and faculty of the
college who were not members of the elite objected. They did
not make their feelings known aloud, but the dissatisfaction,
the growing anger at the reign of lawlessness was evident.
One day the issue came to a head.

Alex Schardheim, the political science teacher who had
been a member of their discussion group and who Walter had
once described to Guido as a machine more than a mind, was
accosted by a group of young toughs one afternoon following
one of his classes. Earlier that day, in a course on eighteenth
century world political history, Schardheim had innocently
and briefly mentioned the role of the pre-Germany states of
Hessen and Braunschweig on the side of Britain in the American Revolution and their defeat at the hands of the colonists,
as well as the support of the Americans by Baron von Steuben
and the recognition of the new country by Prussia's Frederick
the Great. In quick chronological order he also mentioned,
in passing, the overt effect of the American revolution on
the French revolution. He did not comment, but stated the
historical dates and events, leaving any interpretation and
significance to the students. Schardheim was a man not given
to political imagination and he taught from the official textbooks, simply and directly. He had absolutely no conception
that in that class he might be disturbing the equilibrium of
conformity in any way.

But the Nazi youths in the class objected. Facts were no
longer facts when they contradicted belief. Nazism was to
the young people of Germany, as well as to the adults, like
a religion which does not admit of truth if truth is contrary
to catechism. Discussion of German failure, even before

confederation, or aid to despised America, even almost two
centuries earlier, was not acceptable to them. Schardheim saw
the angry faces in class, but didn't understsnd why and paid
no attention to them. He did not know their motivation.
And even if he did, it would make no difference, for he knew
he had done nothing incorrect, that he had had no motives
other than to teach as be had been ordered. Immediately after
the class several of the Nazi youth held a hurried conference.
They organized a plan. Several of their fellows who were not
in Schardheim's classes and who were unknown by the professor were contacted. They stopped Schardheim several blocks
from the university as he turned onto a business street to pur-
chase food for that evening's meal. It was close to four o'clock
and the street was filled with shoppers. There was only one
question asked.

"Are you Herr Schardheim?"

Schardheim smiled. "Yes, of course." He saw no fear from
the swastika imprinted armbands on the brown shirts of the
four husky young men. He was curious only as to what they
wished to speak to him about. He opened his mouth as if
to protest a grievous error, a mistaken identity, an incom-
prehensible surprise as he saw the full open hand of one of
the youths come toward his face. He was more concerned
with trying to catch his glasses as they flew off than with the
sting on his cheek. His mouth opened wider in disbelief as
he heard a coughing laugh and saw a foot twist down onto
his glasses on the ground, breaking the lenses, cracking the
frame. He had not time to even look up into the face that
went with the foot, as a sharp blow of a fist caught the back
of his head and sent him tumbling onto the sidewalk. A kick
into his side, then another, then the pounding of fists and feet
on his body forced him to roll over into the gutter, his arms
and hands desperately trying to cover his face. As he turned
on the ground he could see the faces of his attackers, the same

half-smile of satisfaction on each face, the same anticipation
in each one's eyes of destroying a living thing with their own
hands, the open mouths breathing hard in dedication to the
goal of hurting, of hearing the sounds of suffering. As he lay
in the gutter he tried to bend his head into his body as the
feet trampled at his neck, as the kicks slashed at his shoulder
and arm, as the pounding blow of a fist into the small of his
back shot an incredibly sharp pain through his body, forcing his chest and belly out, his arms askew. And as his body
pushed outward the fists and kicks came from the other side,
at his face again, into his stomach. He caught his breath,
gagged, gagged again. His chin and neck and belly were
wet and he could feel his own vomit covering him. His eyes
were wet and as he tried to catch a glint of the world outside
through the fingers that covered his face and he could see the
dripping blood on his fingers.

He saw that there were more than just his assailants.
People had gathered. Men, women, children. They were
standing around him, above him, surrounding the four
youths who continued to pound and punch and kick him. He
opened his mouth to scream. He thought he cried "help." He
wasn't sure. No one moved. He moved his hands apart wider.
They were there, all right. The German people. His friends.
His neighbors. Was it a dream? Was it a fantasy on a stage?
The people, standing, not moving, watching as he thrashed
and rolled and bent his body in two in the gutter of a public
street of Heidelberg while four young men with swastika
armbands and brown shorts continued to beat him. Had the
entire German nation become unconscionable, murderous,
bestial animals? He closed his eyes in despair and in the next
moment saw and heard and felt nothing.

It was fortunate that he was only forty-five years of age
and in good physical health, the doctors in the hospital told
him. Outside of a broken arm, a fractured rib, broken nose

and multiple cuts on his face and back, there was no life-threatening injury. With a few days in the hospital, he could be released. Complete recovery was only a matter of time. He could, in fact, return to his teaching duties within a few weeks, if he wished.

The injuries were not utmost in Schardheim's thoughts. What disturbed him was his inability to fathom even the slightest reason for the attack. This was hooliganism of the worst sort, he thought. This was disturbance of the orderly, progressive forces of growth of the new regime, he thought. This was, undoubtedly, the work of imposters, saboteurs, subversive agents posing as Nazis. As soon as he left the hospital, he reported the details of the beating to the police. He gave them descriptions of the attackers, as best as he could remember them. They made note of the complaint and promised to investigate immediately.

The next morning, patches on his face, his side encased in bandages, one arm in a sling, he marched into the university chancellor's office. The chancellor had been informed of what had happened and expected Schardheim.

"I have thought of it carefully, Herr Chancellor" he said. "I am sure I have seen those faces before. I know they are students here."

"I am certain they could not have been," the chancellor replied.

"I am certain they are," Schardheim continuted to insist, with every one of his protestations meeting an equally strong "I am certain they are not" from the chancellor.

"They were undoubtedly hoodlums, from the other side of town," the chancellor maintained. "Subversives. Probably communists."

"Subversives and communists, true," Schardheim countered, "but students nevertheless."

Finally, the chancellor stood and cut Schardheim short. "I am sorry you were injured, Schardheim. But now it is in the hands of the police. We can accomplish nothing by discussing the matter here. Leave it to the police." Then, as though it was an afterthought, off-handedly: "It is best forgotten."

Schardheim fumed. "Leave it. Forget it. With an arm in a sling, with a rubber corset tying my rib together, with a nose that can barely breathe, with an aching backside that prevents me from even enjoying a beer sitting down? I'll find them myself, Herr Chancellor."

He found them. That afternoon, leaving the school immediately after his class, on his way home Schardheim saw them, the same four, marching briskly together in step alongside one of the gates surrounding a university building. He yelled and as best as he was able gave chase, half-running, half-walking. The youths began to run easily in front of him, staying a fair distance in front of him, but not moving out of his sight. They turned a corner and moved toward the direction that led to the far end of the campus. As they ran they looked back, shouted obscenities, taunted him to follow. Finally, a hundred yards in front of him they stopped, waited. Schardheim, wiser for his experience, stopped, too. That there were many students around made no difference, he now knew. He did not go to them. He turned away, seemingly going back to his office. He turned back, stopped a group of students, pointed toward the four youths still easily within sight at a recognizable distance, and asked for their names.

"My four students, there," he demanded, "what are their names? I have some materials to send them from my home, but have forgotten their names and do not have my class roster book with me. I don't wish to return to my office now." After several piecemeal recognitions, he got their names. He returned triumphantly to the chancellor's office.

"I demand their punishment and dismissal," he insisted.

The chancellor was conciliatory. "I know these young men," he said. "Upstanding young men. From good families. I am certain it is a mistake. Your assailants could not have been the boys you have mentioned."

"They are. I am sure of it."

"It is a mistake."

"No mistake."

The chancellor thought for a moment, then quietly: "I suggest it best be just forgotten. A playful prank." He did not look at Schardheim as he spoke.

"You will not take action?," Schardheim asked incredulously.

"No. It does not warrant it."

"Amazed. I am amazed," Schardheim exclaimed. "Then, Herr Chancellor, I shall tell every one at the university, every student, every professor. I will shout it to my classes, proclaim it to the skies. Rowdyism, gangsterism, and you let it go unpunished, sir. I will . . ."

The chancellor stood curtly from behind the large desk, interrupting, "That is all, Schardheim." His tone was sharp and definite.

Schardheim stopped and stared, unbelieving. "Yes, sir," he said quietly and left.

The next morning Alex Schardheim was dismissed from the university. His dismissal notice gave no reason. By that afternoon the entire university population knew what had happened. It was virtually the only topic of conversation. Some were violently in favor of the chancellor's action, condemning Schardheim as a "weak woman," a "crying Jew," although he was not Jewish; others, silent in their opposition, were concerned for their own physical safety, something they had heretofore taken for granted. Many times during the day Walter heard the whispered frustration: "it could have been me; what can I do?"

The issue that the small group of professors and students had been waiting for had arrived.

Guido contacted Walter during lunch, asked him to meet him promptly at four o'clock that afternoon. Walter anticipated the importance of Guido's request. To preclude suspicion if anyone saw them together, he purposely took time, in as offhand a manner as he could manage, to tell his students that he was meeting with other professors that afternoon to discuss examinations and grades. He tried to make it as casual as possible, tried to make a little joke out of it. "Who knows?" he told them, "but with a few good drinks and a good cigar for us this afternoon you might end up with less work and better grades." He watched the class carefully as they exited and wondered if anyone suspected. He felt he had handled the situation well.

He met Guido at a corner several blocks away as if by accident. Puzinger was with Guido. They stopped and exchanged pleasantries.

"Shall we synchronize our watches?," Guido asked laughingly, as they talked. They avoided any show of deliberate seriousness.

"You mean 'this is it'?," Walter joined in.

"If you are agreed. We wanted your opinion, Walter. Puzinger thinks so. The others do, too."

"Then let's get on with it," Walter said.

Guido nodded.

"At my place, seven o'clock tonight," Puzinger said.

"In the meantime, you write the copy for the flyers," Guido told Walter. "Strong. Sharp. We call a protest meeting in front of the chancellor's house at six tomorrow, after classes are over, as it begins to get dark. Put all the information into your copy. We arrange at our meeting this evening to run it off and distribute it wherever faculty and students can be found, off and on the campus, to be certain that everyone has the information in the morning. Those that don't see the flyers will hear by word of mouth."

For a moment Walter felt a chill of excitement and fear. It was one thing to talk about it, another to do it. Perhaps he ought to suggest to Guido that Schardheim, after all, did not deserve this effort? After all, he thought, Schardheim had permitted the restrictions to grow even more oppressive and had, indeed, even contributed to them. But in the same instant Walter knew that it was not a person, not Schardheim, who was either the cause or the solution. It was an issue. A principle. For him to back out now would be to proclaim himself a Schardheim. He nodded to Guido in acknowledgment of his duties.

Guido patted him on the shoulder. "Nice bumping into you, Walter."

"Likewise, Herr Professor," Puzinger added, giving a slight bow of courtesy.

Walter nodded to both of them and continued on his way. He was excited and and trepidatious. He was proud and fearful. He envied Guido, envied the young student. He was not a man of action and the time for action had come. He had, somehow, become involved in a way that was neither clear nor even fathomable to him. Now that the time of danger had almost arrived he began to feel his stomach tighten and feel sweat on his hands. He walked toward his house, started to cross the street, then stopped. He watched a small, thin, grey-haired man moving slowly, hunched over, walking by the boundary of the university. He recognized him as a former professor of literature, Max Gruenberg. There were many Max Gruenbergs now, Walter thought. Professors who were Jewish, who had given a lifetime of teaching to Heidelberg, now no longer teaching, remaining in their little houses or small apartments near the university, walking on the sunny afternoons past the campus gates, looking at the buildings that had been the source of their life for so many years and wondering whether the classrooms in which they had lectured for twenty and thirty and forty years were decaying with their own disintegration. Walter wanted to stop and speak with Gruenberg, to tell him what he felt, to tell him that he was sorry, to let him know that he, Walter, was actually doing something to halt the injustice that had harmed Gruenberg.

He began walking toward him, then saw close and clearly the face of this man looking hopefully straight ahead, his hands grasping the bars of a university gate as if the iron would suddenly dissolve and put him back inside. What purpose in giving sympathy to a man who needed action?, Walter thought. What sense in compounding sorrow with pity? Quickly, he crossed back to the other side of the street and walked faster to his home.

Phillipa was not there when he arrived. A note informed him she had gone shopping with a friend, would stay at the friend's house for dinner and continue with her to a piano recital at the university that evening. It was better this way, he thought. He made a quick supper for himself, intently washed and dried the dishes, then went to the living room. He walked to the large front window, closed the curtains and walked back to his desk at the other end of the room. Carefully, he made sure the front door was latched. Returning to the desk, he just as carefully took out several sheets of notepaper, a pencil, and began composing the message that would announce the protest meeting.

The work was accomplished smoothly and easily that evening. The meeting at Puzinger's was short. The protest would be broad in base, with no identifiable leadership. No signs and no speakers. It would be a show of numbers. There would be no force and no violence. Standing, shouting, talking only. The protest would be strong in content and peaceful in form.

The mimeograph was run and the flyers distributed. There was barely a place in the city or on the campus where distribution was not made. Yet, at all times, they were secretive and careful. Only when they were certain that no one was watching, especially in the public places of the town, was a small pile of handbills dropped in an appropriate place. They returned home and during the sporadic times when they slept that night it was with a feeling of a job well done. But anticipation of the next day kept most of them awake most of the night.

The next school day did not pass quickly enough. In their personal awareness It seemed to them strange that there was a lack of official comment. A murmuring of students clustered in small groups indicated that the flyers had been found and were being found. The unusual quiet of the campus attested to the sudden intrusion of something different, something of concern. Most of the flyers had been picked up and destroyed. As soon as their existence had became known to the administration, a special detail of custodial help plus a group of Nazi youth volunteers had scoured the university area. But by the time they had covered all of the ground many of the handbills had already begun extensive circulation in the houses and apartments and bierstubes and meeting places.

The Nazi youth, many now attending classes openly in their brown shirts and swastika armbands, wore deep scowls throughout the day. Occasionally a whisper would be exchanged even in the classroom. Some of the Nazi youth did not show up for classes. Walter and Guido, meeting for lunch, were concerned over this obvious, but unanticipated reaction. Perhaps a counter-protest was being planned. But the forewarning was overshadowed by the feeling that seemed to permeate all the university, as if one large whisper was going through all the walkways and corridors and classrooms and offices: "protest tonight!"

Schardheim, learning of the protest, walked deliberately and prominently up and down the walkways, through the buildings, in the streets, stopping everyone he saw, telling them of the event, not in a whisper, but in loud, forceful tones, insisting that they be there. They ran from him, they walked away from him, they laughed at him. Some listened to him, a few shook his hand, and some spat in his face.

By four o'clock that afternoon there was hardly a person in Heidelberg who did not know of the protest meeting and more than two thousand of them carried tightly folded in their pocket the little flyer.

After each class of the afternoon the campus became more and more deserted, each person purportedly going off to some other part of the city for a visit, a meeting, a dinner, an event that would clearly keep him or her away from the university area, especially the chancellor's residence, for the rest of the evening. Few would risk being seen, lest it be thought that they were remaining for the protest. At five o'clock the campus was virtually empty. Walter went directly home from his last class. He waited impatiently, uneasily in the easy chair in his study, waiting for ten minutes to six, at which time he would casually put on his jacket and walk just as casually, as if out for a late afternoon stroll, toward the chancellor's house. He would arrive there at exactly six o'clock. This is certainly what everyone else has in mind, he thought. He envisioned a swelling mass of humanity converging precisely at six o'clock, shouting and waving flyers and calling for Schardheim's reinstatement.

The time moved more and more slowly. He reached up and plucked a book from his bookshelves, smiled at it disapprovingly when he saw that it was by Schopenhauer, and put it back in favor of a first edition of Heine's poems. Light, easy poems. Comparatively.

He tried not to think about Phillipa and what she would say about his evening's intention. Despite the cold strain of

their relationship, he did love her and he felt guilty assuming
for both of them so great a danger without her knowledge.
Yet, he could not consult her because he knew beforehand
that what she would say and do was not what he wanted her
to say and do. Still, things could not be perfect, he reasoned.
No philosopher had ever found or even expected much,
if anything at all, in a life or an age that could be called
perfection, he told himself. But she did fill what had once
been lonely hours for him with companionship. He admired
her Venusian beauty and her sophisticated manner. He was
warmed by the occasional closeness and softness of her bed.
No, there was not perfection, but there was enough, he believed, for him to love her. Indeed, he held upon his own conscience the fact that he had not more time for Phillipa, that
his duties of teaching and his desires for research and writing
took him from her demands for complete time devotion to
her needs, and he blamed himself in this respect for the lack
of complete understanding and idealistic compatibility that
he wished would be between them. He thought again of what
he proposed to do that evening and how, just as it endangered
him, it endangered her. She should know, he told himself. He
should, if not share it with her, at least warn her of the possible consequences.

Now he was pleased that she would be away that evening. He would not have to follow his dictate of the moment
to tell her. Though he felt strong as he thought this, strong
enough to combat any attempt at dissuasion, he did not want
to weaken himself in argument. He would need the set of his
ideas and the stolidity of his purpose at the protest itself.

Phillipa unexpectedly entered, a piece of paper in one
hand, a package in the other. Walter sensed from her a feeling of restrained anger. She put the package down slowly,
removed her coat, all the while holding and shifting the
piece of paper from hand to hand. Walter recognized what

was to come, waited in trepidation, sorry now that he had not departed a few minutes before. The confrontation did not disturb him as much as did Phillipa herself. Had he been a psychologist, self-analysis might have shown reality to be just the opposite. Because all his life he had shunned action and physical danger, the meeting, the confrontation was, indeed, what really frightened him. Subconsciously, he transferred the fear into the figure of his wife. It was easier to accept and understand that way.

Phillipa smiled almost superciliously as she handed Walter the flyer, standing over him and looking down over his shoulder as he looked at it.

"I wanted to be sure you were not involved in this idiocy," she said briskly. "I hurried home and will go to the concert later. One would think they would know better by now."

She laughed. "Well, stupidity, I suppose, remains a lifetime thing with some people." She paused just long enough, then turned and walked unconcernedly to the stairs. "I almost feel sorry for them," she said. Her tone was deliberately condescending, yet, in it Waiter could hear the essence of bitterness. "Not really for them," she added, "but for their families. They will deserve what they get. But their families will suffer for something they did not do." She sighed as though she were well rid of this moment of sympathy. "Oh, well!" She paused at the staircase: "I am glad that you are not involved."

Walter's musing conscience now broke into his consciousness.

"Phillipa," he called, without taking time to decide to do so, without planning what he would do or say. She walked a few steps up the staircase, then turned. Now he needed to take a moment to find the sense of what he meant to say. It didn't come quickly.

"Phillipa," he said again, his mind stalling for time.

She turned and looked at him. "I heard you," she said.

Walter looked at his watch. It was twenty-two minutes to six. There was time yet. He stood up, half because of
manner, half to give him the bodily freshness and control of
walking.

"I would like to talk with you," he said, almost inanely.
But he meant the words for he knew that he had to let her
know. She had clearly indicated, without accusing him directly, that his actions should not jeopardize her own security.
She deliberately began to walk up the steps again. She would
not make it easy for him.

"I've had a terrible day shopping," she called to him.
"I'm tired. I want to rest."

He was almost tempted to let her go now. But her very
obviousness of forcing him to ask her back prevented him
from doing so.

"This is important," he said slowly. "Come down for a
moment. To talk with me. Then you can go."

She did him the obvious favor of coming back down the
steps, slowly and carefully. She sat in the easy chair, Walter
standing in front of her.

"The situation at the university is far worse than ever
before," he began. "The longer we wait, the worse it gets . . ."

Phillipa started to interrupt, to tell him she had heard
this same concern many times before. But Walter pressed
forward and did not accept her interruption.

"Let me finish before you say anything," he insisted. "Let
me get my words out first."

Phillipa sat back and remained quiet, trying to appear
unconcerned, as if she were listening from politeness and not
interest.

Walter tried to review quickly the progression of
events that had brought him to his present commitment.
"First a ban on speakers," he said. "Then the loyalty oath.
Then all teachers suspected of being communist. Then

Jewish members of the faculty. Then the list grew from those who were suspect to those who were accused of being suspect, to those who were simply suspect of being suspect." Walter let the words carry him along, stronger and militant, not so much for Phillipa's sake, but because he needed to hear them to reinforce himself.

"First we protested a little," he continued. Then when it was hinted that those who protested might become suspect themselves, the protests stopped. When the professors were silenced, the students spoke. Youth does not fear for the stomach as does the older person who has already felt hunger. But the students, too, were dismissed. Dissent became a prisoner. Only whispers. Constrained to the small rooms of student quarters, to the desks in faculty offices, to street corners, to the toilets in the university buildings. And it became quieter and quieter."

Phillipa was annoyed at his obvious distress. His weakness, she felt. And she didn't like being lectured to. "I've heard all this before," she said, as if she were unconscionably bored. "I'm not interested." She got up.

He turned to her sharply. "I do not tell you this to amuse you," he said. I tell it to you because what I propose to do about it will affect you as much as it will affect me.

His voice had risen and Phillipa could see that he was now angry, his self-control about to be lost. She would have no problem now. He would show the usual guilt and apologize and accede to whatever were her demands. She would simply tell him that if he wished to act rudely then she had no obligation to listen to him. This would force him, as always, into her control. But before she could speak he broke in again. Only this time it was in a way that she did not expect. It was as if he had decided to play her game, but play it better than she did.

As quickly as he had become provoked, he became composed and quiet. "I'm sorry," he said. "If you wish to go

upstairs, Phillipa, then of course you may. I shall not try
to force you to listen." He stopped for a moment, just long
enough to indicate that she was to answer, and then before
she could do so, added: "If you wish to stay, then I shall speak
with you." He was aware of what he had done, and there was
no turning back now.

Phillipa had no trouble controlling her husband on her
own level. It was when he was able to submerge his emotional weakness and deal from his intellectual strength that
she found difficulty, when he was able to put himself into an
intellectual position of solicitousness. Now it had been a simple schoolmaster's trick that had trapped her. She looked at
him, her eyes dark and clear and full. They met his without
wavering. Her eyebrows tilted slightly forward as if, now, she
would be the solicitous one, appeasing the willfulness of the
schoolboy. Slowly, with a forward movement of her shoulders
to underscore an indifference, she sat down again.

Walter's sudden surging energy was marked with the
premonition of oldness. At thirty-six his body moved slowly
and his voice hung with the heaviness of a man fifteen years
past his age. The feeling of guilt could not be set aside, and it
took hold of his face. His face was dark, its brooding length-
ened and punctuated by the small goatee that still verged on
the perpetual precipice of growth, but somehow never quite
began to blossom. The fact of Phillipa's staying was in itself
a surprise, a victory so unexpected and satisfying that one
might not ever need to seek another. His words were like
himself, fully weighted, deliberate, serious.

He turned away from Phillipa and walked toward the
drawn curtains.

"It may be too late, it may not be," he said loudly. "But
if we don't do anything now, then we know we have lost our
last chance." He pointed to the flyer, now lying on the desk.

Phillipa didn't change expression, even to the blink of an eyelash. Walter sat on the arm of the chair, removed his glasses from his face, weighed them in his hand as if he were weighing an important thought. The scales were tipped and he caught the glasses by a temple as they started to fall to the floor. He stood up.

"Several of us decided to take that chance. If there are enough of us tonight, if we all join together, there will be no retaliation. They can't fight the whole populace. If we do not take this chance now, there is no telling when, where or how this thing will end." He stopped, looked at Phillipa, waited for her.

"And?" She nodded for him to continue.

He paused, tilted his glasses upward, balanced them carefully between two fingers. "This is a serious step, Phillipa. There might be serious consequences. That is why I felt I had to tell you."

There was no hesitation now. She got up from her chair, moved to her husband, fluffed her hair over her shoulders as she came to him so that it hung longer and blacker and deeper. She stood directly in front of him. He sat back on the arm of the chair now, watched her closely. He watched her hands, her hair, her dark eyes, her smooth skin. He watched her feet gently lifting as they moved, the outline of her calves as they brushed against the tight hem of her skirt. He watched the sharp curve of the hips into the waist, the breasts, firm, yet yielding, salient in front of him now at eye level.

God was an unknown. Intellect, for Walter, shared the intimacy of a patron saint. This other, this Phillipa, was a Goddess.

"I don't wish to stop you from doing anything you want to do, Walter." She spoke softly.

He thought he should laugh at the obviousness of what she was doing, but at the same time he knew the seriousness

of the real struggle that was taking place between him and
her, within himself, and there was no humor in it for him.

"We are all independent," she continued. She felt her
dominance. She continued her advantage. "We are individuals. I think we should remain so. As you say, this is a dangerous thing you do. If you wish, you may jeopardize our safety
and well being. I allow you that." Then, without changing
the pace of her speech, "I wonder only if there is a valid reason for doing this. You cannot really change an entire society.
You must live your own life, for yourself"—then more slowly,
deliberately—"and for me."

She bent toward him, kissed him on the lips, turned
toward the stairs. He remained sitting, motionless, watching
intensely. At the foot of the stairs she turned back to him.

"You must do what you think best, Walter. But remember, these things that have happened have not affected us, so I
don't see why we should try to affect them." She thought she
had won, but she had to make certain. "You are free, Walter.
Just remember that your decision may prove a terrible hurt
to me."

He looked at her. His eyes moved from hers, purposely
downward, lingering and gradually traveling down to her
toes. She watched carefully, waited until the pilgrimage had
been completed, then, almost imperceptibly, without seeming movement, turned and went upstairs.

Walter sat rigidly for a moment, rose and went to the
front window. He was about to look out, didn't dare to. He
turned, picked up a newspaper that had fallen to the floor,
folded it neatly and placed it on a table, picked up the flyer
from his desk and without looking at it tore it in half, tore
it again, tore it once more and dropped the pieces into the
wastebasket.

He went back to the easy chair, picked up the edition
of Heine's poems from the floor next to the chair, sat down

heavily, leaned his head back securely deep into the cushion
and tried to read. He couldn't. His stomach began to ache
inside. Then to pain. Then to boil. It regurgitated and he
wanted to vomit. He was sick. He felt his forehead. It was
hot. The guilt feelings both for Phillipa and for his alter-ego
tore him apart. He wanted to crawl under a bed and stay
there until blackness took him and all his senses. He got up,
walked around rapidly looking over the titles on the bookshelves. He saw them but did not read them. They would not
occupy his mind. He tried to think of the countryside, the
museums. He tried to recall a soccer match he had seen the
past winter, tried to remember every play, any play, tried to
busy his mind in its remembrance. He couldn't. He looked at
his watch. Six-fifteen.

'Too late, anyway," he said, half aloud. Then: "Almost too
late." Then, only in thought, but shouting clearly through
his mind: "Not yet too late."

He walked to the window, opened the curtains. It was
almost completely dark outside. He wondered what was happening at the chancellor's house. He thought of the others,
particularly of Guido. He remembered that first meeting they
had had and their first attempted protest against the loyalty
oath. How long ago was that? Months? Years? Decades? He
chastised himself for his self-recrimination. He had done his
share, he told himself. He had spoken at the meeting, helped
organized the plan, written the flyer, distributed it. He had
done his share. He believed in their cause. He would always
believe in freedom. His motives could not be questioned.
Then he remembered Guido's words to those at that meeting
who proclaimed their sympathy to the ideals of liberty, who
lent verbal encouragement and even funds when needed, but
who refused to take any direct action.

"Hypocrites," Guido had said. "They think they can redeem their freedom like some of them think they can redeem

their souls. They put a handful of gold in the collection box but do nothing about practicing what they say they believe. Stupid, frightened hypocrites!"

Walter squirmed in his chair. Suddenly he was aware of Phillipa coming down the stairs. For a moment he resented her, resented really whatever it was within himself, the snake within him that ate of his bowels, that crawled around on a slimy stomach and made him want to throw up the dirt inside into his own face.

Phillipa stopped under the doorway arch, smiled to him. "I will get supper ready. Then, if you like, we can go upstairs early." She spoke to him gently, offering him his reward for good behavior. She started for the kitchen, turned again.

"I would not worry, Walter," she said. "Your decision is a wise one. I heard downtown that the protest meeting was doomed to failure, anyway. You might have gotten severely hurt. The youth organizations and the police were going to take care of the radicals just as soon as they were all gathered together." She paused a moment, then added: "I heard it in the strictest confidence, of course." She went into the kitchen.

Walter leaped up, grabbed at his coat in the hall. Without a word to Phillipa, he ran out of the house, down the street. He ran all the way to the university, turned toward the chancellor's house. He looked at his watch. Six-thirty. Hopefully, it was not too late to warn them, to prepare them! As he ran, alone, feeling the wind smarting against his face and making it feel alive, he felt strong, confident. If only it were not too late to help them, he thought.

Two blocks from the chancellor's house he stopped, abruptly. He stared in front of him, unbelieving. In all his lifetime he never thought he would see what was now before him.

Chapter X

"It is too late," Walter cried. His tears were real.

He wanted to sink to the ground, to join the others, the dozens, perhaps hundreds who lay scattered on the sidewalks, on the street in front of him. The scene looked like the pictures of battlefields he had seen in books, of the aftermath of civilian uprisings against authority, of almost every painting of the streets of Russian cities after a citizens' protest against the Czar. Men and boys in strange, awkward positions on the hard concrete, some moaning, others stiff, tight against the ground. Some crawling, a few, here and there, standing. In the blackness of the evening they looked like eerie shadows dropped from heaven into some hell, into Milton's hell, the beaten, confused figures unable to understand what had happened to them. Lights from the chancellor's house shone at the end of the two blocks of the strewn field. The lights burned into the street, a flicker every now and then catching a moving body. There was no order, no logical movement or position in what Walter saw. It was a mangled pattern, dark, strange, unknown. Its unbelievability was heightened by the quiet. Not a sound except for an occasional, bare moan. From the distance, blocks in front of

him, emanated a rumble-like noise. It sounded to Walter like
a background of sound effects, like the babbling and shouting
and yelling of men's voices. Walter stared—stupidly, ineptly,
transfixed, trying to reconstruct what had happened. A few
minutes before and he would have seen it. A few minutes before and he would have been part of it. It was as Phillipa had
told him. The Nazi youth and the police had been prepared.
The quiet of the university earlier in the day, the absence of
any statement from the chancellor concerning the meeting,
the apparent unconcern of the authorities where there should
have been concern: This was the calm before the storm that
should have warned Walter and his colleagues. In their excitement, they had not seen it. In their inexperience, they did
not look for it.

At precisely six o'clock they had arrived in front of the
chancellor's house. Into an empty street, at exactly six as
the clock in a church tower in Heidelberg tolled, poured
hundreds of young men and women, Not only students, but
wives, sweethearts, friends. Not only professors, but men and
women of the town. Not the tens of thousands that might
have proclaimed the end to tyranny then and there that evening, but enough hundreds to serve notice that at least one
part of the German society of Heidelberg was concerned, was
ready to protest.

As the crowd gathered, Guido, Erich De Sola, and Maria
Anneman moved on the fringes, encouraging those who were
still a bit trepidatious to move up forward. Ernst Puzinger,
Heinrich Weiner, Willy Baler and Felix Lindner moved
through the throng, urging it along, thickening it as more
and more persons joined it. At five minutes after six more
than a thousand people were in the area, filling the wide
street in front of the chancellor's house, spilling into the side
streets.

Guido began the shouting. "Reinstate Schardheim, rein-state Schardheim."

The cry grew louder. The slogan quickly became inad-equate and the cry "Down with Nazism, down with Hitler," began to filter through and soon one loud, screaming pro-test of yells filled the air, settling into an indistinguishable chant that grew louder and louder. It was not as much as they might have hoped for, but it was more than they had expected. The others looked for Walter, but not seeing him thought nothing of it. They were separated from each other by this time.

By fifteen minutes after six the chanting had begun to die down. Alex Schardheim pushed his way forward, up to the front lawn of the chancellor's house. There was no sign of life inside. Every window was dark.

"Listen to me, listen to me," Schardheim shouted to the crowd.

No one heard, or if they did, they were too busy shouting to pay attention. Heinrich Werner pushed his way forward, was lifted above the crowd on the shoulders of several others.

"Quiet," he began to yell.

Several in front took up the yell. "Quiet."

In a moment it became a roar, then, following the roar, a shout, then a whisper and, finally, sudden silence. They had not planned for this, but the opportunity was there and they took advantage of it.

"Professor Schardheim wants to make a speech," Werner announced.

A tremendous roar of applause went up. It was Schard-heim's day, Schardheim's honor, Schardheim's meeting. He was the issue. The crowd was immediately silent. Guido moved through the mass, to the front. Another cheer went up as some of the students saw him, their favorite professor,

pleased that he was there. Guido got to Schardheim just as
the latter was being hoisted on shoulders so that he could be
seen.

"Speak not only for yourself," Guido advised him. "Make
it an object lesson."

Schardheim smiled. "I know. I learned the lesson." He
waved his hands for silence. They gave it to him.

"I am not standing here as a man dispossessed," he began.
"I stand here as a man possessed."

A cheer. His voice, ordinarily clam, sober and ultra-ob-
jective to the point of droning boredom, was now passionate.

"I have lost my job," he continued, "but I have found a
desire for freedom." Another cheer.

A few people at the fringes of the crowd had run to their
rooms and were returning now with candles, lighting them,
passing them through the crowd. The little flickering lights
appeared like fireflies buzzing through a forest of thick bushes
and trees. Several flashlights were found, the beams shined
from either side and in front onto Schardheim. His head,
large, shiny in its baldness, stared out at the crowd like some
surrealistic sculpture.

"I let my chance go by before," Schardheim continued.
"When the loyalty oaths came, I said this will not happen to
me. When the communists were fired, I ignored it because
it did not affect me. When the Jews were fired, again I said
this is none of my business. I am a teacher, I told myself, not
a politician."

He took a deep breath.

"I took no interest because I thought the honest, sincere,
loyal little man who went about his job without causing a
fuss was safe. Was I safe?," he shouted. A roar of "no" shot
back from the crowd. "Am I safe with my arm in a sling,
with my ribs taped, with my head and face lacerated, without

a job, without food to eat?" The roar of "no" was even louder than before.

"By my silence I made Germany safe for the dictators. By my silence I made Germany unsafe for myself. At the crossroads I followed the path of least resistance. Now we are at another crossroads. Which way do you take?"

He waited a split second for the thought to sink in, then, with all the strength of his voice: "Will you continue to follow the dictators?"

The roar of "no" was deafening, the cheer that followed it even more so. There was no need for Schardheim to say anything more. Guido strained as he climbed onto the shoulders of several students, who held his bulk uneasily. He waved his arms, calling for attention. In a few moments the noise lessened enough for him to be heard.

"Don't give in again," he shouted. "Don't give up anybody's freedom, no matter whose, for in doing so you give up your own. We have found friends here tonight. Many good and unexpected friends. Let us take a stand henceforth together, united, as friends in the cause of freedom."

Another cheer went up. And then another. The crowd was impatient. Youth had heard the words, believed them, and now it wanted more. Someone in front began shouting for the chancellor. The cry was taken up by the others until it resounded through all the streets of the area.

"Chancellor . . . Chancellor . . . ." The house remained dark.

"Let's see what the chancellor will do about Schardheim," someone yelled.

"Let's see the chancellor about Schardheim," the call was taken up.

"About Schardheim. About Schardheim. The Chancellor. The Chancellor."

The mass moved forward, pushing, straining against itself, one against the other, moving slowly toward the house. Werner, tall, strong, straight, the hero of the crowd, the athletic idol of Germany, led the way, calmly, fearlessly, as he had often led the way on the football field. Suddenly the house was ablaze with lights. As if by magic, every window was alight, a uniformed policeman, gun in hand, at each window. The crowd stopped as if a mechanism controlled by a remote button. The chief of police, flanked by two Nazi youth in uniform, also carrying guns, emerged from the front door of the house. Three more policemen followed directly behind them, German Army rifles at their shoulders, at the ready.

"Go back," the police chief shouted, "go back immediately."

"We wish to speak to the chancellor," Werner shouted.

"You," the police chief ordered. "You are one of the leaders? Come forward. Alone."

Werner did not move.

Guido stepped forward. "I am one of the leaders, too. And so are we all. All thousands of us. Do you want us all to step forward?"

"Are you a professor?," the police chief demanded.

"I am a professor."

"Then you come." The police chief pointed to Werner: "You go back." Werner stood his ground.

"We want to see the chancellor," he repeated.

"I will count to three, then shoot" the police chief warned.

"We do not wish to cause any trouble," Guido said softly. "Just have the chancellor speak with us and we will leave quietly."

"One!," the police chief began to count.

"If the Chancellor speaks with us, there will be no bloodshed." Guido took a step forward. "Tell him that."

"Two!"

"Let him speak with us and avoid bloodshed," Guido said.

"Three!"

The others in the front line moved back. Only Guido and Werner and Schardheim stood still.

The police chief nodded to one of the policemen with the guns.

"My God," Guido heard some one say, then heard the sound of a shot. The bullet struck him in the left side, went through his heart. He felt a brief clenching of his stomach, felt a chill go through him and then felt no more. Guido crumpled to the ground, dead.

The crowd became a mob, pushing and scratching to retreat. Those on the fringes ran toward the side streets. Mounted policemen on horses suddenly appeared from nowhere, shutting off the exits. Many managed to run past the horses, but many others were trapped in the center. The policemen marched their horses into the mass, trampling, swinging their clubs indiscriminately. A woman holding her two year old child tried to hide, was pushed toward an oncoming horse, felt the child beaten from her arms by the policeman's club, bent to rescue the baby and was killed as the horse's iron hooves pounded her head into the ground. Those who escaped the first gauntlet, the horses, ran into the second. A hundred yards behind, ringing the area, the Nazi youth stood, dressed and ready for the occasion, no longer merely bullies with sticks and stones. They had been armed by the police. They stood at the edge of the quickly scattering circle, shooting into it, taking delight in their aim, counting the number that fell with their bullets, adding one or two or three to their total so that they might boast even more strongly when they met afterwards with their friends and families to drink beer and tell of their roles on behalf of the Fatherland.

Just as Guido fell, Heinrich Werner had started toward the chief of police. He stopped, went to Guido, saw in an instant that he was dead. In the chaos he looked for help, for an answer. The police chief had moved away now, retreated to a place of safety closer to the house as the policemen and Nazi youth attacked the dispersing mass. Several Nazi youth remained with the police chief, guns in hand. The other police and youths had moved past Werner's position. Werner moved toward the house, toward the police chief. He had no notion why, no idea of what he intended to do, except that he felt he must somehow take some action. The police chief saw him coming.

"Stop, idiot. One more step and you'll get what we gave that other traitor."

Werner didn't stop. He moved slowly, his eyes set on the chief of police. It seemed almost as if he were smiling. The chief turned, frightened, for a moment, forgetting the guns in the hands of the Nazi youth next to him. Then, turning to them: "Shoot!"

There was no gunfire.

"That's Heinrich Werner," one of the Nazi youth muttered. "I play football with him. My God, I can't kill him, I play football with him."

"Shoot," the police chief commanded.

"That's Heinrich Werner," another one of the youth urgently, fearfully told the police chief. "You can't shoot Germany's greatest football player. You can't . . . ."

There was panic in the police chief's voice. Werner was within two yards of him, his eyes unmoving. "Shoot! Shoot!," the police chief pleaded.

Werner was almost upon him. One of the Nazi youth lifted his pistol, held it point blank at Werner's head and fired. The bullet shattered his brain, killing him instantly.

The carnage continued. Two, three falling to the ground, dead, wounded. Then a dozen. Then thirty. Then a hundred. The policemen on their horses, the Nazi youth with their pistols moved through the fallen mass, watching for any who might move, any who tried to get up and run or crawl away.

On the lawn of the chancellor's house four Nazi youth stood laughing. One of them pointed to a body on the ground, the green of the grass matting into a yellow-rust as the life blood of the prone figure returned into the elements whence it had come. The body was that of Schardheim. One of the youth, no more than eighteen, giggled with delight, "We didn't do a good enough job last time, so we finished it tonight." He proudly held up a red-stained gun-butt.

In twenty minutes it was all over. The police and the youth disappeared as quickly as they had come. The crowd had dispersed, most of them behind bolted doors, shuddering, crying, nursing their wounds. The street regained the solemn silence it had known a few minutes before six, hardly more than forty-five minutes before. The only difference was the three hundred dead and wounded, lying like dark angels of independence without order or hope. Somehow, the blackness of the night seemed deeper and more permanent.

From down the street a voice called sternly, hurriedly.

"Get out of here. Get out of here quick. Before we come and get you."

Walter stood a full minute, daring the voice to show itself. Then he turned and slowly, defiantly, walked with heavy steps back to his house.

Chapter XI

The spring semester melted into the summer's heat. The university went on holiday. Some of the faculty went to England. France, Belgium, Italy. Others preferred the quiet relaxation and cooler climates of Garmisch, Scandinavia and Alpine Switzerland. Many remained in Heidelberg, some because they did not have or did not wish to spend the money needed for a vacation; others because they elected to devote the three months of recess to a continuation of intellectual pursuits: to read an author, to study a period, to begin or complete a thesis. Walter took Phillipa for a one month's vacation in Vienna, traveled west into Switzerland for several days of skiing near the Jungfrau at Interlaken, and then for another few days to lower Bavaria, to rest by a quiet lake, to find comfort and escape in the lofty, unburdened mountain tops and the cool, fresh air.

Upon their return to Heidelberg Walter went back to work on a book he had been writing for several years and which, in the few months past, he had made the center of all his out-of-classroom thoughts, concentrating on its needs as if they were the only ones in the world and all else was unneeded and unwanted unreality. The book was an analysis

of Immanuel Kant's philosophical attitude toward an interpretation of world government. He stressed Kant's philosophical justification of a united world nation as opposed to
nationalism and chauvinism on a multi-local level. Even as he
worked, he knew the book would not be published. He had
no intention even of submitting the manuscript to a publisher or even of making it public. It was a kind of penance,
an atonement. In bringing the work to maturity, he would be
creating a subjective, personal fiery cross.

Except for occasional weekend trips to Berlin or Brus-
sels or Paris during the August hiatus, he and Phillipa
remained in Heidelberg for the remainder of the summer.
Phillipa stayed in the house most of the time, reading a
great deal of the time. Social intercourse had become almost
non-existent in the heretofore intellectual circles of Heidelberg. Doomsday was too often determined by guilt through
association.

Walter had never spoken with Phillipa about that evening in April. It was, between them, as though it had never
occurred. Every once in a while he wanted to. One September evening, after returning from the university just before
the fall session was about to begin, he tried to. All through
dinner he felt as though he must begin, and each time he
thought he would his speech became impotent, reflecting
the demoralization that he had felt all through him since
spring. He had gone to the university that afternoon to see if
the formal contracts for the school year had been distributed.
They weren't there. Erich Da Sola was. He held a paper in his
hands when Walter met him. It was not a teaching contract
but, as Erich said, another kind of covenant.

"The terms are not stated," Erich said, smiling and bitter
at the same time. "Maybe a little shorter than a year. Very
likely, I am afraid, a little longer. It is an order to get ready
for transport to one of the detention camps."

Walter didn't know how to answer. But he didn't have to.

"Someone must have recognized me at the protest, and they have just gotten around to me," Erich continued.

Walter's face hurt as his cheeks narrowed and pinched him. It was the first time they had spoken of the matter since it had happened. They had all avoided it.

"At that," Erich said, "my penalty is lighter, much lighter than some of our colleagues who were also guilty of . . . thinking." Da Sola had not known of Walter's late-coming to the protest. Walter had not mentioned it to anyone and never intended to.

"What will you do now?," Walter asked, even as he realized the futility of the question.

"There is nothing I can do."

"If you need money . . . ," Walter offered.

"To run away?" Da Sola laughed. "There is no running away. The moment I leave this building there will likely be someone following me. If I try to escape, I may be put away for five years or ten years instead of . . ." he glanced down at the piece of paper and crinkled the corners of his mouth, this time not in irony but in resignation, ". . . instead of I don't know what!"

Walter nodded. He waited a moment. "There is nothing I can do?" He knew there wasn't. But he had to offer, anyway.

Da Sola tried to brighten the sadness. "Don't cry for me, Walter. The time for crying is past. I do not cry. I will only remember that I have held on to my ideals. I hope that other people remember that they are entitled to ideals, too." He spoke softly now, making the most of what he knew might be his last opportunity to do so for a long time.

"There's one thing people don't seem to understand about Fascism, Walter. They can't bargain with it. Once they let in even the first smell, they can no longer escape it. I've read about Polycrates, Caligula, the Ch'in Dynasty,

Atilla, Nicholas I, John of England and others. I've seen
Mussolini in action and I've felt Hitler. The people don't
understand it. They always cooperate with it until it's too
late. Until they are the victims. And as much as they believe
it will be otherwise, sooner or later it is always them." He
shook hands, strongly, firmly.

"Auf Wiedersehen, Walter."

Phillipa was seated in the easy chair after dinner as Walter told her about his meeting with Da Sola. For the thou-
sandth time since April he cried inside as he thought of all
the Erich Da Solas and Guido Terminis who had not been
afraid to be human beings who could respect themselves.

"I should be one of them, Phillipa," he chastised himself.

"And you would have been if I hadn't stopped you."

He walked to the other end of the room. "That's not what I
want you to say. That's not the kind of help I need." He wasn't
belligerent. Neither was he resigned. He could no longer tac-
itly join Phillipa in her aloofness and unconcern. Not ever.

"Would you rather be in a detention camp, a concentration camp as I've heard them called? Or dead?"

"Sometimes I think it might be better," Walter answered. At least more honest."

"What do you want me to say?," she responded angrily.
"That I'm sorry. Yes, I am sorry for them. But it is not my
fault that they made fools of themselves. Just remember that
it is my doing that you did not!" She got up to leave.

"Maybe I should have!," he shouted. "Maybe I'd be able
to sleep nights! Maybe I ought to now!"

She stayed. She had felt this time might come. She stood
by the chair, then came to Walter, put her arms around his
neck. She looked at him, her eyes wide. The deep, hard blackness suddenly seemed soft to Walter. He felt the pressure of
her breasts.

"This is really so important to you?," she asked. She was deliberately not condescending. She deliberately tried to be understanding, to have him trust her.

"Yes."

He stood still, his body not responding to her. She waited for his physical acquiescence, for his need to melt against her and depend on her. It didn't come. Slowly she moved her arms. He let her. She moved away from him. He let her. As Walter watched what was happening as if through the eyes of an observer, it did not surprise him. More importantly, it did not hurt him, not even disturb him.

"We've said this all before," he told her. I can't live like half a man. I can debate philosophy, but I can't repudiate humanity. I can't burn my conscience."

She sensed, deep in her stomach, that she had lost control, completely and definitely lost control. Inside the tight little knots began. It made the world feel ugly. It made her feel ugly. But there was no threat of tears. She was and would always be above tears.

"One thing I ask, Walter."

"What?"

She had to ask now. She could no longer demand. It had come to that and she knew it.

"If anything happens to you," she said, "I will be sent to a concentration camp. As your wife, it is expected. Because I am Jewish, it is assured. Before you do anything or say anything, think of me."

"I always think of you, Phillipa. Don't I, Phillipa?"

He was surprised at his own self-assurance, at the ease in which, without plan, without purpose, he had become his own master, had achieved an independence of spirit and will from Phillipa. Could it have been this easy all this time, he wondered? Perhaps all he had to do was to relax, to be himself, and it would have been done? Now he had accomplished it, now he could truly be himself.

"I always think of you, Phillipa," he repeated. "Don't I, Phillipa." There was the slightest trace of self-satisfaction in his voice.

Phillipa didn't tempt it. She came close to him again. He felt the invitation of the lower part of her body pressing against his. She smiled inside, some of it touching the edges of her lips. He was not entirely gone from her.

"Promise me you'll do nothing that might send me to a concentration camp," she said.

He didn't answer. He looked at himself, at her, as if from outside of the picture. He saw himself search for the strength of a few moments before, saw himself laugh at the thought of forcing himself to do anything, now that he had clearly proven what he had to prove. He could be himself, he could let his feelings do just as they wished. He had accomplished what he had wanted to.

She kissed him lightly on the lips. She waited for an answer.

He felt her warmth go through him, more deeply than he had known it for some time. She was exciting and comfortable at the same moment. She was the part of the good life that waited and belonged to him outside of the classroom. What, indeed, could he do that might result in either of them going to a concentration camp, he asked himself? There had been a time for doing, he reprimanded himself, and he hadn't taken advantage of it. Now it was too late.

She waited another moment, then carefully, softly moved from him. She stood and looked at him, from a few feet away. "I'm going to bed now, Walter." Then, gently: "Are you coming?"

She was halfway up the stairs when Walter called.

She stopped. "Yes?" She waited.

"I promise."

Chapter XII

The next few years saw a new and stronger Germany. National security became the essence of German life. A thousand watchfires flamed in defense of the State. The politically suspect, the racially diverse, the ethnically different, the intellectually independent were reduced to ashes in the flame.

Walter continued in his position at Heidelberg. He taught his students what the Ministry of Information told him to teach. Because she was Walter's wife, Phillipa continued safe from the infliction penalties upon the German Jewry. Once she went to Munich after her father had had his business and personal property confiscated. She found him living in a small room in an old building in the center of Munich, in a neighborhood much like the one she would always remember, with distaste, from her fourteenth summer. The man who had been strong and sure in his castle of plenty now sat old, tired, confused, his fortress reduced to the incongruity, for him, of a small wood stove, a wash basin, a bed, a table with a single chair, solitary window, one door, and only four walls. He sat on the chair and looked out the window.

He watched the world pass in front of him and didn't understand it.

"I gave money to the Nazi party," he told his daughter. "They told me that was all they wanted. Then they took my telephone away and they said that was all they wanted. Then my newspaper, and I thought that would be the end. After that my social clubs and business clubs and my meeting places and I knew it must stop there. I protested a little, but not much because I knew it couldn't go any farther. The decent people would stop it. After all, this is Germany. Now I find myself living in a hole-in-a-wall without my business, without my home, without my money and . . . and, Phillipa . . . I don't understand!"

The sun went down and the sky grew dark. Phillipa's father sat by the window, looking out into the darkness.

In 1938 Germany invaded Austria.

Austrian Chancellor Schuschnigg quickly found himself among the disinherited. The word "ghetto" became a part of the Austrian vocabulary, too. In Germany, however, it began to disappear as each day, trucks and trains began leaving the cities, transporting to other places the ghettoed human threats to state security.

Phillipa received a letter from Munich during that year, from a man who had once been a business associate of her father's and who had since, as a non-Jew, been given control of the entire brokerage house.

"Please destroy this letter as soon as you finish reading it," Phillipa read, "I am taking a great chance in writing it to you, but because your father and I were once such good friends"—'good friends' had been crossed out and 'business associates' had been written in its place—"I feel I must write to you and let you know. This last Tuesday, in the middle of the night, your father was taken and put on a transport. Where it was going I do not know. But I have been told by the people who told me about your father that the rumor was to the east. This is all I can write to you now. I need not tell you of my sincere regrets. If there is anything I can do"—and here, in self-sufficient parentheses: '(within existing circumstances, of course)'—"I shall certainly try to do so. With my best wishes . . . ."

At the bottom of the page a P.S. urged: "Please destroy this letter now."

Phillipa was in her bedroom when she read the letter. Holding it in her hand, she went to her bed, lay across it, pressing her face into the bosom of the pillow. She had never felt strong affection for her father and consequently, through the years, had not thought about him much. Now she did. Not from a sudden paternal devotion but because of her own fear. Now that it had happened to her father, the threat automatically came closer to herself. She remained almost motionless on the bed for an hour, listening to and feeling the inner movements of her body, trying to determine whether the pounding in her stomach that she became acutely aware of would become knots and whether the knots would become tears. She read the letter again. For a brief moment she wondered whether tears would help. As she wondered, the muscles of her stomach began to relax and the decision was made. She stood up, put the letter carefully on the marble-topped dressing table in front of her bed. Slowly and deliberately she combed her hair, tied it back in a clasp, powdered her chin, cheeks, nose, forehead, and put on fresh lipstick. She took an eyebrow pencil and looked in the mirror at her eyes. She noted with satisfaction that they had remained smooth and dry.

As she received more letters and more reports about people she had known, about people she knew, about friends who were being sent to the concentration camps, she became obsessed with the orderliness of her own person. She guessed at the violence of the camps and this disturbed her. Things which were not pretty were necessarily ugly. Ugliness, to her, was disorder. The thought of hundreds of thousands of people in concentration camps was inescapable disorder. More and more she found herself seated at her dressing table, looking in the mirror at her soft face, properly rouged and powdered, her bare, unblemished shoulders, her clean, manicured fingers, her shining smooth hair neatly clasped behind her. She found a mental refuge from disorder in the structure of her own physical being.

At first she was able to think about the camps, for the stories about them were sparse and unconfirmed. It was easy enough to dismiss the rumors as unbelievable exaggerations. Strangely, it seemed to her as she thought about it, she was even able to find a place for her father in her thought patterns. Sometimes he would even intrude himself. After a while he would invariably be part of her reflections when she thought about the camps. His presence did not disturb her. She pretended that she was a spectator looking at a play that somehow contained real people but that was nevertheless restricted to a stage and could not conceivably actually reach into the audience. She found herself able to think about the camps less and less, however, as the rumors about them became statements and the statements became reports and the reports became graphic descriptions of sadism. Knowing what the truth was, she and all of those who had known a certain amount of tolerance and humanity before Hitler had to shut out from their moral responsibilities the blood that figuratively and in some cases literally flowed through the gates of the concentration camps into their own homes. The more she learned about the camps, the more she put them out of her mind. It wasn't long before, knowing fully about them, she thought about them not at all. Or, rather, almost not at all. There was one thing she could not shut out. She was still a Jew.

Walter could not forget it, either. Not because he didn't want to. He had the woman to look at, to watch the dark hair and soft body, to feel the physical realization of. Despite an affection that was intermittent, a relationship that was more in his anticipation than in reality, he could find a base of mutual concern, of at least mutual acceptance. Now that it was unavoidably obvious that Phillipa remained free only because she was married to him, a Gentile, he was disturbed. It was an unwelcome factor. It thrust upon him an ethical morality that contradicted his emotional and physical wants. It was wrong for him, he thought, to desire a dependency or devotion, even solely in his own mind, because its achievement might be entirely due to something entirely outside of his and Phillipa's personal reference. He could not accept as honest or real, without questioning the motivation, overtly or unconsciously, any warmth between Phillipa and himself.

The thought plagued him. First, because trying to eliminate it from his subjective thinking he necessarily included it in his objective thinking; and trying to eliminate it from his objective thinking he unwillingly included it in his subjective thinking. Second, because he was a philosophy professor he could not, no matter how theoretical he might be, long remain in intellectual vassalage to Thales, Protagoras, Anaxagoras and the Nazied hymn-singing glory of Nietzsche. The consciousness of Hegel, Marx and Croce subsisted, even if solely in personal application, in Germany in 1938.

Walter began to spend more time by himself. He would wait until he was alone in the house, then go into the study and talk to himself. Sometimes he would think of something humorous and smile. When was the last time he had smiled? A day? A week? A month? A student in one of his classes was discussing the superman theories of Nietzsche, the National Socialist declaration of the right of the pure and strong.

"Dr. Goebbels was correct," the student said. "In the early days he helped assure us of our moral and ethical right with the slogan, 'Gott Mit Uns!'"

"That is right," an anonymous voice from the rear of the classroom called. "God Is With Us. The government used to have that sign all over. Now they don't advertise so much any more."

One student laughed. A few others, unthinking, joined in. Walter caught himself laughing, stopped, his heart beating faster, his palms beginning to sweat. He quickly changed the subject.

"We are discussing philosophical fact, not opinion" he said.

No more twinkling eye or hushed exchange of words. He hoped that no one had noticed who the dissenting student had been. The academic lie was the only safe truth.

Walter paced back and forth in the study, thinking of this incident. "This is not easy," he said aloud. "I have taught and thought and lived free thinking. And it has come to this. I go to class and talk platitudes and pace this room and think more platitudes." He stopped, walked to the front door. He became angry because there was no one there to interrupt the pain of his thinking. He resented himself because he gave himself no choice but to think and suffer this intellectual pain. He took off his glasses, held them in one hand, drummed on the desk with the fingers of the other.

"This vise on the mind," he said to himself, "this stagnation of German culture and philosophy, this waiting, waiting, waiting "

He turned and looked defiantly, then fearfully, at the empty hallway leading to the world outside. He turned back and sat in the easy chair, slumping into it in total resignation, divorcing himself from the discomfort of time and place and ideas. His relationship to his work and his philosophy, his relationship to himself, his relationship to Phillipa, all were troubling him, all were painful, all were unresolved, and he lived in a continual atmosphere of nagging suspension.

The summer of 1939 was a normal one for Germany. Normal for the times. The heat had come early that year. In March, Hitler embraced Memel, Czechoslovakia becoming virtually a prisoner of the Nazis undeclared love. The snow melted on the roads to northern Switzerland and the silvered Alpine steeples watched stoically as the German generals marched armies south to the Italian border where, in May, Rome and Berlin concluded a binding military alliance.

It was unexpectedly warm in the north. The ice melted early and the Baltic Sea carefully covered the remains of the first trainloads of bodies that had been gassed, just as the new leaves began to find their way to the trees. The sea cleared itself of the carloads of ashes of bone that had been melted in the furnaces just as the last blotches of white snow disappeared from the German farmlands.

During the sweltering heat that Germany knows during July and August the people went on about their business as usual, stopping only to listen to an important speech or to see a new movie about the Jewish menace or to talk about the latest gains on the diplomatic front. Or, occasionally, to hear a new story about the concentration camps.

"But of course, Herr Deckel, that is certainly no concern of ours!"

Perhaps things weren't altogether what might exactly be called usual. They seemed a little slower, more sluggish. The heat didn't come in waves, as it frequently did, but came in a great mass and stayed. It hovered over the people, keeping them in a state of deferred action, as though time were standing still, waiting for something important to happen before it could move on again.

On September 1, Germany invaded Poland. Two days later England and France declared war against Germany. The heat cloud passed and the weather suddenly changed and pushed forward. The air became cool and fresh and exciting. The people worked harder at their jobs, read their newspapers with more care, listened to more speeches, talked with more ebullience, and words and pleasures accelerated to keep up with the fast changing news. Gratification was not only mental. Packages by the hundreds, then the thousands, and before long in the tens of thousands began to pour into Germany from the soldier sons and husbands and sweethearts. Clothes, perfumes, books, jewelry, gold and silver ornaments—all the inevitable interest-on-investment of a victorious army. The battlefields of the eastern and western fronts yielded all this and much more.

Life seemed fuller, more worthwhile, as destiny forged ahead with the tanks and guns that pressed onward through Europe. The German people were beginning to feel the flush of their place in the sun. In Buchenwald a German woman official ordered lampshades made out of the skins of people who were serving the Germans' march toward destiny.

By the time the roads leading west from Cologne had been filled with snow once more, by the time the streets of Belgium and France began to be submerged under the heavy boot that ground relentlessly into the overflowing rain and mud, by the time April, 1940, found its way into creation, the German armies were well on their way toward a ten-strike over the entire continent. In the German cities, in the towns, the villages, the farms; on the cobbled streets, the concrete highways, the manure-covered paths; under the tall buildings, the high arches, the shading trees—the individual German, the multitude, was spirited and proud.

"This is not a triumph only for the country, Karl, this is for me, this is a personal triumph!"

In a hospital a doctor asked himself what was it that had made a scientist devoid of scientific truth. In a studio an artist searched for an answer to art without integrity. They wondered, not because they couldn't know, but because abstract questioning was easier than seeing oneself reflected in the reality of naked answers. In Munich, Berlin, Frankfurt, Stuttgart, many wondered, and continued to live. In Landshut, Kauffering, Auschwitz, Dachau, many stopped wondering and knew. They did not live.

The streets were full with slush and the lawns were thick with mud as Walter walked home from the university one afternoon in that April of 1940. It was raining and the air was warm. He thought about the soldiers on the battlefield. For a moment he envied them. "They have only their own lives to worry about," he mused. He thought about another April, five years before, and about a man named Termini and about a boy named Werner and about many other men and women and boys and girls whose names he no longer remembered. "They had so many other people's lives to worry about," he said to himself. And he went into his study and closed the curtains and sat at his desk, his head buried in his hands, as he had done every April for the past five years, and cried tears for Guido Termini.

What had begun in infinite space was now a narrow vice around the private life of every subject of the master race. Phillipa still had her handsome, expensive wardrobe. But she no longer wore it. There were no more parties or concerts for her. There was something incongruous, particularly distasteful, for a woman like Phillipa to wear her long black hair flowing over the back of a gown with the six-pointed yellow star sewed on the front. In the torment of her isolation she first found indifference, then resentment. If there was anything she could have done in what was to her the ultimate of humiliation, she would have. But there was nothing. So she began to think. Since there were no longer events or personalities to talk to Walter about, she searched for something else, for something more. What seemed to be random thoughts moved inexorably toward the demands of necessity. The understanding of her own mind, the metamorphosis of society, the life and death of people. It was still only verbal. It meant little more to her than it had before, except that before it had been general. Now it was specific. Now it affected her.

"I still do not understand," she told Walter one day. "For a time it was enough not to be a political leftist. For a longer time it was enough not to be so poor as to be unable to bribe the proper officials."

Walter wished he could help her, this woman, strong, confident, sure, proud, who looked for an answer and whose independence and strength, even after seven years, still would not let her see it because the answer was too big and too close and too strong.

"Then it was sufficient not to be an orthodox Jew," she continued, "and later, enough not to be 100% Jewish. After that, because I changed my religion through marriage, there was a little more time left." Her mouth relaxed and her eyes became almost brown in their softness. "Now, it seems, the postponements have run out."

"Postponements, somehow, always do," replied Walter.

Now that she did talk to him about these things, Walter wished that they could go back to the innocence of the enforced marriage contract. For the first time in their eight years of marriage Phillipa really needed him. And anything he could do for her now would be eight years too late.

He had hurried home early from the university. He stepped onto the sidewalk, scraped the soles of his shoes against the edge of the curb, erasing the tight clumps of mud. He walked up the narrow pavement, wiped the rest of the mud from his shoes on the straw mat in front of the door.

There was something incredibly immoral, he thought, about
the flowers that had begun to blossom in his yard this particular spring. He closed the door slowly, almost reluctantly.
His feet were unwilling, almost lifeless as he walked into
the living room. Phillipa was seated in his chair. He looked
deliberately around the room, trying to suppress the morbid
excitement of what he knew he would find, hoping against
hope that it would not be there. It was. A neatly folded white
piece of paper placed on the top of his desk. He looked at this
woman who, more than ever before, he wished he could love.
When he left that morning her hair had been flowing freely,
her face clean, without rouge. Now her hair was tied severely
back with a clasp, her mouth uniformly red with lipstick.
He looked at her eyes. For a moment he wasn't sure; then she
looked at him, forward and direct and her eyes were clear and
wide, neither red nor wet. He pointed at the white piece of
paper.

"I heard at the college that they had been around."

Her voice was cold. "They came this morning," she said.

"How many?"

"Two."

"When will it be?"

Her lips rippled, as if a knot had found its way into her
stomach and then, abruptly, been thrust away.

"Tomorrow morning," she answered.

Walter tried to understand what she felt, tried to feel
what she was feeling so that he could know what to say and
what to do. He didn't know. After eight years of marriage, his
wife was a stranger.

"Tomorrow," he thought. "From sunset to sunrise and
that makes a tomorrow." For eight years he had backed up,
stopped and backed up again. Now he had reached the wall.
The tragedy was Phillipa's and he tried to find an answer for
her. But he knew the drama was just as much his. "It is Phillipa

I must think of now," he told himself, "not myself." He took the white piece of paper, unfolded.it, sought for some words with which to begin.

"The order reads that no one who has non-Aryan blood in any degree can no longer be exempt" He paused. "It's a general order," he said. He knew, even before he stopped talking, that his words were incorrect platitudes.

"It's a specific order," she corrected.

He sought for more words, to console her. Even as he spoke he knew that she didn't want consolation. It was he who wanted it.

"Someday it will be all over," he told her.

"Someday we shall all be dead," she answered.

The word-playing of sympathies annoyed her. Yet, she didn't know what, at that moment, she really wanted. It puzzled her. It was all too unreal, too abstract to have the precise meaning she knew that it did have. Even more than the order or transportation to a concentration camp, this lack of completeness disturbed her. At that moment she should be thinking, she told herself, of the gas chambers and the blood ditches and the open pits of shoveled earth. But they, indescribable as they seemed, were realities. They could be seen and, in all probability, would be felt. She could cope with such things. But the other was insubstantial, an event happening in another place and time, in another world to other people that had no relationship to her, to what she knew herself to be. She had always gotten what she wanted because she had always known what she wanted. But now she didn't know. What was it? Walter? She watched him as he walked over to the bookshelves, retreating for a moment into the security of what was most real to him, and then turning and walking back toward her. Was it something she wanted from him now? What was it? Her world was slipping away and she could find nothing to hold on to.

The quintessence of Phillipa Kohn. She felt her outside body diffuse into the nothingness of the air around her, her entire self melting into a vacuum, only a thin center line from her head to her toes remaining. She felt naked.

Walter was talking. "If we had a month, even a week, we might get you to Switzerland. At least we could try."

The thin-center line began to grow for a moment, as if the words of this man who was talking fulfilled some sort of requirement. What was it she demanded, of herself and of him? She felt it was no longer only a desire.

Walter leaned against the bookshelves. "You're not afraid?," he questioned.

"I am afraid, but I am not afraid,"

"It will pass," he blurted out, and then bit his lip, for he had long hated the sound of those words.

The inconclusiveness pushed at the shaky center structure of what Phillipa felt herself to be. The emptiness became more acute. Now she not only knew it, but felt it "What do I want?," she asked herself again. "What do I want?," she thought. And then, "What do I need?" The realization brought her back to her own reality.

"You can say that," she said sharply to him, "You can say a lot of things, but you do nothing. Your wife goes to a concentration camp and you say it will pass."

Instinctively he began to back up. The edges of the books prodded into him. They were round and the small of his back curved around them and they didn't hurt. He could have remained there, defensively, apologetically. Instead, he sought an intellectual way out, he looked for an analogy of this physical sensation to his own conscious will. By rote he began to remember some words of Freytag, Schopenhauer, Shaw, then, stopping, saw himself simply and boldly as part of the entire drama. He moved away from the wall. He was hurt, as he usually was when his wife was displeased with him.

But he was also angry. He felt a fire he had not put into words for a long time. It had been easier to retreat to the bookshelves. He walked to the chair, took his glasses into his hand, twirled them a moment, held them steady, and looked at Phillipa. Now he did not measure his words. These were words he felt he wished to say and he said them.

"I said it will pass," he told her. "I said it will pass because this is what you have been telling me for almost eight years. With each new happening, you said it would pass. When, at the university, men were being fired, you said it would pass. When we could not express our own thoughts publicly, you said it would pass. When I might have taken steps to put an end to all this, you prevented me and said it would pass. Well, I let it pass. I waited and watched and waited and it has passed—to the point where my wife is being taken and I can do not a thing about it. Not any more. Now that I want to, now that I am ready to, not any more."

Phillipa felt the thin line of her being grow again. Her person was no longer an imponderable. The transparency of the air solidified into what she knew was herself. The completeness returned. She knew again what she had to do, what she could do. To herself she tried to understand the reason for the reformation. "Was it this? Was it Walter?," she mumbled to herself. She did not really care.

"What did you say, Phillipa?"

"Nothing. Nothing."

Then, to herself: "But what is it I wanted?" The need had gone and so had the words. She looked at Walter. She wanted to be very angry with him. He had stepped out of his place, the place she had made for him. She should put him back there, through condescension, superiority. She put together the words she would use. The deliciousness of her past control hummed the words to herself: "You are over-dramatizing yourself again, my sweet," she could say. Or could she?

Something had happened that now made the words inappropriate. She had gotten something from Walter without telling him first what it was she wanted. Or needed. Yet, she didn't know what it was she had wished or even what she had gotten.

Walter should be comforting her, not berating her, she thought. Yet, in some perverse way this confrontation by Walter was more important than platitudinous words of comfort. It made her angry and anger made her defiant. And the strength of defiance made her both grateful and proud. To Walter for meeting her needs on her level, not as a supplicant but as a peer. And to herself for overcoming the momentary lapse bordering on self-pity. Her self-confidence in her own status as a human being, above and better than other human beings, gave her even more resolve to face the future with a certainly that she dominate it, not succumb to it. Others might try to survive, she would strive to conquer. She strengthened her self-assurance that she could somehow, ultimately, still control the people and the world she lived in.

"Save your energies for yourself, Walter," she told him. "'Your wife is a Jew. Maybe soon you will need them, as I need mine now."

Walter felt her need and wanted to love her and wanted to hate her. He wondered which it was, let the dichotomy pass. He stood in front of her.

"I love you," he said.

He said it simply, softly. That was all. His voice had become heavy again, but not the heaviness of despair. It was like the air that is heavy with the dewy freshness of the morning. It was a feeling he had not known for years, and for a moment he didn't know what it meant or where it was going. But it felt good inside and he didn't care.

"You're not afraid," he said. This time it was not a question, but an assurance.

"Only the weak are afraid," she told him. "Some go and cry. Others go and suffer. Many go and die. But none of these are going to happen to me. They are weak. They feel. their stomachs tie up into knots and their tears bring them fear. But not I, Walter."

She stood up. She was complete again, self-confident. She wanted to say, "I always had more then the rest, I always was more than the rest, and I shall always be so." But she didn't. Somehow, this once, with Walter standing unmoving in front of her, she couldn't. Somehow, this once, she had the slightest feeling that perhaps she might wish for a moment that it didn't have to be so.

"You are right, Walter," she said. This is only temporary. "This, too, shall pass."

She waited a moment, then turned away and walked to the stairs.

"Phillipa?"'

"Yes?"

"We shall make it pass."

She stopped and waited until he reached her side.

Phillipa left the next morning. She took a small canvas pack: her two best dresses, several pairs of silk hosiery, a small box full of cosmetics. Walter packed it neatly for her as she bathed and dressed. He went to the kitchen, wrapped a pound of Swiss cheese in waxed paper, placed it with half a loaf of pumpernickel bread and a box of store crackers in a brown bag, took it back to the bedroom and folded it into the pack. He did it quietly. She would reject carrying it, he knew, as a compromise with weakness. He put it out of sight, but where she could find it easily. He reasoned that before the day was out she would open the pack to look for powder or lipstick. By that time compromise would have become expediency.

He went back downstairs. As he prepared breakfast for
Phillipa, he wondered how long she would he traveling, how
she was going, where she was going. He began to picture
Phillipa in many situations: a crowded barracks; on a long
line begging for bread; in dirty, torn clothing scrubbing a
sidewalk (it looked, surprisingly, like the sidewalk in front
of the university administration building); in a gas chamber,
her face and body slowly becoming a blur, the blur reform-
ing into a black outline in a brick furnace; lying naked on a
floor, surrounded by uncountable shining, black S.S. boots.
He laughed out loud to assure himself of his irrationality in
thinking these thoughts. But the black boots continued to
bother him and he concentrated on the breakfast. Phillipa
came down in a few minutes. She wore a dark grey suit, her
hair tied tightly in back, her face serious, but soft and calm.
There was no trace of anything but self-assurance.

"Phillipa . . .," Walter began.

She didn't answer and he understood and did not call to
her again. They remained silent throughout the meal. Walter
watched her closely, studying her for any sign that would tell
him she needed his help. He was ready to anticipate it, to
give what was needed. But she needed nothing. Only herself.
At seven o'clock two S.S. men came to the door, knocked.
Walter answered the door.

"Our apologies for disturbing you so early, Herr Professor. We have come for Fraulein Kohn."

"Frau Penmann," Walter said.

"Fraulein Kohn," one of them, holding a sheet of paper,
repeated. "This is what our orders read. This is the right address, Herr Professor." He looked at Walter with a mixture of
disgust and pity. Walter studied their faces. He was thankful, at least, that his own position and Aryan acceptance had
spared Phillipa the initial brutality and degradation of others
who had been collected for the transports. He remained

silent, unmoving, as if he were waiting for the temple to crumble or the sea to part.

"We are in a hurry, Herr Professor," the other S.S. man told him.

"There are no miracles in Nazi Germany," Walter wanted to say. Instead he turned and went for Phillipa. They were very polite, these S.S. men, he thought. He wondered what the hangman acted like as he pulled the release. He guessed he knew.

As they walked up the stairs to get the pack, Phillipa moved slowly, as if to imbue herself with the things of security and comfort that she would need to hold on to for a long, long time. There was little Walter could say, he knew. Yet, he felt compelled to offer some kind of hope, some kind of reassurance. He would try in every way to help her, he said, to seek her freedom, at the very least to make things easier for her at the camp as soon as he could find out where she was. She thanked him. More an acknowledgment than thanks, accepting as perfunctory the unreality his assurances. His words were, after all, something she should expect and yet did not really believe. She was not the same as the evening before. The hard frame had encompassed her again, more forcefully than ever before. They returned to the hall. Walter stopped, put his arms around her shoulders. She accepted the embrace, did not respond to it.

"Before you go, my darling"—he said this slowly, without dramatics—"I want you to know that I truly love you."

"I know, Walter."

"And last night, Phillipa . . . ." He hesitated, uncertain whether to continue. "Last night, Phillipa, was the most wonderful of all we have spent together."

The sentimentality was lost.

"I must apologize for last night," she said.

"Apologize?"

"I was rather foolish," she told him.

"Because you needed me?"

"Because I may have given the impression that I needed you." Her voice was firm, almost cold. Even her body seemed to stiffen, "There was no reason for it. I have never needed anyone. I don't now." She wasn't sure she really meant to say these words to Walter, but saying them gave her strength.

"It isn't a weakness," he told her, "we all need someone. We must all live together and work together. Whether it is a husband or a wife or a friend or just the people who are in the world with us. Now, more than ever, you must understand that."

"My cheeks are still soft and my eyes are still dry," she said.

She turned away from Walter, then stopped and looked at him. He did not try to stop her. She knew it was not she who was walking away, but he who was letting her go. It was his decision, not hers. She felt a strange respect for this man that she had not known twenty-four hours earlier. The night that had passed had not been a mistake. She faced him and was not ashamed to look up, evenly, into the depths of this man's eyes. She spoke softly, the softness letting him know that there was not a wall, but a truth between them.

"Walter, you may have been right years ago."

"May have been right?"

"I won't say any more. I am a proud woman. I can see, but not what I don't wish to. If I said you were right, then it would mean I was wrong."

That was all. Nothing more was necessary. She picked up the pack, hung it by the strap over the crook in her arm.

"I respect you, Phillipa" Walter said. Perhaps, when one's life is trembling, he thought, and it is too late to fight the foe together, fighting alone, in her way, would enable one to survive where another way would not.

"Your cheeks are soft and your eyes are dry," he said, "and that has made them beautiful." He smiled, held her body for a moment against his. "Keep them that way," he whispered.

A heavy knock sounded at the door, then a boot kicking against it and a voice insisting: "We are waiting, Herr Professor."

Phillipa smiled, wondering if Walter understood her now, at last. He looked at her, wondered if her smile meant that, at last, she understood him. He kissed her lightly, walked with her to the door, and she was gone.

He waited several minutes and then walked to the railroad station, where the day's transports would be loaded. He stood at a corner of a building across the street from the station square where he could watch, unobserved. They came. Phillipa, along with several dozen others, some young, some old, herded into a tight group, molded into line by the leather strips of rawhide carried by the S.S. men. Walter winced each time a whip struck, his academic mind unable to avoid the thought that their seeming politeness, after all, was only semantic. He had heard stories of the early morning transports. He wondered why he hadn't gotten up at seven o'clock in the morning before to see this. He wished that all of the people of Heidelberg would see this. How differently they would feel, he conjectured. The people came, with their bodies bent, their heads low, pushing against one another to escape the sting of the whip. Mothers, holding by the hand small children confused by this strange game of policeman. Young women, already fearful of the eyes of the men in the black boots. Old men, wondering whether they would have the strength to live long enough to take the showers of gas that would cleanse the life from their bodies, Then, for the first time, Walter saw the others. The people of Heidelberg. A goodly number of them, entering and leaving the rail-way station, passing by on their way to work: the business men, the factory workers, the clerks, the shopkeepers, the

housewives on their way to early market, the government
workers. Some paused long enough to look at the group of
frightened, beaten, crying people. All of them walked on, accepting what they saw as a scene of every day life (and in fact,
thought Walter, wasn't it?), something of necessity, not even
regrettable any longer, something unrelated to their own
particular world. Human beings being tortured, unrelated to
the world of the German people, thought Walter. Weren't the
German people human beings? Was he not a human being?
Did the fact that all this was being done under the law make
it more palatable, make it less reprehensible? Was there no
moral law, no law of humanity for himself, for his wife, for
his neighbors, for his countrymen and women?

Walter thought this for only fleeting seconds as suddenly,
seemingly standing out from the rest of the group, he saw
Phillipa. Her body was erect, her stomach hard and still. As
she walked past the place where he watched and away from
him, he saw that her head was high, her hair firmly in place,
her lips still neat with lipstick, her eyes clear and dry. He
stared for a moment after the group had disappeared into the
railroad station and toward the long row of boxcars on one
of the tracks. He tried to keep Phillipa in his memory. He
started to cross the street to go to the university to teach an
early class. Suddenly he stopped, closed his eyes and saw Phillipa again, and now, next to her, the big man with the beard
of a disciple, Guido Termini. And next to him Erich Da Sola,
who had taken his transport five years before.

"There's one thing people don't understand about Fascism, Walter," Erich had said. "If they let it start at all, then
they can't escape it. They always cooperate until it's them.
And it's always them."

Walter re-crossed the street, away from the university.
He didn't care that he might be late for his class. He wanted
to walk and to think. He had some planning to do.

Chapter XIII

For three days Phillipa sat silently in a corner of a boxcar. Humanity crowded in upon her. The smell became part of her own constipation. She wanted to run away, but could only press her back tighter and tighter against the cold wood of the train wall. There were eighty people in the one boxcar, packed together, and yet each one alone. Each covered with the hood of his or her own existence, the first mantle of that perpetual fear when one wonders what the next moment will bring and knows that he or she will have no say in it. At first, under the cloak, come the thoughts of the future; then, when the cold and hunger become more than thoughts, comes the present; and when the cold and hunger are accepted as part of a weariness that can no longer be fought, there remains only the past.

A little girl cried from one end of the car, and the mother took her to the hole that had been torn in the floor; the others turned their heads politely. For a moment they combined the exigencies of the present with the amenities of the past. Soon they would see people forced to drown in their own feces and they would blink an eye only because the eyelid helped shut out the smell.

It would take some of them months, others only a few days, but all would look back to the large sign reading

"Heidelberg Bahnhof" and know that walking under it they had gone from one world into another. The past would dissolve into an enigmatic make-believe, the present would be rejected in the impossibility of its deformity, and the future would not even enter into their consciousness. They would look back and remember and know only that from that moment on they were no longer alive.

Phillipa was grateful that first evening, as much for the physical symbol that took her mind momentarily out of the night-darkened boxcar as for anything else, when she opened her pack and found the food that Walter had put there. On the second day of the journey the train stopped and Phillipa, with the others, was taken off and lined up alongside the tracks. The weather was a little cooler. There seemed to be more trees, less farmland.

"It's Poland," Phillipa heard someone whisper. "I have a sister in Poland." Then, the hasty correction: "I had a sister in Poland."

An S.S. Corporal, apparently in charge of that part of the shipment, began separating the males and females. In a few minutes the men and boys stood on one side of the tracks, the woman and girls on the other. Phillipa noted how quickly and effectively the S.S. lash worked. Phillipa tried not to look when a little boy, no more than five, suddenly broke away from the men's group and started to run across the tracks, back to his mother. The S.S. Corporal called to the child to stop. He didn't. He tripped and fell across the tracks with a bullet in his head. Phillipa thanked God that she had never been a mother. She turned to the side as the child's mother was carried, hysterical, into the boxcar. The men watched silently, screaming silently and helplessly as the women were put back on the train, the large sliding doors shut and bolted on their wives, mothers, daughters, sisters, friends. A command from the S.S. Corporal and the men turned their backs on the train and marched away.

It was not yet to be believed. It could be only a bad dream, not acceptable into the world of reality. The unreality of the nightmare stood out even more in contrast to the S.S. men, who went about it all calmly, businesslike, as if it were merely the routine of an everyday job. It was.

The third day the train stopped again. Phillipa, choked by the stink of dung and sweat and vomit, hardly cared now what happened to her. Her only wish was to get out of there, into fresh air. They remained another night in the sealed, unmoving boxcars. Phillipa stayed awake, trying not to, not being able to permit herself a sleep that might miss an opportunity for a moment of what had now become luxury: A breath of air, a place for bodily relief, a taste of water, a piece of food. Artificial light filtered in through the cracks and holes in the roof of the train, making half-ghostly figures of the other women in the boxcar. Phillipa stared at them. Some were propped against the walls of the car, like herself, half-asleep or half-dead, she couldn't tell which. Others, their dresses and skirts entangled, their clothes disarranged, their hair dirty, unkempt, huddled with their backs to one another, their knees pulled up against their chins. She had moved twice during the past day. Once, when an old woman next to her wretched, splattering her shoes and stockings and legs. The helpless, apologetic look in the woman's eyes didn't abate Phillipa's contempt. Later, when she herself wanted to throw up, her contempt turned to anger. Not for the woman, but for herself. She moved again when two lesbians huddled against the wall next to her head, making love. She wondered when her anger might turn to pity and, worse, become self-pity.

On the morning of the fourth day the train started again. She watched carefully the cracks in the ceiling of the car, watched the blackness become grey, the grey become white, the white become yellow. A single sunbeam pushed its way into the car. Phillipa wanted to reach out and take it into her hands and squeeze it and hold it close. She didn't have the strength.

Suddenly the train halted, the doors slid open and a voice ordered "Schnell aus." A woman by the door screamed as the cut of a whip tore the skin from across the front of her face. They marched down a ramp from the train platform. Those who had the strength looked up and saw the large letters "Oscwizm" on the banner hanging above the entrance to the camp. A large gate with the words "Arbeit Macht Frei" spread across its frame greeted them. They marched through the gate, all of them afraid now, all of them hurrying, staying tightly together, trying to keep away from the outside edge of the moving mass where the whip would reach them more easily. Phillipa told herself not to be afraid, not to succumb to the indignity, but she pushed with the others, trying to surround herself with the protection of other bodies.

They stopped just past the main gate and were herded into a long, low building where they waited while a young Lieutenant wearing an S.S. armband counted them as one would count cattle in a pen. They passed through the building and continued to march. Now they were a distance beyond the main gate and Phillipa could separate herself ever so slightly from the mass and walk almost by herself, in the line, erect and purposeful. The camp looked like the pictures of military training bases. One-storied brown wooden barracks, row on row, along both sides of the street. Larger buildings, stone grey, were at the end of one side of the street. In the distance she could see other streets duplicating the one she was on. At all sides were tall towers with soldiers in them, and surrounding everything were high barbed-wire fences.

A young girl, perhaps no more than nineteen, walked alongside her.

"Do you think they will give us food now?," she asked.

"I don't know," Phillipa answered.

"These buildings look so good, after the train," the girl insisted. "Do you think they will let us sleep now?"

"Perhaps?" Phillipa was too weary to speak.

"Oh, I am so tired," the girl said. "And so afraid."

Phillipa wanted to tell the girl not to be afraid. She felt strong because she could hide her fear. The other could not. She didn't have time to tell the girl anything.

The group stopped and a man dressed in an officer's uniform, but without insignia, stepped forward. His black boots shone, his uniform clean and meticulous. The riding crop he carried was handled delicately, as if it were an exstension of a ballet costume. He pointed it first to one side and then to the other, dividing the group into two parts.

"One to the left, one to the right."

He counted them off neatly and precisely, and they moved where he pointed. His voice was cultured and soft, almost gentle. His face was handsome, almost angelic. His manner gave hope and confidence. Phillipa began to feel better. Here, at last, was a gentleman. Perhaps it would not be as bad as she thought. She turned toward him, to get a closer look, listened to hear if anyone knew who he was. All she could hear were the half-whispered words, "the Doctor." She wouldn't learn till much later that his last name was Mengele.

Phillipa found herself in the group on the left. She smiled at the young girl as the latter stepped off into the group on the right. Those on the left were told to put their belongings down and wait. The others, on the right, began to march off.

"Nach Birkenau," the Doctor said quietly, smiling to them as if to assure them that all was well. The young girl waved to Phillipa.

For a moment Phillipa envied the other group. In the
distance she could see the buildings toward which that group
marched. They looked cleaner and whiter than those of the
street in which she stood. The cobbled streets almost seemed
to become pavements and there seemed to be trees and small
gardens in that direction. It wasn't until a few days later that
she learned that the sharp odor she smelled that first evening
had come from the crematoria, from Birkenau, where that
same afternoon the group on the right had been burnt to
ashes.

The individuality Phillipa had known all her life all but
disappeared during the next few days. She felt it, she still
had it, she told herself. But if it was to remain, it would
remain only inside of her. They spent the first night in one
of the barracks, an empty one, without heat, without beds
or mattresses. She was thankful that she could stretch out.
There was plenty of floor space. It is funny, she thought,
how even the bad things sometimes seem good. They had
been four days without decent food, some of them without
any food at all. During the night she could hear the scurry-
ing of hands into tightly grasped packs or bags that each of
the women carried, searching for the last crumbs of nourishment, hastily devouring them before another inmate
through the strength of uncontrollable hunger stole them
away. She felt the softness of her dresses, pulled a corner of
one from the edge of the pack and, in the darkness, held it
caressingly against her cheek as she half-slept, half-dreamt of
the sense memory of the rustling silk in other places and in
other times. Suddenly a twinge of panic came to her. What
if they should confiscate all the belongings? Indeed, this
seemed more than likely. She thought for a moment, calmed
herself and carefully removed from the pack her comb and
hand-mirror, found a deep, wide crack in the floorboards by
the side of the barracks where she lay and silently stuffed

them down, out of sight. With reassurance now, she took the edge of the silk dress and pressed it against her face, the vanity of the past and the promise of the future safely hidden, and she tried to go to sleep.

The next morning they were lined up with their belongings. At first they feared the worst. Phillipa began to tear inside. Not alone the fear of dying, but the fear of the helplessness of going to die and not being able to do anything about it. They were marched to another large building, told to go inside. As they entered a soldier took each one's belongings and threw them onto an ever increasing pile. With the satisfaction of not having given away all of her worldly possessions, Phillipa didn't mind as much as she thought she would. The gently persuading "Doctor" was not there. But a corporal's whip was just as effective. Inside the building a group of soldiers stood with water hoses.

"Undress," the women were told.

They stood still. The corporal stood in front of them, his face flushed, a bit unsteady and wavering. He walked once up and down the line of women. Phillipa could smell the stench of liquor from him even as he passed.

"I am Corporal Kadeck," he told them. "Some of you may have already heard of me. If you haven't, you soon will." He laughed, made a full sweep of his body toward the men behind him with the water hoses, his face smiling in anticipation of their laughter at the nuance of his little joke. They laughed.

He turned to the assembled group of women again. He looked at them slowly, carefully, enjoying the anticipation of what was to come. This was apparently something he did every day, something he enjoyed just as much every time he did it. His mouth stretched into a broad smile as he repeated, with a purposeful matter-of-factness.

"Undress!"

No one moved.

"But in front of men," someone in the group muttered.

This was what the corporal was waiting for. It was apparently a routine expectation which prompted the daily procedure of events. He struck his whip on the ground.

"Achtung!"

He looked in the direction where the voice had come. He pushed aside those in his way, took the arm of one woman, about thirty years of age, pulled her to the front of the group. Phillipa could see her hands shake, her whole body crying inside. Phillipa wanted to cry for her. But she hadn't yet learned how to cry for herself.

"You are concerned about the men," the corporal said, delighting himself with his own mock irony. "They, too, are concerned about you. Undress."

She remained still, frozen with fear. Corporal Kadeck moved to her aide, grabbed the top of her dress with one hand, tore it away from her body. She screamed. The corporal slapped her across the mouth with the hand holding the whip, at the same time tearing away the rest of her clothes with the other. She stood naked. She tried to cover herself, awkwardly bending her body, folding her arms across her breasts. Kadeck put down the whip, grabbed her arms and thrust them apart, turning her full view toward the men with the hoses.

"Now you will do what I say," he yelled at the shocked group of women. The other soldiers broke out into laughter, pleased with their leader and with themselves. At Kadeck's command they turned the hoses on the one woman who stood in front of them, slamming her against one side of the building with the heavy stream of water. She made no attempt to resist. There was nothing she could resist against now. The corporal turned to the others.

"We Germans must protect our country from the con-
tamination of you Jewish vermin," be shouted. "So we start
by giving you a well-needed bath." He laughed. He slapped
the whip against the floor again. "Undress."

The women still stood unmoving. He began to walk toward one group huddled against a corner. Quickly, they began
to take their clothes off. He stood and watched, then faced
another group. They looked at the others and began to follow
suit. The woman who had been first had fainted, slumped
bruised and half-drowned onto the wood floor. The soldiers
turned their hoses off. They began to point and laugh now
at the naked parts of the women's bodies in front of them.
Kadeck walked slowly past the two naked groups, studying
them as one might judge cattle at a state fair exhibit. He
pointed to one girl, a thin, whispish girl with soft, stringy
blonde hair, barely formed in body, perhaps no more than 15
or 16 years of age. He reached in, took her roughly by the
hand and pulled her forward. He turned back to the soldiers.

"Willy," he called.

A young boy, perhaps no more than eighteen, stepped
forward, obediently. He looked sheepish, embarrassed. He
stood close to his fellows, unwilling to move any further.

"Willy," Kadeck said again. "Come. A present for you.
Just about right for a young boy your age, no?"

The other soldiers laughed. One reached over and
pinched Willy on the buttocks. Another leaned over and
whispered something into his ear. Willy's face blanched, then
with the bravado expected of him, stepped forward. For a
moment the girl did not realize what was obvious to everyone else. Then, as the boy approached, her face and body
broke into the ageless lines of fear. "Oh, God. Oh, no. Oh,
please, no." The boy half-pulled, half-dragged the screaming
girl through the door leading into the small room at the rear

of the hut. The other men shouted obscene encouragement
to the boy, their voices barely heard above the screaming
of the girl. Most of the women turned their faces, lowered
their heads. Suddenly the whip flashed at the two groups of
already stripped women and they ware herded toward one
corner of the room, the hoses burst on again and the flood
of water beat into their bodies, splashing them across the
ground, into the wall and over and into and onto one another. Perhaps one of them, even at that moment, had a memory
of a few days earlier of watching her own child in a bathtub
splashing with glee around the tub filled with rubber dolls
and toys of childhood.

In a few minutes the small door at the rear opened and
the young girl walked in, slowly, without trembling, without
a tear. The boy was shaking as he picked up a hose and joined
the others and in a few moments the water from his hose had
washed away the blood that had covered the girl's legs.

The sound of the thrusting water, the laughter of the S.S.
men, the screaming commands of the corporal grew louder
and louder until they echoed back and forth throughout
the whole room. Phillipa watched, heard, unbelieving. The
eyes of the soldiers, the pointing, the laughter, went into
her, through her. She felt as though she were being raped, as
though she had already been raped. As the corporal turned to
the group in which she was, she slowly began to undress.

They returned to the barracks later that morning, naked, resigned to the shocking unbelievability of anything
that might be done to them now. They pushed themselves
against the bare walls of the barracks, as if to find warmth
and protection in whatever barrier separated them from the
world outside. Suddenly the door of the barracks flew open
and a load of striped, pajama-type uniforms were thrown in.
For a moment they all stared. Them, almost as if in joyous
exultation of a priceless gift, they ran, stumbled, fell, crawled

to the pile, grasping, pulling, jerking, tearing out of it and
from each other the piece of fabric that would restore to them
a dignity that was worth more at that moment than any they
had ever known before in their lives.

At first it was desperation, the need for self-salvation.
In each one's mind occurred the thought that perhaps there
would be not be enough clothing for all and each scrambled
into the pile of clothing, now strewn and scattered over the
floor of the room, searching for the top and bottom of immediate deliverance. The naked arms and legs and buttocks
and breasts rolled one on top of and into another, a mass of
flailing, twisting naked women fighting for a last vestige of
honor and decorum. Phillipa stayed in a corner and watched,
knowing her need to obtain her share of clothing but unable
to join the indignity of animal competition. And yet, she was
not altogether immune. She moved to the edge of the group,
waited, and as an item of clothing was accidentally thrown to
the side she jealously grabbed at it and ran with it to a side of
the room, to put it on before someone else could take it from
her. She went back again and reached into the group and tore
from the flimsy grasp of a young girl a second piece of clothing and donned that. She sat at the side now, breathing hard
and wanting to vomit at the bestiality of common behavior
she had permitted herself to indulge in.

Now, in the center of the room, the naked, half-naked
and clothed bodies of the women began to realize that there
was enough clothing for all. The tearing and pushing and
scratching and fighting were no longer necessary. A huge
woman, still naked, with huge hips and legs and swaying
breasts stood up in the center of the group, surveyed the
scene around her, lifted high over her head the two pieces
of clothing she had salvaged, and then laughed. The others stopped, looked at her, looked around, looked at themselves and also laughed. The titter became a roar and the

roar became an hysteric and in a moment they were rolling once again on the floor, over and through the spilled pieces of clothing, laughing and shouting and yelling like children playing in the shallow water of the ocean's edge and piling on top of one another as each new soft wave came to lift their bodies and buoy their spirits. The women who were on the side of the barracks, one by one gradually leaped back into the joyful play, the building resounding with the shouts of girl-children in the glory of youthful exuberance. They knew their behavior was stupidly outrageous, that bitter tears were more appropriate than laughter for the situation they were in. But they also felt—they knew—that this was the probably the last moment they would ever have for any more moments of life's exuberance.

In the early afternoon the women had begun to know each other, to talk, some furtively in whispers, others in the residue of the elation of the late morning. Phillipa looked at them and wondered whether she, too, should make a friend or friends. Not yet, she decided. If she remained separate, her strength would be all her own. The stronger she remained, the better chance she would have to survive. She moved herself into the corner of the room where she had slept the night before, scratched with her fingernails along the edge of the rotted floorboard, pushed up above the level of the board her comb and mirror. With deliberate, deft movement, she began to comb out her long black hair, admiring herself in the mirror as she did so. This was assurance. Assurance of her grooming, of her beauty. When she controlled it, she controlled part of her strength. She lost herself in satisfied thoughts of the past as she stroked the comb through her hair.

That afternoon they were lined up again. The lieutenant was there. He spoke softly as he had the day before.

"I have good news for you," he told them. "'You will not go to Birkenau . . . yet. We need workers and you have been

chosen to work . . . for a while . . . and to live . . . for a while.
You will be assigned to permanent barracks and to jobs in the
camp, in the fields, on the roads or in the factories, as your
services are needed."

"Will we eat?," someone ventured to ask. The others
turned and looked at her. Then, realizing their betrayal,
turned forward again, stood a long moment, waiting.

The lieutenant spoke calmly. "You will eat," he said quietly. "As soon as your assignments for this afternoon are completed." He called to Kadeck. "Corporal, they're yours now."

As Kadeck marched them off, Phillipa heard the woman
next to her chance a whisper. Without turning her head the
sound of the woman's hushed voice reached her ear. "This
Kadeck. This morning was not an accident. I have heard of
him. A drunk. Vicious. A torturer. Completely unpredictable.
Look out for him. One moment, like anyone else; the next, an
unbelievable monster."

Without looking back, Phillipa nodded her head, not so
much for acknowledgment, for she knew the woman next to
her would not dare turn her head to look at her, but in self-
assurance that she had, from that morning, already come to
this conclusion about Kadeck.

Kadeck led them to a building containing a row of small
tables with two chairs at each table. On one of the chairs at
each table sat an inmate with a small needle-type machine,
like a large hypodermic. At first a wave of fear passed over the
women. They had already heard of one of the standard death
techniques: the injection of carbolic acid into the heart. But
in a moment they realized that the lieutenant's promise of
work rather than death was true. This was not yet the place
or time. Each inmate at the tables had a list containing the
names of the new inmates, a number next to each name. As
each women took her place at the table, her arm was bared
and a number tattooed onto her forearm. As each series of

numbers was completed, an S.S. guard checked the number on the arm against an official number on a list. Phillipa looked at her number, then stared at it, her flesh shivering with the repulsion of this foreign substance encroaching upon her body. She looked away and told herself she would never look at the tattooed number again.

When all the women had gone through the procedure, Kadeck lined them up again. He stood in front of them for a moment, then walked once up and down the line.

"Now you are officially registered," he said. "Now each of you is officially one of our most esteemed guests." He bowed low, with a sweep of an arm along the floor. He tottered a moment, then quickly straightened up, his hand pushing back into his inside jacket pocket a flask that had begun to slide out as he had bent over. The broad-mouthed smile returned to his face.

"And I will wager that some of you thought that this was a heart-injection center." He paused a moment, as a lecturer about to make an obvious point, so simple that only he was wise enough to see the answer. "I see questioning faces," he said. "Apparently, some of you don't know about the heart-injection procedure." He paused another moment. "Is there anyone who doesn't know about it who would like to?" There was no response. He expected none. He pointed to a woman directly in front of him, a woman of perhaps fifty years of age who Phillipa had taken special notice of because, like herself, she had seemed to stay separate from the group, had thus far been silent and apart.

"Frau," Kadeck said, "come forward and tell us about the heart-injection procedure." The woman came forward.

"I am sorry," she stammered. "I do not know how it works."

"Oh, what a pity," smiled Kadeck. "Then I must show you."

He pointed to two inmates at the tables.

"Here!" They came quickly, fear and pity on their faces at the same time. Without having to be told, they each held one of the woman's arms, pulled them back against her sides. Her face suddenly broke into lines of horror. Her eyes stared, unbelieving. She opened her mouth to scream, then turned her face to Kadeck's, staring into his eyes, almost challenging him. Kadeck stopped for a moment, surprised, then broadened his smile. He reached up and tore the top part of the uniform from the woman's body. From his jacket pocket he took a large needle-tipped syringe. With the air of a professor demonstrating an important experiment to a class, he held up the syringe with a flourish.

"Now, watch closely," he said. "I shall demonstrate the heart-injection technique." He turned to the woman being held in front of him: "Especially for you," he told her, "since you didn't know what it was."

The woman wet her lips, opened her mouth and spat in his face. His smile disappeared and awkwardly, viciously, he lunged at the woman with the syringe. She screamed as it pierced her breast. He pulled it out, saw that it had not released the fluid, caught himself, found his smile again, and this time, more carefully, searched for the heart region, plunged the needle in slowly, as deliberately and slowly as he could, pushed forward the release, waited perhaps a half-minute as the woman began to slump, half in faint from pain, half in the beginning moments of death, against the tight arms of the men who held her. Triumphantly, Kadeck pulled the syringe away. The woman slumped to the floor.

"Throw it out," he ordered the two inmates. They dragged the body across the floor and out the rear door of the building.

Kadeck turned to the women. "Now you stupid Jews have learned something," he said. The smile was gone.

"Perhaps we shall have more educational lessons for you from time to time. We Germans have a lot to teach you."

In silence he lined them up again and marched them to another building in which a long line of men stood with barber's shears and clipping machines, These men were not soldiers, but, like those in the previous building, also inmates of the concentration camp. Phillipa understood then why some were allowed to live, what kinds of jobs justified to the Nazis an extension of human life. There was no protest, no hesitation as the women moved slowly down the line, past the S.S. man who stood with his whip ready, each woman getting her head shaved clean.

Kadeck seemed a little tired when the shearing was all completed. As they were to see him do many times again,   . he turned his back to the group, withdrew the flask from his inside jacket pocket and took several hurried, almost frantic gulps of whiskey. The stimulation of the morning was gone. But he found words for his one more little joke.

"See how well we treat you," he told them. "We give you baths and we give you haircuts. Permanents, shall we say! You certainly cannot say that we do not look out for the cleanliness and beauty of our guests." He snapped the whip and they lined up and marched out.

That evening Phillipa took her hand mirror and smashed it to the floor, grinding up the pieces under her bare heel.

That night, several hours after darkness had shut the sixty women in Phillipa's barracks out of the outside world and had shut out the outside world from them, permitting them a sleep of resigned exhaustion, the door suddenly slammed open, the single electric bulb hanging from a loose cord tied to a wooden peg in the center of the ceiling flashed on, and Corporal Kadeck and two of the S.S. men from the line of water hoses stood in the doorway.

Turning her head toward the heavy footsteps, Phillips saw the three pairs of heavy, black jackboots, the dress uniforms, the lightning patches of the storm-trooper elite shining on the left shirtsleeves. They carried rifles. They took a few steps into the room. One went back to the door, paced off several feet toward the center of the barracks, and drew an imaginary line with the heel of his boot.

Kadeck faced the women.

'Who is from Munich?," he shouted, his voice overly-deep and overly-loud with drunkenness.

For a moment the thought of a special assignment raced through Phillipa's head, a magic opportunity for release from what she knew must come in her present situation. But she knew better. And her home was not Munich any longer, but Heidelberg.

A woman lying a few feet from her stood up, apparently entertaining the same teasing thoughts that had crossed Phillipa's mind.

"Come here," Kadeck ordered.

She walked forward.

"Here," he pointed, his foot touching the imaginary line on the floor. She stepped on it, looking at him, obedient, expectant. Kadeck motioned the inmates in back of her to get out of the way and at the same moment the man who had drawn the line suddenly stepped back a foot, pulled back the butt of his rifle and slammed it with all his force into the neck of the woman in front of him. Without a sound her neck jerked back and her body flew across the room toward the far wall.

The third man slowly and with serious deliberation paced, foot by foot, the distance from the imaginary line to the place where the woman lay. He took a pencil and piece of paper from his inner pocket, jotted down the information.

Then he bent, felt along the woman's neck, felt for her heart-beat. After a moment he rose, thrusting the paper toward the first soldier, who held the rifle butt still thrust forward where it had made contact, his head and face forward with it, anxiously awaiting word from his comrade.

"Dead," the third soldier said. "Broken neck. Sixteen feet distance." He reached in his pocket, peeled off several bills. "Twenty marks," he said. "Here. But I will win the next one."

The first soldier smiled, pocketed the money, threw his arm around his friend.

"Twenty feet next time," he said. "And thirty marks." He laughed. "Is it a bet?"

"All right," his companion protested as they left the barracks, "but next time I choose the target."

"Then I must have odds," the other answered, as they walked away, laughing in good fellowship.

"You," Kadeck said, pointing to two women cowering on the floor nearest him, and nodding toward the body. "Throw it outside." He waited while the two women dragged the body to the door, dragged it around to a side of the barracks, and hurriedly returned.

The pounding step of his boots was the only sound Phillipa heard as he turned off the light and pulled shut the door.

Phillipa was assigned to her work-job the following day. With the other inmates in her barracks she lined up at six in the morning, the sun barely aloft, marched briskly to a long, low building, inside past small teller-like windows where she was given a round bowl filled with a dark porridge-like substance that smelled like stale coffee, and a large round piece of hard bread. From there she was seated at a narrow, low table, side by side with the others. A guard called out "zehn minuten" and they began to eat hurriedly. Most stopped immediately after tasting the contents of the bowl. It was harsh and bitter, much like unsalted or unsweetened

cooked oatmeal, lumpy and cold, surrounded by its own
thin, flavorless juice. It had the consistency, when chewed, of
sawdust.

Phillipa, less hungry perhaps than the others by virtue
of Walter's small food package that had lasted through the
long train trip and until their belongings were confiscated,
and sustained by a brief handout of food the afternoon before, sat stolidly, not touching her plate. Across the table a
stout, youngish man—not much more than a boy, Phillippa
thought—from the men's barracks who, with a few other
males, occasionally was assigned to work near the women's
barracks and permitted to join them at the evening meal,
watched her and did likewise. Several others followed their
lead. Soon half the long table sat without eating. A guard
walked down the aisle, watching the table. He smiled at the
full plates.

"Don't eat if you don't want to. You won't get any more
until evening. You'll wish you had this food."

"This is food?," the fat young man across from Phillipa
said. An involuntary titter went up around the table, then
died as if suddenly stamped on as the guard turned. He stared
at the fat young man, the corner of his mouth twitching. In
one motion the guard's hand reached out, the whip lashed
forward and caught the young man across the face, pulling
skin and blood after the leather thong.

The young man didn't flinch. The half-smile was gone,
but his eyes continued to stare at the guard. The guard didn't
notice, or didn't care to. He turned and walked casually on
his rounds. No one else ate anything more. In a minute the
whistle blew, they heard another guard call "raus."

They were led at a fast walk through the gate they had
come through the first day, up, over and down the ramp, and
out of the camp. They marched at almost a trot for a half-
hour, the older men and women gasping, stumbling, falling,

rising again as the guard's lash slapped at them, bit into them
and forced them on. They stopped finally, in front of a factory,
a dirtied brick building with small, barred windows. Uncer-
emoniously they were led inside. Outside, there had been an
odor like that of a dump or, for those who had came from the
northern port and railway centers, like that of a stockyard.
Inside, the smell was unbearable. It was raw and thick. No air
circulated into the building, letting the stench pile onto itself
until it was so thick it could almost be seen. Quickly, they
were assigned to jobs. Phillipa found herself at a sink-like
table, one portion of flat, rough wood, another portion a basin
with a short length of rubber hose hanging into it, running
cold water. A rough, wire scrub brush was on the flat, wood
part. As Phillipa stood there a piece of skin, thin, soft, flesh-
white skin was handed to her from the person standing next
to her. Without question she knew what she had to do. The
skin was wet, with a glutinous-type substance clinging to it.
Here and there were small clumps of wet blood, on some of
it soft, short hairs. She placed the skin on the table, began to
scrub it until it was smooth. She worked in easy, long strokes,
finding that the short, swift ones began to put a cramp into
her arm. Before she had finished the first skin, another was
thrust at her. Before she had barely begun on the second, a
third. A guard paused, glanced at her table, and she felt the
sting of a whip across the backs of her legs. She jumped,
wanted to cry out, but caught the scream in her throat.

"Mehr schnell," the guard yelled. "You're too slow. Work
faster."

She worked faster. As a pained cramp grew in her right
shoulder, she shifted the brush to her left hand. The skins
were interminable. Sometimes they came to her fairly clean,
at other times covered with slime. After a while it didn't
matter. They looked all the same, they felt all the same. A
numbness grew over her body and her senses. Every little

while she glanced toward the barred windows. The sun shone. It seemed to get brighter and brighter every time she looked. She gritted her teeth and waited for darkness.

As the work became part of her, she was able to glance around the room. At her end of the room were dozens of similar tubs. She recognized many of the people in her barracks working at them. At the other end of the room there seemed to be larger tubs, surrounded by people working packed close together. A mist, a steam vapor surrounded them, seeming to be emanating from the tubs. It seemed, too, that when an unusually sharp odor stung her, it came from that direction.

She noticed, also, that besides the guards there seemed to be supervisors. Inmate supervisors. At one side of the room a young, strong-looking woman walked, a short stick in her hand, poking those who seemed to be slowing down. She had no whip. That apparently was the guards' prerogative. At Phillipa's side of the room there was an inmate supervisor, also. At first Phillipa noticed just her shadowed profile passing. Then, once, close-up, she saw her face. It struck a responsive note, but she couldn't place it. Large features, big mouth, round eyes, large flat nose, short brown hair beginning to fluff as it reached out in back. Phillipa felt the sweat on her forehead, reached up to brush back her hair, and pulled her hand back quickly as if she had touched a hairless dead thing. The supervisor must have been there for some time, judged Phillipa, to have grown so much hair on what must have been, like the others, at first a bare, cropped head. The supervisor wore the same clothing as the other inmates, the vertically striped pajama-like uniforms, alternating blue and white. Only she had more: A short, wrap-around sweater and, most important, Phillipa noticed, shoes. They had been given no shoes, only the uniform. She must have turned her head and stared too long, for at that moment the supervisor poked her in the back with the

club. It hurt, but even as she buried herself deeper over the
sink Phillipa saw the woman's face again. For a second the
woman saw Phillipa's face, hesitated, looked closely again.
She held back the stick that she had reached forward with to
prod again, uncertain who this newcomer was, but equally
certain that she knew her.

The supervisor had a certain power, Phillipa noted. At
one time during the day, when one of the inmates at the other
end of the room apparently was unable to continue and was
removed from the building, a guard came and pointed to a
young man standing near Phillipa. The man hesitated.

"Please. Not the solution," he begged. "I can't stand the
smell and the pain. It'll kill me. Please."

Phillipa began to understand what was happening at the
other end of the room. It was the beginning of the tanning
process, where the stripped skin was first cleaned, soaked in
boiling water and a solution of formaldehyde to cleanse it and
disinfect it of hairs, flesh and other extraneous matter. Phillipa felt thankful for her job. The guard pulled at the balky
young man, raised his whip. The man began to move. At that
moment the supervisor came over.

"He is good here," she smiled to the guard, turning at
the same time and smiling at the young, good-looking man.
It made no real difference to the guard. He smiled a knowing look at the supervisor and at the young man and walked
down the line and took someone else for the steam solution.

The supervisor passed Phillipa a while later, stopped,
watched her work for a moment and then, as if she were officially satisfied or dissatisfied—one could not tell which, the
tone was always the same—asked Phillipa her name.

"Penmann," Phillipa replied, without ceasing the scrubbing motion of her hands and arms.

"Penmann?" The supervisor was puzzled. Then, understanding: "Real name, schnell."

Phillipa wanted to turn away, to pay no attention. What difference now, anyway, she then thought. "Kohn," she said. "Phillipa Kohn."

The supervisor's eyes brightened. A quick smile caught her lips, just as quickly disappeared. "Phillipa Kohn," she muttered, almost inaudibly. Leaning forward, she said ever so slightly, "Carol Sperling." Then she walked quickly away.

It took a moment for Phillipa to remember the name. Carol Sperling? Of course. Her childhood friend. From Munich. Long ago. Long, long ago. How old was she then? Eight? Ten? Of course. Carol's father had lost his money, had moved from the neighborhood. She had not seen her after that. It was funny, she began to think, how the fates could take the poor and the rich alike and . . . but she stopped that thought for a more immediate, more important one. She now had a friend here. In a position of importance. It could be easier for her. Much easier. She remembered how close friends they had been as children. She forgot, for the moment, how, when Carol needed her at the age of ten, she had turned her back and walked away.

Her thoughts were diverted by moaning sounds a few feet from her. A woman not far away slipped to the ground from exhaustion, got up again. Phillipa could see her table piled with skins not yet done. A man next to her reached over, took several for his table to relieve her burden. A guard saw him, struck his whip across the man's back.

"Zuruck," the guard said. "Put them back." The man did as he was told.

The woman slipped to the floor again, hung against the side of the basin. She was perhaps sixty, thin, frail. She had fallen several times during the morning walk to the factory. A guard walked up to her, slashed at her with the whip. She arose slowly, tried to grasp for the scrubbing brush to begin her work again.

"She is no good," the guard said, as much for his own
benefit as for the edification of the inmates. He called to the
front door. "Here. She is no good." Two guards walked from
the front door, rudely lifted the woman by her arms. "To
Birkenau," the first guard said casually. The woman began to
scream. A pistol butt thumped onto her head. There was no
more sound. The guards dragged her out.

Phillips quickly turned back to her work. "At least she
won't feel the fires," she thought, in an attempt at unconcern.

Phillipa busied herself in her work, trying to lose her
consciousness in repetitive automation of her labor. She
thought of Heidelberg, she thought of Switzerland, her
thoughts kept going back to Munich and to her childhood
and to Carol Sperling. Once, on a late afternoon, she was
shaken from her mental escape as she looked down at one
piece of skin that reached her table. On it was tattooed, in
réd, a heart, and in blue letters, in the center, the letters
MUTTE. For a moment, for the first time, she thought of her
own mother. She had died at the right time, she reflected.
She thought of her father, then, and understood, now, how he
might have felt when had died. Suddenly a hand of one of the
guards reached in front of her, hastily took the skin with the
tattoo and surreptitiously stuffed it into his pocket. Phillipa
hurriedly turned back to the skins on her table and lost herself and her thoughts in the routine of physical movement.

Night finally came. Even the guards seemed tired, grateful for the end of the day. The sky had just turned completely
dark when they stepped outside of the factory again. The
return to camp took longer, was not quite so hurried. Phillipa had no way of knowing the time, but estimated it was
about eight o'clock. They plodded back, a supervisor in front
leading the way with a kerosene lantern. They walked in
single file, each one several paces behind the person in front.
A guard walked up and down the line, counting each inmate.

The line halted. They were ordered to remain absolutely still. Several guards moved away from the main line, off to the side of the road. In the near distance Phillipa heard what sounded like a thump, the sound of a body tripping and falling. In a split second the shouts of guards were heard, then were mixed with rifle shots. Then silence. For a minute or so Phillipa could hear only the sound of the guards' boots. Then two shots. After a moment, another two shots. Not far away, perhaps only a hundred yards, a lighted match touched a cigarette, then another. In a few moments two guards had rejoined the main line and they moved once again, slowly, toward the camp.

When they reached the camp they went directly to the dining hall. The walk back had taken perhaps an hour. It was beginning to drizzle now and low moans of shivering and coughs and sneezes echoed through the line. They stood in twos outside the hall, waiting. They could see groups of other inmates, apparently returned from their jobs, moving in and out of the building at ten minute intervals. They stood for about an hour. Then they were led in, on the run, past the counters where each received a bowl and a wooden spoon. The meal was essentially the same as they had had in the morning, except that in most of the bowls there was added a small, almost scorched, half-steamed, half-boiled potato. Most were rotten. But no one, this time, refused to eat.

Phillipa dunked her lump of bread into the watery part of the bowl, let it soak, closed her eyes and bit into it. After it got to her stomach, it didn't taste too bad. When she returned to her barracks she found it changed. Alongside the walls bunks had been installed, three-tiered wooden bunks, each about six feet in length, about four feet in width, and perhaps three feet of space between one bunk and the one above it. Scattered bunches of straw had been piled onto each wooden bunk enclosure. The bunks stretched all around

the barracks, covering the four walls, and leaving only room
for the front door. There were forty-five bunks.in all. When
they arrived they found many of them already filled by a new
group of inmates who had arrived only that day, some of the
bunks occupied by two or three women. Phillipa found a
bunk against a far corner wall, the third bunk, on top of the
rest. She quickly grabbed it. It was some kind of separation,
she felt. Some kind of superiority and independence, if only
through the physical advantage of being able to turn on her
side and look out over most of the barracks, of being above all
the other women in the barracks. She hoped no one would be
put in it with her.

The following day the pattern of the previous day was
repeated. The morning meal, the march to the factory, the
scrub-basins. She assumed that this was to be her job, at
least for a while. She would survive this, she thought. She
could numb herself to it with disdain, she could adjust her
physical being to do the work and move her thoughts to
something else or to nothingness. When she arrived at the
factory she made a point of smiling at her supervisor, Carol
Sperling. Perhaps there were even better jobs in that factory,
she thought, Perhaps Carol could transfer her to one. At the
very least, she thought, she would have some protection on
that one. That afternoon another of the inmates at the steam
solution had faltered, been removed, and shot. The guard, at
random, grabbed Phillipa hard by the buttocks.

"Go, over there," he pointed to the steam solution tables.
Phillipa was about to say "please," then hesitated, turned
instead to Carol, who stood close by, watching.

Phillipa did not move, waiting. "Come on," the guard
repeated.

Phillipa looked directly at Carol, into her eyes. "I do a
good job here, don't I?," she asked. "Wouldn't you want me

to stay here?" She felt dirty and ugly inside, begging. But the results would be worth it, she told herself.

Carol didn't move, her eyes remaining fixed, her face motionless, as if she were lost in a moment of long, long ago.

"I will be going to the steam solution," Phillipa repeated. "Don't you want me to remain here?"

Carol still made no move, no sound.

"Please," Phillipa said in desperation.

Carol looked at Phillipa for another moment. Then she turned her back and walked away.

Chapter XIV

For several weeks after that Phillipa thought of trying to become a supervisor, There were several kinds. Some were overseers of work details. Others were in charge of individual barracks. Some supervised entire blocks of inmates. The barracks supervisor was usually one of the original group and took charge of the other inmates to and from work each day, seven days of the week (Phillipa had lost track of the days and knew when Sunday arrived only because of the freshly cleaned and pressed uniforms of the guards as they went to and returned from church services), and was responsible for maintaining correct behavior, order and discipline in the barracks. Any infractions were to be reported by the barracks supervisor to the S. S. corporal in charge of the block. In exchange for this service, where the other inmates slept in their three–tiered bunks, frequently two or more in a bunk, with the by-now lice-infested straw over the wooden slats, the overseer had a separate bunk with a regular mattress, freedom of the street block for one hour each evening— a privilege denied to the regular inmates—and larger food rations. Phillipa weighed the advantages and disadvantages. The responsibility of being a supervisor suggested a stronger

emotional drain. And she told herself that the less emotional
strain the better chance for survival. On the other hand, the
material relief available to the supervisor provided more of a
physical chance for survival, Most important, she speculated,
when the time came that all others would be found no longer
useful and sent to Birkenau, it was possible that the supervisor might be permitted to live.

One evening, when she was turning the matter over in
her mind, the woman in the bunk next to her, on the top tier,
was smoking a cigarette butt she had found on the line of
march, apparently dropped by one of the guards. The supervisor was out of the barracks taking her nightly privilege of
freedom of the block. Where the woman got a match to light
the cigarette, Phillipa could not guess, although she knew
that many inmates had somehow obtained bits and pieces
of forbidden goods which they had managed to successfully
conceal around their bunks and in the barracks. The woman's
name was Jahda. She knew only her first name. Last names
were unimportant. Names were needed here only for identification with the tattooed number and, besides, who would
ever get to need a last name again?

Before anyone could whisper a warning the front door
opened and the supervisor stood there, unexpected, before the
end of her allotted free time. All that Phillipa knew shout the
supervisor was that she came from Hungary. The rumor was
that she was a nymphomaniac and slept freely with almost all
of S.S. and military guards assigned to that block. She was a
short woman, thick-legged, with thin, hollow cheeks and a
large month and nose. It was said that she was jealous of the
other women, in particular the pretty girls. Phillipa glanced
quickly at Jahda who, despite only a bare fuzz of hair beginning to grow on her head, was nevertheless not unattractive
in a sexual way. She was about 20 years old, Phillips guessed,
and she likened her to the girl she had smiled to on the very

first day at the camp. She saw Jahda quickly put out the fire
of the cigarette between her fingers, stuff the butt between
the edge of her bunk and the side wall, and quickly jerk her
head forward as if she were doing nothing, merely staring
into space. Phillipa could see the terrible fear on her face, her
body beginning to shake as a thin whisp of smoke curled up
into the air from the last puff she had taken. The supervisor's
eyes moved around the barracks. Without a word she turned
around and walked out. That night Jahda was pulled screaming from her bunk and did not return.

Phillipa did not think any more about trying to become
a supervisor. She did her job at the tanning factory, kept to
herself as much as possible. Those who were too weak to
work, who did not do their jobs well, who in any way upset
the normal flow of daily life of the job detail, of the barracks or of the block were removed and disappeared. Whenever that happened the whispered word "Birkenau" reached
knowing ears. Phillipa conserved her emotional and physical
strength. More than ever she knew she would need as much
as she could of both.

The fat young man she had met across the mess hall table
when she first came to camp worked more frequently near
her barracks and she saw him often at meals, on the marches,
at the factory. He helped keep spirits alive. He was a jolly
person, always smiling or laughing if the situation permitted, always bringing words of hope to the old, the tired,
the crippled, the weak. He did not laugh at people, ever—
except when the butt of his laughter could be the guards,
the supervisors, or the Nazi state in general. He was intelligent, cautious in his humor, sharp in his satire. Phillipa was
surprised when she learned his age. Willy, as they called him,
admitted to twenty-four. He looked much younger, not even
twenty. Secretly, when their supervisor was not around, he
would sneak over to where the women were gathered, huddle

with them, talk and make little jokes and they felt a little
less sad. Phillipa often thought of him as a student, as a boy
who at that very moment should be carrying books to class in
Heidelberg. He was not Jewish, she learned, but a political
prisoner. He had been in jail before, he jokingly told them.
For two years. This was his first experience in a death camp.
The next step was the gas chamber and the furnace, so he
hoped he would stay here for at least two years, too. Maybe
the war would be over by then? It gave them all a small moment of hope in a dark and hopeless situation.

One day, in conversation, he mentioned Heidelberg University. One of his stories, told in hushed whispers in the cold
darkness, was about a teacher he knew who did not drink beer,
who objected to drinking on principle, and who came to class
one day to find several of the students reeking of beer. To teach
them a lesson he came in the following day with several bottles
of liquor and carefully and deliberately walked around the
classroom, pouring them over heads, clothing, books and desks.
Instead of presenting a coherent lesson, he made the class sit at
attention for a full hour, imbibing the strong smell of alcohol.
It was funny for a while until, unexpectedly, the chancellor
came in and saw what looked like as entire classroom of inebri-
ates, with the whiskey smell reaching clear into the corridor.

"You were at Heidelberg University?," Phillipa questioned.

"I studied there. Well, let us say I attempted to study
there."

"Did you know Professor Walter Penmann?"

For the first time Willy's face stopped smiling. He did
net answer, but waited until he could move away from the
others with Phillipa.

"What about Professor Penmann?," he asked?

Phillipa did not understand his suddenly serious attitude. She had only wished to make conversation, to find a

link, to find in him the roots for some intelligent cultured conversation that might ease her thoughts into the gentleness of the past.

"What about him?," the young man demanded, as if it were a matter of utmost importance.

"Nothing," Phillipa said simply. "It is just that I am his wife."

The young man's face brightened, then sagged. "It would be a lie for me to say I am glad to see you," he said, "for I am not happy to see anyone here. But it is an honor to make your acquaintance. Perhaps the Professor told you about me? My name is Willy Baier."

Phillipa did not recognize the name. But she nodded as if she did. She did not want it to seem that there was anything her husband did not tell her.

"If only we had started sooner," Willy Baier sighed. "If only everyone had protested sooner!"

They heard the boot sounds of a guard making his rounds. Willy bid a hurried "wiedersehen" and disappeared toward his part of the camp.

Phillipa spoke with him often after that. She made no special attempt to because it was too painful to recall Walter and Heidelberg and the past—all of which had now blended into a comparaive image of incomparable comfort, pleasure, happiness. But whenever she and Willy were near each other, whenever the opportunity presented itself, they talked about Heidelberg and the university and Walter. Indeed, she knew that she deliberately took advantage of such occasions. She could not admit it openly to herself, but speaking to the young man brought her a little closer to Walter.

When she had been at Auschwitz about six months she received a package from Walter. This was not altogether unusual. Every so often this link with the outside, made possible through the International Red Cross, was opened for a brief moment. The Nazis allowed it, particularly for those who had non-Jewish connections, such as Phillipa with an Aryan husband, however illegal and invalid their marriage was now considered by the State. The Nazis kept track of the people who received packages. It made good propaganda for the rest of the world. "These people are merely in a work camp," they would tell the press representatives of various countries. "They are security risks, so they naturally are segregated. Without harm. Without discomfort, except as necessary in any crowded community. But they are in no danger. See—they even receive packages from their friends and relatives."

Phillipa wondered whether anybody in the world really believed that. It was a bitter realization for her to think that some probably did. Nevertheless, for the people inside it was important to know that someone they knew outside was alive, even if they themselves were virtually not. What was important, too, was the food they received: the biscuits, the raw potatoes. Anything of value—hard-boiled eggs, tins of meat or fish, fruits—were confiscated by the inspecting guards who received and examined every package before it was decided whether to forward it to the inmate.

Phillipa had been called by a guard to the block supply building to get the package. It was after her return from work. She took it and crushed it as flat as she could against her body under the uniform to prevent any of her barracks-mates from seeing it. Carefully she climbed up to her bunk. Cautiously she began to remove, in silent split-seconds, the package from under the uniform. The package had, of course, been opened. If there had been a letter from Walter, it had been removed. Phillipa grasped the dried biscuits, the several raw potatoes, greedily bundled them under her straw pillow. She wondered how Walter would know to send these goods, usually the only ones left untouched by the guards. She was happy that he had had this much foresight. It gave her a sense of personal confidence and strength to be able to say to herself, "Walter, for once you used a little foresight and did something right without being asked or told."

When the others were asleep that night she would eat the food. All of it. She dared not attempt to keep it. Food was the most valuable possession in the camp, and as such it had no owner. Whoever reached it, ate it. It made her feel guilty to sneak and hide like this. But only for a moment. Her physical survival made her part of the crowd now. She was in it and under it and she had to squirm to keep from being stepped on and crushed out of existence. She learned to squirm.

The others knew. If they couldn't see or smell it, they sensed it. Slowly her bunk was surrounded by silent, drawn, determined faces. If there was any food to be had, they would get it. Quickly, she pulled the box out, slipped from it a biscuit, one potato, then held it out, her hand clutching the loose rewrapped paper covering. With one roar a dozen hands in front of her tore the box from the paper, spilling it onto the heads of those below. There was no energy expended on shouts and screams. Virtually silent grunts came from the suddenly entangled mass of bodies and hands scratching and tearing at the few biscuits and potatoes that had slipped from the now shredded cardboard box onto the floor. As one hand clutched a bit of potato another tore onto that hand and wrenched the potato from it, to be scratched at in turn by another hand fumbling in desperation for the piece of food. It took only a few moments. Every scrap, every crumb disappeared into some mouth, to be swallowed as quickly as possible, not even to be chewed for fear that the delay would permit someone to disgorge the precious bit of food and take it for her own. As quickly as the crows had come, it disappeared. Silently, quietly, as if nothing had occurred, the bodies slowly drifted back to their respective bunks. One woman

squatted in the center of the floor under Phillipa's bunk and
stared at the bare boards, as if by some miracle the scraps of
food would suddenly reappear. Another woman slowly and
carefully picked up the remaining pieces of cardboard, folded
them into a neat pile and carried them to her bunk, secreting
them in one corner of straw along the wooden side-rail.

Phillipa propped herself against the wood wall of the barracks, her head bent low to escape the low ceiling, raised her
knees slightly and spread the wrapping paper flat out against
them. The postmark was still visible. It said "Koln." Willy Baier had brought back the past to her—more than she told herself
she wanted— and she had thought frequently of Walter in the
past weeks. She thought of many things, not only of things that
had been, but things that might have been. "So many things
we wanted to do," she mused, "so many things we could have
done. In the early days. Before the concentration camps." The
thought made her feel weak and she put it from her. Was there
ever a world, she contemplated, without concentration camps?

She looked at the postmark again, tried to make believe
that it said Heidelberg. That would mean she wouldn't have
to think about it any more. But it did say Koln—Cologne.
She stretched her legs out wide in front of her. Her mind was
cramped. Her body could lie free. "He must be on vacation,"
she thought. "Or perhaps he was transferred?" She knew this
couldn't be. "Of course, they fired him," she admitted to herself. "They fired him and he went to Cologne to seek another
job." But she knew that once he was fired there could not
be another job. "Or to escape," she then said. There was too
much pain in speculating any further. "At least," she satisfied
herself, "he isn't in a concentration camp."

The transports came in regularly and each night she
smelled the stinking burning odor from the other end of the
camp, from Birkenau. In the mornings, on the march to the
tanning factory, she saw the trucks full of ashes and charred

skeletons. For a while she wondered what they had looked
like, who their families were, what they did, what they
thought, how they felt when the gas jets were turned on or
the fire began to reach their flesh. After a while she looked
at them without thinking anything, as if they were part of
the landscape, as if they had always been there and would
always be there. Sometimes at night and even at the factory
she could hear a high, molting wail. She tried to imagine that
it was an air-raid siren. For a time she could pretend. But she
knew that it was the screams of hundreds and thousands coming from the mouth of the German craw.

The word whispered quickly through the barracks with
a hush and a whimper: "Mengele." It was said with hesitation, with fear, with disbelief, as if it signified something too
horrible to be accepted as being real. They had all heard of
Dr. Mengele, the inspector, the commander, the determiner of
life and death, of a quick end or an interminable torture. The
stories had grown all out of proportion in the minds of many.
Phillipa could not accept them: The medical experiments on
inmates without the benefit of anesthesia, the amputation
and regrafting of limbs from one to another; the determination of the extent to which the human body could withstand
pain before death through experiments on the eyes, nose, ears,
tongue; the experiments on the male genitals and the female
breasts; the breeding experiments between women inmates and
animals; the special use of children for new physical forms of
human shape through German medical technology. She shut
her mind and ears to these stories, for in her deepest moments
of despair, in her strongest moments of revulsion and horror, she could not further distort her brain and emotions with
these stories. Even when Willy Baier assured her of the truth
of these stories and more, she could not accept it. But she did
accept the ordinary, every day actions that she had heard about
Mengele: His penchant for sending anyone, for no reason at all,

to Birkenau; his apparent delight in having inmates clubbed to
death in front of other inmates; his pleasure in providing himself, the guards and inmates with sexual diversion performed
by other inmates in a barracks or, more often, in the center of
a barracks block; his satisfaction in forcing inmates to torture
other inmates to death, nakedly, openly, as the others stood at
attention, commanded to watch without blinking an eye.

Mengele was coming to their block the next morning,
the word was. The usual exhaustion that both pushed one to
and pulled one from sleep was more fitful that night. Each inmate prepared herself for resignation to death and hoped that
it would simply be Birkenau, without the torture of a circus
performance for the German overlords or the everlasting suffering of becoming a guinea pig for medical experiments.

Before sunrise the word came again. A barracks inspection. Perhaps it would not be so bad? The lice had long since
been accepted as a permanent part of their existence and the
thin red splotches of welts that covered every woman's body
were no longer even noticed or scratched. Yet, it would be
fine to have a fumigation, a cleansing of the barracks. At
sunrise they were lined up, marched to the center of the street
outside of their barracks. All the barracks on the block had
been similarly emptied, with lines of inmates standing at
attention in front of each. In the middle of the block stood
several officers, among them, his face hidden from Phillipa's
sight, a man in a dark civilian business suit. There was not a
sound on the block. Phillipa could hear his voice as an echo.
It was not ominous, not dark, but a refined voice, reflecting
brightness and pleasure.

"I wish to inspect these barracks, Captain."

"Jawohl, Herr Doktor."

"Disgraceful to have our guests live in such unclean
circumstances, Captain. We must think of their comfort. We
must clean and disinfect them entirely."

Phillipa saw him now. She thought she had recognized the voice and now recognized the person: The Doctor who had separated them near the main gate the day she arrived. She was puzzled. Could this be Mengele, this man who reflected in his bearing, his manner, his appearance, his speech all that Phillipa had associated with good breeding and cultural superiority?

"Jawohl, Herr Doktor," the captain answered again. Then, after a moment: "It will be difficult, Herr Doktor. These inmates have been here for almost two years. Their natural filth has multiplied. They and the barracks are crawling with filth."

"Oh, a pity," came the reply. "Well, we must cleanse our guests. A complete fumigation then. We must have a clean, orderly inspection, must we not? Before I enter the barracks you will send exterminators to fumigate them."

"Jawohl, Herr Doktor." The captain motioned to a group of soldiers carrying long hoses attached to cylinders strapped to their backs. They wore what looked like gas masks. The men moved in a body to the barracks at the farthest end of the block.

"And don't forget the human vermin, too, bitte," the Doctor said without a change of emotion in his voice, the warm resonance continuing as if he were proclaiming an act of compassion and kindness. "De-louse them. Give them showers."

A shuddering moan went up from the groups of inmates. The rising and falling sound of scattered moaning continued for several seconds, then hushed weeping, then silence. The Doctor looked around. For a moment it seemed as if he were about to suggest something more, then he stopped.

"I am very busy this morning, Captain. I have some special work to take care of at the hospital. I will not wait for a personal inspection. I leave it to you to clean up this block quickly."

He turned, followed by several officers, walked to a late model Ford automobile parked nearby, was helped in by an orderly, and driven off.

The captain waited only an instant. "Nach Birkenau," he ordered. Led by their supervisors, each group was turned toward the main street and started on the march to the other end of the camp.

It was a moment Phillipa had thought about. Each time she did, she consciously tried to plan what she would do when her walk to Birkenau came. What ruse she would use, what excuse she would find, what subterfuge she would invent, what violence she would resort to, what way, any way, to escape Germany's final solution to minority existence and political non-conformity. But like all the others, she simply walked. Like all the others, her thoughts had never found fruition but always ended in an abortive frustration of having no answer, in a cloudy incompleteness that drifted her away from the immediacy of thought. There was no plan. There was no escape. There was only hopeless, fearful, enervated resignation.

Like corpses moving toward their own burial grounds, the people walked. There were moans, there was some crying forced out of bodies with no energy for tears. There were murmured prayers and pleas that disappeared into empty air and reached no one who could be moved by them. For most it was the inevitable expectation, come sooner than some might have expected and later than others might have wished. For many it was only the fear of the unknown, the bias to live under any circumstances that made the walk one of pain. For others it was a welcome walk, an organized finish to an existence they had many times since they had come to the camp wished would end, but which they had neither the personal will power or courage to do anything about.

They passed the dining hall, for a moment thinking of it even in terms of comparative pleasure. Indeed, it had provided ten minutes of physical sustenance twice a day. Phillipa, as had the others, knew about the showers, the gas chambers. If it were that and not the experimental hospital, not the torture rooms, it would not be so bad. A few minutes for the hoses to release the gas, a few minutes of choking agony. And then it would be over. At least she could lose herself in the agonies of hundreds of others at the same time. It somehow would not be altogether a personal suffering, a personal death. Even as she felt this, Phillipa caught herself and intellectually pushed away the thought. If she had to die, it would be as an individual, she told herself, separate, complete, aware. If she had to die, it might be by someone else's means, but death itself would come on her terms, as she would think it and feel it.

They came to a part of the camp she had not seen before. The neat wooden cottages, labeled with the names of Majors and Captains and Lieutenants. Carefully swept front walks and delicately planted flower gardens, orderly encased behind low white fences. Clear glass windows bordered by trim, ruffled curtains. Children's toys and bicycles properly placed on rear porches. It hurt and at the same time pleased her to see this, the cleanliness and order of the German people.

They walked on and came to an area of larger buildings, some wood, some brick, some looking like offices, others like apartment house residences, still others like small business or storehouse or factory buildings. More and more soldiers were to be seen, more and more of them in officers uniforms. And more and more civilians, men and women, seemingly there on errands of everyday business, going about their affairs with briskness and efficiency as if this world were the same world as any small city anyplace in Germany. It was as if they didn't see the long line of striped-pajama clad, emaciated, head-shaven, moaning, falling, lashed, foot-bleeding, soul-less people trudging past them on their way to what everyone knew existed but shut out of their eyes and minds and consciences.

The line stopped. At first a wave of fear passed over the line. The final walk was finished, the last breath of air was about to be taken. Some thought that it would be better if they had come to one of the blood ditches to be shot to death. At least the final moment would have the freedom of the earth and sky. Perhaps this would be it, after all, for the gas chambers and furnaces were only part of the well-planned and managed death factory of Birkenau. Then a different feeling crept into the line. One of hope, even for those who had by now looked forward to the gas chamber and had accepted that the end had come. This was not yet Birkenau. The ever-present thin thread of hope caught firm hold. Perhaps a change of plans and they would be returned to their jobs and barracks? Perhaps, possibly, a reassignment. Perhaps . . . but that was as far as their imaginations, shriveled by the reality of experience, could take them.

Two officers and two Polish civilians began walking up and down the line of the inmates, who were spread out in two rows, each one easily and clearly visible from the front. Phillipa caught hasty snatches of conversation as the officials walked past.

"Everybody is going into the Army," one of the civilians was saying. He was a man about sixty, portly, round-faced, red-cheeked, who looked like the kind of man who probably would stop on the way home that evening at a sweet shop to buy chocolates to feed to his grandchildren as he held them on his knee and told them stories of princes and princesses and fairies and angels.

"If you don't give us enough men, how can we build a proper sanitation system?," he was saying. His voice faded off. In a few moments they walked past again. This time Phillipa heard the words of a uniformed major in the group, a well-dressed, clean-cut man who reminded her of the efficient clerks in the efficient shops of Heidelberg.

"I will give you every strong-looking man you need. But you will assume all costs and responsibilities. I will provide a guard to march them to town in the morning and back every evening. When anyone's work falters you will inform the guard. They will dispose of each useless worker as necessary. Replacements will be available for one month only."

The portly civilian said something about one month being all that was needed to complete the job, as they faded again from Phillipa's hearing.

Phillipa's resurgence of hope was dashed. Some men would be spared for a month, at least. But the women would apparently continue to Birkenau. She watched as the portly civilian, a guard alongside him, walked back down the line again, this time pointing to male bodies as he passed. On occasion he would stop, motion to a man to turn around, look at his shoulder and back muscles, make his decision and walk on. Phillipa could see the men suddenly grow straight and tall, flexing what muscles remained in their bodies, tensing their backs and chests and shoulders. One man who was passed by suddenly threw off his pajama shirt, ran to the portly civilian, flexing an arm to show a muscle.

"Take me," he shouted. "Take me. I'm strong. I can work."

A whip held by the guard lashed around his neck, throwing him to the ground. He held out an arm, the muscle still flexed, to the portly civilian. A rifle butt crashed down on the muscle. With a scream of pain, the man withdrew the smashed arm and elbow. As the rifle barrel itself was tilted toward him he crawled hurriedly away to find a place in the line.

A sliver of elation passed over Phillipa as she saw Willy
Baier among the fifty or so males now lined up in front of
the group. The portly civilian made a half-bow, shook hands
with the major, smiled in the condescending gratitude of
a successfully concluded business agreement, walked to his
Ford automobile and drove away as a corporal marched the
newly-selected and newly-spared men in the direction the car
had gone.

In the manner of cattle ready for a command, the inmates
prepared to turn and march again toward their final destination. But their guards didn't move. It was if they were waiting for something. The inmates stood motionless for perhaps
half-an-hour. Some collapsed from the exhaustion of the walk
and the wait, got up or were helped up by another inmate
and stood some more. Others lay there, unable to rise again,
were dragged out to the front by other inmates on orders
from the guard and were lifted, pushed and thrown into a
waiting truck. There was no doubt about their fate. Most of
them didn't seem to care any more.

From one of the brick apartment buildings across the
open street where the inmates stood, a captain and a woman
of perhaps forty-five years of age emerged, smiling and jok-
ing, and walked to the line. They stopped near where Phillipa stood, were joined in a moment by a major and a young
lieutenant.

"Do you think you can find any out of this group?," the
major asked the woman.

"If I can't, I may have a revolt on my hands," the woman
laughed. "We've run short and with the lack of discipline of
some of your men, if they don't get their nightly . . . and
daily . . . woman . . . ."

"Begging your pardon, sir," the lieutenant interjected,
"after a day on this job, the men have to have some relaxation. As Special Services Officer, I feel . . . "

"You needn't explain, Lieutenant," the major interrupted. "I know the needs of the men as well as you."

"We had hoped not to bother you again, Major," the captain said. "But our healthy German boys are sometimes too strong for these weakling Jew-women. They don't last long. And others get pregnant. We can keep them two-three months that way, but then it becomes a little inconvenient for the men, so we have to get rid bf them. This means a rather steady need for replacements."

"Oh, I was never so embarrassed as last night," the woman said. "There I was, assigning the boys to rooms as they came in, when suddenly I get this call from upstairs. Why, right in the middle, mind you, right in the middle, this Jew-girl expires. Just like that. Dies, right in the middle. And she had been one of our good ones, too. Not more than sixteen or seventeen years old. Sometimes on busy weekends we gave her as many as twenty a night. I wouldn't have minded so much, but the man—well, he was an officer. A captain, mind you."

"These are old ones," the major said, pointing at the line. "They have been here two years and more, many of them. Not very good for this sort of thing anymore, I'm afraid." He shrugged his shoulders. "But if you can use them, take what you want. I don't think they'll last long."

"Well, I do need some for tonight," the woman said. "If they work out, we'll keep them, and if they don't, we'll dispose of them."

"We run an efficient organization," the captain added.

"We have other plans for some of these," the major said. "But take what you want."

The captain walked down the line. "All women, all clothes off," he ordered. There was no hesitation.

The woman walked to the end of the line and studied each female body carefully, making her choices after a moment of deliberation for each.

"My God, my God," thought Phillipa to herself. "To beg to be allowed to become a whore. My God, my God." Her breath came in gasps, Her arms and legs shook, she felt a sweat covering her body. As the woman came to where she stood she thrust her breasts forward, sucked in her stomach, tilted her legs and thighs out at an angle, thrust her head high and hoped that there were no obvious unsightly lines on her stomach or face or chin.

Phillipa was one of fifty women left standing in the street as the remainder of the inmates, re-formed into the same line that had left the barracks several hours before, walked away to the end of their journey. It was as if Phillipa didn't see them, didn't notice them, didn't know they were there. She had been saved. Whatever would come next, she had for that moment survived, and in her own exhilaration of continued life there was no room for the others.

Again they were made to stand, their camp uniforms in their hands, waiting, The major whispered to the captain and the captain whispered to the woman and the lieutenant tried to enter the conversation and was shunted aside. Finally, the whispering stopped and they approached the group of lined-up women, the major saying, "Twenty-five and twenty-five. If you need more, you can get them from the next transport."

"That will do for a few days," the woman answered. "Your promise for the next transport?"'

"Did you not hear me?," the major said swiftly and sharply.

"Yes, Herr Major," the woman said hurriedly and obediently.

Once more the woman went down the line. It was impossible for Phillipa to speculate now. Which should she hope for? Which twenty-five. If only she knew, she thought; and then, did it really matter? Would one group be any better or any worse than the other? As long as both meant life. But did they? She had no time to think any more. The selection had been made. She was not one of those chosen by the woman this time. The chosen were herded into line by the captain and quickly marched off behind the woman to the large brick building across the street, to the brothel. The lieutenant saluted the major and, with his job apparently satisfactorily done, returned to his office.

"We have another assignment for you," the major told the remaining women. "Why we clothe you I don't know, but we do, and so we need more uniforms. Today and tomorrow. A large transport is arriving soon. With some of your friends and relatives, perhaps?" He paused and chuckled at the friendly, homey thought he felt he had instilled in his charges. "And you are to provide the uniforms immediately. You will be taken to work now. And you will work until the uniforms are ready. Twenty-four hours, forty-eight hours, or an entire week. Without stopping. And if you slow up, you will be disposed of."

He motioned to a corporal, who made ready to march off the inmates. "Consider yourselves fortunate," he said to the women. "All right, Corporal. Mach schnell!"

It was as if a whole new world had opened up to Phillipa and she could smell the freshness of the air and the perfume of the flowers. And yet, as she marched, light-footed and light of soul, she was unhappy. For a long moment there was a twinge of disappointment, a twinge of regret, a feeling of personal despair that somehow she was not considered pretty enough of body and face to be chosen for the brothel.

The job in the clothing mill was an easy one. For two days and two nights she went without sleep, sorting and packing uniforms for distribution. But when they were finally permitted to stop, marched to a dining hall for food and led to a barracks—a new one, a different one, similar to the one she had known in her first year at Auschwitz, but a bit larger, the bunks a bit more packed with straw, the cracks in the walls a bit more sealed against the cold winds—she went to sleep with a feeling of contentment, a feeling of well-being and certainty that now, indeed, she would survive. Her regular work day was sixteen hours. Her new job, after the tanning factory, was an easy one. She sorted various sizes and shapes of clothes after they came from the seamstresses and tied them into piles of twenty for shipping to the barracks where new inmates were quartered. She found she needed less sleep than she had needed for the tanning factory, she was less exhausted when she returned at night, and she even found the strength to sit up and walk around the barracks at night after the evening meal, feeling the satisfaction of independence of sitting and moving and walking. She even got used to the meals. The bad taste gradually disappeared and soon there was no taste at all. It became something to fill the stomach, to keep life going. This area of camp was different. The guards seemed less brutal, the officers less punishing. Even the food varied from time to time. Sometimes a piece of meat in the soup and occasionally the meat would not be rotten. Sometimes a whole potato, occasionally boiled and palatable.

There was not a contentment or an acceptance. But she did begin to feel a solidity. It was life. Precisely in terms of the usual pattern of the camp, it was life. And life, above all, was the important thing. It could be bare, ugly, sniveling, crawling, painfully unbearable—but it was life. She knew, too, that her situation was an enviable one, perhaps one of the best in the entire camp. She had time now to notice things around her, to look at people, to think in the abstract instead of having to concentrate all energies on her own immediate, specific problems of remaining alive from second to second. The more she looked at the people around her and the more she thought about them, the more she began to see how much they looked like her and behaved like her. Conversely, she had to admit to herself that she, in turn, looked like them and behaved like them. Were they that much like her? And, finally, she had to ask herself, was she that much like them?

The walk to the clothing mill from her barracks to the dining hall took perhaps thirty minutes. She passed several sections of the camp on the way: the barracks for special prisoners, those who were prominent in some way in society and who were being withheld from Birkenau to avoid giving the outside world, should it learn of the person's demise, undesirable propaganda materials; the children's block, something she had vaguely heard of previously but had not seen and, indeed, had not really believed existed, where children under twelve were segregated, given no food or sustenance since they contributed no labor, and who lived like small animals in a jungle until their turn came to be used for Mengele's special experiments or to be sent to Birkenau to clear their quarters for incoming transports of more children. She was marched past one of the main offices of the camp command into which, in early morning, she sometimes saw civilians enter who were fawned upon as though they were—and, indeed, must have been—important members of the government and outside society, and into which went high ranking officers, including those in the uniforms of generals and marshals.

Each day, not far from her own barracks, by the special prisoners section, she passed a smaller, older, dirtier looking building. In front of it, never moving, always in the same position, a small white-haired man sat, his legs bending from the single barracks step onto the ground, his back hunched, his head thrown back almost in a contorted position. His hair was long and white, falling over a face chiseled like the lines made by a stonecutter whose mallet slipped too many times. His ears were scrawny and stood straight out from his head. His eyes stared as though blind, looking at everything and nothing. His mouth alone moved as if he were constantly babbling something, but no sound came out.

Phillipa asked one of the older inmates about him one day.

"An inmate," she was told, without meaning or emotion.

"But how come he's still alive? They kill the old ones, the feeble ones immediately."

"They are soothing their conscience," the other inmate told her. "They are keeping a thin thread tied to their national pride."

"I don't understand."

"The old man," the inmate said, "he is . . . he was" came the correction "Germany's great comedian, the film actor, Theodor Harz."

Phillipa began to play a game. She began to count the months by the seasons, four at a time. When summer came she was happy because she still lived. She waited for autumn and was satisfied because she had existed another quarter-year. When winter found her still alive, she began her eager wait for spring. Spring had once meant beauty and freshness and freedom. Now it meant she could wait for summer again. She waited, waited, waited for something to happen, secure in her survival that nothing did.

She did not need to solve her own problems now. She would be satisfied simply to exist. Now and again the thought crossed her mind that someday this would all be over, that Germany would lose the war and that this nightmare would be at an end, would turn out to be something unreal, to be pushed aside into a hidden memory and never thought of again. But she could not speculate on such a possibility long, for the impossibility of it happening was made manifest by one look around her, by one morning's march to the clothing mill. Some other inmates were more practical, it seemed, and in their desperate need found solutions to their problems. The children, for instance.

She had not noticed it before, although it had apparently happened many times, but one morning as her group passed the children's block a truck carrying victims to the gas chambers rumbled slowly by them. Suddenly, from one of the buildings three children ran, one of them no more than five years old, the others perhaps eight or ten, although their emaciated condition made them seem smaller and younger. The children dashed into the street, toward the truck heading for Birkenau, with a special effort grabbed onto the chains of the tail gate and pulled themselves up onto the truck and desperately squeezed in among the people riding to their deaths. It happened quickly and all Phillipa could see were the children's faces: empty, drawn faces, completely devoid of all emotion, the large extruding eyes staring into nothingness, looking for an end to something apparently much worse than nothingness.

Later that night, after their return to the barracks, Phillipa asked about the children. All day, as she worked at the mill, the faces of the children kept coming back to her.

"Wouldn't you do the same," one inmate asked her, "if you were where they were?"

"Don't you know?," another inmate added. "Don't you know?"

"I have heard some things. But I've not noticed it before."

"They're living like cannibals," another inmate told her. "Like wild animals. Like animals in a cage in a laboratory. That's what they are."

"That's their only salvation," another one said. "That's their only escape."

"I was assigned once to bring some to the hospital," one inmate said. "I have seen them." She closed her eyes and shuddered. "They are thrown into a large room. Forty, fifty. No food. No facilities. They don't work, so they don't get food. At first they cry. Then they sit and die, stinking and filthy in their corners. Five-, six-, seven-year old little children." She stopped. Have you ever had any children?," she asked.

Phillipa shook her head.

"I had two," the woman said. "1 try not to think of them any more." Then, after a moment: "I hope they're dead—better than the children's block. Do you know what happens when they get hungry enough. The older ones, they become cannibals."

Phillips gasped, turned her head aside.

"Yes," the inmate insisted. "They eat each other. They find the younger ones who are too small and too weak to fight back and they become cannibals. What in God's name do you expect them to do!" She buried her head in her hands for a moment, then looked up again. "You want to know more?"

Phillipa said nothing.

"At night the guards come, sometimes drunk. The brutality. The games they play to amuse themselves. The physical torture, the sexual perversion and torture of these children by the guards. Some of these children, in one night, have gone stark, raving mad, like a wild dog that has been beaten and kicked and tortured too much." She stopped for a moment, then continued. "Look at that building tomorrow morning. Try to see into it. Watch what you see. Many of these children have been used for the medical experiments. You'll see them. Stumps of legs, stumps of arms, blind, no ears, no tongues. They came back instead of being disposed of and the others then knew about the medical experiments of the master race. What have they to live for, these children? Torture, starvation, murder, to wait until they are brought to the hospital for Mengele's doctors or, if they're lucky, to the gas chambers to make room for a new transport of children. When you see them jump onto the trucks going to the gas chambers, you can be sure that they go willingly, that they go eagerly. It's the only solution to their problem. Death is their salvation."

Phillipa didn't want to hear any more. When they walked past the children's block the next day she tried not to look toward the buildings. A commotion halted the line of march. She could not see clearly what was happening, other than that a group of children had arrived, apparently from a new transport, and were being herded from a truck toward the children's block. A lieutenant she had not seen before strode from the direction of the block toward the new group. His high-polished black boots reflected the bright morning sun as they lifted high and forcefully with each step. A whisper went up and down the line. "Borg. Borg." She had heard of Hans Borg. Inmates had spoken of his cruelty. It didn't matter whether you confessed first or not, if he was inclined to find a victim to take to his special room in order to amuse himself with the efficiency of his sadist techniques. He also liked to spend time at the children's block, bringing the children bits of fruit or chocolate or crackers. He called himself "uncle" when among them and liked them to call him "uncle."

Phillipa began walking again as the line of march resumed. Without her being aware of anything about to happen, two small children appeared in front of her, crowded between her and the inmate next to her. One was a little girl perhaps seven or eight. She held tight to the hand of a little boy, a child of perhaps five years of age.

"I am Phillipa Goldenstern," the girl said to Phillipa, looking up at her face and talking even as the children tried to keep pace with the adult step. Phillipa gasped and looked down at the child.

"This is my brother, Morris," she said. "They took us from Mummy and Daddy. A few days ago. Now I'm afraid they will take my brother from me. He is too little. He is too young. He could not stand that."

A shout from fifty yards or so away indicated that the children had been spotted. Phillipa turned. She saw Borg himself, his face smiling, his large step easy-gaited, walking after them.

"You will help, us, won't you?," the little girl said to Phillipa. "Please help us."

Phillipa remained silent. She wanted to give the child some reassurance, to give the child some hope. But all she could think of to say was that she could no nothing. So she said nothing.

The little girl tugged at her sleeve. "Please." Phillipa looked down and saw the child's large eyes. Firm. Unafraid. But alone. She reminded her of herself at that age.

The little girl turned and saw Borg only a few yards behind them. He did not seem to hurry. His naturally long steps and precise gait were enough to catch up quickly.

Phillipa heard the girl whisper to her brother. "No matter what happens, Morris, don't cry. Do you understand? Don't let them know we're afraid. Don't let them think that they are better than us and can make us cry."

The little boy did not understand. But he nodded his head and held tighter to his sister's hand.

"Come to Uncle Hans," Borg said. He was in step with them now and Phillipa moved aside, giving him full room to walk alongside the children.

"Come to Uncle Hans," he repeated and held out his hands to them.

The little girl looked straight ahead and kept walking, clasping her brother's hand tightly in hers.

To the left was a brick building, a storehouse. Borg stepped in front of the children. "Halt," he shouted. The line of march stopped. The children stopped. "You must come

with Uncle Hans," he said once more, his voice soft and
enticing, though insistent. At the same moment he reached
down and took each child by a hand, leading then off to the
side, toward the brick building. The children did not resist.
They stopped at the side of the building. Borg reached down,
picked up the little boy by the ankles, swung the small body
back into the air and then smashed the child's head into
the brick wall, splattering death onto the wall and onto the
ground. Without hesitation he reached for the little girl, her
face unmoving, her eyes dry and unblinking, grabbed her
ankles, swung her body back and smashed her head, too, into
the brick wall. He turned around, his face a gentle smile.
Only his mouth moved, his tongue tip licking the sides of his
lips in satisfaction. He walked back to the line.

"You," he pointed to Phillipa. "Clean that up." He
turned and walked slowly and easily back to where he had
left the transport of children.

Phillipa drew her head back involuntarily, her mouth
gaping open. She tried to breathe air as if she had suddenly
been choked off from it, her mouth opening and closing as if
in convulsions.

A corporal who was standing nearby looked at her, waiting for her to begin her ugly task. Her stomach heaved and
her heart pounded. Slowly she walked toward the wall. She
could not see and could not think. She bent her head and
vomited, on her arms and hands and belly, legs and feet.
She bent her head and retched again and a fire tore across
her stomach and nothing came out of her mouth. She got
a broom and pan and a pail of water and scrub-brush from
inside the brick building. Two male inmates had already
disposed of the remains of the bodies when she returned.
She stared into nothingness and pushed her thoughts into
nothingness as she cleaned up what was left. Than she joined
her group and the line of march began again. From then on,

when she walked past the children's block she kept her eyes straight ahead. She never permitted herself to look at it or at any of the children in it again.

She began to look forward to the days at the clothing mill. There was no rest, her body ached and her stomach pounded as the days wore on, but it removed her from the beastiality and torture that seemed to mark all the other activities in the camp and it was infinitely better than the tanning factory. Thoughts of the skins fresh from their source that she had so long cleaned in the boiling vats still made her double up her body and dry-retch until her stomach ached with exhaustion. At the clothing mill even the guards seemed less brutal. There were the usual incidents. One day when the man working next to her fell to the ground with an intestinal pain, one of the guards prodded him onto his feet again. In a moment the man doubled-up to the ground again, screaming in agony at the pain in his middle. The guard grabbed a stick and began to poke the man.

"Here?," the guard questioned, "here?," and with each poke the stick went deeper into the man's body, finally breaking the skin, going into the flesh. Within minutes the man was thrashing about on the floor and had to be dragged outside. Phillipa heard later that he died of abdominal bleeding. But such incidents at the clothing mill were the exception.

Even discipline there was more relaxed and one afternoon, when the supply of uniforms had slowed down and Phillipa was standing at attention by her table waiting for more work, one of the guards approached her.

"You are Phillipa Kohn?," he asked.

The sweat of fear came over Phillipa.

"Yes," she said, tentatively.

"From Heidelberg?," the guard continued.

"Yes."

"You were the wife of a Professor?"

The guard seemed not to be playing games with her, but instead, she felt, was quite seriously interested in talking to her. She relaxed for a moment.

"Professor Walter Penmann, Chairman of the Department of Philosophy." Then, trying to conceal her eagerness: "Do you know something of him?"

"No," the guard told her. "I was a student at the university. But I did not have any studies with Herr Professor Penmann." His voice was almost reverent, almost reminiscent of the eagerness of youth as it enters the university, its hushed respect for the professor and for the source of knowledge. The hardness moved out of his face, reflecting for perhaps the first time in several years the remaining freshness of a twenty-three-year-old youth.

Phillipa was surprised at the respect given by the boy in his use of Walter's title, surprised at the boy's manner and appearance. Perhaps this was a trap? Experience had taught her that conversation between a guard and an inmate existed only for special purposes and always to the disadvantage of the inmate.

She said nothing more. She would take no chances. In a few minutes her table was filled again with uniforms and she turned with speedy, now-trained hands to the sorting and packing. The guard seemed to understand.

"We will talk again," he said as he walked away.

In a few days an opportunity came. She had carried a load of uniforms to the shipping station at one end of the building and was on her way back when the guard stopped her.

"You," he said loudly, for all to hear. "I want to see you." The other guards looked over, smiled, and went about their own business. Arrangements of any kind between a guard and an inmate remained a personal prerogative.

"Frau Penmann," the guard said. In a moment he had been transformed from the soldier into the student once again. "I know you have reason to be distrustful. But we are not all alike. I thought we might just chat every now and then."

"If you wish," Phillipa said. If he was what he seemed, Phillipa thought, he could do a lot for her or, at least, serve as a buffer in case of trouble. She wanted to trust him and, for her own hopes of survival, told herself that she felt she could.

"This brutality, this sadism," he said, "we don't all agree with it. I think back to the university and at night I wake up in a sweat at what I have been forced to do here. Do you understand?"

"Yes."

"Do you think of Heidelberg and the university, too?"

"Yes."

"I think of the Bierstube and the songs and the patriotic speeches. I am sorry now, in a way. Maybe if I had spent more time going to concerts . . ." he smiled ". . . or taking studies in philosophy . . . ."

"I used to go to many concerts," Phillipa said.

"I didn't really learn how," the guard said. "Maybe if I had spent more time with the humanities and the arts, I would not have allowed myself to be where I am." He was silent for a few moments.

"It is time you return to your work," he finally said, as firmly as he could, without the harshness of tone that marked guard commands, but loud enough to be heard by others She turned and walked quickly to her table,

They talked frequently after that. Every few days the guard would stop by her and she would talk with him. Rather, he would talk to her, telling her of his unhappiness with what he was doing, of how not only he but so many others who he knew were being forced to participate in the torture and extermination policy of the camp against their own natures and wishes.

"What I say to you is completely confidential, of course," he told her one day.

Phillipa kept the smile inside of her. As if any one would take my word against that of a guard, she thought. She understood his caution, nevertheless. Despite their frequent talks, he had at no time offered her his name.

"I look at all this brutality, this sadism, and I wonder what has happened to my Germany, to my people. Have we all become monsters? But then I look at myself," he continued, "and my friends and I know that it is only a few, only a handful, who force us to do this. We have no choice. We are given orders and we must obey. Even the big ones, some of them have no choice, either." He pondered a moment, feeling the need to convince her, in turn convincing himself. It did not overtly occur either to him or to Phillipa that if she were convinced it would be an expiation of the guilt that he felt so deeply inside.

"You have heard of Adolph Eichmann?," he asked.

Phillipa nodded.

"Even him. Even the ones in charge of the final solution for the Jews, even some of them are under direct orders from Goebbels and Goering. So what can we little fish do?" He looked at her seriously. "I hope you understand that, Fran Penmann. I hope you understand that."

Phillipa nodded. She really didn't understand, but she wanted to. She thought about it over the days, the weeks, the months. Truly, the people themselves, as common and uncultured and uneducated as most were to her, could not be so brutal, so bestial, so sadistic had they a free choice. She knew the discipline, the efficiency, the need to follow orders, and she began to think that, indeed, the guard was right. The more she believed this, the more hope it gave her, the more possibility there became for her that the very fact of such coercion meant that the true feelings and beliefs of her guards

and captors might eventually emerge and save her. She became convinced that, in great part, the S.S. men, the soldiers,
the German and Polish civilians who were responsible for the
horrors of Auschwitz were only obeying orders and had no
choice.

One morning the dining hall line was slowed up by the
refusal of a number of inmates of one barracks to eat. Several
in that barracks had suffered what seemed to be food poisoning the evening before and during the night and early morning had been so seriously ill that it was clear they would not
be able to put in their day's work. As was frequently the case
with those who became ill, the easiest and cheapest method
of curing them was taken. A truck pulled up at the barracks
and they were thrown on, to be transported to Birkenau.
Anyone who was ill did everything to conceal it. Typhus was
the illness most feared. The conditions of the barracks bred
lice and lice carried the disease. Once it spread, it became
an epidemic and in many barracks screams of dying inmates
frequently filled the air all night long. They could not report
to the hospital or to the doctors because the standard cure for
typhus was either Birkenau or carbolic acid in the veins.

This morning the remaining inmates of the stricken
barracks refused to eat, afraid that whatever caused the food
poisoning the night before was still present in the morning's
meal. While extra guards were called to dispose of those who
balked—and the arrival of the special guards resulted in immediate consumption of the feared food—Phillipa's barracks
stood on line, a hundred yards away, behind several other
groups waiting their turn. It was because of this that she was
able to see and hear an incident that seriously questioned the
attitude she had developed about the responsibility of her
captors.

Walking from the direction of the children's block were
several officers and several civilians. One of the officers was a

colonel whose name she didn't know, but who she had seen several times before in situations that indicated he had an important command at the camp. His voice and that of one of the civilians were raised in loud argument with each other.

"I don't care what your supposed morals are, Dr. Paeltzer," the colonel was shouting. "We are all duty bound to the State to perform whatever tasks we are ordered to."

"You can perform whatever tasks you are ordered to, Colonel," the civilian answered, "But I will not deliberately participate in such crimes. What you are, I cannot say, but I like to think of myself as a human being."

"A human being, you say," the colonel retorted. "You are a weakling, a traitor. You think you are something special. You think you are above the rest of us. Well, we may not like some of what we do any better than you do. But we are following orders. We are doing what the country needs us to do. We have laws governing the Jews and the communists and the Gypsies and the homos and the subversives, and we are obeying those laws. To do otherwise is not only to be a traitor to our country, but to deliberately break the law."

"Have it as you will. This tour of the camp was enough for me. I shall not participate in cold-blooded brutality. I shall not be a party to mass murder."

"You are throwing accusations at better men than yourself," the colonel said.

"Better men? Maybe I once thought so. Never have I been so shocked than to see my old professor from Prague in charge of the children's medical treatment. Treatment?," he added bitterly. "Torture is more like it. Yes, I once thought he was a better man than I. If murder is your concept of a better man, then he still is."

The colonel tried a different tack.

"You act like this is all news to you, like this is the first time you have heard of or seen a concentration camp. You are a hypocrite, a frightened, spineless, woman hyprocite, Dr. Paeltzer."

"I have heard about the camps. I have heard about what went on here. Of course, all of us in Germany have. And I knew, too. We all of us knew. We would have to be not only deaf, dumb and blind, but have no sense of smell not to know. But I didn't want to believe it. I put it out of my mind. But now I have seen it. The gas chambers, the crematoria, the medical experiments. I have seen too much of it. No, Colonel, I shall not participate in this barbarism. I am a human being! Report me if you like!" He turned and walked toward the headquarters area of the camp. 'This is no job for my mother's son!"

Some time later Phillipa asked the friendly, unnamed guard at the clothing mill whether he had heard of this incident.

"Everyone has," he answered.

"What happened to the Doctor?," Phillipa asked.

"Nothing," the guard said softly, "nothing."

"Have you heard of any punishment happening to any S.S. men who actually refused to obey such orders?"

The boy pondered a moment. He started to say something, stopped, then barely moved his lips. "No," he said. "No, I have not." He stood facing her a brief moment more, then turned and walked away, not able to look at her any longer. Phillipa watched as he went out the door. Then suddenly the realization of where she was and what she had done was upon her. A horror seized her.

"Oh, my God," she told herself, "oh, my God, what have I said, what have I done?" And her stomach began to tighten into knots as she watched the door, waiting for it to open again, waiting for what now seemed the inevitable.

Chapter XV

Walter did not go to his classes that day in 1940 when Phillipa was taken away. He walked for several hours, up and down the crowded shopping streets, along the small, cobbled walks of the residential areas. He knew from the first moment that the S.S. men arrived at his house that there was nothing he would be able to do for Phillipa. Since even before they were married his every action had been predicated on what effect it might have on her. Now she was no longer there. There were no more reprieves from self-duty, no more conferences of compromise with himself. Mentally, spiritually, physically he was free. Free to think and do as he wished. The price he might have to pay would be reckoned only in terms of his own conscience, perhaps in terms of his own blood. He knew, at this moment, only that he had to get out of Germany.

He phoned the university and said that he was ill. He went home, not quite decided that he was ready for the decisiveness of action, but enough on the edge of necessity to pack his essential belongings in preparation. Clothing, the more expensive pieces of silver, and Phillipa's jewelry. All the money he could gather together. For an hour he sat and looked at his bookshelves. It hurt most to leave his books behind. Not even one book could he take. He could not, however, leave his unfinished manuscript work. That was still part of a possible future. His manuscript on Kant, the sheets of typing paper now bent and beginning to yellow, was stuffed into the suitcase. Someday, he thought, he would finish it and it would be published.

The next day was Friday and in the early morning he called his secretary and advised her to cancel his classes for the day. He said he was still too ill to leave his house. He gave her assignments to give to his classes for their first meeting of the following week. He hung up the phone reluctantly. He knew that the click of the receiver was shutting forever the part of his life that had been the most important. But even in his reluctance he was not hesitant. Now he stood naked and clean in the world. No more connections, no more ties.

The past was gone. The present offered nothing. Only the future counted. What kind of a future could there be? He let his speculations become airy and idealistic. A peaceful and democratic Germany where he could raise a family without fear? The thought of a family jarred him. How much he had wanted a family! But Phillipa did not. Her freedom, her individuality, her good times, her body were not to be marred. Later, for different reasons, Walter agreed with her. He feared to bring up a child in the political noose he saw tightening around his country. Was there ever to be an extension of him into eternity? Only a faint glimmer of the future held out even the smallest promise. As long as the promise was there, he had no choice but to look for it. Perhaps even to fight for it.

That evening, as soon as it got dark, he left Heidelberg. He locked the front door securely. He put the key carefully into his wallet, knowing even as he wondered whether he would ever use it again that he probably would not.

He walked to the Bahnhof. The bright evenings of spring had not yet fully arrived and the dull grey remnants of winter still hung over the city, easing into darkness before seven o'clock. He saw no one he knew. He tried to carry his suitcase as though it were lighter and emptier than it was. He moved with purposeful nonchalance. Nothing suspicious. Merely a pleasure trip over the weekend.

Even as he approached the ticket window and heard the clerk ask "where to?" he had not yet decided where he was going. "Where to?," came the urgent repetition.

He put a fifty-mark note on the ledge, pushed it under the wire bar to the ticket seller.

"Well?"

Even as he mentally forced himself to try to think of a destination, it struck him funny that he had not thought out where he would go. Only that he would go. In a matter of seconds thoughts of the irony of his urgency and his concomitant lack of preparation raced through his mind. He laughed to himself. For a philosopher, he had certainly reached the bounds of impracticality. He looked around hurriedly, at the train gates, at the little black boards posted in front of each gate on which were chalked the destinations of the trains. The first was "Berlin." He turned back to the ticket window, about to make that his choice. Then he was uncertain. He felt that it was wrong. He did not want to go east. East went further into Germany. He wanted to go out of Germany. Then a vague indefinite idea struck him that he must cross into France. Perhaps to the little town of Givet on the Belgium border where his former housekeeper, Mathilde Berrun, had gone to live with her sister on a small farm. He wondered if Mathilde was still alive. Or perhaps to Paris, to the Sorbonne or the University of Paris. He was known there and would be welcomed. Perhaps be could even teach there? The thought of teaching again disturbed him. It was not what he felt he wanted to do now. It had become stagnant to him. Was it peace and quiet and rest that he needed? Perhaps the peace and quiet and rest of intense physical labor as opposed to intellectual pressure?

"If you can't make up your mind, get out of line!" a voice shouted from in back of him. Scattered laughs came from the line of people behind him. He turned back to the ticket window and as he did his eyes caught the chalked names in front of another gate: Mannheim, Mainz, Weisbaden, Koblenz, Bonn, Koln.

"Excuse me, please," he told the ticket-seller. He said it again, louder, for the other people in line to hear. "Bitte enschuldigen!" He chose the farthest point. "Koln," he said to the ticket-seller.

It was a three-hour trip. The stops were short. Civilian passengers were few. Soldiers in bright new uniforms. Soldiers in neatly pressed but worn uniforms with battle decorations. He found a seat in a small compartment with three soldiers. They looked at him with disdain, unhappy with his civilian status. He stared from the window. He didn't wish to speak with them. The train continued north, past the rich farms and the lush castles of the Rhineland. Now for the first time, as the occasional blinding lights of the dark landscape made a repetitious blur in front of his eyes, he thought about what he would do. He thought about how he would get to France. He bit his lip to keep from laughing. How ludicrously impractical can a man be, he thought. At that moment the German Wehrmacht stood at the borders of France, ready to strike. The French forces stood armed and ready to repulse any alien attempt to enter their land. Did he, Walter Paul, expect to simply walk across the Siegfried and Maginot Lines?

His musings became more serious. He had heard of German agents who reportedly crossed the border every day. By the same token, he presumed there were French agents

who came the other way. If he were able to contact one of
these French agents, offer himself to the anti-Nazi forces, he
might get to France. He laughed to himself in satisfaction,
then closed his month hard as the soldiers turned to stare at
him. He nodded to them shyly, as if he had suddenly remembered an extraordinarily good joke. The satisfaction remained
within him. Even for a man who doesn't plan, he thought,
necessity sets up its own road-markers.

He arrived at the Cologne railroad station a little after ten
o'clock. He took a cup of coffee at a restaurant adjoining the
station. He took stock of his situation. He had made the right
travel choice. Cologne, on the map, was northeast of Givet. If
he could make his way toward Aachen, at the western border
of Germany, and then get into Belgium, he could follow the
main route of the Meuse River past Liege and eventually into
Givet as it jutted as a tiny finger of France into the southern
edge of Belgium. Because Cologne was a large city it would
be easier for him to hide there. And he knew he must hide.
On Monday the university would begin to look for him. The
police would be notified, especially in light of his relationship
to Phillipa. The only place of safety in Germany was in a large
crowd. By Monday evening he would have to find a good
shelter. After that he could begin to try to learn how one goes
about making contact with French agents or Belgian agents.
The very thought was ridiculous. Secret agents were something he had seen only in the cinema. He wouldn't know a
secret agent if he were speaking with one face to face. He had
not the slightest idea how he would even begin to go about
seeing his plan to fruition. As soon as he finished his coffee
and his thoughts he walked along a small dark street next to
the Bahnhof, looked for a cheap hotel.

"Just for the night," he told the fat, sleepy woman at the
desk. "I'll have to take another train very early in the morning. Probably before you are up."

"Good," she told him. "As long as you pay in advance. And I won't worry about you having left when I clean your room tomorrow." Then, as if in anticipation of an unasked question, "We clean the rooms every day here,"

"I can see that," he told her. He thought he had never seen a dirtier hotel. He slept till five. Then, careful that no one else was in the hall, he went to the common bathroom, shaved off his beard and mustache. That was the way such things were done in the movies, he reasoned, when someone was trying to hide from the authorities. He was surprised at the way he looked. He seemed to be ten years younger, youthful, not even thirty years old. As he studied his new face he was glad that he had grown the Van Dyke beard years before; it certainly had given him the look of dignity that one expected of the chairman of a university philosophy department.

He left the hotel without anyone seeing him, stopped to get some breakfast, then walked aimlessly for a while, trying to become acquainted with that part of the city. He watched the center section of town fill up with workers, shoppers, travelers. The streets suddenly became crowded with military personnel. He turned down a side street, walked a few blocks away from the main section and found a transient rooming house.

The woman who ran it seemed gentle and kind, although as he looked at her appearance he wondered whether it was simply relaxed and apathetic. She was tall and thin, in her late forties, stringy in appearance, with unkempt long, uncombed blonde hair, wearing a brightly flowered unshaped dress, rumpled stockings and scuffed bedroom slippers.

"We have a number of rooms vacant. I'll show them to you and you can have your choice." She took him up to the third floor of the old, wood-slatted building. "You're not a soldier run away, are you?," she asked. There was no

bitterness or accusation in her voice. It was lethargic, like
the rest of her.

"No," Walter said quickly. "I expect to be in the Wehrmacht soon. But not yet. I am a writer."

"Oh." Her face was sad for a moment. "Rent in advance."

Walter chose a small room in the cradle of the chimney
eaves on the top floor.

"For a month," he said. He gave her thirty marks. "I'm
not a very successful writer," he continued. "I'm writing
a story set in Cologne and I wanted to come here for first
hand experience. My home is in Munich." He felt somewhat
surprised, relieved and proud at the ease in which he had
concocted and told the lie. She seemed to be satisfied with his
story.

"If you don't stay a full month, I'll refund whatever is
due you," she told him. "You seem like a nice young man."

He registered under the name of Johann Becher. He remembered having gone to primary school with a boy of that
name. It was nondescript and common enough to be reason-
ably safe.

Walter spent the day in his room, trying to determine
how he would go about implementing his plan to escape
from Germany. He took a sheet of paper and a pencil and
began to write down in logical order the various possibilities and procedures, as if he were solving a philosophical
problem by the method of logical analysis. He wrote on the
paper, under the Roman numeral I: '"Groups and Individuals." Then, under that: "A. Discontented, anti-Nazi elements
still in Germany." He thought for a moment. He was in that
category. He thought of others like himself. What kind of
people were they? Under Arabic number 1 he wrote: "Read-
ers, thinkers, intellectuals." Then he set up another category,
B, next to which he wrote "Sources." Where could he find
such people? He wrote: "1. Schools." He crossed it out.

It would be too dangerous for him to be near any educational institution. He thought a moment and substituted the word "Library." He had said he was a writer. It would be logical for him to spend time in a library. Perhaps there, sooner or later, he would meet the right intellectual, overhear a conversation. He crumpled up the sheet of paper, thought a moment of what a spy in the movies would do, put the paper in an ash tray, touched a lighted match to it and watched it burn into ashes. He did his speculating and reasoning in his mind for the remainder of the day.

He spent the next two weeks in the library, from morning until evening. He watched and listened, but without success. The time was not wasted. He read voluminously, began to take notes for a new book, the philosophical development of higher education in Germany, with an emphasis on government control. The subject was of special interest because, at that moment, it was only too frightening to him to speculate on how it might end. After two weeks he had to come to a different kind of decision. How much longer should he spend at the library, hoping for the desired information, and how much chance should he take attempting to find other sources? His enjoyment with his research project clouded the sharpness of his original intention.

He began to spend some of his evenings sitting in the front parlor of the rooming house with Frau Ritter, the landlady. Her conversation was quiet and limited, reflecting the same lethargic unconcern of her appearance. Most often they would listen to the radio or Frau Ritter would work her needles and yarn while Walter would read a newspaper or a book. Rarely did another tenant enter the parlor and then, it seemed, only to quickly ask Fran Ritter a question of apparent unimportance and then disappear. In fact, in the first few weeks at Frau Ritter's he met only one other tenant, a man of some seventy years of age, and this by accident when they both tried to get into the hall bathroom at the same time one morning. After a little joke about cleanliness not being one of the virtues of rooming houses with limited bath facilities, Walter went back to his room and the old man, after a mumbled apology and offer to let Walter go first, which the latter declined, went into the bathroom.

"Herr Stauffel has been here for ten years," Frau Ritter told him that evening. "My oldest tenant." And then, without change of expression and with no discernible hidden meaning, "But not my favorite."

The only thing Walter learned about Frau Rlitter was that, somewhere, she had a husband. She spoke of him only once.

"A very selfish man, Otto," she said. "I married him for love. He had no money. Only this house. But I never got any real love from him." She blinked her eyes, as if a tear might somehow blot the flowered brightness of her creased, loose dress. "Never." She didn't mention Otto again.

From time to time and for brief moments Walter saw one visitor. A young girl, perhaps eighteen or nineteen years old, a thin, almost permanently sad face, well-defined pinched nose, narrow lips and tight cheeks. The thinness was not sharp, but rather ethereal, almost like a combination of light and shadow that created an effect of aesthetic unreality. Within the sadness of the face there was a special beauty, a hidden but absolute premonition of warmth and brightness. She was the lightness of youth and at the same the seriousness that man had created in the world—in her gestures, her speech, her walk.

The first time Walter saw her she had entered without knocking, come into the parlor and was about to speak when she saw Walter. His presence was unexpected and she hesitated imperceptibly, turned, waited for Frau Ritter to rise, then followed her into the kitchen, emerging barely a minute later, leaving as quietly as she had come in. Frau Ritter returned to her knitting and Walter continued to read his book as if he had noticed nothing worth commenting upon.

"A neighbor girl," Frau Ritter said casually a few moments later. "Has boy-friend trouble. Comes to me for advice." She gave an obviously forced laugh. "I'm well experienced in such matters. Well experienced."

Walter glanced up, smiled in acknowledgment, saw Frau Ritter's eyes meet his. He smiled again, lowered his eyes, lifted them again and saw her still staring at him. He excused himself and went up to his room.

Walter remained at Frau Ritter's. The library afforded him none of the contacts he had hoped to make and his time there was of value only for his research. Indeed, the research provided him with the academic satisfactions he had willfully tried to forget. He feared they might distract him from his immediate purpose and as he buried himself day to day in his research he found the ease that comes from the safety of non-controversial activity. His conscience grew flabby within the pleasurable walls of his self-constructed ivory tower. But even in the warm corners of the library, even through the heavy leather bindings of the books, fear crept. He knew that the Gestapo undoubtedly was looking for him and he knew that soon he would have to find a means of escape if he was to escape at all. At random, he sought accidental contacts at focal points of cultural gatherings, expecting that the intellectuals, the artists, those who might be likely to actively defend their freedoms against tyranny, would also likely be found at concerts, ballets, plays and art exhibits. But he met empty faces and blank people. Everyone seemed constrained, displaying as their only overt emotion and activity a middle-class pomposity, a safe and sane mask to conceal any suggestion of nonconformity of any kind. He even began to frequent the beer halls in the hope of bumping into some soul of kindred need. But the bierstuben were invariably filled with soldiers and Nazi youth, boastful, drunk and disorderly to the point of anti-social excess. In desperation he even began to risk walks in the street at night, thinking that by some miraculous unknown talisman be might somehow find what he sought. Yet, even evening walks were laborious and depressive, for he knew he walked in vain, he knew even as he looked from one face to another as he passed men and women on the streets that he would not know what he sought even if he met it, and if he found it he would not dare determine if it were really so. More and more fearful, more and more depressed, he returned to the evening quiet of Frau Ritter's parlor, ostensibly reading a book but instead letting his mind seek the many alternatives that he was certain must be there but which totally eluded him.

He saw the young girl at Frau Ritter's frequently. Each time she followed the same procedure. She would enter the hallway, wait for Frau Ritter, disappear into the kitchen with her, then leave a minute or two later. One evening, when Frau Ritter had gone from the parlor to her apartment for a moment, the girl appeared. Walter rose politely.

"I'm afraid I make it difficult for you to talk with Frau Ritter," he said. "Please accept my apologies."

The girl seemed to want to speak. Then, as though she were too shy even to acknowledge his thoughtfulness, shook her head, indicating at the same time her appreciation for his comments and her assurance that he was not inconveniencing her. Walter was about to sit down when something, perhaps the feeling of what lay behind her manner and her appearance, pushed him into further talk.

"I have noticed you frequently," he said. "Perhaps some time you will join us for the evening." Then, realizing that he had left her with no response, he added, "My name is Johann Becher. I am a writer."

The girl hesitated, pursed her lips as if to keep them from opening, then allowed a wisp of a smile to lighten her mouth: "My name is Jeanine Hoffman." As if in habit to explain her given name, she added, "My mother was French."

She looked at him, turned her eyes away quickly, but not before Walter saw into them. For a moment whatever barriers may have existed between them not there.

Frau Ritter suddenly entered, aware of something that displeased her. Her voice was almost too loud.

"My dear," she said to the girl, "more boy-friend trouble? My, you do have problems these days. Come, let me help you." And she led the way into the kitchen.

Walter looked for the girl during subsequent evenings, even began to anticipate hopefully her coming. But she did not come again. Frau Ritter didn't mention her. Walter still felt the uneasiness of that brief meeting, not an uneasiness of himself or of the girl, but of Frau Ritter, and so he did not mention her, either.

At the end of five months be had made no friends in Cologne, had made no acquaintances from whom he could even begin to draw information. In fact, Frau Ritter was the only person with whom he could find any communication.

In his desperation he began, as unobtrusively as he could, to move the content of their limited conversations toward what he wished to know. She did not hesitate when he discussed the war, the front lines, the French. But the moment he tried to lead into the subject of political action in Germany she had no further thoughts and no further conversation. Once he pushed her by speaking of rumors he had heard of a political underground. With surprise and innocence on her face she assured him that no decent German would be involved in such an affair and that, therefore, nothing of the kind probably even existed. She excused herself and left the room for a few minutes.

When she returned she resumed the conversation on an entirely different subject and from that time on would not he drawn into conversation with him on that subject at all. Yet, in a different way, her attitude toward him seemed to change. He now found coffee waiting for him when he arose in the morning. Sometimes she invited him to dinner with her when he returned early from the library. She baked special little cakes for him and if he returned to his room late at night he might very well find a dish of freshly baked cookies on his night–table. He became embarrassed at what became a constant smile from Frau Ritter each time they exchanged a word between them that might he construed as warm or personal. And he became disturbed as sometimes he caught her off guard and concluded that she apparently stared at him when she thought he wasn't aware of it. Her conversations with Walter more and more concerned themselves with romance, with boys and girls, with men and women, about love. Could it be, thought Walter, that this woman really was what she seemed to be, an incurable, eccentric romantic?

Then one evening Frau Ritter excused herself from the parlor. She was not gone more than a minute when the girl, Jeanine, entered. She stood in the hall, at the arched doorway to the parlor. Walter felt a moment of excitement, wanted to rationalize its existence, and then let whatever thoughts he might have had remain unverbalized. Instead, he let the sudden feeling of warmth and exhilaration decide his actions.

He stood quickly. "Fraulein Hoffman," he said. "Please"—he motioned with his hand—"please come in."

To his surprise the girl entered, sat on the conch directly across from Walter's chair. They sat for more than a minute looking at each other, with no words. Walter didn't feel embarrassed at the silence. He wondered whether the girl was. He felt he ought to say something.

"Do you . . . do you like to read?"

The girl looked at him softly. "You do," she said, nodding to the book he had dropped on the floor by his chair.

He looked down, forgetting that it was there. He picked it up, leaned over to put it on the table in front of him.

"Yes, I do."

"What is it you like to read?"

"Philosophy," he said. Then realizing that this was not Heidelberg, not a pleasant party in an academic atmosphere, not an existence of an eternity before, he hastily added: "And poetry. And fiction. I read anything. Anything that I find interesting."

"What are you reading there?," she asked.

He had to look to see. "A play," he said. "I am embarrassed that I got so caught up in it that I forgot what I was reading."

"What play?"

"Hauptmann. *The Weavers*."

"Not many people read that play today."

Walter was startled, but not altogether surprised.

"But Hauptmann has declared his support for the ideals of our country, has he not?," Walter demanded.

Without a change of expression the girl nodded her head. "Yes, many persons seem to have voiced their support."

They sat for a minute more, not speaking. It was pleasant for Walter, not having to talk and yet feeling that there was a satisfying communication between them. It surprised him when he said his next words because he did not do what he had always done before, that is thought them over carefully so that they would come out precisely as he meant them to come out.

"Jeanine . . . I hope you do not mind my calling you Jeanine . . ."

She smiled and made the word "no" with her lips.

"I do not know how you and your boy friend are getting along now," he said. "What I mean is, I know you had some disagreement and whether it is settled I do not know. But . . . I would like it if you would come with me to dinner tomorrow night. We could find a quiet place in the city. Perhaps with a bit of music."

"I should like that very much," she said. Then, as if a script had been written for the evening and the proper place for an act ending had been reached, she stood up, reached her hand toward his. "I will meet you here at seven o'clock tomorrow evening. Good night, Johann."

He held her hand for a brief moment. He wanted to squeeze it, but was embarrassed to. Then: "But you have not seen Fran Ritter this evening."

"Apparently she is occupied. I can see her another time."

He walked with her to the door. She offered her hand again. This time he held it tight. Then she was gone.

It took Walter many hours that night to make a decision about Jeanine. His loneliness, his fears, his needs—all this colored life for him and gave him a vulnerability to romanticism that he knew was not true or practically possible. He loved Phillipa. This alone was sufficient to put aside the thoughts and feelings he had had earlier that evening. To become involved with Jeanine might even be the temptation and the delay that would prevent him from making the escape to France that still had to be the purpose of his immediate existence. And even if all the rest were not so, he argued to himself, he was approaching forty and Jeanine could not yet be twenty. A man approaching middle-age with a child not yet fully aware of life. He decided that he would not take her to dinner the following evening. He would be certain not to see her again at all. With this determination he went to sleep.

When he awoke in the morning the day seemed especially bright and the sun seemed especially warm. With a light step he took his papers and walked to the library, anxiously waiting for seven o'clock in the evening to come so that he could spend the remaining hours of the day with Jeanine.

In the days and weeks that followed they met often for dinner, for lunch, for strolls in the park in the early afternoon, for walks through the busy city streets in the late morning, for visits to the museums, the concert halls, the ballet, the theatre. And always he found, when with Jeanine, an openness, a freshness, an eagerness for life and for the future. His thoughts, his feelings, his experiences, his ideas suddenly seemed to mean more to him, to his ego, to the world, because they meant something, it seemed, to Jeanine. Sometimes, when Jeanine told him of her ideals of freedom, of her stimulation by the novels of Thomas Mann or the poetry of Bertolt Brecht, Walter would talk about Mann and Brecht and about Theodore Dreiser and Sinclair Lewis and Bernard Shaw and would feel a gentle touch of fingers on his hand and turn and see a glow of satisfaction in soft brown eyes and he in turn would feel his eyes glow and know that what he thought and felt, what he was, meant something to more than himself.

Sometimes they would walk for hours without a word. At first it would discomfort him.

"Don't feel uncomfortable," Jeanine would say. "We don't need words. We both know how we feel. We can exchange all the beauties of the world without words."

It was the warmth of September now. The heat of August had gone and left behind a glow of gentle satisfaction that mixed with the freshness of fall. Where spring to most was the season of rebirth, autumn to Walter was the return to students and books and classrooms and was his intellectual rebirth. He felt the relaxation of the summer's sun within him at the same time that he felt his body tense, as if in conditioned response, for a new year of ideas and thought. But now he felt something more. Intellectual dedication, this autumn, had not claimed his whole being. Part of him, his emotional self, was held back in a warmth and expectation of its own. He felt an alternating emptiness and fullness when Jeanine was not with him and when he saw her again. For the first time in his life it was something that he did not use words for, did not need rationale for, did not want thoughts for. His feelings, for reasons that he did not fully understand and did not care whether he understood them or not, were sufficient.

The first week of September bloomed hot, as if the year reached backward in time to play just once more with the days of August. Along the edge of the east bank of the Rhine, several kilometers south of the city, Walter and Jeanine walked, she with a picnic basket in one band, he with a blanket over one arm, their free hands clasped tightly together between them, their legs brushing each other's as they stepped almost in rhythm through the grass and foliage along the bank, their heads up, straight, ahead of them, looking with smiling open months into the blue sky and every once in a while turning to each other, Walter feeling Jeanine's hair gently moving across his face, his head bending and his lips lightly kissing her hair and, deliberately affecting the pose of a schoolboy stealing a kiss, his mouth rubbing gently across the nape of her neck. He brightened inside with satisfaction as he felt her body quiver at his touch and then quickly and softly he touched his lips to hers as she lifted her head toward his. They walked on in silence, feeling each other without touch, exchanging thoughts without sound.

Walter spread the blanket by a large linden tree that bent toward the river and that spread its branches in a circle, inviting and protecting at the same time any who would sit under

it and enjoy its hospitality. Jeanine put the picnic basket
at the corner of the blanket. She lay back, her hands outstretched. Walter lay by her side. He propped his head on one
arm and stared at her. No thoughts, no words came to him.
Solely the feeling of contentment, of looking at the face of
the woman lying there. He lifted a finger in front of his eyes,
shut one eye and figuratively traced the finger across her lips.

Had he ever kissed her?, he thought. So many times, he
mused, and yet perhaps never. Not really ever. Not ever really. He looked at her and felt a moment of trepidation even
as his body moved down toward hers and his lips moved onto
hers. He felt her lips rise to him, her body and breasts arching up toward him, her arms pulling at his shoulders, around
his neck and molding his body fully and completely against
hers. He closed his eyes and touched her tongue with his and
felt for the warm wet of the inside of her mouth and felt the
tickle of her tongue against the roof of his mouth and the
fullness and wetness of joining his face with hers and then the
crinkling of the corners of his mouth into a broad smile as her
teeth grasped gently and firmly onto his outstretched tongue
and her throat shivered with a soundless giggle of pleasure
and teasing.

Slowly, imperceptibly, the warmth still clinging between
them, making a bridge between them, his mouth moved
from hers. He lifted his head, seeing her eyes, deep and light
brown at the same time, his body still full and close on hers.

"Have I ever kissed you before?," he said.

"A thousand times and never," she answered. "All my
life. And for the first time."

He lifted his body, put his hands on her face, touched
her lips with his fingers, her eyes, her forehead, ran his
hands along her hair, across her neck, down her shoulders
and rested them on her breasts. Her face and body remained
completely relaxed, her smile of pleasure and satisfaction

unchanging. He felt he should say something. Somehow he ought to find words of explanation, and yet, he thought, why did he have to.

"It feels right," he said. "You feel right."

"It is right," she said.

It was as if this is where he belonged, he thought. Where they belonged.

His hands left her breasts and moved along her hips, against the inside of her thighs. He pushed his hands up, cupping them firmly against her, feeling the soft give of hair, the heat of her body through her clothes reaching into his hands. His movements were not planned or even deliberate. It was as if there was nothing else that he should do, as if his touch was as necessary and natural as taking his next breath. Jeanine did not move a muscle but remained smiling and relaxed, as if she too felt the security and trust of what was right and appropriate.

"I am a virgin," she said without change of expression or tone. "No, don't move," she continued as she felt his hands beginning to move away from her body. He relaxed again. "I want you to make love to me," she said. "I really do. But I am afraid." She paused, not quite sure how to explain or whether she had to explain. "Do you understand that? My wanting to and not being able to. I'm not teasing you or leading you on. I don't want you to dislike me or be disappointed in me."

Walter smiled, then laughed. "You are a little girl. A very little girl." Gently he removed his hands from her body, then lifted her to him, sat with his back propped against the tree and held her against him, her head resting into his shoulder, his arms enveloping her breasts and waist.

"Today, right now," he said to her, "you bring life to me. A life, a warmth, a trust, a kind of . . . love"—he didn't want to use the word because he was not sure it was yet the right word—"that I have never known before." Now he searched

for the right words, not for rationalization, but for clarity.
"Would you understand, Jeanine, if I said to you that I do
want to make love to you . . ."—he corrected himself—"with
you . . . and it would be all right if I never made love with
you."

"I think I understand."

"1 don't know how to say this without saying something
that I don't want to admit. But I must say it, if only for my
own need to admit it out loud. What I get from you is youth,
a brightness, a hope, an enjoyment of life that I have never
known. It is not that I am old. But indeed, I am. Not in
numbers, perhaps, but in spirit. Sometimes, I wonder if I ever
was young. I am over thirty-five years old now, and when I
was twenty I was thirty-five. But now, for the first time in
my life, I can feel what it really is to be twenty. No, that's not
right. What I should say is, what it really is, is to be aware of
the goodness and excitement and beauty and potential of life
that make themselves known only to those who have youth,
whether they are twenty or thirty-five."

She began to say something, but he put his fingers gently
over her lips. He needed to say this to the end.

"Don't you know that I have thought of this many times.
You are twenty and I am almost forty. To me, I suppose,
that does not seem to be such a difference because I know
now that you can make me feel like I am twenty or whatever
numerical age that is needed to match twenty. But I am concerned about what you feel. When I was twenty and in the
university I had a professor I liked a great deal. He seemed
younger than the others, always took an interest in us, not
only in our academic development but in any personal problems or adjustments we might have or need. I looked on him
almost as a contemporary. One day I learned how old he was.
Thirty-two years of age. Suddenly he appeared old. An old
man. Or an older man, at least. The numbers were some kind

of magic and I looked at him a little differently from then on. Maybe with more reverence. Certainly not as one of my contemporaries. Now when I think of that age, thirty-two, it seems so young. But that is because I am now older than that and I say to myself, how can one reconcile forty and twenty?"

Jeanine laughed.

"I am not laughing at you," she said, gently reaching backward and touching his cheek with her hand, then turning her head and kissing him tenderly on the lips. "I like you as you are. I am not here with you because you were born in a certain year, but because you are what you are."

"You are a woman," he said. "And yet, at the same time you are a child. I know I shouldn't, but I can't help worrying about our age difference."

She turned completely around now, her body facing him, sitting in his lap, her arms free, her hands holding onto his.

"Who is the child?," she said softly. "I am ageless. I am twenty and I am an eternity." She took his hands and pressed them to her lips. Her eyes sparkled as she looked into his. She laughed. "Why, don't you really know who I am?," she asked in a voice filled with mock seriousness. "I am a witch from centuries past. I was spawned in the Black Forest. I am in reality hundreds of years older than you."

He stroked her hair, held her face close in front of his, looked at her a long while, then kissed her full on the month. Now the seriousness had gone from his face. "I know that," he said. "I do know it."

They sat close, unmoving for a long time. They listened to the soft movement of the Rhine waters against the bank, the sounds of a distant automobile horn, the laugh of a child, the earth moving through the wind, the faint hushing sound of the blowing leaves. They listened and felt each other's presence.

After a while Walter's pleasure of just being was intruded upon by thought. He did not reason out his ideas or words.

For a fleeting, almost subconscious moment he mused at the fact that he did not, but then, before he could analyze his motives, as he had done his entire life, he was speaking, somehow secure that no matter what his words were, they would be all right. They would have to be all right.

"You don't know anything about me, Jeanine," he said.

"I don't have to know more about you than I already know. I know all I need to know."

"We must sometimes think in terms other than abstract romanticism," he said. "I mean about my past, my personal life."

"I must ask you something . . . for me," Jeanine said. "For now, for the time being, I would prefer that we do not discuss your life other than what it is now, what you are now, at the moment when we are together. It is only that which we have together that has any meaning. The rest I don't even want to think about."

Walter smiled. "That makes me happy. But I can't accept that happiness without saying at least one thing that is important. Whether you care for me to speak or not, I will say it." He paused, now trying to find the words that would be most gentle and least painful without being melodramatic. But he could find none that did not seem trite. "I am married," he said. "I am now separated from my wife. Not voluntarily. Circumstances have made it necessary. But you should know that I am still in love with her." He paused, "At least, and I say this in honesty because there must be complete honesty between us, that until just very recently, until I have gotten to know you, I thought I was in love with her. And I may still be."

He looked at Jeanine. "I don't need for you to say anything," he told her. "I just wanted to tell you." He released his arms, his hold on her, so that she would not have to pull to move away from him. He wanted her to be able to leave

freely and openly if she wished. But she didn't move. She lay
close against him, as if he had not said a word, as if it didn't
matter what he told her or what he did, that their closeness
was not something arranged by duty or agreement, but was
there by the very nature of their both being there.

Walter thought about Phillipa. Had he really loved her,
he wondered. This woman here, this girl here, who came to
him and yielded to him and seemed to be part of him, not
challenging him because she might not care for his words
or actions, gave him a security of being able to feel, to be,
to love, without worrying that at any moment he might be
rejected because what he was or did or said was not what was
expected of him. He thought of Phillipa and his constant
fear of making a mistake, of her criticisms, of her continual
fault-finding, or her being unable to respond to his questions
without sharpness or sarcasm. Even in their marriage bed his
fear of reaching over and touching her because of the expected
turning aside of her body, her rejection of his self or, even
worse, the passive acceptance of his physical love without
response, without eagerness or desire, as an arrangement to
satisfy the terms of a marriage contract. He looked at Jeanine
and his body welled with the happiness of being needed and
wanted, of knowing that someone felt enough about him,
what he was in himself as a person, to give themselves to him
without fear or reservation, to belong to him and to provide
him, too, with a belonging.

He felt her body coming closer to his, his to hers, and he
held her head, his fingers entwined in her hair as she rolled
backward, lying on the blanket, his body coming on top of
her. He spread her hair out along the edges of the blanket surrounding her head, ran his hands down and held her breasts,
felt for her nipples with his fingers and squeezed and rubbed
them in an aesthetic satisfaction of tactile pleasure. He felt
his penis grow rigid and push against his clothing, against

her clothes and, as if their clothes had suddenly disappeared, against her legs and her thighs in order to find on the inside of her thighs the soft vaginal indentation. Her body began to move and her lips reached for his and pulled and sucked against his, her teeth grasping for his tongue, her body turning and twisting and raising toward him in a rhythmical motion. He felt his own breathing come hard, his gasps suddenly finding-counterpoint as her breaths became short and sharp. He raised his body slightly, felt with one hand for her vagina and, through the soft silk of her clothing, began to rub against the welling hot wetness. Her body began to jerk now, as if anticipating spasms of uncontrol. He reached up, took her hand, carried it down and against the hard erection of his penis, felt her fingers close tightly, massaging on him, felt with his fingers once again for the inviting inside of her body, and together they moved against each other and across each other and with each other in a mutual satisfaction of warmth and closeness and understanding.

He searched for words to understand what was happening to him, but couldn't find any. He knew only that it was right, that it was proper, that it was what had to be, the only thing that could or should be done by him, by them, at that moment. Suddenly her body lost its rhythm and began to jerk upward toward him and then away from him, almost uncontrollably. She tried to speak through the open-gasping of her mouth.

"I can't, I can't," she whispered. Quickly, but gently, he removed his hand, eased himself away from her and, with his arms holding her close around the waist, let her down, stretched out on the blanket. He rolled next to her, still holding her, moving her head against his chest, giving her comfort and a place of safety. They lay for a few minutes, their breaths gradually slowing in intensity, their bodies gradually finding relaxation in silence. Jeanine looked up at him.

"I can't," she said. "I want to. But I am afraid. I am afraid
I will be hurt, I don't know why. Maybe something that I was
taught as a child. But I have such a fear of being hurt. Oh, I
want you to make love to me. And you will make love to me.
Someday. Maybe soon. But I am so afraid."

She buried her face in his shoulder, reached up and
rubbed her eyes.

"I don't want to cry." she said. She looked up and
laughed. "I suppose I am a little girl, after all."

"A little girl and a grown woman."

"I often wonder why it is," she said, "that I am afraid to let
someone really love me. Why I am afraid to really love someone.
Perhaps it was because I was not very pretty as a child. When
I was thirteen and fourteen. When I was sixteen." She laughed
again. "It is funny because that seems a thousand years ago
to me now." She paused. "I never thought anyone could love
unpretty me," she said. "I always thought that I would have to
get someone's love some other way, with my body, by offering
my body, when I didn't want to, when I didn't really love that
person. Having to give myself when I didn't really want to made
me afraid." She laughed once more. "Maybe I will solve the
problem by simply remaining a virgin for the rest of my life."

She looked up at Walter. "No. I know I shall not remain
a virgin. I won't let you let me," she said.

"But you know better now, don't you?," Walter said.
"You are pretty, you know. Very pretty. And I am sure that
there are very few men who would not fall in love with you,
for what you are and not for what physical satisfactions you
may give them, if they had the chance to get to know you.
You don't have to offer anything for love, Jeanine. Men will
offer you whatever you desire."

She kissed him lightly on the lips. "Even if you are just
saying that to make me feel better, I am glad that you said
it." She pushed herself back into his arms.

"I am sorry that I distressed you by being so physical," he said.

She turned her face to his. She was not smiling. "Please, you must not ever say to me that you are sorry again. There is nothing to be sorry for. I want you to be and do just what you want to, whenever you want to." Then she smiled. "For such an old, old man you don't understand much about love."

Walter thought again of Phillipa. Yes, he thought to himself, for such an old, old man I do not know very much about love.

"But I am learning," he said to Jeanine. "This is what you bring to me," he said, "this fullness and joy of simply being."

"I mean what I say about your making love to me," she said.

"And I meant what I said about it really not being why I want to be with you," he replied. "Shall I be intellectual?," he asked, with a short laugh. "I am what is known as an intellectual," he said.

"If you wish, be intellectual," she answered. "Or be emotional. Or be whatever you want to be."

He felt her warmth inside of him. "I feel there are many kinds of sharing between people. There can be satisfaction, there can be happiness, and there can be a kind of love with only one of the sharings, or with two or with three." He paused. "Does this sound too complicated?"

"Not yet." she said.

"There is one kind of sharing we have done. The sharing of the skies, the flowers, the river, the wind, the beauties of nature. There is another kind of sharing we have also had, the intellectual understanding, the sharing of ideas, of enjoyment of the arts, of words. There is a third kind of sharing we have known, an emotional sharing, an unspoken feeling of oneness, of desire, of need. And there is a fourth kind of sharing,

the physical sharing, the sexual completeness of a relationship between two people. As I have said, when one or two or
three are present there can be love. But only when all four are
present can there be the fullness of life, the kind of love that
makes existence a constant brightness of a thousand suns,
enabling people to reach the highest of whatever they have
evolved on this earth for."

He touched her face with his hands and turned it toward
his. "Now, are you thoroughly confused?"

"I understand," she said softly.

He kissed her, barely touching her lips.

He settled back, holding her easily against him. "I shall
make love to you," be said. "When you are ready. When we
are ready. We shall know the right time. You are a woman
and yet a little girl. And it will be soft, slow, and gentle. It
shall be a warm fullness for you and shall be for you what is
right and proper and part of what we share together. And you
shall not be afraid. You shall not be hurt. It will come to you
easily, softly, naturally." He held her lightly against his chest,
stroking her hair with one hand, saying over and over again,
"gently, gently, gently."

They remained that way for a long time. A soft chill began to blow along the river. They did not feel it. Across and
up the river the spire of the Cathedral of Cologne splashed
with gold and edged into black as the light of the setting sun
moved slowly upward on the building, finally leaving it with
a golden crown.

Walter pointed to the picnic box, still at the edge of the
blanket. "Are you hungry?," he asked.

"No," she said.

They stood up.

"Somehow I know you now," she said. "Who you are.
What you are." Her tone was casual, matter-of-fact.

She reached for the picnic basket as he began to fold the blanket.

Without stopping and with lightness in her voice, she said to him and to no one in particular, "I love you."

He stopped just for a moment, looked at her, feeling within him gratitude to her, just for being her.

Hand in hand, they walked slowly, buoyantly along the bank back to Cologne.

Chapter XVI

Walter pleasured in the feel of this autumn. What had in recent years been a chill wind became a fresh breeze; what had seemed a heaviness in an overcast sky became a blanket of softness. He awoke in the mornings with anticipation and went to bed at night with warm satisfaction. His mind, his body, his manner became relaxed, open, young. It was as if he were seeing himself for the first time, a self that he never knew even existed, a self that opened outward more and more each day to reveal feelings and actions that blossomed from within and made him feel ten feet tall. The days passed as a montage in a film, images of color shared in seeing, experiencing, touching, tasting, looking, knowing. When he awoke in the morning and knew he would see Jeanine in an hour, a minute, seconds. The self-imposed intellectual restrictions, the societal-imposed conformities were no longer there and Walter entered into the world as if new-born, with a virginal nakedness of thought and emotion that thrust him far beyond the confines of sedentary earth.

One evening he and Jeanine sat side by side at a table in a bierstube near Frau Ritter's house, her foot twisting around his, her ankle rubbing against his calf, his arm crooked around hers, their fingers twined together tightly. He smiled as he looked at himself and this girl next to him. "When I was a schoolboy," he thought, "I considered this so wicked, so daring, so thrilling. When I was grown I considered it so childish. But it is neither. It is right, proper, natural." He looked at her, looked down at the awkwardness of their position and anticipated her thoughts. "How else should we sit?," he said silently to himself, as if there could be no answer to the question.

They drank of the beer, slowly, in gulps, in long draughts. They sat without words a long time. He didn't have to speak. He knew she was feeling as he did. They exchanged thoughts and feelings without words. It was as if he were in a state of self-hypnosis, as if any verbal sound would break the spell.

Jeanine, without moving, without changing her smile, without even looking at him, spoke.

"Next Tuesday, Johann," she said.

He hesitated a moment, still momentarily startled when addressed by the protective name he had given himself.

"Next Tuesday, what?," he asked lightly, without seeming to really need an answer.

"Next Tuesday we will make love. Next Tuesday I will give you my virginity."

He let go of her arm, disentangled himself, and looked at her. He was embarrassed. But only for a moment.

"Next Tuesday you shall give me your complete love. And I shall give you mine," Walter said with too much seriousness. "I think that is what you mean, isn't it?"

"Yes," she said.

They moved close together again and sat silently as before. Walter felt a brimming of satisfaction inside, felt himself smiling. It was peculiar, he thought, what he felt. These many weeks he had been in love with this girl, these many weeks of longing to find fruition of his love within her, and now that they had set a day, somehow it didn't seem to make the difference he thought it would. No more important, in a way, than going to their first concert together, than sharing an afternoon of bright yellow rays of sun flashing down to them through the incongruous patterns of branches and leaves of the trees on the hilltops overlooking the Rhine. Physical love was another part of themselves that would bring them even closer, and it was this that made him feel full and happy. It was not a conquest, not an accomplishment, not a seduction. It was a natural development of what they were to each other. Intellectually, it seemed strange to him that in all these weeks of closeness they had not made love. Emotionally, he had identified with Jeanine's fear, with her uncertainty of her self and of her motives. He had told her they could wait, should wait until she felt she was ready, until the gentleness and closeness of what they were to each other reached the day when she knew it was the right time. As he walked her to her home that night, his arm about her waist, he felt his body tingle a little more, his step move with a little more assurance of her love.

The next few days were ordinary days, ordinary in their extraordinariness of his daily rebirth in the time spent with Jeanine. His attempts to contact the underground, his goal of escape from Germany seemed to have lost meaning. If life could only continue as it was, there could be no more idyllic place in the world. Yet, he knew he had divorced himself from reality, that the special circumstances gave him a moment of hiding from the world that would soon burst again onto him and destroy his new world by its increasing evil. He knew he ought to make new efforts, especially now that he would not be alone, that wherever he would go he would take Jeanine with him. Though he had still not mentioned this to her, he knew somehow that it would happen. And even as he

told himself that he must take some positive action, he felt
that none was necessary. He felt that some deus-ex-machina
was waiting to pluck him from his desert of indecision and
transport him with the wings of eagles to his promised land.

He had almost forgotten what day it was when he met
Jeanine Tuesday evening for dinner. But the moment he saw
her he knew. Their actions were no different on the surface.
But it was as though they were both too calm.

"I have no fear, none at all," Jeanine whispered to him
over the dinner table. "In fact," she smiled, "I can't wait!"

He reached his hand across the table and held hers. "Cold
hands," he said. "Cold feet, too?"

"You'll warm them." She pulled his hand close to her
breast. "Warm inside. Oh, very warm inside with love for
you."

They walked slowly to Frau Ritter's. She was not in
the living room when they arrived. Without stopping they
walked straight upstairs. Walter held her close for a long
time, tight and gentle at the same time in his arms after he
shut the door and bolted the latch behind them.

"My beautiful girl-woman," he said. "I shall love you."

"Be loving with me."

She held her arms out and up, as a flower blossoming to
the touch of the sun. He unbuttoned the back of her dress,
gently let it slide to the floor. She stepped out of it, and he
laid it carefully onto a chair. He loosened her slip, draped it
slowly down to her ankles, held it as she stepped from it. He
looked at her face, saw a smile of trust and pleasure. He took
off one of her shoes, carried it and placed by the chair, did the
same for the other. Slowly, ever so slowly, he unhooked her
brassiere, slid the straps across and off her arms, let his hands
almost imperceptibly move over the corners of her breasts,
slide gently until his palms rested fully against her nipples.
He smiled in pleasure as he felt her body give a slight shiver.

He removed his hands and stood full in front of her, close as
he could without their bodies touching. His arms remained
by his sides. She stood straight, too, not bending, not shrinking. He looked into her eyes. She smiled, her face full of joy.
Her mouth formed the words "I love you."

He bent down and put his hands against her hips, began
to slide his fingers down along her sides, rolling the edge of
her underpants as he did so, letting them half-roll, half-slide
down over her hips, past her thighs. Without looking at her
body, but his eyes steadily on her face, he walked over to
the chair and carefully placed the underpants on top of the
other garments. He walked back to her, this time standing a
foot or two away. Then he reached out his hands and stroked
her hair, around her neck, along her cheekbones, touching
his fingers to her forehead, her eyes, her nose, her lips. He
brought his hands down the length of her arms and up again,
then along her shoulders to her breasts, touching her nipples
gently between his fingers. She smiled as she moved, twisted
her body, her mouth opening in satisfaction, as if to say, "I
can't help moving. I don't want to, but I do want to."

She breathed heavily, lifting her breasts out toward him,
and even as she did so his hands went along the soft part of
her stomach, his fingers twined around her hips, and then
he brought his palms together fully, up along her thighs
until they joined in the stiff, curled hair. He let the sides of
his thumbs and fingers work tightly toward her vagina and
felt its hot moistness as she moved and turned her hips to
accommodate the feeling of his hands. He bent on one knee,
touched her thighs with his lips, placed his mouth against
the springy hair, brown and full as he saw it for the first time,
and pressed his lips hard against the rounded lips inside
her body, gently kissed her naval as she giggled, moved his
mouth slowly against her body, up to her diaphragm, kissed
each nipple softly, his tongue leaving a wetness, her body

curling in pleasure, a light, moaning "ooh" coming from her lips. He touched his tongue to each ear, along the back of her neck, then with closed lips lightly kissed her forehead, her eyes, and with a culminating fullness pressed against her lips.

Their bodies seemed to teeter in space for a moment, reaching out at odd angles away from each other, only their mouths touching, and then slowly, each knowing what the other knew, they brought their bodies together. They didn't need words as he lifted her and carried her to the bed. She lay there, body open, her arms wide, waiting, as he took pains not to rush as he undid his clothes and placed them next to hers by the chair. He lay on the bed next to her, rolling his hands over her body now, against her breasts, between her thighs, across her back and neck. She reached over and began to touch his body, his back, his chest, across his hips until she brought her hands together tightly, holding and pressing his erect penis. Slowly, slowly, they continued, almost as if it were movement in slow motion, each action in fractions, every moment to last the maximum time, to have the maximum effect. He put his mouth on her breast and sucked at her nipple, and as she began to squirm and roll against him, he withdrew his mouth. "Gentle, gentle," he whispered, more to remind himself than her. He put his mouth more gently on the other nipple, licked at it until her body began to move upward in an arc toward him, seeking more depth of his touch. He held her close and lay her back gently on the sheet. He let his body roll over onto hers, bringing their faces close to one another. He kissed her full on the mouth, let his lips remain there even as his hands touched along the sides of her body and his fingers stroked inside her thighs. She opened her thighs, began to arch her back, pulling her knees back, her buttocks lifting slightly at an angle. "Come in," she said. "Please come in."

He felt the hairs of his body tingle against hers, felt his penis glide through the mass of springy, curled hair, slide between her legs that contracted to hold him there. He lifted himself slightly and with his hands guided his penis to the tight passage within her. He kept his balance, lifting himself above her so as not to bring the force of weight of his body too strongly onto hers, and slowly, carefully let his penis push into her, at first amost imperceptibly, then as it grew moist and wet, with short, restrained thrusts, gradually moving forward a fraction of an inch with each thrust.

Jeanine held her arms tight around his back. He kept his face close to hers, his lips full on hers, stopping only for short moments to breathe in deep draughts of air. Suddenly the passage grew smoother, seemingly wider as he felt her virginity gushing out onto him and onto the sheet beneath them, his body entering more deeply into hers. He let himself be carried along with an increasing rhythm, with longer strokes. Suddenly she pinched hard into the small of his back and her body tightened. "Oh, not too hard," she gasped. He stopped, not altogether, but long enough to hold his body in control, and he resumed slow, short movements, barely sliding back and forth against her and in her.

"I'm sorry," he said. "I forgot for the moment. As if this were not the first time, but something we had been doing all our lives."

"Don't be sorry," she said. "It wouldn't have hurt if we had been doing this all our lives. As we should have been."

"I feel myself getting closer and closer to a completion of fullness with you," he said.

"Oh, I wish it were already," Jeanine answered. "Little by little, a little more, it will come." She paused a moment. "You didn't hurt me. Really, you didn't."

Gradually he felt a smoother friction, and controlling the depth and speed of his thrust went further and further inside of her. Soon he found a flowing rhythm again and began to relax his body on top of hers, feeling the pools of sweat as their stomachs touched, feeling a delight in the mixing of their bodies as he slid along the top of her and at the same time slid so easily now inside of her.

"It's all right now," she said. "It's good now."

Her body began to move in rhythm with his, her breasts heaving up toward him and away again, her buttocks twisting and rising and falling at the same time. Now their lips were separated and her mouth opened and closed in steady short gasps, the gasps becoming louder and fuller. Walter felt his own body begin to lose control and shivers begin to shoot through him, his anal muscles contracting, trying to hold back his release, to keep himself longer inside of her.

Their bodies were moving together now in steady, increasingly faster rhythm, the sounds from their throats getting louder and more abandoned, his body thumping down onto hers, the sweat rolling onto them and between them and off of them.

"Oh, darling, oh, darling," Jeanine began to moan. "Deeper, deeper."

Walter looked at the woman beneath him now. He wondered at the slightness of her body, the thin wisp of a girl-woman, yielding all the physical being of herself to him. She seemed so fragile, as if she might shatter if he used her roughly. She seemed to sense his thoughts.

"Don't be afraid," she said. "Let yourself go. Let yourself be you."

"If only I could," thought Walter. "If only I could." And then he ceased thinking and moved deeper and fuller than he ever had before. Someplace from within him came a yearning and strength and a freedom that he had not known existed and he melted into a physical love with the woman under him, thrusting all of himself into her, not thinking of her, not thinking of himself, but using whatever there was that they were sharing between them for his own immediate emotional and physical fulfillment. He could hear the high-pitched half-screams coming from her mouth and heard himself shouting in involuntary deep, low tones. And then he half-moaned, half-cried, and at the same moment felt Jeanine's fingers pull deep into his back and her voice cried out, "Oh, my God, oh, my God," and her body arched up, carrying him with it, and then suddenly she dropped back and he grew limp inside of her and they both collapsed into a pool of wetness. They smelled all around them the sweet odor of love.

For a long time, how long they couldn't guess, they lay there, clasped to one another, as one physical being. Then he rolled off her, lay on his back next to her. For a brief moment he deliberately caught his breath, tried to regain his normal breathing. He turned on his side, propped himself on an elbow, patted her hair and her face with one hand.

"I love you," he said. "I don't know why I have to say it," he added, "you must already know it."

"Yes, I do," she said. "I love you, too," she added. "Although I don't know why I have to say it, either."

They smiled at each other's understanding and with the little strength that gradually began to return to them giggled to each other, pulled each other close and kissed. Walter sat up and looked down to the bedding tangled beneath them.

"Frau Ritter is going to think that I am shaving in bed," he said.

Jeanine looked down at the blobs and smears of red all over the center of the bed. "Oh, my, what will she say?" Jeanine got up, very businesslike, shooed Walter off the bed. "I had better fix this right away."

"What are you going to do?

"Wash it out with cold water. Perhaps it will be almost dry by morning."

"Nothing is going to be dry by the time we leave in the morning," he said, smiling.

"Oh, I know that," she said, slipping on Walter's robe and carrying the folded-up sheet to the door, looking down the hall, seeing no one, and walking with it to the bathroom.

Jeanine seemed almost shy when she returned.

"Are you all right?," Walter asked.

"Lovely," she smiled in answer. "Never lovelier."

She stretched the washed sheet from across the top of a chair to the bureau, where she wedged a corner into the top drawer. Her body moved with complete relaxation across the room, then to Walter on the bed. Walter watched her body as she removed the robe, then at her face as he knew she was watching him looking. He half-expected to see embarrassment or at least reticence on her face. He felt warm to see wide-open eyes, staring at him with a fullness and pleasure of being.

"This is where I belong, how I belong, and with the man I belong," she said.

He held her close in his arms, sensing all the parts of his body as he felt the parts of her body against him, and he consciously waited for a tingling in his loins, anxious to find completion with her again. She looked up at him, not moving her body away, but her face reflecting once more what had seemed to him shyness when she reentered the room a few moments before.

"What is it, Jeanine?"

"I'm almost afraid to say. And yet I have been looking forward for weeks and weeks for the pleasure I would have the moment I could tell you."

"You've already told me."

Her eyes narrowed, as if she had been caught in an indiscretion. "Oh?," she asked simply, without implication.

"Yes. You've told me. And now I'll tell you. It's no longer a secret. He put his mouth close to her ear and whispered "I love you."

Jeanine laughed a delighted "ooh," and pulled his face toward hers, kissed him full on the lips, then again and again and again, all over his face.

"You silly, wonderful, virile man. I love you." Then she grew silent again. After a moment: "No, Walter, I cannot put it off. I must tell you."

His face grew serious. He pitched his voice low, gave it a slow, worried quality. "I knew it all along, what you're going to tell me."

She smiled. "You're teasing."

"No. I knew it all along. You're not only married, but you have two children hidden in the attic of your house, you never got a divorce from your husband and your lover is a captain in the S.S." He hastily corrected himself as he saw the look of game-playing turn to distaste in her mouth. "No, I'm sorry," he said. "That last part wasn't funny."

"For a moment, let's not play. I must be serious," she said.

Walter wondered if this is how all the people he had ever known had felt about him when he insisted on being serious when the others, for reasons he could not fathom, sometimes wanted to play games that to him seemed childish and irresponsible. "But who gives a damn," he muttered to himself. "If its irresponsibility, then I am irresponsible. But oh, what a freedom in just being myself." He turned to Jeanine in understanding.

"Yes, we shall be serious."

"Do you know who I am? I mean truly who I am?," she asked

"If you mean, do I know that I love you and that you are the person I love, then I know who you are. But that is not what you mean and so I don't know who you are." Then, after a pause: "But you need not tell me anything."

"I have to. Because it is important to you." She moved a bit away from him now, lay on her back. Walter turned on his side, propped himself up on an elbow so that they could see each other as they talked.

"For weeks now," Jeanine said, "I have been hoping the time would come when someone would say to you, come, here is the anti-Nazi underground, here is your chance to fight Hitler, here is your chance to escape. And I have so anticipated the look on your face when those words would be said."

Walter sat up. He pulled the blanket up from the foot of the bed and covered the lower part of his body. He suddenly felt exposed. Then, looking at Jeanine, he pulled the blanket up over her, too, until it reached her shoulders. He deliberately remained quiet. After a few seconds Jeanine continued.

"I thought perhaps you knew all the time. Did you?"

Walter forced a laugh, more to create a reality of his own being from the strange silence that was within him than because of any amusement.

"I felt it," he said. "In a way I am shocked, but I am not surprised." He relaxed now, lay back on the bed. "Did you know about me all the time?," he asked.

"From Frau Ritter," Jeanine answered.

Walter sat up even straighter. "Of course, of course," he exclaimed. "How stupid I have been. An elephant in front of me and I thought it was a mouse." Now he laughed in bitter amusement at his own lack of perspicacity. "Frau Ritter. That explains so many things." He turned to Jeanine. "Do you know my real name?"

"Walter Penmann," she answered. "Professor of Philosophy at Heidelberg University. Wife Phillipa Kohn, transported to Auschwitz. No report on her since departure." And then, without pause so that there could be no mistaking her intent, "But Johann . . . Walter. . . "

"Johann, now," he corrected. "Johann is the person you have loved and who loves you. We'll keep it that way."

Jeanine smiled. "Johann . . . it was truly you I fell in love with. I was not playing games with you. I meant all we did and all we felt. I must tell you that I did not plan it that way. Shortly after you arrived, Frau Ritter informed us about you and I was told to find out who you are and whether it would be safe to make you one of us. At first I did have an ulterior motive. But it did not last long. Perhaps it was even the first time I came to see Frau Ritter and we didn't speak, perhaps it was even then that I knew I was in love with you. I only hope you can forgive what may seem like a deception to you."

Walter thought a moment. "No, I understand. In a way, I have been practicing a deception, too, not telling you who I really was, although you already knew."

"Part of me knew. But that part was set aside when I was with you. I only knew Johann Becher, the man who exists now, to me, for me. Do you understand?"

"Of course I understand." He pulled Jeanine to him again, holding her tight and close. Now he could feel free with her again, even moreso than before because now even the secret of his true identity was something shared between them.

"Why do you tell me now?," he asked. "Is something about to happen? Has the time come to tell me that I am accepted, that I will be helped to escape?"

"Yes. And soon." She said the words sadly, her face worried. "Tomorrow night. There are several of us who need to move into France to work with the underground there in setting up lines of supply and escape routes. On the way to the border there is one important task. In Heidelberg. To help the escape of several underground leaders there. We need your help because you know Heidelberg better than any of us here. Once this plan is executed, some of us, you included if you wish, will be able to continue on the way to France."

"Are you going?," Walter asked.

"I don't want to go. I think I can do more here."

"Are you going?"

"They say that I am becoming too well known. That the S.S. may suspect me soon. That I will have to go."

"Then I will go, too. But I want you to understand, Jeanine, that there is something more important to me now than my political beliefs. You. You have given me a rebirth of life that in my wildest dreams I could not have imagined existed. And I cannot give that up, and not giving that up, I cannot give you up." He paused. "You see," he laughed, "what a selfish person you have made me."

"And you see what a selfish person you have made me," she answered. "I would die not being with you, no matter what the reason."

They lay clasped together, Walter feeling the energy throb through him again, felt his pelvis growing hot against Jeanine's. He was ready to make love again. Jeanine knew this, too, pushed against him, rubbed her body against him. Then suddenly she sat up. He reached for her, attempted to put her gently onto the bed beneath him, but she squirmed away.

"Oh, you university professors. You intellectuals. Pretending to make love when all you know is to lie on top of a girl and go through the motions of something you read in a textbook."

Her mouth was serious, but her eyes were laughing. Nevertheless, Walter felt a tinge of anger within him. Maybe the teasing was too close to the truth? He reached over, placed a hand on her breast, felt for the nipple.

"You seemed to like what I gave you before," he said.

She pushed his hand away and moved to the other side of the bed.

"Well, after all this time with you and all the money you've spent on me," she said, "I thought I owed you something." The laugh stayed on her narrowly opened lips, contrasting with the fullness of warmth and sparkle in her eyes.

He tried to match her game-playing, but his growing flushed anger prevented him from reaching the sharpness of her tone and gave him only heavy, flat defenses.

"You owe me nothing. In fact, proper business arrangements indicate that I owe you something. I will check my wallet and if you will just let me know your fee . . . ."

He hoped, he felt that she would accept the words as a joke. Somehow, inside, her words had upset him, as if there were really some truth in what she was saying. But he had done it well, hadn't he?, he asked himself. He was virile, he had felt a freedom he had never felt before. Was there more? Could there be more? Even more?

"Oh, I couldn't accept a fee from you. An impoverished writer? You couldn't afford me? Not at the prices I get from my regular customers."

She said it almost as if it were true and Walter had to look at the sheet draped between the chair and bureau to convince himself that it wasn't true. She had trumped him.

"In fact," she said flippantly, "I must take time now to figure out who I shall have my next affair with. There is one boy who I have known for some years, who I grew up with, who I've frequently thought of sleeping with. I must arrange it with him next week. And that older man—about your age, I should say—who picked me up on the street in his car a few months ago and who gives me presents and just begs me to sleep with him. I must certainly have an affair with him. He tells me he loves me, and needs me. Isn't it nice to be loved and needed."

Walter felt his shoulders tense and his arms grow rigid. He began to breathe deeply. He wasn't sure if it was in anger or jealousy. His joke had backfired and he didn't want the game to continue.

"But of course," Jeanine continued, now standing at the side of the bed, facing him, her breasts and thighs bouncing and swaying back and forth in front of him at eye level, "you university professors don't need me. You have your books. But this man, why I think he might even rape me some time when I'm with him, if I offer him the least encouragement. But you wouldn't do that, would you? You're too refined for that. You wouldn't know how."

"I don't have to rape you," Walter muttered, lunging for her as if to prove his masculinity. "I will show you how to make love."

She laughed as she pulled from his grasp. "Naughty, naughty," she said, "musn't be so fierce. You might upset your equilibrium. Why, what would all of the professors in their white collars and ties think of you if you acted so beastly?"

Walter wanted to strike out at her. He felt tears in his eyes, anger shaking him, a tightness and tenseness surging through him, knowing that what she said was true, feeling that he wanted to take her and beat her and shake her and thrust his penis so far and full and hard into her that she would scream with an anger of her own.

I can't act like that, he thought. It's not possible. That is for beasts. I cannot hurt anyone, no less this woman who I love.

"Why do you hesitate?," she teased. "Afraid of me? Afraid that you might find out you are a man? Really a man? Or really not a man?"

Walter stopped thinking. If he had any thought at all, it was "God damn it, the hell with it, I'll do what I want to do, and to hell with everything."

He got up from the bed with a rush. "You bitch," he shouted to her, "you rotten, beautiful, wonderful bitch." He grabbed her wrists and turned her body toward him.

The mocking smile was still on her face, the fullness in her eyes unchanged. Walter didn't consider how he might look. For that moment he just felt. He kissed her mouth, bit into her lip, bit at her ears, bit his teeth into the white of her nipples until she yelled, then lifted her and threw her onto the bed, threw himself onto her with wildness, crashing his body onto her, thrusting his penis deep into her until once more she screamed, the sounds and yells giving him a satisfaction that he heard and felt and didn't believe. It was if he were both himself and someone else, divorced from the being that for more than 35 years had been Walter Penmann. Suddenly he stopped his thrusts and with a smile of conquest and satisfaction on his face pulled himself from her.

"Did you want something, little girl?," he asked, with mock bitterness. "Were you looking for a man, did you say?"

Her face was wreathed in smiles, her chest heaving to catch its breath. "Yes, I want something," she gasped, her fingers clinging to the sides of his back, trying to pull him down. "Do you know where I can find a man, a real man?"

"To do what?," he countered. "To climb on top of you and rape you? Any man will do for that. To make love to you, you need a special man."

She was ready now. "Yes, a special man. Where can I find one?"

"To do what?"

"To fill me with love and turn my world upside down."

Walter laughed in a full, deep, open-throated bass. "To turn your world upside down? Really? Is that what you want?" He grabbed her ankles and pulled her off the bed, thrusting her feet high in the air in front of him, her body dangling in front of him, her hair flowing down and almost touching the ground. He pulled her, roughly, easily, whatever way he felt, around to the aide of the bed where the carpet was, pulled her body close to him, moved his hands down to her knees, still holding her body upside down, pulled her legs apart, bent over and thrust his penis into her, and with the exultant shouts of the barbarian hun pillaging the virginal treasures of the temples, pulled her body like a toy meant to serve his pleasures, into him and out, walking around the room, using her for the moment, caring nothing but for his instant emotional and physical satisfaction.

Jeanine gasped and cried and moaned as her body was pulled repeatedly toward him, his penis plunging again and again deep into her. She twisted and squirmed and writhed in the air in front of him as a marionette on a string being used for some perverted unrealistic purpose. In one continuous movement he swung her legs high and out from him, her body plunging onto the bed, falling with abandon. She lay there, her legs and arms stretched out, open and loose, unable to move of their own will. He leaped onto her, thrusting himself inside of her again, felt her hands and arms press with all their strength around his back, tightened his legs around her, rolled with her over and over on the bed, fell together, she on top of him, onto the floor, their physical union remaining tight and together. He began to push her body, now resting on top of his, into a sitting position on top of him.

"I can't," she muttered. But her body responded, as if by rote.

"You damned well will," he said. She moved into position on top of him. "Now you work," he commanded. She began to slide and move on top of him. He saw her face begin to contort as he lay back, his hands folded at the back of his head, his face smiling in supreme satisfaction. Then, as she began to move on him with ever increasing rhythm and her mouth began to open and shut with low moans, he pushed her off, pulled away from her.

"Do you want to call that friend now?," he asked. "That boy you grew up with. Or that pickup from the street? Since you didn't think the man you wanted was here."

"Oh, please, oh, please," she moaned, moving toward him. Without a word and with a firm gentleness he lifted her, carried her to the bed, placed her beneath him, and in unspoken understanding they moved in rhythm together, reaching a climax of closeness and warmth and satisfaction that was beyond their intellectual comprehension as human beings.

They didn't talk much more that night. They held each other in each other's arms, snatching bits of sleep, feeling for each other in the darkness, thrice more meeting each other's physical and emotional needs in the act of love.

Walter was awake, staring at the ceiling with no thoughts at all, watching the reflected rays of the sun gradually move across and light up the dark patches of unpainted plaster on the ceiling, following the light as it moved toward the molding at the other end of the room and oddly contemplating the evenness of the pattern it might make. Jeanine turned, her hair brushing against his face, being pulled back by her hands, and her warm lips gently touching his.

"Good morning, my love."

"Good morning, my love."

"How long have I been sleeping?"

"A half-hour. A long time," Walter said.

"Is that all?"

"It's not much more than that since the last time," he said.

She moved her hand down along his thighs, felt his body. "Are you ready for more?"

He laughed without moving. "I'll be lucky if I can climb out of bed without help."

"But I don't want you out of bed. I like you in bed," she
said.

He pulled her to him, cradled her down on his chest, in
his arms.

"What have you done to me, young lady?"

"I'm not a young lady. I told you I was ageless?"

"Yes, I know. You are." He sighed. "Where did you learn
all that?"

"I've known it for centuries. I was just waiting for you to
bring it out."

"You really are a witch, aren't you?"

She pushed her head into his chest, snuggled close
against him. "Oh, Johann. I do love you."

"Not Johann. Walter."

She smiled, didn't move. "Oh?"

"Didn't you know? For the first time in his life, Walter
has come alive. He was there all the time, but I didn't know.
Nobody knew. You brought out the real Walter. So now he
can use his own name and be his own being. It's me with
you, Walter with you, whoever he is, whatever he is, but
him. Me."

She turned her face toward his and kissed him softly. "I'm
glad."

"I wish I could tell you, Jeanine, what I feel for you. It's
not just a love, it's something I can't describe. It's a dependency on you to make me what I really am. What I never
really knew or even dreamt existed within me. My inner self.
A kind of glory and power and fire that was constrained. My
intellectualism or whatever, it doesn't matter, constrained
me. Now I feel like the flower whose seed has blown from
a cave and found the sun and the rain and uncovers its head
and breasts and belly and blossoms outward to the world and
to itself. And each time tonight there was more and more, a
growing and learning."

"And each time it will be more and more. Oh, Walter, I am so grateful to you. And I love you so. I thought that perhaps you would be the teacher and I the pupil, on different levels, and in a sense this is true. But that we are growing and learning together makes our love that much more, that much stronger."

Walter darted up as a knock sounded on the door.

"It is I, Frau Ritter."

"I . . . just a moment, Frau Ritter," Walter called.

"It is all right . . .," she hesitated a moment, "Herr Becher."

Walter looked at Jeanine.

"She knows who you really are," she nodded to him.

"I wanted to tell you," Frau Ritter continued through the door, "that breakfast is ready for you. Come down as soon as you can." Then, with only momentary hesitation: "Both of you."

Frau Ritter was talkative at the breakfast table. "I'm an expert on love, as I told you," she chattered at Walter. "I knew all along. I knew from the beginning. Even an outsider can feel those things if they have any sensitivity. And I'm pleased for you, for both of you. In these times it is important that we have something of the goodness and fullness of life since everything else is so rotten and gangrenous in our country."

After breakfast Jeanine went to her home, returned in less than an hour with a small traveling bag. "Only the essentials," she said. Nothing to slow one down in the event one has to run, nothing to reveal anything in the event the bag is lost."

Walter obtained a similar small bag, almost like a briefcase, from Frau Ritter, put in only a few essentials. He gave Frau Ritter his manuscript on Kant.

"If there is anything such as a life's work for a professor, this is my life's work. There is much to be done on it yet, but someday it will be an important document."

"I understand," she said. "I will take care of it."

He gave her his other important goods and documents and writings to store for him.

"Your room will remain as is for a while," Frau Ritter said. "In case anyone comes, as far as I know you are still residing here. What you do by day and by night, when they do not find you in, is not my business. I can't keep track of the business doings or the nighttime amusements of all of my roomers."

Walter and Jeanine spent the afternoon and evening in the room. Their love was quietly intense as though they were trying to find the depths of each other with deliberate care, to give and take as fully as possible, all of each other, in anticipation of the unknown and the uncertainty of the days that were to follow. It was 11 o'clock at night when Frau Ritter knocked at the door. Walter opened it and she stood a moment in the dark, closed it and came close to them.

"They are here. The car is parked around the corner, on Schleystrasse. It is time for you to leave. Jeanine will go to the car." Then, with a smile, pointedly using his pseudonym, "Johann will walk a few blocks to Weberstrasse where the car will drive and where he will join you." She walked to the door, stopped. "Now, I shall not see you again. For a long time," she added, to avoid the feeling of finality. "Good luck."

Jeanine ran to her, hugged her closely. "I don't have to tell you, Frau Ritter, what you have meant to me. I shall never forget you."

"Of course you shan't. For I shall see you before too long. This monstrous thing that has taken the conscience and loyalty of most of our people will pass." Then, in a determined tone, "we will make it pass."

Walter shook hands with her.

"I thank you, Frau Ritter. I am grateful to you for my life. In many ways."

"I understand," she acknowledged.

He held her hand a moment, then impulsively leaned over and kissed her on the cheek.

She laughed, pleased. "That makes it all worth while." She quickly opened and closed the door behind them and they were gone.

Chapter XVII

There were three others in the car besides Jeanine when Walter joined them. Walter was given no names.

"You are new at this," the man who sat in the back seat with them said. "It is easier for you and safer for us if you cannot talk, if you honestly do not know who we are in case of some unfortunate eventuality."

He was a large man with a large belly who looked as though he ought to be behind the counter of a butcher shop, chatting pleasantly with his customers about the continued triumphs of the Third Reich while drinking from a bottomless bottle of beer. But his manner was gruff, unsmiling, almost sad in its urgent efficiency.

"You call me Max," he said. "That is all you need to know about me."

The two men in the front seat said little, other than acknowledging Walter's entrance and conversing with each other from time to time about the road, the directions, and the trip to Heidelberg. They were both thin, in their forties or fifties, with slight, bristling mustaches. They could have been twins, Walter thought, but attributed this impression more to their similarity in behavior than to any genetic conclusion.

Walter recognized the route most of the time along the main roads on the east bank of the Rhine except for detours taken every time they came close to a village or town. Sometimes their detour would last for many miles, continuing over dirt country roads and bumping over cow paths at ten or fifteen kilometers an hour before the car emerged again at the edge of the Rhine River. The two men in the front seat consulted a hand drawn map frequently, the one on the right pointing out to the driver specially-marked warnings that indicated the need for a detour and noting the roads that were considered safe. Once, as they drove through a village—Walter did not recognize which one—they found themselves approaching an S.S. patrol car cruising slowly along in front of them. Unless they slowed down to a suspiciously slow speed, they would have to pass it. There was no place to turn off. They would overtake the patrol car before they reached the next cross street. Max quickly ordered the driver to stop in front of a two story building on the right hand side in the middle of the block. Walter noted that the building seemed to contain a number of apartments. The S.S. car noticed them, stopped, began to back up.

"Schnell," Max said. "We have just come from a party and we're going in to wake some friends to have another party."

Walter looked at his watch. It was 2 A.M.

With Max walking in front singing loudly, the other two men swaying with their arms around each other, muttering, interspersing their language with profanity, Walter and Jeanine held tightly to each other, stopping every other moment to kiss and touch each other. As if in a drunken oblivion and not aware that they were in public, they all walked unsteadily to the front door of the apartment house.

The S.S. car had drawn alongside theirs by now, an S.S. man leaning out of the window, a flashlight in his hand.

A man poked his head out of the first floor window of the building.

"Quiet. We are decent people here. Go home, you drunken fools."

Max stopped, walked deliberately up to the window in pretended surprise and annoyance at the man's objections. "We come from celebrating another glorious victory for our Fuhrer and Our Fatherland. And we shall continue with our friends upstairs. They appreciate their country. Don't you want to join us in celebrating."

He flashed his arm up toward the man. "Heil Hitler."

He turned toward the others, facing the S.S. car as he did so. "Heil Hitler." His colleagues answered him with arm salutes in uncoordinated unison, "Heil Hitler."

The man in the window stared at them, saw the S.S. car, hesitated a moment, weakly raised his arm, muttered "Heil Hitler" and withdrew, closing the window behind him with a loud slam.

The S.S. men laughed, watched Walter and Jeanine fondling each other, not paying attention to Max and the other two as they forced the front door open. The S.S. men kept their eyes on Walter and Jeanine as they half-stumbled into the open doorway and seemed to disappear upstairs. Inside the darkened hallway Walter heard the S.S. men laugh again and then heard the sound of their car driving away.

They waited several minutes. Then the driver of their car walked out, started slowly up the street, came back in less than a minute. He motioned for them to get back in the car. They walked slowly and quietly. The driver backed down the street, took the first cross avenue east, and disappeared into a myriad of dirt farm roads, after an hour or so finally returning to a main road near the Rhine again.

They continued without further incident. Max explained Walter's purpose.

"We have had an underground developing in Heidelberg over the past few months, mainly to harass the officials and perhaps provoke some of the university community into at least passive resistance to the Nazis. If even a few persons in the community made some public indication of non-cooperation with the transports or if only a few gave some help to the Jews who are trying to avoid going to the concentration camps, this would give hope to the others. But I am afraid we have failed."

Walter nodded his head, as if in agreement. Max looked at him, expecting an explanation.

"I know," Walter said. "I know the fear. Somehow those who should be most understanding of the differences between democracy and fascism are the first to capitulate. We had a small group at the university, but we were virtually alone, especially after our first public protest ended in defeat . . . and death for many. Most of the faculty were content to do nothing."

"The leaders of the underground there are now known," Max said. "If they are captured it would mean whatever tortures were necessary to get the names of others. So we must get them out. They are in hiding. I have the addresses " he pointed to his head "up here, but I don't know Heidelberg that well. None of us here do. We expect you to guide us in the most inconspicuous manner to the right places. Willy"— he pointed to the passenger in the front seat—"and I will stay in Heidelberg. We will merely be visiting friends and will make our way back to Cologne in a few days. But that is not your concern. "Hans"—he pointed to the driver—"will stay with you. Jeanine and you will act as you did so expertly earlier. As lovers. This will give you some protection against being on the streets during the daytime, a protection which you would not have if you were by yourself."

Walter glanced at Jeanine. Her eyes were smiling at the wisdom of Max's instructions. Max paused a moment, changed the tone of his voice.

"You know that Jeanine must get out of the country?"

Walter nodded.

Max continued. "The three from Heidelberg will join you in the car. Hans knows the route from there. First to Stuttgart and eventually across the border near Strasbourg. I hope you are prepared to walk. And maybe run. Perhaps thirty kilometers or more."

Walter nodded again. There was no further need for instructions.

They reached Heidelberg at eight in the morning with no further incidents, mingling with the cars driving into the city for business or pleasure purposes, becoming anonymous in the early morning congestion of city traffic. Hans parked the car in the center of the city.

"We make our first pickup at two this afternoon," Max told them. "You can move around the city, but protect yourselves. Melt into the community. Have breakfast, have lunch. Go to a kino, walk through the department stores, but act always as if you have a purpose, as if you are on some business or pleasure errand. Do not loiter, do not arouse suspicion. You, Johann, be especially careful. You may be seen by people who know you."

"They might not recognize me. I had a beard. I don't think they would recognize me," Walter was quick to inter-ject.

"Be careful, anyway," Max said. "Having Jeanine with you will be a decoy. Do not leave each other's side for a mo-ment."

Walter and Jeanine looked at each other again, amused by the ludicrousness of any other possibility.

"Be here at ten minutes to two. Ten minutes to two exactly."

They went their separate ways.

"Come," Walter said, taking Jeanine's hand. "Let me show you my city." With trepidation he walked with her through the business section, pointing out the bierstubes, which ones were for which student groups, explaining the political orientations of the years previous when groups of all shades of opinion chose their individual eating and drinking places.

"But now it's all the same," Walter said. "One people, one belief."

They walked past the university, Walter deliberately moving at a brisk pace on the far side of the street, attempting not to seem interested in the academic buildings, afraid to stop and look with any feeling of nostalgia. They finished circling several blocks of the university and were about to return to the center of town.

"I would like to see your house, where you lived," Jeanine said.

Walter hesitated. "I don't think so. I don't think you should."

"It will remind you of your wife?"

"Of course."

"I know. That's why I think we should go there. I don't want you to feel that I am taking you from her. I want you to feel only that I am adding something to your life that no one else could add. She is one part of your life. I am another part."

"I will have guilt feelings," Walter said. "But you are right. And I would like to see it again."

They walked past his house, staying on the other side of the street. Nothing had changed. The shrubbery on the sides of the narrow walk leading up the door was a bit overgrown. The long window curtain in the front room was pulled down.

He wondered whether the house was empty or whether any-one lived there now. He squinted to see if there was a name under the bell on the side of the front door. He made out the letters, suddenly squeezed hard on Jeanine's hand, then let go, pulled out his handkerchief even as he continued to walk, wiped his face, poked the handkerchief at his eyes.

"My God, my God," he muttered. Then, after a moment, he took Jeanine's hand again, feeling what seemed to be a special warmth and dryness in her hand, realizing that it was only the sudden contrast with the wet dampness of his.

"Peter Lewald," he muttered to himself, then, feeling he ought to explain, said it louder to Jeanine. "Peter Lewald, he is now occupying my house. He was a young professor in my department. A fearful, insecure, weak young man. He was one of the first to give in. I remember a hearing—it seems so many years ago now—where he was frightened that he would be accused of something and began to give names. Of some of his professors. People who were completely innocent of anything. But they needed names and he gave them. I don't know what happened to his professors. Concentration camps, probably. But he had made it easier for himself. Probably chairman of the department now, I suppose." He thought a moment. "They couldn't do that," he muttered, half to him-self. "No," he admitted out loud, "that is precisely what they would do."

They walked for another few blocks, Walter slowly regaining his calm. As he walked hand in hand with Jeanine, he looked straight ahead, did not look at her, felt only the feminine hand in his. He thought of Phillipa. How many times had he walked with her, hand in hand? Had they ever walked hand in hand? They must have, he thought, but he couldn't remember a single instance. His chest began to hurt. He felt for Phillipa, wondered where she was, wondered if she were alive, wondered what physical and psychological degradation she was undergoing if she were still alive. He thought of the moments of love with her, the moments of peace and satisfaction, the rare moments when he had from her what seemed like a love and confidence that made him feel whole and strong. He thought of the early months of their marriage. Even the later years. There was a security, if nothing else. He thought how fine it would be if nothing had changed, if he turned a corner, looked about and saw Phillipa next to him, and they would walk home and sit and talk for a while and he would prepare his class lesson for the following morning and then they would get ready for dinner and an evening at a concert or a play or a reception. He remembered the parties of the early years of their marriage, the parties when he was the center of intellectual attention. He smiled to himself in satisfaction.

"I'm glad that something pleases you."

Jeanine's words brought him out of his dream world.

He smiled to her now. "You please me," he said, putting the daydream thoughts away. He pointed ahead. "About a half-kilometer ahead is a woods. I sometimes used to walk there by myself. It's a thick woods. Hardly anybody else ever walks there, except the students. But that is mainly in the evening." He looked at his watch. "It's not yet noon. We have time."

They walked over a small dirt road, turned down a narrow path, overgrown and blocked with the branches of young trees and thick bushes. They crossed a small stream, turned up an incline. Walter held Jeanine tight by one hand, leading the way, pulling her up the slope at times, at other times standing to one side and holding aside the tangled branches and brambles so she could get through. At the top of the small hill he stopped. The ground was level and they could look around from the apex and see the downward slope around them.

"On top of the world," Walter said. He gathered dry leaves from the ground, pulled several thick leaved branches from the trees, spread them out on the ground. "Better than a man-made pillow," he said. Without a word, like children in a garden of Eden, they took off the coverings of society, faced each other bare, standing on the leaves. Gently they lay down together, rolled into each other's arms. They stared up at the surrounding trees, the green leaves, the red-berried bushes poking through the foliage, the patches of blue sky showering streams of sunlight on their bodies.

They lay together a long time without moving.

"I have never felt so peaceful," Walter said.

"Nor I," Jeanine said. Why do people make love in bed, in a closed room, in the dark? It's as if they have something to hide, something to constrict, rather than to open themselves fully to nature and to the world!"

Walter loved her gently and fully. He put his whole being into her and felt a completeness in return. It was an equilibrium with nature, smooth, continuous, growing, moving through an unending cycle of fulfillment.

"I could stay this way forever," Jeanine said.

"This is forever," Walter said. "This is the closest to forever that any man or woman has ever come or will ever come."

They lay without a word, only their fingertips touching side by side, their bodies open to the freedom of the universe.

"This is like that day, so long ago it seems, of that picnic by the Rhine," Jeanine said. "That first one."

"I remember how we walked for a long time without a word. I kept wanting to say something, trying to say something, thinking I ought to say something. But I really didn't have to," Walter added.

"We knew, both of us, what kind of love we had, didn't we?," Jeanine said. "I really didn't have to tell you I loved you. We neither one of us had to say it. We understood."

"We knew it," Walter added. "As in the hours when we knew each other's thoughts only by the touch of our hands or the sound of our footsteps down a darkened street or hearing each other breathing, lying side by side. As we know it now. As we shall always know it."

He reached toward her and at the same moment she came to him and they fused their love tightly, once more as if it were the last time, as if they had to become so much a part of each other that nothing could ever pry them apart.

They returned to the car at precisely ten minutes to two. Max gave Walter an address not far from the university.

"It is possible that the house may be watched, so you are to direct Hans in such a fashion that we drive past on the opposite side of the street. Then, if I say it is all right, we drive around a corner to stop in front of the house. The party will be ready and will come out the moment we stop. From there we must go immediately to this next address."

He gave Walter an address on Darmstadtstrasse, in the center of the city, the old section, where there were many student apartments.

"Why, I recognize this address," Walter said. "A student, Puzinger . . ."

"I know," Max interrupted, quieting him. He smiled now, the first time Walter had seen him show any sign of sentiment. "We checked on you, Walter. We know what you know. And we trust you. Say nothing you don't have to."

Walter gave Hans block by block directions. They were turning the corner into the street where the first address was located when Max shouted, "Straight ahead, Hans, straight ahead, don't turn." Without any indication of a change in plans Hans continued straight ahead. As they passed the cross street Walter could see several cars down the block, ostensibly ordinary civilian cars, parked near one of the houses.

"The Gestapo," Max said. "They have apparently found out. Let's try the other address, quickly. The same precaution, Walter. You too, Hans."

The street where Puzinger lived was empty. They drove slowly down the side opposite Puzinger's address. From a doorway a woman appeared and stepped into the street, in front of the car. Hans slammed on the brakes.

"Schweinhund," the woman screamed at them. "Murderers. You shouldn't be allowed to drive in the streets." She stayed close to the car, so close that Hans could not continue, and walked up to the side window. "You belong in jail, trying to run over innocent pedestrians. Why don't you go after some Jews instead of us good Germans?"

She stuck her head through the open window, whispered something quickly and hurriedly to Max. Walter could not hear all the words. Then she withdrew, started to complete her crossing of the street. "Pigs," she shouted. "I have your license number. My lawyer will sue for everything you have."

"Hochwaldstrasse, 32," Max said.

Hans turned to the back seat. "Which way?"

Walter hurriedly gave directions.

"The fastest way?," Max asked.

"Yes, so I figured," Walter said, guiding Hans through the streets.

"We may yet save two," Max explained. "The Gestapo found them too soon. One is taken. The others have gone to Hochwaldstrasse. Do you know it, Walter?"

"A quiet residential block, small houses."

"When we get there you and Jeanine go inside as if you are merely visitors. We will drive to the end of the block and wait there. Willy will get out and start walking back up the street in the event you need help."

Willy reached into his jacket pocket, took out a Luger pistol, examined it briefly and returned it to its place.

"If all goes well," Max continued, "you will pass Willy on the street, the four of you, and come to the car. I will be gone. Walter, you will direct Hans through side routes out of the city. Once out of the city, Hans has alternate roads to Stuttgart." He paused. "If there is trouble, Willy will be prepared to distract attention and perhaps give you some gunfire cover. In that case we will all, all of us, get to the car if possible and try to get out of the city. If we can't make it, we shall abandon the car downtown and strike out separately, to lose ourselves in the crowd. We depend on you, Walter, to help us elude any pursuers."

"I will try," acknowledged Walter.

"And if worst comes to worst, whoever can get to the car, get there. Anyone who cannot, he is on his own, to run and hide as best as he is able." And almost as if an afterthought, as if in assumption that it had been taken for granted all the time, "Of course, if we find trouble already existing on Hochwaldstrasse, we do not stop, but return downtown, Willy and I leave the car and the rest of you continue to Stuttgart as planned."

Hochwaldstrasse was quiet, only one car parked on the street. Number 32 was a small, two story frame house, a small garden in front, a stone fence covered with rose vines separating the side yard from its neighbor. The car stopped in front of the house. Walter and Jeanine thanked the others in clear, open voices for the ride and did not look back as the car drove off. They walked directly to the house, acting in the good humor of people come to visit friends. They knocked once and the door opened a crack. They could see part of a face peering at them.

"We're friends of Max, from Cologne," Jeanine said. The door opened a little wider.

"I'm sorry, I don't know any Max from Cologne," the face behind the door said.

"Well, we might have the wrong address," Jeanine said.

"Yes, we made an error. At first we went to Darmstadt-strasse," Walter added.

The door opened all the way.

"Who is it you are looking for?" The face and voice belonged to a thin, tall woman of perhaps fifty, now erect without suggestion of fear or defense.

A door to the right of the main entrance, a few feet into the hallway, opened.

"Come," said a voice.

Walter turned, recognized the face. "My God," he said. "My God," he ran to the door. "Is it really you? Maria, is it you?"

Maria Anneman took his hand, then embraced him.

"And is it really you?," she said. "No more beard, but I thought I knew the voice. We thought you were dead. We thought the S.S. had taken you."

Walter smiled. "Hopefully, they are not looking for me."

Maria introduced the woman who had opened the door for them. "Frau Bretthausen. A good friend. This is her house."

Jeanine interrupted. "We have no time. The car is waiting at the corner. Where is the other?"

"It is Felix Lindner," Maria said. "You remember him, Walter?"

"The quiet one," Walter said. "Is this the Heidelberg underground, all my old comrades?"

"Mostly," Maria answered. Frau Bretthausen went into an inner room. "Maybe in atonement for not having followed through as strongly as we should have when there was still time."

"No, we tried. You remember the Schardheim protest massacre." He felt the gorge of guilt and defensiveness at his own role returning.

"Or maybe it is because we so-called intellectuals should have been perceptive enough to see what was happening at the beginning," Maria said, "and now we must make up for it because so many of us didn't see."

Frau Bretthausen returned with Felix Lindner. He and Walter shook hands warmly.

Jeanine pulled Walter by the arm. "Come, let us hurry." Maria kissed Frau Bretthausen, Felix shook her hand and they all walked to the door.

"We walk slowly, openly up the street, as though we might be going on an everyday shopping tour downtown," Jeanine told them.

They opened the door and started walking. Walter got next to Maria, intending to talk with her, to question her about what had happened in Heidelberg in the time since he had left. They were no more than a few yards from the house when two cars, from opposite directions, careened around the corner in front of them.

"Keep walking," Jeanine said, "as though nothing is wrong."

From behind them they heard the screech of other cars turning the corner. The two cars in front moved in a diagonal line down the street, toward the spot where they were walking.

"Try to remain calm. Try and bluff them," Jeanine said quietly.

One of the cars reached the curb near them. A uniformed Gestapo officer pointed a pistol through the open window, another opened the door of the car on the street side and stepped out, a submachine gun in his arms.

"We know you, Anneman, Lindner. Come with us quietly. All of you are under arrest in the name of the Third Reich."

With a push at Walter, as if to give him a head start, Jeanine shouted "run," and like a flock of frightened birds they dashed toward the corner. At the same moment, now no more than ten yards away, Willy began firing his pistol at the Gestapo men. The man with the sub-machine gun grabbed at his wounded arm and dropped the weapon. The man with the pistol began firing at them. The second car had now stopped and several of the Gestapo got out and blocked the way to the corner. In back of them the two cars that had come from the other end of the street stopped and men came out of them and blocked that avenue of escape. An S.S. major began to run from that direction toward them.

"Capture them if you can," he shouted to his men. "Capture them if you can. But don't let them escape."

Walter saw Felix dart across the street, trying to reach a small alleyway between two houses. A burst of machine gun bullets sounded and Felix was thrown forward on his face, the entire back of his head, body and legs welling into a pool of blood that obliterated the visual contours of whatever was left of his human torso.

Walter saw Willy stand for a moment, firing, then saw him turn and run, then stop suddenly and sink to the ground as several shots rang out. He saw Maria rush headlong toward the S.S. men on the sidewalk in front of her. As their attention was diverted to Felix and Willy, Maria made a sudden movement of desperation, her arms flailing, her knees kicking high. For a brief moment she was past the group, then two men reached for her, ran a few steps and pulled her to the ground. In a matter of seconds, the two men, each twisting an arm behind her back, had pushed her face down into the back seat of the car. Walter could see her body stuffed onto the floor, and then heard her screams as the men, one from each side of the car, jumped with deliberate heaviness, feet first, into the back of the car and onto whatever lay in their way.

Walter and Jeanine stood transfixed, unable to do anything, with no way of escape. They turned back now, each

one thinking to get to Frau Bretthausen's house, perhaps
to make their way out through the rear. But even as they
turned together, they stopped, both hesitating to betray Frau
Bretthausen on the chance that the Gestapo did not know
which house they had come from. They hesitated just long
enough. Several of the men at their rear had now reached a
point closer to Frau Bretthausen than they were. They could
not beat them there, even provided they were not shot in the
process of trying. Then it didn't matter as two men, their
guns ready, turned up the walk and toward the house.

Walter grabbed Jeanine's arm, pulled her close to him,
said "I love you" without even looking at her, and pushed her
face forward, sprawling her in the gutter of the street. At the
same moment he began to run toward the Gestapo in front of
him who had begun to converge upon him. He stopped short,
shouting as loudly as he could, and ran part way to the men
who were walking toward him from the opposite direction.
The attention of all of the Gestapo was momentarily drawn
to this sudden strange behavior and as Walter turned and
repeated the process he saw Jeanine running across the street,
past Felix's body and toward the alley that Felix had tried
to reach. As he turned again he saw two men running across
the street after her, their pistols firing, their aim distorted by
their movement. Out of the corner of his eye he saw Jeanine
reach the entrance of the alley, caught a glimpse of her face as
she looked back and saw her disappear down the alley. Then,
in sudden exhaustion, he stopped and let himself slump to
the ground.

"Maybe she made it," he said to himself. "Dear God or
whatever you are or whatever it is, I hope she made it."

"Stehe auf," said a voice towering over him.

He started to stand, looked up and saw the uniformed
body and officer-capped face of Erich Dresser. Awkwardly,

half-up, half-crouching, he froze. It was like an impossible dream, like a perversion of the worst Kafkaesque nightmare.

He almost wanted to laugh. For a moment he was outside of himself looking on, seeing himself crouching on a sidewalk in Heidelberg, with dead bodies in the street, bodies of his friends, and seeing his old university colleague, his friend of the discussion group days, Erich Dresser, standing over him with the life and death power of an S.S. major. It was not Walter there, it could not be Walter there. It was so completely alien to everything Walter had ever thought, known, or felt. As he stood, it was with the numbness of disbelief. It was as if he no longer had any thoughts or feelings of a human being, but was some fabricated figure taking part in a ludicrous drama that happened to be taking place in real life.

Dresser slapped Walter's arms to his sides with a riding crop, slapped him across the knees, forcing him to stand straighter. Then he looked in Walter's face, hesitated, shook his head from side to side. He lowered the riding crop, seemed as if he were about to reach out and touch the prisoner in front of him, to come close to him. Then, as if he had caught himself in an unforgivable weakness, he stepped back a short pace. His voice was not quite a sharp or loud as it had been.

"You are Walter Penmann?"

"Yes, Erich. I'm Walter."

"What in God's name, Walter, are you doing here? I knew you had radical ideas, I knew your fuzzy thinking, how you had been taken in by the communists at times. But a spy, a traitor, a saboteur? I never thought it would come to that. I am sorry for you."

"It may be, Erich, that when history is finally written, I will be the true patriot."

"If we lose, yes. History always favors the victors. But if we win, no. And most assuredly, Walter, we shall win this war against Godless, atheistic communism and the Jew-run democracies."

"So it has come to this for you, Erich. A butcher's uniform." Walter pointed to the major's insignia. "A legal mandate for murder. It is you who one should be sorry for."

Dresser's face hardened. He tightened his grip on the riding crop, but did not move his hand.

"It is lucky for you that I am a sentimental person." He saw what seemed like a half-smile on Walter's face. "Oh, yes, I am. For old friends, for old colleagues. Any other enemy of the Reich would be dealt with quite harshly for what you have just said, no less done."

Walter began to speak, but Dresser hurriedly continued. "But you are overwrought. You were not the criminal type and I can understand how all this could make you say things you would not say were you in possession of your senses. Yet, Walter, you are still a criminal and must be dealt with accordingly." Dresser waved his arms to the men surrounding him.

"I will talk to the prisoner alone." They walked away. He did not have to explain his motives to his underlings.

"Believe me, Walter," he said when they were alone, "I still do think fondly of the good days we had together. As a close friend I was unhappy, of course, at your ill-advised marriage." He paused, decided to say no more of that, the implication of his words quite clear. "But we remained friends. I am disturbed now, indeed, saddened now, for it is clear that you are involved with the underground. And we must have whatever information you possess."

"I possess none," Walter said. "I met the underground only yesterday."

"Where?"

Walter hesitated. "In Cologne."

"Good. I hoped I could trust you, that you would tell the truth. We have their automobile and know it came from Cologne."

Dresser offered Walter a cigarette. Walter declined it. Dresser lit one for himself. "What information about them do you have that you can give us?'

"None. I don't even know the full names of the people I came with. They were taking me to Stuttgart to get me across the border."

"I believe you," Dresser said. He took a long puff on his cigarette. "But, unfortunately, the others at Gestapo headquarters will not. I am sorry to have to tell you this, Walter, but they will overlook no opportunity to get information. They will torture you for it."

Walter's face suddenly cringed. He had thought of capture, of death, but had not let the thought of torture cross his mind. He didn't know if he could stand it. He didn't think he could.

"And it will be worse if you have nothing to tell," Dresser continued, "because they won't believe you, and they will torture you until you say something, until you make up something that sounds believable. And then they will kill you, anyway."

Dresser paused a moment. "Terrible thing," he said, "and I regret that it must be so. But we are fighting an evil foe and in defense of our country and our way of life extremist measures are sometimes necessary."

Walter did not know what to say. He tried to think of a book or a play he might have read where the hero was in a similar situation. What had the hero done to get out of it? How had he escaped the fate worse than death? He couldn't laugh at this childish grasping at straws. A fear and resignation gripped him at the same time, and his thoughts were blocked by visual images of what his impending torture would be like.

"As an old friend I will give you an alternative, Walter," Dresser said. He did not hesitate. "I can have you shot now."

"The gift of a friend," Walter mused aloud. "Murder." He turned to Dresser. "Do I have a choice?"

"Do you believe you have?"

"Where?," Walter asked.

Dresser pointed to the stone wall next to the Bretthausen house.

"When?"

"Now."

Walter turned and walked slowly in that direction. Dresser waved his arm and two S.S. men followed after him to the wall. The stubs of dead roses, moldy and black, the vines thin and withered, stuck to the stone.

"This may go ill with me, you know, Walter," Dresser said. "I hope you know what I am doing for you."

Walter did not answer. The two S.S. men twisted a short piece of cord around his wrists, tied them behind his back.

"You understand, too, that it is my duty, Walter," Dresser said. "You are an enemy of our country and one way or another, to protect our country, you must die. I am truly sorry and wish there were another way."

Walter looked out into the sky, tried to put his thoughts on the moving patterns of the clouds in the sky, tried not to think of anything.

Walter heard Dresser's commands as the two Gestapo men, submachine guns in their hands, stood some ten feet in front of him.

"Ready."

He thought of Jeanine. He thought of Phillipa. And then he thought of Guido.

"Aim."

Who shall I think of first?, he thought. Phillipa, Jeanine or Guido? Jeanine, Guido or Phillipa? Guido, Phillipa or Jeanine? . . . Mama . . . Papa. . . .

"Fire."

He thought he heard a loud noise, felt a hot blackness overwhelm him, vaguely tried to suck in the air of the living world and then felt and thought and knew no more as all of his senses vanished into death.

Chapter XVIII

After a while, to those few who survived at Auschwitz, life and death, given or taken abruptly, became routine, dull, inescapable. Sadistic murderous frenzy became the commonplace, everyday, normal behavior of the everyday normal German and Polish citizens who worked at their duties in Auschwitz with the same efficiency and loyalty that they would give to their jobs in the bookkeeping office or in the butcher shop. Phillipa consciously fought to retain a continuing fear, a defensiveness that would make her constantly alert to any situation that might require whatever ingenuity she possessed to save her from the gas chamber. She dreaded the ever-present, ever-growing atmosphere that pushed upon her, as it did upon the others, a capitulation to resignation. It seemed as if nothing was important in Auschwitz. Nothing mattered until it happened to you, and even then the grotesqueness of what was happening made the event itself impossible of belief. Only when the needle was raised for an injection, only when guns pointed at you in the blood ditch, only when the doors of the gas chambers were slammed and bolted, only when one of the myriad of unspeakable horrors of torture to death actually began was there a realization of self and reality. For the fortunate few, the realization didn't happen even then, but pain and death came upon them as in an opiate dream.

Phillipa knew, more and more as each day passed, that her survival had continued past all bounds of reason in Auschwitz. Seventy-five per cent of all who entered were murdered shortly after their arrival. Virtually all the rest, assigned to special work details, to guinea pig roles in medical experiments, to servicing the physical needs, sexual and otherwise, of the camp personnel, were used up and discarded into death in a relatively short time. A few, here and there, by accident, by will, by bribery, by whatever means desperate men and women discover and have the opportunity to apply, continued to exist. Phillipa was one of these. How she remained alive she could not fully understand. A chance assignment to a work detail, a chance selection into a line of marchers that was not going to Birkenau, a chance meeting with a guard who for reasons known only to him gave her special protection and special privileges. But as the years passed she did continue to exist. She watched the development of the camp around her, the coming and going of personnel, the special pleasure and relief of the German soldiers who were assigned to Auschwitz instead of being sent to the eastern front, and the showing of their appreciation in their special zeal to forward their country's final solution to the problem of the Jews, Communists, Gypsies, Homosexuals, and assorted Catholic priests, Protestant ministers and other political non-conformists. She learned when not to be in a certain place where there was danger of being noticed, for being noticed was analogous to the invitation to destruction the fly on the wall invites when it permits itself to disturb the orderly nature of an otherwise efficiently clean vista. She learned when to be at a certain place where there might be an opportunity for an extra bit of ration or a few moments of peace and quiet under a sky, otherwise

clear except for the continual pall of smoke hanging heavy
from the chimneys of the Birkenau ovens. She learned about
the camp underground, the inmates who somehow managed
to virtually lose themselves in the morass of mechanized, efficient violence and who established by some means she could
not fathom a communication system and means whereby
messages, food and even weapons were sometimes smuggled
in from the outside. But in her self-protection she was careful
not to open herself to any friendship with anyone or overtly
to indicate any interest in anything other than her own self-
preservation, and her knowledge of the camp underground
was limited only to rumor, overheard snatches of conversation
and the vague feeling that even in the ashes of despair there
was human ferment and a desire to rise again to the status of
humanity.

There was occasional news from the outside world when a
new transport arrived. The legacy of those who were destined
for the gas chambers and furnaces was a hope-giving bit
of information to those who remained. America was in the
war, she learned. The Soviet Union had joined forces with
the west and was fighting Nazism. The news was not always
hopeful. Japan was beating the United States in the far east.
Germany had almost conquered Russia and was at the very
gates of Moscow. There also were small encouraging signs.
A threatened uprising in Poland. An underground rebellion
and the seizing of a railroad terminal in Hungary. A rebel
force in Yugoslavia. Partisan harassment in occupied France.
There were even rumors of salvation for the inmates: That
the United States might bomb the concentration camps, thus
giving those who survived the bombings a chance to escape
the furnaces; that the Pope in the Vatican might publicly
condemn the German mass murders of Jews and others and
by this religious pressure put an effective halt or at least a
slowdown to further concentration camp atrocities.

From the east came stories of one man who became a
symbol to the inmates. A "Mister K," as he was called, who
led a small band of guerillas near the Soviet-Polish border
and who struck in the daytime as well as at night, waylaying
small groups of Nazi soldiers on foot, in cars, along the roads,
in the fields, in dark alleys. The guerilla harassment forced
a turning of attention from the persecution and transporting of the few remaining non-Nazi civilians in the area. The
exploits of "Mister K" and his group became a symbol for
others in eastern Europe and gave the impetus for other small
clandestine anti-Nazi freedom forces. Fear of that which
could not be seen and, for many, not understood, became part
of the existence of the German occupying forces. Unexpected
death was something new to them and, being new, it was especially fearful. With each new story of "Mister K"s exploits
the inmates exulted, glorying in what was for each a bit of
personal revenge.

The German overseers of Auschwitz began to feel, too,
the incessant boredom of efficiency of the camp. For most the
initial excitement and thrill of ordering death and execut-
ing life gave way to the tedium of sameness. They sought for
ways to make their jobs more interesting. More often than
not they found them and exulted in their ingenuity. Phillipa
watched the creative German mind at work. In the summer
of 1943 she watched as one particular transport came in from
Poland. It was composed entirely of men. She watched them
as they came down the ramp, marched through the gates into
the long, low reception building. "The furnaces need more
fuel," she reflected. She watched the attempts of the men to
walk with strength, with pride. "Don't you know you are going to burn, you fools?," she muttered to herself. She saw the
transport again the next morning. They didn't burn. At one
corner of the camp was a gigantic cesspool into which all the
filth and scum and feces of the camp found its way. She was

with her work group on the way to the clothing mill when they passed it. The Germans had found a new way. She heard the cries of the men as they choked and stifled and clutched at the filth of a nation as they sunk to the bottom of the cesspool. The laughter of the S.S. men, guards, and civilian workers standing at the sides of the cesspool echoed after the cries. She turned her head as she continued to walk along the road and vomited.

In her own barracks the turnover was constant. Everyone was expendable. There were a hundred rules and regulations. The slightest violation was sufficient for an order to Birkenau. The young girl who did not understand the order of the S.S. man; the older woman who did not move quickly enough in fulfilling a command; the pretty girl who was envied by the female overseer; the lonely girl who was discovered writing poetry or reading from the torn sheets of a book that had been smuggled in; the girls who were caught smoking; the proud girls who refused the S.S. corporal.

Philippa remained. She was defensive, careful, anticipating. She did occasionally and surreptitiously talk with other inmates and found occasional pleasure in sharing memories and in the warmth of the common bond of past experience and future hope. But by and large she kept to herself. Aloof from what she considered the petty friendships and intrigues of barracks life, she did not put herself in a position that might cause her to commit any action that might be counter to the stated conformity or even sudden whims of the block administrators. After a while, as she watched many come and go and she remained, she began to feel a sense of superior accomplishment, a superiority of being able to live in a world of constant death. She even began to feel a slight sense of security. Her hair had grown back, she found the long-hidden remnants of her comb and at night, when she was sure no one was watching, she combed her hair with pride, feeling it

grow longer and thicker with each passing month. Indeed,
she had reason to feel secure. Winter had come and it was
now the beginning of 1944. Four years was a long time to
remain alive in a concentration camp.

Phillipa noticed that the transports from the east had
decreased in recent weeks, a good sign that the Russians
might be moving, might be pressing forward out of Russia
into Poland, closer and closer to Auschwitz. Stories of underground activity grew more frequent. "Mister K" was spoken
of constantly. One evening in early March a whisper flew
through the camp.

"Mister K is captured. Mister K is here!"

"Where? In Auschwitz?"

"Well, where is here, dummkopf?"

The center street of the camp separating the blocks
of Phillipa's section was lit that night. Rarely in the past
year had it been lighted after dark. Frequently, bombers
came close to the area and though the inmates prayed that
Auschwitz would be hit, the authorities made certain that
the camp was well blacked out. Although the rumors had it
that the Allied command said it couldn't bomb Auschwitz,
as Jewish organizations throughout the world had asked
it to do, on the grounds that the distance from its bases in
England was too far, factories just next to Auschwitz were
sometimes bombed. The inmates couldn't understand the
Allies reasoning.

This night the lights were on, shining a dull yellow
onto the cemetery-like silent wooden boxes that made up the
inmates quarters. The sound of marching feet came from the
direction of the railroad ramp, resounding like bullets against
the hollow-shelled barracks over the winter-hard ground.
Slivers of doors opened, cracks in walls were crowded, and
thousands of eyes poured out onto the barracks street.

A squad of German riflemen approached, stepping high, their knees reaching forward like the waddle of geese. In the midst of them, hands tied behind him, walking erect, was a man of perhaps fifty, not too tall, with broad shoulders, a bull neck, husky arms. His face was lean and tanned, his features sharp, as if they were standing out from the rest of him, searching for something. His hair was white, balding in the center. He did not look heroic, neither tall nor handsome in the manner of the fiction hero. But his bearing gave him a dignity that let all who saw know who he was.

"Mister K." The whisper passed from lip to ear.

Thousands of eyes staring and not a sound. A man walking in emptiness. Then suddenly, as if it had been planned, simultaneously from the darkness of every barracks a thousand voices rang out: "We shall avenge you, Mister K."

The soldiers stopped momentarily, turned their guns toward the barracks. No one moved. Not a face withdrew.

And then, from the midst of the soldiers surrounding him, a surprisingly soft and gentle voice filled the silence of the black night: "Live and fight. We shall yet win."

"Go on," the S.S. Captain ordered. "Schnell." They continued marching, the click, click of their boots echoing in the stillness again, as if the interruption, the voice of hope had been a hallucination, as if the soldiers were the center of the universe and nothing existed beyond the tips of their bayonets.

As they passed Phillipa's barracks, she squeezed to a place by the door and looked out. She saw the man's face as he marched by, clenched her fists and bit her lip to keep from gasping in surprise. She knew him from a world past. Richard Kazorin. From the university. One of Walter's friends. He had been a communist, she remembered. She had snubbed him, had disliked him, laughed at him, had no use for him. Now he was a symbol of whatever hope lay outside of the

barbed wire and she felt that she wanted to run out onto the
street and shake his hand and kiss him.

Once more the voices echoed, without emotion, "We
shall avenge you."

Phillipa saw Mister K smile. The marching passed and
faded into the distance. Silence encompassed the camp again.
Five minutes passed. Ten. Then, filling the earth and sky
and air, came the sound of a volley of shots. Only then did
the faces withdraw back into the barracks. Slowly, without
any visible emotion. But they all knew that a little bit more
of whatever life remained within them was outside in that
graveyard that was their world.

The weather began to thaw and the hard, snow packed
ground turned into sink-holes of endless, oozing mud. The
camp seemed to gird itself for a springtime of renewed activity, even as it was slowed down by the forces of nature's own
physical reawakening. The spring of 1944 came and on a
warm morning in early June a new transport arrived. Not
from the east this time, but from the west. One of the girls
in the barracks who worked near the gate heard the rumor.
Almost within seconds it hurtled through the entire camp,
speeding from person to person. "The Allies have invaded
the mainland. They're pushing the Germans back from the
coast of France." For the first time that they could remember,
people began to look at each other with a glimmer of positive anticipation. Phillipa could almost feel the smiling. But
not quite. Smiles were a thing of a remote and forgotten past,
part of something called pleasure and hope. This news was
not yet worthy of a smile. They had learned too often that the
reality of hope was much harder to come by than the rumored
whisper of it.

Several of the women from the new transport were assigned to Phillipa's barracks that night. She sat on the edge
of her bunk, watching them come in, watched the shadowed

distortion of their beings on the ground from the yellow flickering of the single light bulb high up on the ceiling. One of the new women, with a long thin, ageless face that chronologically might have been in the middle-twenties, was going from bed to bed. Phillipa kept her eyes on her. Always, whenever she saw a new young woman, a thin wisp of a girl, she was reminded of her first day at Auschwitz, of a time when she was incapable of believing the horrors that awaited, of the girl who walked alongside of her who just happened to be put into another line, a line she might have been in. She wondered if it would always be like that, always a reminder. "Always?," she asked herself. "What is always?"

She looked up to see one of the women in a nearby bunk pointing to her. The young woman she had been looking at came toward her.

"Are you Phillipa Kohn?" The young woman stood by her. Her voice was soft and low, but she spoke hurriedly, as if there were no time left in the world.

Phillipa felt a warning of fear. There was no sliding scale of values at Auschwitz. As long as one's routine, one's continuing conformity was allowed to remain untouched, there was safety. The moment security was disturbed in any way, one was not safe. Nothing that could happen could be for the good. Only a vacuum could avoid disorder.

"My name is Jeanine Hoffman," the young woman told her.

She understood Phillipa's hesitation. "I'm originally from Cologne. I have been in camps in the west. I arrived on the transport here today."

The name Cologne meant something to Phillipa. Many years past. Too long ago. She could not find a niche for it in her immediate consciousness. She looked at the girl blankly.

Jeanine waited a moment more. Then softly, gently: "Frau Walter Penmann?"

Phillipa jerked upright to her feet. She felt her face begin to flush. She wanted to do something with her body, to hide herself, to move about, to do anything but remain where she was.

"Sit down," she finally ordered the young woman.

Jeanine sat on the edge of the bunk. Phillipa stood for a moment more, still could not find controlled composure. Then she sat down next to Jeanine.

"What do you know about Walter Penmann?" Phillipa looked around carefully before she spoke. She didn't know why, except that caution had become habit and could never be overdone.

"You needn't be afraid of me," Jeanine whispered to her. "I was in the resistance."

This meant nothing to Phillipa. She questioned again: "What do you know about Walter Penmann?" Now her manner was careful, cold and demanding.

Jeanine became cautious. "Where did he teach?," she asked Phillipa. Now she was testing.

Phillipa did not want to play games. "Heidelberg University," she answered quickly.

"What did he teach?"

"Philosophy."

Jeanine stopped, satisfied. Phillipa waited for her to make the next approach.

"I knew Walter," Jeanine said softly. Her voice was almost muffled.

Phillipa caught her breath in her chest. She felt her muscles pinch her. This was her link with the past, with the real world and, perhaps, a link with the future. A slow, calm anticipation began to move through her. She leaned back and then caught herself with a sudden fear.

"Is he all right?"

Jeanine tried not to say it. "I'm sorry," she began slowly, to try to prepare Phillipa as best as possible. Then, quickly: "No, he isn't."

Phillipa pulled back as though she had been thrust at with a hot iron. "You don't know him. You never knew him. You lie."

"Four years ago you received packages from Walter postmarked Cologne." Jeanine hesitated. "They were sent to you when packages to camps were still permitted by mail."

Phillipa stared at the girl for a moment, then put her hands to her mouth. "Oh, my God," she said. "Oh, my God." And then, just as quickly, pulled her hands back, held them stiffened in her lap. She reached up, wiped a strand of hair from the side of her forehead, feeling at the same time for the corners of her eyes. They were dry.

"I didn't mean it to sound so pitiless," Jeanine apologized. The lines from her eyes to her nose, across her cheekbones to her mouth, tightened. "After so many years of fighting Nazism, I sometimes forget the niceties of sentimentalism."

"I don't need sentimentality," Phillipa said.

"Neither do the Nazis," Jeanine said sharply. Then, softly: "I think we all need it. Sentimentality is part of being human. I need it. I want it. I apologize only because I sometimes forget how to use it."

Phillipa would not argue. "Tell me about Walter," she said.

"Not long after you were taken away he went to Cologne," Jeanine said. "He tried to contact the underground to leave the country. I was with the underground. I met him. We were on the way out of the country. We stopped in Heidelberg to help some others escape. We were trapped there. He did not get away."

"Killed," Phillipa said, as if asking the question was superfluous.

"Yes."

Phillipa consciously made herself move closer to Jeanine so that nothing would be missed. She stared at the other woman. Inside she began to hurt. Not the knots of losing a loved one, but the hurt of a womb that was never filled. It ached empty.

"How did it happen?," Phillipa asked. "Tell me in detail. I want to know it all." There were no faltering tones. She was ready to take the truth and hold it, not let it step on her.

Jeanine tried to hold back her own feelings as she remembered the circumstances. She tried to make it sound matter-of-fact so that she would not inadvertently reveal her own relationship to Walter to add to Phillipa's concern.

"I'll tell you in detail, Phillipa," she said. Her tone was warm and friendly.

It had been a long time since Phillipa had been called by her first name, as one would speak to a friend. For four years it had been almost solely a means of communication. Now it sounded sincere. She wanted to like this woman. She tried to understand why. Perhaps it was a link with something that often intruded upon her thoughts, something that could have been? Perhaps it was a common bond, an imperceptible closeness of sharing between the two of them that could not be seen or told, but somehow was there to be felt?

Jeanine moved closer to Phillipa so that the sides of their bodies touched. Even as she talked, part of her thoughts stayed on an objective plane, looking at this woman whose dreams of a past life she was even then waking with her words, and whose strands of hope for a future life she was verbally bringing to a final and unwakable end. Jeanine finished her story.

"Walter pushed me aside and as he ran back and forth, distracting their attention, I managed to run across the street, down an alley and I got away. For a while. It was only later that I learned that after questioning him, they shot him right then and there."

She put her hand on Phillipa's arm, more to comfort herself. Phillipa reached up and for a brief moment their hands touched as if in common bereavement.

Phillipa wanted to cry for Walter now. This man whom she once accepted without love, but who now, with a better understanding of herself, with an understanding of others born out the misery of a concentration camp, she thought that she could have loved and perhaps, this very moment, did love. It was as if she were suddenly thrust, with the thoughts of Walter's death, into the humanity of life. That in some strange manner he had purged her of some kind of guilt and inhumanity. Perhaps she should cry, she thought once more. Perhaps she should allow herself this debility of the rest of the human race. Perhaps, for once in her life, there was something of importance that transcended her own self-protection, her own self-interest, her own defense of superiority to the needs and weaknesses of ordinary humans. She looked around and saw the others in the barracks watching her. They knew from their own experiences what the visit from the new girl meant. This was the way they found out about the life and death of their own families, if they hadn't already seen their loved ones torn from their own arms and beaten into destruction in front of their own eyes. And they knew that, in what the world had become, it was not possible that the newcomer brought news of anything but death.

Phillipa looked at the faces that watched her with the usual, resigned blank stares. "No tears," she told herself. "No crying. When one cries in Auschwitz, then one has weakened and is ready for death," She repeated to herself the maxim of those who were able to achieve the brutish stoicism, lack of sentimentality, and strength needed to remain alive in a concentration camp.

"Why," she asked herself, "when once, a lifetime ago, it did not matter if I cried, I did not want to and now, when I want to, it does matter?" She did not cry. Instead, she sat up straight. She ran her fingers through her hair, dug beneath her straw mattress and pulled out the remnants of her comb, pulled it through her hair, then just as quickly put the comb back, put her hands in her lap again, reflecting her usual stolidity. Whatever she felt was no longer on the outside; it was all buried inside. She turned to Jeanine, now only making conversation.

"What have you done these four years?"

"I ran. For a while, with forged papers, I worked in an airplane factory in Stuttgart. Then back to Cologne. But I had no place to hide. I found that my parents had both been killed in an air raid. The Gestapo found me out. Because I am not Jewish they did not send me to the gas chambers, but simply to a detention camp. To Dachau at first. Then to Buchenwald. Two years there. Now, with the Allies moving on the continent, they sent me here. For liquidation, I suppose. The final solution for everyone before the war is lost. The Germans will have achieved one of their goals, at any rate." She clipped her words with bitterness. "I used to think of myself as German. No more."

Phillipa began to ask about the war, the movements of the Allies. Jeanine interrupted her.

"I must say something more about Walter," she said. Phillipa looked at her, silent.

"I know what you are feeling," Jeanine continued. "But I want you to know that I feel something, too. I owe my life to him. He was a person to be proud of. He was a wonderful person. I hope you believe that."

"Why would I think otherwise?," Phillipa asked pointedly.

"I just want you to be assured of that," Jeanine said. "It is important that you know that." She hesitated. "Phillipa, Walter did love you." She stopped again as Phillipa's eyes met hers, questioning. "He spoke to me a great deal about you. I know much about you. I know about some of the difficult things. But he did love you."

Phillipa looked at her a long time in silence. Then, very softly: "Thank you."

"I'm sorry, Phillipa, for all the good things that might have been. For too many of us, it is too late."

Phillipa held out her hands, grasping those of this girl next to her. "Tell me, Jeanine," she said.

"What?"

"In so many things, why do so many people wait until it is too late?"

It was like a heavy music, the left hand of the pianist sounding a chord that played the same notes deeper and deeper and louder and louder until they broke the eardrums and went into the mind and the brain screamed "when is it going to stop, when is it going to stop?"

Gradually, the smell from Birkenau grew dimmer and the music slowed. The transports came in again and it grew fuller and went faster and faster and faster and the human being became a black key on the piano—pounded and pounded and pounded. Then one day the pounding stopped and for a moment the notes began to dance, freely, as once before, long, long ago.

In November, 1944, Hitler ordered the crematoria blown up. In January, 1945, Auschwitz was liberated by the Russian Army. The Russians marched through Hungary and Poland

and into Berlin, the Americans and British across the Rhine and into Czechoslovakia, and the war was over. The flames of Birkenau became only glowing coals, a dimming reminder of the tons and tons of ashes beneath. The people of the concentration camps were free. But the heaviness of the music remained and in its lament lay thirteen years of fascism and death.

"We live," Phillipa heard those around her say, "but we shall never be alive."

The captors had fled, the camp was open and its inmates, those pitiful emaciated, diseased, ill few who remained, moved through gates and into the freshness of a free air. Into an open, smokeless sky.

"Hallo." Phillipa and Jeanine passed a girl with smiling teeth, hand in hand with a boy whose head tilted upward, looking toward the sun. "We walk the high road and there is no furnace for our final step."

"Hallo." The woman stopped with the child in her arms and the man shifted the pack from one shoulder to another. "We travel the pock-marked fields and we are not buried under the rubble."

The ragged, barefoot, starving, sick skeletons of human bodies stepped with hope along the paths of salvation chocked with humanity throughout all of Europe. "We will reach the promised land," they said.

Chapter XIX

There was no joy for Phillipa on the day of her liberation. Only a numbness of relief. A relief that the constant fear, the continual expectation of sudden ugly death could now sink away, sink into a lethargy of nothingness. For indeed, what was there left that was vital to existence? There was no pleasure for Phillipa as she saw the S.S. men and the kapos and the civilian overseers and the guards rounded up by the Russian soldiers and herded now, as the people they had thus-used for so many years, into the blocks of barracks, prodded by bayonets, hit by clubs, thrown into fear by the men and women of the now conquering enemy, thrown into what was worse, the disorder of the scrambling self-protection for survival against their own guilt feelings that assured them that this enemy would now seek revenge in much the same manner that they had only a while before subjected the enemy. And knowing what they had done, the expectation was more than they could stand.

"They have not done enough to the Germans," Jeanine said to Phillipa the day after liberation. "They let them live. None should be let to live."

"And then the Russians would be hardly better than the Nazis," Phillipa answered.

"The Americans and British feed them, they house them. And ten years from now no one will remember what inhuman beasts the Germans are," Jeanine retorted. "The rest of the world will even be shaking hands with them, as they click their heels and bow and say 'I was not a Nazi,' and smile to themselves as they fool the world once more."

"I suppose I am too tired to be bitter," Phillipa said. "You have been in Auschwitz only a year. I just want to get away from here. I just want to forget, as if I ever could, that any of this even existed."

The remaining inmates roamed the camp. Some searched for possible traces of family and friends, others searched for remaining pieces of clothing from those who were murdered in the few days preceding the Russian arrival, so that they might start out with shoes on their feet and clothes on their bodies for the journey that would take them away from Auschwitz. Where they would go they didn't know. An endless journey to a nonexistent place. As long as it was away from Auschwitz.

A woman in their barracks said goodby. "I am going back to Latvia," she said. "I will go to my city, I will go to my house, even if it is no longer there, and I will sit in front of it day and night, and sometime, somehow, I know my husband and my son and my daughter will come back and find me there. I know it."

With a pack containing an extra pair of shoes she had found and an extra dress for warmth, the dress hardly cold from the dead body of its former owner, she trudged toward the main gate, to pass once more through the long, low building that divided the world of reality from the world of insanity.

"How many will go back to their homes and sit and wait?," Phillipa said to Jeanine. "Her husband and children came here with her. They've been dead for two years!"

Phillipa and Jeanine walked slowly through the camp, toward the furnaces dismantled by the Germans two months earlier, but the buildings and the gas chambers remained, clear evidence of what had been.

"Just some shoes and a warm coat," Jeanine said. "There is no food here. We'll find what we can on the way."

They passed a street lined with huge wooden boxes. A woman crouched close to one, its side open, ashes spilling from it onto the ground, across her feet. She sifted her hands through, lifting up palmfuls, letting the ashes trickle through her fingers, then frantically grabbing fistfuls, opening them close to her face and letting the ashes drop heavily down in front of her. "Henry, Henry," she kept repeating. "Is it you, Henry, is it you, Henry?"

Several woman sat on their haunches near the childrens' barracks, silent, still, staring. Just staring, their faces without expression, staring at the empty buildings.

A few men wandered through the women's block where Phillipa's barracks had been, calling women's names. There were no answers.

Auschwitz was an open camp. Most of the Nazis had gotten away. There was no trace of the Doctor. A shadow would appear from around a corner, wearing a uniform and black, shiny boots, and a survivor would freeze, then quiver and whisper "Mengele." But Mengele was gone.

Phillipa and Jeanine wandered through the disorder of the camp, the moving and running and confusion of thousands of people having no relationship to anyone else and wanting only to find their own individual salvation—or their revenge. The stench of rotting flesh from corpses piled into a series of small hills throughout the camp made it almost impossible to breathe. Open pits with half-burnt bodies were eveywhere. Former prisoners who would never again be free from the nightmares of their confinement crawled along the ground, too weak and ill to stand or walk, begging for food, looking for physical salvation that was nowhere to be seen. A young man, perhaps no more than twenty years old, lay on the ground, his arms outstretched, his eyes expressing gratitude to the Russian soldier who was giving him food and water and covering him with the soldier's own jacket. Summoning all of his strength as he looked up at the soldier and the sky, he brought dignity to his voice as he said, "Now I can die!"

Phillipa and Jeanine found blankets, some extra shoes, some pants and jackets that they could wear, string to tie their belongings into packs, and they started for the main gate. They passed a Russian soldier, his rifle butt pushing alternately against the heads of two S.S. men partly in uniform, apparently caught before they could change into civilian garments or, better yet, inmate uniforms that might find them freedom. They were less lucky than most of their compatriots.

"To the blood ditch," the Russian soldier commanded. He spat at their slowly moving backs. "To the blood ditch, where every captured Russian soldier was sent. You German filth. Every one of you will die. Every one I see will die."

Another Russian soldier came up. "You would behave like a German?," he said to his comrade.

"Like a human being," came the answer. "Like a human being who once had a family that these scum murdered."

"They burnt down my house in Moscow," the second soldier said.

"So you lost a house? You lost a relative? I lived in Kiev. Do you know what they did to the people of Kiev? To my wife? My little girl? My father? My mother? My brothers? Do you know what they did? When a dog becomes mad and begins to destroy human beings, then you must shoot him. These are mad dogs. They must be destroyed. I am a human being who must protect the rest of humanity from these mad dogs."

Phillipa and Jeanine walked on. A man dressed in the striped-pajama uniform of an inmate joined them, walked next to them for a few minutes. They paid no attention. The man stared at Phillipa as they came close to the gate. Russian soldiers were checking all those who wanted to leave.

"You remember me?," the man suddenly blurted to Phillipa. "The clothing factory. I was once a student at Heidelberg. I was nice to you at the clothing factory. You remember?" His voice was almost frantic with pleading.

Phillipa looked at him. "Yes, I remember," she said.

"You must let me go out with you. You must help me go out with you. Please. I was good to you."

Phillipa said nothing.

"I know what I did was wrong," he said. "I am willing to pay for what I did. But not with the Russians. They are monsters. The British, the Americans, they are civilized. They will understand that this was a war. Now that they have won, they will forgive and forget. Your husband, Professor Penmann, would understand that. The Russians will be vengeful. But the British and Americans, in a few years we shall be friends again. They will need us, you will see. Before the Russians become too strong. They will need us to keep the Russians in their place." His words came quickly, hurriedly, urgently. Before he could even think, they were out. Any words, any ideas that might lead to safety.

They were at the gate. The Russian guards asked Phillipa and Jeanine to roll up their left sleeves. They did so. Their concentration numbers were clearly tattooed on their arms.

"I came in on a recent shipment," the man with them protested. "There was no time to tattoo my number."

The Russian guard turned to Phillipa. "You know him? A friend of yours?"

Phillipa turned her head and with Jeanine walked out into the other world.

Skeletal bodies wearing striped pajama-uniforms pushed
bloodied footsteps across the far reaches of Europe. Phillipa
and Jeanine could not walk. They trudged. They pushed.
They were carried in the morass of bodies around them,
against them, a mass, a crowd, a mob filling the roads, the
streets, the fields, moving, crawling, oozing, like a giant
amoeba. They saw around them the men and women and
children in ragged clothes, torn shoes, barefoot, carrying
small sacks of the destitute personal relics of life, filling every
inch of ground that led from one part of Europe to another.

How far Phillipa and Jeanine went that first day they had
no idea. Slowly, inches at a time, stopping for long periods
as the amoeba shivered and slowed down and waited for its
forward part to slide ahead again.

For days they moved thusly. At the pace of the crowd.
And each day more and more people filled the space that now
bulged to capacity. People from concentration camps, slave
laborers, volunteer workers, prisoners of war. It seemed as if
all of Europe had been uprooted and now, in the days following the end of the war, were all at once seeking a return to
some part of the past that, no matter how bad at one time,
was now a cherished dream. For most, it would never be
found again. For many, for the Jews, they would find only
rubble or a home or business stolen by their German or Polish or other countries' neighbors. For some, they would find
only the death that they had eluded in the concentration
camps, murdered as they returned to their homes by their
own townspeople who continued to blame them for the war
and its destruction.

For some of the German soldiers and civilians who
sought their way back to their homes, it was a psychological
nightmare. The glory of triumph, of conquered cities, of gold
and silver and jewels, of human beings to be used as they
wished—all of the material and idealistic, moral and amoral

spoils of a decade had suddenly disappeared and the end of the war became a personal tragedy that was compounded by their sudden immersion into a world of fear for their personal safety. Many posed as slave laborers, as victims of Nazism, and joined the mass migration.

"We will go first to Munich," Phillipa said. "Perhaps my father's house is still standing? With the Nazis out of power, it will be mine again. And my father's business. That will belong to me now. I can sell them and start a new life. I can sell them and we shall have money to go on."

"Go on where?," Jeanine asked.

"I don't know. But I can't stay there. Not in Munich. Not in Heidelberg. Not in Germany. I don't know. I will see when I get to wherever it will be."

"I have relatives in France. Near Paris. An uncle and aunt. On my mother's side. Perhaps that is a place to be?"

"I have always loved Paris," Phillipa said. "Perhaps there is hope for life there. We'll see."

Through Poland and Czechoslovakia and into Germany they walked. With one stream of humanity going one way, passing another stream of humanity going another way. Old people dropped in the roads, died, were carried off to the sides of the roads into open fields and buried in shallow graves dug by hands clawing into the mud of the brown soil. Young people and children stopped, clawing at their stomachs, tearing at their heads. Dysentary and all the diseases that spring from no sanitation and weakened bodies and bare bits of food and no will to live scourged the lines of march. Soon dead bodies were simply left along the sides of the roads, joining the decaying cadavers of soldiers who had been killed in the final days of the war and whose bodies had not been removed and who were now lying naked, their bodies and belongings stripped by the displaced persons whose needs, as the living, was greater than the needs of the dead.

Even at night the movement continued. Rest was something taken when needed. Soon they began to see small settlements alongside the roads. Hovels dug into hillsides, shacks made out of the rubble of bombed buildings, tents tied together from blankets and torn clothing. These were the new homes of the displaced persons who had stopped to rest and found that they could no longer go on, who had no place to go to and no reason to go on.

Food was nowhere to be found. Each day individuals, families, friends would disappear from the line of march into a nearby town, some few returning to the march some hours later, some with the satisfaction of having found some nourishment, others hoping to continue another day without food, trusting that some would be found in some other city along the way.

Jeanine and Phillipa went to the towns frequently. First they stopped at the City Halls. In the Russian zones of occupation they found Red Army officers in charge. As often as not they would receive food.

"We do not have much," they would be told. "But whatever there is, you people will get it first before any of it goes to the fascists." The officers would point their hands at the town in front of them over which they were the chief occupying officials.

In the American zone in Germany things were somewhat different.

"But we have hardly any food for our own population," the Mayor would tell them.

"But your population has eaten for five years," they would answer. "We are from Auschwitz," and they would show their identification number tattoos.

"Judische schwein. Enemies of the State. You get out of my city before I have the police take care of you."

"Then we shall go to the American Military Government."

"Go," the Mayor would answer. "I have been Burgermeister here for eight years and I shall be for eight years more. The Americans are our friends. They know who can run Germany in an orderly, efficient manner."

At the Military Government offices the German secretaries who did the translating for the American officers in charge would tell them that there was no food, that the officer was not in, that they had better leave the town immediately before they were jailed as public nuisances. In one town the officer himself met with them. He was a young man in his mid-twenties. Phillipa spoke English with him.

"I wish I could do something for you," he said, "but we have no special orders to give food out to displaced persons roaming the countryside. My orders from General Patton are to distribute what food we have on a calorie basis to the Germans. Remember, they are not our enemies any longer, but defeated people, and we must act accordingly and feed them."

"But what about us, those who have been tortured and murdered for so many years by these defeated people who you are so solicitous about?"

"I have no orders for you. You don't fit into any special category. Maybe in a few months when General Eisenhower's headquarters get properly set up for administration, then we'll be able to do something for you."

"And in the meantime all the concentration camp victims that survived Hitler will starve to death?"

The young man looked at Phillipa, unhappy with her attitude. He looked at Jeanine, ran his eyes up and down her body, his consideration unmistakable.

"I think we might arrange something," the young officer said. "You," he nodded to Jeanine, "you can be my personal guest for lunch . . . in my apartment . . . and you will have some extra food to take back to your friend."

The first time it happened, Jeanine spat at the feet of the officer. "You say you are an American. You are a Nazi pig."

After that, when American Military Government officers made similar propositions, they simply turned, silently, and walked out.

In one town the American officer who met with them walked to his desk, withdrew some papers. "Here are some special ration cards. Not much, But enough to get you through a few days." He gave them some military government scrip. "Not much money, but enough to buy some food. I'm sorry I can't give you more. Fortunately for you, not too many displaced persons come directly to my office as you do or I would soon be out of food coupons. I don't know how they get food. If they do at all. You can use these at any Mathaus food distributing station. But don't tell them you're from Auschwitz," he warned. He mused, his tone bitter. "Some of our higher ranking officers have felt that it's all right to leave the same Nazi mayors and other officials right where they were. And Auschwitz makes these officials especially self-conscious and defensive."

Phillipa and Jeanine walked through Germany together, toward Munich. "It's easier when there are two of us," Jeanine said. They stopped in the towns and found torn sheets of old newspaper and padded the soles of their shoes. The hard cobbled stones, the mud, the gravelled dirt all ate through the thin ersatz leather easily and quickly.

The roads became more crowded the closer they got to cities. Frequently they were tumbled into a tangle of arms and legs and bodies into the ditches alongside the road as the blaring sounds of the horns of Army trucks and jeeps pushed slowly against the mass blocking the way, the soldiers frequently trying to push from the backs and sides and tops of their vehicles the people who were even more frantically trying to save precious energy for their journey by hitching even the shortest of rides. The infrequent civilian truck barely moved, even in a clear space, with every possible inch of space occupied by the clinging bodies and hands and fingers of displaced persons trying desperately not to fall off. Once Phillipa and Jeanine almost got a ride, climbed to the erect tail-gate of a truck, but were pulled off by two men who ran after the moving truck, reached up and grabbed their legs, hurled them heavily to the ground and leaped up to take their places.

Close to Munich, Phillipa began to see places she had known before. She took Jeanine into Landshut to show her a restaurant that she and Walter had sometimes driven to when he had come up from Heidelberg to see her and they wanted to get away from Munich for an evening. Some of the fear was gone as she walked through the streets, confidence coming with familiarity. As they approached the restaurant two German women stood in their way, blocking their path. They attempted to walk around them, were forced into the gutter. The German women stared at them as they continued past.

"Filthy Jew swine. Coming back to take over our sidewalks and streets. Pretty soon they'll try to take over our businesses and homes again. Der Fuhrer didn't do a good enough job!"

They passed the people at the lunch hour sitting in front of their shops, by the kitchen windows of their homes, munching their share of the rationed black bread and potatoes. They passed two soldiers, still dressed in their German Army uniforms, who stared at them in anger.

"We have no food," one of them said loudly, "and we have fought for our country."

"And they let these Jews and Communists come back to take the bread out of our mouths," said the other.

Phillipa and Jeanine left the town quickly, wondering how many of the Germans who saw them and watched the lines of displaced persons moving on the roads outside of their cities were wondering why they had let so many of their enemy live to pollute their countryside with debility, hunger, and sickness.

In Munich they found the large house still standing. The tall green hedge was now low and uneven. It was broken through in many places.

"The hedge doesn't give much protection against the outside," Jeanine observed.

"No, it doesn't," Phillipa agreed.

They went to the front door. It was open and they walked in, stood in the front hall. There was the feeling of safety to Phillipa, the sense of memory of security and independence, as she wanted it and willed it. Suddenly, unexpectedly, a man came from an inner room. It was her father's former business partner.

He was compassionate. He gave them some clean new clothes and shoes. After they had bathed and eaten, he gave them some money. It was as if he expected Phillipa to go now.

"I am sorry for what has happened," he said. "But, of course, it was no fault of mine," he told them regretfully. He smiled apologetically. "I cannot be responsible for what the government has done, can I?"

Phillipa had no strength or wish for recrimination. Not now.

"No, it was not your fault," she said. "But now I am back, and I shall not blame you. You took good care of the house and, I am sure, of the business. You shall get a good share for having done so when I sell them."

"The house? The business?," he said. He seemed not to understand.

"Now that I am back I will, of course, take the house and business back. Naturally, they belong to me, through my father."

"But my dear. The house and business were given to me by the government. It was all quite legal. I cannot just go ahead and break the law, can I?"

The Burgermeister, the Mayor of Munich, was equally sympathetic. "We regret the terrible things that have happened over these past years." He stood behind his desk, studying carefully the American flag that had displaced the Nazi swastika flag that had hung on the wall. "But the house and the business have been legally deeded to Herr Tesser. It would be impossible to take them from him without breaking the law."

"It was given to him by the Nazis. This woman is a victim of the Nazis," Jeanine angrily said. "Do you propose so blatantly to continue the Nazi policies."

"It is not I who makes such decisions," the Burgermeister answered curtly. "If you want the law changed, go see the American occupation commander, go see General Patton." He sat down at his desk and, not looking up at them again, busied himself with some papers.

"It will take time," the American colonel at the Munich Military Headquarters told them. "We cannot disobey the laws and change them just like that. Eventually, we will see that justice is done." Then, more quietly, confidentially to Phillipa: "But, after all, there is nothing for you people here anymore, anyway. Why create trouble? It's hard enough for us to get these people's cooperation without making them angry by taking away the property they acquired over these past years. Look, you'd be much happier going to Palestine or some place like that than staying here. Why don't you just plan to do that and let bygones be bygones!"

Phillipa and Jeanine stepped over the broken concrete in the Munich street below, waited for a jeep to pass carrying a young German blonde talking excitedly to her American lieutenant, and began walking toward the city limits.

In Heidelberg they found the little house with the flowers growing in the front lawn. But only the flowers remained, growing now through the scattered bricks and decaying wood that had been a home. Phillipa looked at it for a long time.

"I don't know why I am standing here," she said to Jeanine. "I have never been one to be sentimental." She walked around the rubble. "Here was the kitchen . . . here was the living room. . . ." She stopped. "These memories are only for the dead," she said aloud. She walked into the midst of the rubble and began poking about with her foot.

"Don't bother," Jeanine said. "The scavengers have already cleaned it out."

In the rubble Phillipa found a small book. She rubbed off the dirt and grime that covered it. At the top of one page was the title, "The Rights of Man," and underneath it the name "Thomas Paine." She leafed through it. At the side of one page was a pencilled notation, now just barely visible: "If one is not free, then none are free," and after it the initials "W.P."

Jeanine stood by while Phillipa stared at the book, then held it tightly. Phillipa looked up, came out of the rubble into the street.

"And now?," Jeanine asked.

"Now I suppose I am truly alone. There is no more. I don't know what I had hoped to find in Munich or here. But there is nothing."

"Nothing?"

"Ah," Phillipa said, almost forcing a smile. "I forgot that one cannot feel sorry for oneself and survive. Yes, I suppose there is something. Some memory of millions left behind. Some memory of one or two or three persons left behind." She thought for a moment. "Before we go on to Paris, Jeanine, one more thing. I thought, perhaps, I might not do this. But I feel I must. Take me to where Walter was killed."

Jeanine found the place. It was hard to recognize. Many of the houses were gone, bombed. The street was covered with bricks and plaster and concrete. The stone wall still remained. It held the only life in the street, bright red roses growing in profusion, covering every inch of space where a man might once have stood and died. They both looked at the wall for a long time.

"My eyes are wet," Jeanine said, finally, "but yours are not."

"No," Phillipa spoke softly. "It is too late to cry for the past. And when I could have, I didn't cry for the future." She took from a pocket the yellowed book she had found in the rubble.

"Are you going to leave it here?," Jeanine asked.

"Part of it." Phillipa tore the string that held the binding. With the heel of her shoe she dug a hole into the earth in front of the wall, placed part of the book there, covered it with dirt and packed it down.

"Half for him, half for me," she said. She put the remaining pages back into her pocket and turned slowly away. Then, her step brisk, her face looking up, almost bright with anticipation, she took Jeanine by the arm and turned her toward the railway station. "Now to Paris. We shall see what the future is like."

Part of the money they had gotten from her father's partner in Munich bought them railway tickets. In the railroad station in Stuttgart they stopped to change trains. Phillipa found a mirror in the ladies room and looked at the reflection. She was only 35, but the concentration camp had made its mark. The long black hair no longer shone when it was combed out; what had once reflected for her the brightness of life was now dulled. The long, sinewy hands were no longer soft. Years of manual work had left sharp, heavy lines and

rough, callused skin. The gently, sloping cheeks were no longer carefree; they showed the deep impressions of a lifetime of
feeling, the thin, hard creases from the edge of the nose to the
mouth, the wrinkles that come to the forehead in a perpetual
frown, the crossed pinpoints from the outer edges of the eyes
that a young woman worries about when she begins to age
before she feels ready for it. The well-rounded mouth had
become narrow and when the sun shone full overhead the
cheeks suddenly seemed hollow and thin.

She was conscious that, as she walked, her breasts shook
more heavily than she had known before; the firmness that had
lifted them high was no more and now they didn't carry themselves, but she carried them. She could see that her shoulders
tilted forward ever so slightly, carrying a burden that could
never be removed. The beauty was gone. But in the studied,
deliberate grace of what remained, Phillipa was still young.

So as she looked in the mirror, she saw more than what
appeared on the surface. The eyes that had once been dark
and sharp were now soft, not with the pity of resignation,
but with a hint of gentleness and understanding. She combed
her hair and straightened her clothes. She washed her face
and with a few pfennings bought some lipstick and powder
from a woman nearby who was loathe to give up these precious, hard to acquire cosmetics, but, perhaps in a moment
of assuaging guilt feelings, did so. Phillipa looked in the
mirror again. This time she forced her mouth to smile. And
then, without forcing them, her eyes began to smile, ever so
slightly. Her hair hung down almost to her shoulders, clasped
neatly behind her. She stood straight and erect and held her
head high. "It is a long time since Heidelberg," she said to
herself, "a very long time, but I still can be pretty." She was
pleased with herself and with the world when she walked out
into the waiting area and saw men, after so many years, turning to look at her again.

Chapter XX

In Paris, Phillipa found a reincarnation of the world. The summer, the sun, the rain, the air seemed to breathe a new life into every living thing, no matter how small or how poor. It was, to her, a disinterment of freedom, and by its very suddenness it seemed to blossom more luxuriously than it ever had before. It was not the unhindered, unending future of her Munich childhood, nor was it the self-determined present of Heidelberg. Although her life as a girl of fashion in Munich and as the wife of a leading intellectual in Heidelberg were pushed into the dream-like fantasy of a world that had physically disappeared from all existence for all eternity, the past was still with her, a constant part of her, a commitment that pervaded her entire being and did not permit her to throw off all memory and be born again with a completely clean slate.

But she did not grieve. She met those without families, without homes, without food, with any seeming hope for the future. For them, in the anesthesia of the present, any reincarnation was far off in the future, if ever. For her, the willing of strength that she had prided herself on all her life, the refusal to succumb to the debility of tears, the shunning of self pity that had enabled her to somehow survive the eternity of

Auschwitz pushed her forward into the life of today and the
expectation of tomorrow and prevented her from falling into
the abyss of yesterday. She made the future begin each day, in
every doorway, in every street, in every shop, with every step
on every avenue. She could assure herself, as she walked along
the quays and through the narrow streets and across the wide
boulevards and past the buildings and monuments and under
the trees and among the flowers, that the next morning, even
if the sun should not be there, Paris would be there and she
would be there.

Jeanine found her aunt and uncle. Her uncle had
a position as a cutter in a leather shop. Although their
subsistence was bare, it was sufficient. They lived in an old
four-story apartment building in the Montparnasse section
of Paris, a short metro ride for Phillipa from the magic of
any part of the life of the city. A storage room in the small
apartment was fitted with a double mattress and Phillipa stayed there with Jeanine. The money she had gotten
in Munich lasted some weeks. Then, unwilling to force
Jeanine's relatives into more sacrifice, she sought a job. Jobs
were not easy to get. The Paris economy, though not as badly disrupted as in many other places in Europe, was a shaky
one, and business and industry operated at an inflationary
level, with subsistence bolstered primarily by the funds
spent by the American military forces stationed in Paris and
in the surrounding areas.

Phillipa learned that the United States Army headquarters in Paris was seeking office personnel who could also serve
as interpreters. Phillipa went to one of the headquarters offices, in a fine, white stone building just two blocks off L'Etoile,
near the Arc de Triomphe. She arrived some twenty minutes
early and already as many as forty or fifty women were lined
up in front of the building. Almost automatically she got
in line and as she did so a fear and resignation overtook her,

filled her with the sense memory of the concentration camp, the dependence on conformity, lines, submission, order and efficiency. Almost trembling, she broke away from the line and walked back to the Arc de Triomphe. She stood under it, walked around it until she began to feel the morning freshness of Paris, the people hurrying to work, the housewives carrying the long, unwrapped loaves of bread under their arms to a last minute breakfast before sending their husbands off to work and their children off to school. The sun began to burn through a grey haze and patches of light splashed at her feet, onto her legs, and she stood fixed, waiting for the full brightness to flood her face. It felt warm and reassuring and she walked back to the Army building. The line had disappeared. It was half-past eight o'clock now, half an hour after the appointment time.

Unhurriedly, she walked in. Deliberately, she tried to recall the feeling of confidence of a Phillipa of years past, a self-possessed security. As she walked through the entrance hall, got the room number from the receptionist on duty, and walked up the two flights of stairs she felt self-assured and controlled. She wanted a position, but she would not compromise for it. They would have to ask her. On her terms. It gave her intense satisfaction to internally verbalize these thoughts.

She walked into a large room rung with benches placed along the four walls. The benches were almost full with women sitting, waiting. Phillipa stood and watched from the doorway. Within seconds an inner door opened and a name was called and a woman arose quickly and scampered into the inner office as another woman left it and walked past Phillipa toward the outer door. Phillipa sat down and waited.

"You have to fill out a card," the woman next to her said. She pointed to a desk in the center of the room.

Phillipa walked to it, found some application cards, took one back to her seat with her.

"The secretary's gone inside. You're probably too late," the woman next to her told her. "Maybe she'll come out and you can still apply?," she added.

"Thank you," Phillipa said. "I'll wait."

Within an hour the room was cleared, except for Phillipa. The last woman came out of the inner office and left. A moment later a woman dressed in an Army uniform came out. She stopped abruptly at seeing Phillipa.

"I'm sorry," she said. "We have all the applications we need today. You're too late."

"I have not come to apply for a position," Phillipa answered, "but to discuss it with your superior." Phillipa remained seated.

The WAC corporal hesitated. She smiled as if she understood. "I'll see if there is time for one more interview," she said. Before she could turn back to the office a man emerged, not too tall, but big, broad shouldered, a large head resting on thick shoulders, his ample uniform tight over a body that seemed to want to burst its restraints. His eyes appeared to twinkle with some secret joy and anticipation. His face was round and full, muscled jaws pulling skin that might otherwise have begun to turn to jowels, putting in their place lines of maturity. Phillipa judged that he was in his early forties.

He stopped on seeing Phillipa.

"I thought we were all through, Corporal?," he turned to the uniformed woman.

"This lady does not wish to apply for the job, Captain," the corporal answered. "She says she wants to . . . discuss it with you."

"Oh?" The captain's eyes narrowed. With deliberate gallantry he strode to Phillipa. "I am Captain Gordon," he said, extending his hand. Phillipa reached up, touched it lightly, as she might have greeted a colleague of Walter's at a reception in Heidelberg.

"Madame Penmann," she said.

The captain looked at the corporal, then back at Phillipa. "Will you wait here, Corporal," the captain said, "while Madame Penmann and I discuss the position." With an almost imperceptible bow of politeness, he motioned Phillipa to precede him to the inner office. He seated Phillipa in a chair in front of his desk, then pulled his chair around to face her.

"I gather you speak English well, Madame Penmann?"

"Yes. English, French and German. Also Italian and some Russian and Slavic. But before we go into that, we can save both your time and my time by determining whether this position interests me or not."

Even as she said this, Phillipa wondered whether she was pushing her self-sufficiency too far.

The captain looked at her for some seconds. "Yes, of course," he said, smiling broadly. Phillipa noted that the smile was genuine, that it was, indeed, almost a laugh, not one of derision, but one that found in her and in him and in that situation as in, perhaps, all situations, a joie de vivre. She liked that, for it was something she had missed for so long.

"Yes, let me explain it to you," the captain continued. "I can already see that your qualifications are more than most." He laughed, then quickly added: "I'm laughing not at you, but because I'm delighted to find a woman of independence and purpose in a world that seems to be filled with people looking for a handout of some sort or another."

Phillipa drew back inside. The insensitivity of the remark disturbed her. Yet, she could not be certain what it really meant to him.

"I can see that you're not simply looking for a job," he continued.

Phillipa felt that she understood how to deal with this man.

"No, you are incorrect. I am looking for a job. But, of course, the right kind of a job."

"Well, this is Special Services," the captain began. "The cultural division." He pronounced the word 'cultural' as if one or both of them might not be sure what it meant. "Culture for the troops here. Plays, music, books, art, and all the rest."

"You sound as though you are not too fond of . . . culture." She emphasized the last word.

"Oh, don't misunderstand," he laughed. "I am. It's just that I don't know too much about it. They assigned me to this division." He leaned forward, almost confidentially. "Frankly, I wish I were in the athletic division. Back home I was a Little All-American. That's football. Lafayette, 1925." He paused momentarily, felt he ought to explain further. "Lafayette College, in America," he added.

Phillipa smiled. "Yes, I know. In Easton, Pennsylvania. A very fine men's college."

The captain jumped up from his chair. "Hey, hey," he fairly shouted. "You know Lafayette." He sat down again. "How do you know Lafayette?" His pleasure was unconcealed.

"My husband was a university professor in Heidelberg," Phillipa answered quietly.

"Hey, what do you know about that! I was a college professor, too, before I joined the Army. I taught mathematics. For engineers. Should've been in the Engineers, but I guess because of my football background they put me in Special Services. I sat out most of the war in England. But the way the Army does things, they didn't even let me get near an athletic field. Information and Education Officer they called me, and now they put me in charge of arts and culture. Just like the Army." He stopped. "I'm sorry," he said, "rattling on like this."

Phillipa was smiling. She enjoyed his enthusaiasm, "No, please do not stop. This tells me much about what it is you do here."

"That's enough for the moment. Where is your husband now?"

"Dead."

"Oh," he paused. "Sorry." Then: "You don't sound French. You're not French, are you?"

She hesitated, but only a moment. "German."

"Was he in the German Army?" His eyes narrowed and his voice hardened. He shifted uncomfortably. Then: "Well, if you're in France and not in Germany, I imagine you must have been anti-Nazi."

"My husband was murdered by the Nazis," Phillipa said. "He was shot while working with the underground. Four years ago."

The captain sat back, half in sympathy, half in relief. He mumbled, "I'm sorry," trying to avoid the triteness of dutiful sympathy. "And you. What have you done since that time?"

"Since that time and before it I was in Auschwitz concentration camp. You have heard of it?" Phillipa thought she might attempt the smile of condescension reserved for those who fall into their own traps of embarrassment. But no smile came.

The captain blanched. "Oh, my God. I am sorry." He sat back for a moment. "You are all right now?"

Phillipa managed the deliberate smile of polite conversation. "Physically, yes. The more you meet those who have survived the Nazi final solution, the more you will know that nothing ever again will be, as you say, 'all right'."

"I didn't mean it that way."

"I'm not chastizing you," she said.

He moved closer to her now, leaning forward in his chair. "Madame Penmann," he said, "I need someone in this office to assist me in the job of bringing culture to the young men in the United States Army in this sector. I assume you know theatre, music, painting and the other arts?"

"The arts were my field of study in the university. They were an integral part of my life as a young woman in Munich and as the wife of the Chairman of the Department of Philosophy at Heidelberg University."

"Then I hope, Madame, you will consider accepting a position as my personal assistant in this office. The . . ."—he searched for the tight words—". . . prerogatives and responsibilities will include advising me on the selection of materials and the ordering and scheduling of such materials for the troops. There will also be"—he could not keep from breaking into a broad smile as he said it, anticipating the pleasure it would bring her to hear it—"the need to preview many of these materials, such as plays, concerts and art exhibits. Will you consider accepting the position?"

"It will be my pleasure," Phillipa said, standing and offering her hand. The captain held it tightly, with a firm grip. Phillipa responded with the handshake of one who was no longer just a first time acquaintance, but not yet a friend and colleague.

"When shall I return, Captain?," she asked.

"Captain Edgar Gordon," he quickly said. "At eight tomorrow morning." Then, almost before he was aware of it, added "Edgar Gordon."

"Phillipa Penmann," she said, concluding the handshake. "Until tomorrow morning." He nodded. She smiled and left the office.

The sun now shone brightly on the Champs Elysees and Phillipa walked the entire distance to the Place de Concorde, breathing in the freshness of life and the anticipation of the arts of Paris that were to come. For a brief moment she realized that they had not even discussed salary. What, indeed, did it really matter, except as something to provide a place to sleep and food to eat and—looming deliciously important again—the right clothes to buy and the correct makeup to wear?

It was a good job, paid well in terms of the French economy, and enabled Phillipa to spend her time in the areas of interest that meant most to her. She found Captain Gordon largely untutored in the values and potentials of the arts and she took pleasure in helping him learn what was considered good and what was mediocre. Her duties were manifold and broad. She procured films, arranged for USO entertainment visits, ordered books, scheduled visits to art exhibitions, museums, concerts, and plays, and planned special events and contacted those people in the arts whose services she desired. It was, in a way, remindful of Heidelberg, except that the social contacts were now professional ones and her judgments were not for herself alone, but for tens of thousands of young men whose lives would in some way be affected by what she decided. She was left more and more in charge of the organization and planning of events and it was not long before the administrative work of the office was hers. The captain signed the papers and issued the requisitions, but it was she who put into his hands and mouth the advice that resulted in the final decisions. The captain enjoyed the relationship. He enjoyed this woman who was so competent and strong and could do for him those things that he either could not do or did not wish to do himself.

Often, during the day, they talked—about university life, about France, about their work. Frequently, during the afternoons, she would take him to preview an art exhibition or watch a rehearsal of a concert she planned scheduling for the soldiers. And always he was like the youth who first finds the heat of enthusiasm for art that makes him stand through rain and snow and cold for two days and nights in front of the Metropolitan Opera House in New York City to be sure of getting standing room tickets for the opening program of the season.

"For a forty-two year old bachelor, fixed in his ways, I'm certainly learning a lot," he would laugh. His was indeed a

joie de vivre and Phillipa felt it and responded to it and soon
found herself laughing and enjoying the wonders of Paris as if
she were a youth again herself.

"When life is taken away," she told Jeanine one day, "how
much sweeter it seems to be when we unexpectedly get it
back. "

She had since moved from Jeanine's relatives' apartment and had gotten herself a small place not far from her
office in a small residence hotel off Rue St. George. She saw
Jeanine often. Jeanine had returned to school to study political science at the University of Paris and during Phillipa's
lunch hour they would meet and together walk in the parks,
through the Tuilleries, along the Champs Elysees. Sometimes Phillipa would take a taxi and meet Jeanine at a small
outdoor cafe along the left bank and extend her lunch time
into two hours. The captain never objected; in fact, he never
mentioned it. Phillipa's time was her own.

Almost always, when Phillipa and Jeanine met, their
conversation turned to Walter. Although this was their link
with the past, more and more they found nothing to say. Each
turned deep into her own thoughts of Walter Penmann, as if
he were two different men they had known. Sometimes they
even talked about Auschwitz and their year together there.
After a while they could talk about it on occasion as if they
had been merely spectators. Often they recalled their march
of many months from the camp to Paris. The harsh experiences were pushed into momentary forgetfulness and they found
moments of laughter about little incidents, forgotten at the
time, but now remembered as something of good humor
out of a morass of despair. Yet, each one felt inside that their
relationship was artificial. Phillipa respected Jeanine's interest
in politics and understood her fervor. But she could not bring
herself to accompany Jeanine to the political speeches and
meetings and rallies.

"The Americans and British and even the French are building up Germany again," Jeanine would insist. "To counter the Soviets. To counter communism. And this is exactly what they did fifteen years ago and look where it led us. It seems to me that only the Russians are making any effort to destroy the evil of Nazism for good."

Phillipa sympathized, but would not participate. "I know I ought to join you at some of these meetings and with some of these action groups," she said. "But somehow I cannot. Intellectually, I understand what you mean. But emotionally I am afraid. No, I don't think I am afraid. Just no longer involved. I just don't believe it can happen again. Here or anywhere. And certainly the Americans will prevent it. I'm sure of that."

"But it starts slowly, Phillipa. Remember Heidelberg. Not with the gas chambers and ovens, but with a simple loyalty oath and the firing of a professor. Once we have let it get that far, then we have opened the gate and there is no turning back. The extremists, the fascists, will have had their opening."

Phillipa had no answer. "I understand what you say. But somehow I cannot believe that it could ever happen again. Too many people have learned first hand what happened this time and no decent person in this world would allow it to happen again."

As she saw less and less of Jeanine, she began to feel more and more alone. At first not lonely, but as the link with the past began to be more and more broken, sometimes lonely. She had no interest in seeing men, in dating, in the romantic conceptions of a male-female relationship. Was there a man who could meet her requirements? Someone strong enough to respect and weak enough to control? After all, she told herself, she had no real need. And yet, as she thought of Walter now, she wondered whether things would actually be different if he were still alive, whether he and she were now different. She assured herself that she was finding sufficient stimulation in her present life, in the intellectual and aesthetic relationships with people through her job. And yet, as she watched her own face and figure bloom with the Paris springtime, adapting themselves to the freshness and beauty and life of her surroundings, she felt occasional periods of loneliness that overwhelmed her. She would not have felt like this ten years before, she told herself, and she wondered, without really understanding, why it was happening now. It was almost as if there had been forged an unbreakable link between her and the rest of mankind, a relationship that in all her life she had refused to acknowledge or permit to exist, but which now pulled her away from an isolation of complete self-dependence.

It was spring and Phillipa felt its warmth along the clean avenues and white buildings. She smiled back at April and she and Paris shared the secret of comfort and vitality at the same time. One afternoon she and Captain Gordon were walking through the Tuilleries after visiting a new exhibit at the Louvre. Always, he was open, almost blunt. There was no philosophizing, no weighing of words to determine whether they were the proper ones to be said. But this day he seemed meditative, almost shy. He pulled her by the hand, down onto a bench next to him.

"Look, Phillipa, something you probably know, but I want to say anyway." He stopped, stood up, "Oh, hell, I guess I won't say it."

"As you wish," Phillipa smiled.

He looked down at her, saw the condescension in her smile, and plopped himself down on the bench again with a roaring laugh.

"Phillipa, you think I'm some kind of overgrown child, don't you?" He stopped and laughed again. "Well, I suppose

I am. Look, I'll tell you this much, and you already know
it, so I'm really telling it to you so it gets said out loud. I'm
grateful to you for having come to my office that day. You've
shown a strength and ability that I thought no woman could
have." He paused. "I guess that's why I'm forty-two years old
and a bachelor." After another pause, his voice full and strong
with the energy of the life around him: "Do you know you've
been with me four months now and I've seen you only in the
afternoons. Now, certainly, with all those plays and concerts
at night we have reason for getting together for official business in the evening. But for some goddamned reason you've
been mighty official and prim and proper about all this, and I
don't like it. After all, this is Paris."

"Let me think about it," Phillipa said. "Come." She got
up and reached for his arm. "Time to get back to the office
and to work."

"Think about it, hell! Work, hell!" His face had the
broad smile of anticipation, as if something exciting was
about to happen and only he knew what. "Phillipa, if you're
going back to work now, you're going to have to run all the
way there to stop me from catching you."

He grabbed her arm and she tried to twist away and they
found themselves stepping off the walk and onto the grass.
He pulled her close to a tree.

"And if you don't go out with me tonight, it's because
you've got your door so barricaded that an All-American
football player can't break it down."

She began to walk toward the far sidewalk, past the trees.
He stopped her again.

"Don't think because I sometimes act like a big lug that
I can't see and feel beneath the surface. I know you're lonely.
And I know that you at least like me and enjoy my company.
And whatever it is that's keeping you tied up in your own
little world, let me tell you that you're too beautiful a woman

to hide yourself from the rest of mankind. And," pointing to himself, "especially this mankind."

He stood in front of her, holding her hands in his. "There's a new performance tonight. At the Grand Guignol. I've got tickets and I'm taking you home right now and I'll pick you up in just about two hours for cocktails and dinner before the theatre."

Phillipa was smiling now. Outside and inside. She was not offended. She was pleased. She was excited. His attention and insistence was not postured, not intellectualized. He behaved as if what he was doing was just the perfectly right and natural and proper thing to do. She wanted to say yes, to take his arm and let him take her home, and to bathe and dress and primp with an abandon and anticipation that she could hardly remember from before. And yet, could she allow herself to be taken over so completely, to let this man decide what she would do, when and how she would do it, at his will? Could she permit a situation to develop over which she had such little control? She started to say something.

He put his fingers to her lips. "Not one word," he said. He laughed, and pointed to the sidewalk at the other end of the gardens, past the bushes and trees. "I'll give you a sporting chance. If you really want to run away from me, go ahead. And if you really want to run fast enough for me not to catch you, well, just try!"

Phillipa wanted to say something to stop him. What was happeening was silly and childish. But it was also exhilarating. Before she could say anything, he was counting, "one, two, three, go." And without knowing what she was doing, or why she was doing it, she began to run among the trees. Not to the sidewalk, not quickly, not to get away, but, for some reason and in some manner she did not quite understand, just to run. She moved around a tree as he lunged at her, missed and fell onto the ground. She looked around the corner of the tree, stared at the foolishness of his sprawled figure. He looked up and laughed.

"Just for that . . .," he said, and with a leap was up and grabbed her hand as she started to dash away.

She struggled, not too hard, but enough to prevent him from holding her still.

"Come now, we must stop it," she said.

She looked around her, at the people watching, embarrassment crossing her face "All those people. What will they think?"

Strollers, approving smiles on their faces, had stopped to watch these two adults cavort like children.

"What do you care what they think?," the captain said between huffed breaths. "It's your garden and your trees, too."

Still not sure what she was doing, still hesitant, Phillipa stopped as if she were giving in. Then, with a laugh, she slipped her wrist from his hand and dashed away.

"If you really want that date," she said, making a bee-line for the sidewalk, "you'd better be an All-American football player again."

Without hesitation Captain Edgar Gordon rushed after her, his roaring bellow mixing with her laughter, laughter that she heard as from afar, not really believing that the giggles and high-pitched sounds of play could be coming from herself. Suddenly he was at her side. She tried to turn away, twisting against a tree, slipping as she did so, her back falling against the flat bark, the captain in front of her, catching her in his arms, then falling with her, their bodies close together, their faces almost touching, nestled against the wide tree trunk. His lips touched hers, not tentatively, not lightly, but fully and strongly, and he pressed his mouth tightly onto hers, his arms pulling her closer to him. Her mind filled with a momentary fear of abandonment, of losing herself, her

control. And then she felt her own mouth tightening around
his, her tongue searching, her teeth opening and biting into
his lip, and she didn't care about anything but what she was
feeling at that single moment of pleasure.

They remained like that, it seemed a long time and it
seemed an instant, and then, with arms about each other's waist,
they strolled slowly, silently, toward the walk. Phillipa released
herself, straightened her clothes, brushed her hair carefully back,
feeling to see that there were no loose wisps at the clasp. She felt
a trembling inside, as if she did not know what was happening
to her, as if the situation was leading her to an end that was not
of her own choosing or making. She stood erect, breathed in
deeply for a few moments and felt her composure returning. She
took the captain's arm and sat with him on a bench.

"Captain . . .," she began to say.

He interrupted her. "If you ever call me captain again,"
he said with mock seriousness, "I'll slug you."

She smiled. "Edgar sounds even more formal."

"My friends call me Eddie." He tried to be humorous
about it. "Since you're a special friend"—he emphasized the
word special—". . . more than a friend, you can at least call
me that."

She thought for a moment. She wanted to tell him that
she had never done anything like this before. She wanted
to say out loud, for the world to hear, that never before had
she lost control as she had then, had she behaved as—she
searched for the words, and she felt, even as she found them,
that somehow they were not the right words—an ordinary
woman. But to say this was to admit it. And as far as he was
concerned, everything that she did, anything that she did
must be because she had decided that was the thing to be
done. Even at that moment she told herself that she must not
let her emotions lead her again to any kind of similar lack of
self-control and command over a situation.

"Now," he said, "I'll take you home." He looked at his watch. "I'll pick you up at five. Cocktails, dinner and the good old Grand Guignol."

"It would be fine for us to go out tonight,"she said. "But if you don't mind, I do not feel up to drinking before dinner."

He looked a bit disappointed, quickly tried to hide it. "Well, sure. All right."

"I am going to take a nap to rest up for the evening," she said. "Will you call for me at seven o'clock?"

"Seven o'clock it is," he said. "Although I'll be miserable, having to be without the company of a pretty girl for another two hours."

They sat for a few moments more. She looked up, as if with a new thought.

"Do you know," she said, "that Maurice Chevalier is at the Club ABC tonight? I haven't seen Maurice Chevalier for more than ten years, since one of my first trips to Paris from Heidelberg." Then, after a pause: "Do you think it might be advisable for us to see the program? We probably could not get M'sieu Chavalier for a booking, but there might be other acts . . . ." She let her voice trail off with a deliberate smile.

With much pomp the captain stood up, reached for an envelope with two tickets in his inside pocket. He walked over to a couple on a bench nearby, handed the man the envelope. "Compliments of the United States Army. To the Grand Guignol. One of our special, extraordinary services to the French populace."

Phillipa saw the other man stand and shake hands with the captain and excitedly open the envelope and show the tickets to his female companion.

"Well, now there had better be tickets for the Club ABC tonight," the captain said as he returned to Phillipa. He took her hand and they began to walk to the Avenue. "Now, let's find a taxi," he said.

"Don't you think you might want to go first to the ABC and pick up good seats?," she said.

"Well, I thought I'd take you home first."

"I wouldn't think of putting you to that extra trouble," she insisted, "especially when you have to get the tickets and then go and freshen up and dress." She didn't let him protest. "Now, I insist." She pointed to a taxi. "You go now. I'll get the next one."

He leaned over, kissed her lightly on the cheek and ran for the taxi. She found another a minute later. On the way to her apartment, for the first time she didn't notice the sights and sounds of Paris but thought instead of what had happened that afternoon. She did not want to think of Walter, but she could not help it. This man was so unlike Walter. She refused to think about the words better and worse, although they crossed her mind. Different, she kept repeating to herself. He was open. Free. He had a joy of the world and was not afraid to use it and taste life, seemingly without inhibitions. The comparison confused her. For this was the kind of Walter that Jeanine always spoke of, the Walter that Jeanine seemed to have known. But then, Jeanine was so young. How could she judge what a person really is? She turned her thoughts back to the captain. He pleased her. The possibilities of their relationship pleased her. She must learn much more about him now. He was someone who, like her in a way, dominated the world. He was in some ways as strong as she. And she liked this. As she had seen that afternoom, he could dominate her. And as she also saw that afternoon, it was she who really made the final decisions. In the ultimate sense, she controlled him. And she liked this.

At first it was an occasional evening, then every evening, and then all day every Saturday and Sunday. Phillipa laughed and played as she never had before. At the opera, the night clubs, in Montmartre, the carnival in Pigalle, the

Follies, the weekend trips to the chateau country, the visits
to Fontainbleu, the rides and picnics in the Bois de Bologne,
the countless aperatifs at the outdoor cafes and the aimless
strolls on the Champs Elysees. The more she thought about
Heidelberg and Auschwitz, the more they became a part of
the past. Something she would not forget, but memories of
the past and not live symbols that intruded into the present.
She could still feel the sense of her life with Walter and now,
in retrospect, understand what was potentially fine and what
was lacking and, sometimes she would feel regret and sorrow.
But she could set them all aside and make her present for the
living and not for the dead. She found with Edgar Gordon a
continuous excitement of the present.

As she began to think of the future, too, she searched
into Edgar Gordon. The more she searched, the greater was
the contrast with Walter. Eddie Gordon was not intellectual,
not a thinker, not a man who could find deep meanings and
who sought his fullness in books and arts and philosophy. He
was a bright man, certainly a man with an excellent memory
and high capacity for details. He had been considered one of
the bright young mathematicians at his college and before he
entered the Armed Forces was becoming known for extending engineering mathematics into other scientific areas. They
talked occasionally, although it seemed to Phillipa that more
often they were too busy doing something to just sit and talk.

One day, as they were discussing his work as a university
professor, he mentioned some of the special contributions of
German scientist refugees to the United States. Albert Einstein's name was predominant.

"You know I am Jewish," Phillipa said. She didn't recall
it ever being mentioned between them before. She told
herself that she assumed he knew all the time and therefore,
unconsciously or deliberately, both had avoided mentioning
it. But now if he didn't know, it was time to tell him.

Eddie sat still for a moment, obviously taken aback by what seemed a non-sequiter.

"Perhaps I should say I was Jewish. I have no religious affiliation, as you know. But my mother and father were Jewish. And that was why I was in Auschwitz."

"That's a hell of a thing to bring up," he said.

"We were discussing Einstein. Jewish refugees in America."

"Well, I know," he responded. "But well, for Chrissakes, you don't think a person's religion matters to me, do you. Why, I've got some awfully good friends back in Pennsylvania who are Jewish." He cut himself short. He saw her mouth suddenly tighten and her body stiffen. He hurried to apologize.

"Now, what the hell, Phillipa! You know I didn't mean it that way. I suppose I couldn't tell you who among my friends was Jewish or not Jewish. Oh, I know the way it sounded. I guess when you're in the majority group you can't help but be condescending at times, even though not deliberately. I haven't been to church for so long myself, I wouldn't know a Unitarian service any more from an Episcopalian one."

Phillipa was quiet and reserved for the rest of that afternoon. She didn't mention it any more and Eddie never brought up the subject again.

In August he arranged for a week's leave to the Riviera. Phillipa took that week as a vacation, too, and they drove down to the little town of Menton, near the Italian border. He proposed to rent a small cottage for them both, one he had stayed at before, facing the sea, with a fenced back yard leading directly onto the sandy beach, perhaps fifty yards from the water.

"On condition that there are two bedrooms. Separate bedrooms," Phillipa insisted.

"Why, Madame," Eddie cried in mock horror. "Have I ever taken the least bit of liberty with your faith and trust in me?"

"No," she laughed. "But we have never stayed together in the same room. It's not quite proper."

"Not quite proper? Why it's positively indecent," he roared. "Why, they'd probably burn me at the stake for it in Pennsylvania. Or in some parts of Pennsylvania, anyway," he laughed. Then, more seriously: "We're adults. We can both handle ourselves. And we both know that you can handle me when you want to."

"I hope it's a nice cottage," she smiled.

They arrived late the first evening, driving all the way from Paris that same day, stopping for supper on the way. It was a small cottage with a parlor, a kitchen, and two small bedrooms next to each other with an adjoining door. Phillipa watched Eddie as he unloaded their things, carried them with boyish vigor into the cottage, and checked all the utilities.

She saw an openness of strength and purpose, a freshness, a youthfullness that began to express itself even more fully away from the formality of the Army hierarchy of which he was so much a part. She watched his every movement and made up her mind.

They went to bed shortly after they arrived. "Be sure to lock your door," Eddie told her as they prepared for bed. "You can't tell what kind of Mr. Hyde I am when I get out of this Army uniform."

"I expect you're as gentle as Dr. Jeckyll," she told him. "You haven't harmed me yet."

"I haven't done anything to you yet," he countered, "and 'harm' isn't the right word, but there's always a first time."

"I'll sleep without worry," she said.

She did not lock her door. She deliberately left it open a crack, enough so that Eddie, from his bed, could see her in hers. Shortly after they were in bed, she switched her light on.

"Anything the matter, honey?," Eddie called from the next room.

"I have a terrible pain in my shoulders," she said. "Must be from the long auto trip."

"Can I get you something?"

"Perhaps a massage?"

"One great big massage coming right up." He jumped out of bed, bounded to her room. He sat on the edge of her bed and began to knead her shoulders. Her nightgown was thin and loose, and she leaned back against him, letting the gown float gently down over her body and outline it against the soft light. She pushed her head toward his, her hair touching his cheek. He shifted around.

"I can't do a good massage job when there's so much other distraction," he said.

"Oh, well then, perhaps we should stop the massage?," she said unkindly.

"Hey, I was only kidding." He continued to massage her shoulders She turned her body again, her breasts moving to the side and toward his arms.

He leaned over and kissed her, first very hard, then more softly. She remained still. His hands moved from her neck and shoulders and moved down her arms, along her sides and onto her breasts. She did not move. Then his body moved onto the bed, and she could feel the heat from him, the trembling of his limbs. His hands tightened around her, and she pulled quickly away.

He sat up on the bed, like a child who had just had his favorite toy taken away and didn't know the reason why.

"I don't understand," he said in surprise.

"No? I did not ask you here to make love to me."

"I didn't say you did," he flustered. "But there you were, and there I was."

"Perhaps we had better go back to sleep."

"I'm sorry, Phillipa . . .," he began. Then, surprised that he allowed himself to be so deterred, he reached for her again, his hands grasping onto her arms, then to her breasts. She pulled back as if hurt.

"You clumsy fool," she shouted. "You have bruised me."

He stopped, sat back. "I'm sorry," he said. "I guess I've just done everything wrong." He started back to his bed. Then he stopped. "Will you forgive me, Phillipa, I didn't realize. . . ." He didn't know what to say.

She smiled to him, condescendingly. "We'll get our night's sleep now," she said, and watched him trudge back to his room, puzzlement and self-abashment mixed with frustration.

"Will you close the door?," she called.

"Yes, of course," and he hurried to do so.

They spent the next few days lying in the sand, swimming, tramping along the shore looking for shells and stones, and evenings walking along the flower-decked streets of the town or driving to Cannes or Nice or St. Tropaze for dinner. Edgar was uneasy these days and evenings and he was careful to make no attempt to embrace Phillipa. He belabored himself for what he considered a faux-pas that first night.

One late afternoon, the sun gradually beginning to slant off in the distance, the cool breeze from the sea beginning to filter through the hot mass of sunlight, they lay side by side on the sand, silently looking into the sky, watching the forming fragments of clouds, the edges breaking off, then trailing behind to disappear into puffs of grey smoke.

Several times that afternoon Eddie had suggested that they dress, to drive to Nice for dinner. But each time Phillipa decided that they should stay longer. She lay close to him and frequently turned and moved her body against his, sometimes putting her hand on his. He would turn to her, look at her with longing, turn back again. All at once she sat up.

"Well, it seems as though we have nothing more to do here," she said in a voice of disappointed boredom. "We may as well go to dinner."

"What do you mean nothing more? I've got a lot more we can do here," he laughed. But he was only half-serious.

"You don't act like it," she said. She remained sitting, not yet up.

He turned on his elbow, reached a hand out toward her. "Wait. Not yet," he said.

She lay back down as he propped himself up to look at her. "Not that you don't know it already, but the sand, the sky, the seas, everything just seems appropriate for me to tell you I love you." She didn't move, didn't respond. Then, more slowly, he repeated, "I love you." He bent over and kissed her full on the lips, bringing his body close to hers, then down onto hers. He waited a long time. Then, in a thin, soft voice: "Please?"

"Please what?"

"I don't want you to be hurt or angry, like the other night. I love you too much."

"Are you a child playing games? I thought you were a man who knew what he wanted."

"You play with me, don't you?," he said.

"We can always stop playing if you don't know how," she told him. She could see his breathing becoming stronger and an anger rising inside of him. She began to get up now, almost as if disdaining his company.

Suddenly he pulled her body to him, lifted her easily into his arms. She began to feel an excitement inside her, unexpectedly, a disorder, a churning, as though she were losing control. She tightened her muscles, relaxed them and felt control of herself again. He held her body up high as it were a doll, and he pressed his lips to hers hard, on the verge of crushing them.

"So we're to play games, are we!," he said.

She began to push her hands at him, to struggle and twist to get out of his arms. He laughed with pleasure at her squirming. She reached her hands toward his face, her fingernails toward him, then turned her fingers aside and instead pushed with closed fists against his shoulders, then with one open hand clenched onto his shoulder as if to twist it away. It would not budge. They were both silent as he carried her through the door of the cottage and to the bedroom. He stood her on the floor in front of him. She stood straight, looking at him Then without a word he pulled the bathing suit straps from her shoulders, slid the suit down over her breasts, to her waist and rolled it down across her hips to the floor. She breathed heavily, feeling she ought to fight, to run from him, and satisfied that she didn't. He removed his own trunks and reached for her again. Phillipa pulled away. She pushed and tore and scratched and tried to run to the next room. He caught her about the waist and lifted her into his arms.

"Yes, yes, yes," she told herself, silently, over and over.

"No, no, no," she cried loudly, over and over, pushing and tugging at his arms, trying to pull away from his chest, trying to get her feet to the floor. "No, no, no," she repeated, then she stopped. She felt her body lowered with great force, yet somehow gently, onto the bed. She twisted her arms across her breasts and pulled her legs and thighs close together. With one motion his hands reached for her wrists and pulled them apart, his knee pushing between hers, spreading her thighs apart, and she felt her body open, twisting up, arching toward his, and then she felt him inside of her, and a hot-cold flash shivered her entire being, and it pounded through her and she felt her arms go about his body and pull him closer to her and she dug her fingernails into him and lost herself in the unceasing strength of this man as he made love to her.

Chapter XXI

It was September, 1946. The heavy warm air over the city had begun to blow away and little puffs of fresh coolness moved from the Seine across the rooftops and through the steel-girded arms of the Eiffel Tower. Phillipa and Eddie were sitting on the balcony of the sleek stone terrace called the Trocadero, watching in the distance the elevator climb slowly up the body of the Eiffel Tower. Eddie had been quiet that entire morning in the office. He had been silent during lunch and now, as they sat there, he obviously was in deep thought. Suddenly, he took her hands, pulled himself in front of her.

"Do you know something," he asked? "Do you know that a forty-three year old bachelor is an oddity in America?"

"I expect a forty-three year old bachelor is an oddity any place," she answered.

"Well, in America and maybe in other places most men get married for the sake of getting married. You don't know what its like to have a mother keep saying, "Eddie, you're thirty years old, you're thirty-five years old, and its about time I had some grandchildren. Haven't you found a nice girl to settle down with yet?"

Phillipa laughed. "That happens in Munich, too."

"Well, one of two things happens. Either you succumb to the nagging and you marry the first half-way eligible girl you meet, or you get so angry that you don't marry at all. I like to think that it was because I never did find the right girl. And I got to thinking that I never would. Not one that was at the same time a woman and still strong enough and capable enough to handle me."

Phillipa said nothing.

"Honey, I'm leaving for the States in two weeks."

She pulled her hands away. Now she needed her own self-reliance again, her independence of everything and everyone.

"I'm sorry. And I'm glad." She looked at him with sincerity. "I know you want to get back to your career."

"My order came this morning. My time of service is almost up and I've got enough rotation points, so . . . ." He stopped. "So, look Phillipa, you know what I'm driving at. I want you to marry me. Just like that. Easy and simple. You know I love you."

He waited for her to say something. When nothing came, he continued. "I'll get back to my teaching job. It's not a fortune, but we can live pretty well on it. If we get married immediately, here, we can cut all the red tape and you can follow me over in just a few weeks."

Still no response from Phillipa.

He took her hands in his again. "Don't be afraid, darling, you know how I feel. I've got big, broad All-American shoulders." He started to laugh, thought better of it. "Tell me what you feel, honestly."

This was not unexpected, but even in the expectation, it was a surprise. "You're sure you want this?," she demanded.

"Yes."

"And you think you know enough about me? We are neither of us children. It will not be easy to adjust, for you or for me."

"I know that. And I know enough about you. If you mean what you were, I now have all the official records in the office if I want to look at them. If you mean who you are, I have known you for almost a year and I have known you in all the wonderful ways that people can know each other. And now I'm asking you to marry me."

"And I will be able to join you in America right away?"

"As soon as it can be arranged."

She smiled to him, even as he leaned over to kiss her.

"My answer is yes," she said. And then, after a moment, "but you must know this. I know I want to marry you, Eddie. I think I love you. But I cannot be sure. I may never be sure. You understand this?"

"Yes, I understand," he said, smiling. "You're thinking about the past. Think about the happiness in the future. Why think about the past?"

"I have put the past away from me," she said. "As much as I am able to. But I am afraid that for me the future will always be, in some measure, part of the past."

He tried to understand this. "I think I know what you mean, darling. And I accept that." He looked at her face. "Your eyes seem sad. Don't cry about the past."

In an instant her body became more erect and her eyes sparkled with brightness and confidence.

"No," she answered. "I thought you knew." She smiled now. "I never cry—about the past or the present or the future."

In a few months Phillipa found herself in the United States in a small house near a large university. The house was much like the one in Heidelberg: The flowered lawn, the stairs leading to the second floor bedrooms, the front parlor with shelves of books. Not quite so many books and quite different in content from those she remembered. But enough books to give her a pleasant remembrance of Heidelberg and not too many to be a rival. The town was fairly large, perhaps 100,000 people in the metropolitan area, but despite several industries it was the university which gave it its major pride and prestige. The streets surrounding the university buildings were filled with what to Phillipa were lovely, almost sumptuous homes, and it surprised her at first to learn that they were mostly owned by faculty members. Unlike Heidelberg, however, most of the students lived in modern dormitories on the campus without appearing to have lost their individuality in the mass living conditions to the extent that their individualities too frequently disappeared in mass class conditions of large lecture halls in the university.

The social organizations, she quickly learned, were primarily fraternities and sororities, very much like the discriminatory secret societies of the students at Heidelberg, with membership principally based on religion or economic status or ethnic background or social standing. The members lived in specially built houses on the campus or in large residential homes near the campus that had been converted for their use. A major difference, Phillipa soon noted, was that where the closed societies of the Heidelberg students had been largely oriented toward political and economic ideas and commitments and, sometimes, action, the closed societies of the American students seemed to be oriented essentially around a self-annointed snobbishness that expressed its primary goals through partying and drinking.

At first Phillipa wondered whether any American students were interested in the arts or politics. She began to see in the student newspaper and in the flyers and posters distributed by some student organizations that a minority was. It seemed to her that this minority was also physically distanced from the mainstream of the campus, living in great part in the town itself, in small apartments or in shared furnished houses. The business section of the town was much like that of Heidelberg, providing for all ordinary shopping needs. One thing that was the same amused her: The profusion of student beer parlors. Only in Heidelberg they were mainly for intellectual stimulation; here they seemed to be used for just the opposite purpose.

Eddie was busy with his work, finding his own adjustment to teaching and research after years away and catching up on new developments in his field that had only vaguely and infrequently reached him during his time as a Special Services officer. During the first year Phillipa spent much time alone in the house, especially in the mornings and afternoons when her husband was busy at the university. During those times she often thought about Walter and speculated how he would have fit into this new life, one that for her was not only new but at the same time a continuation of an old one. There was no recrimination in her thoughts because there was no hurt. A sometimes wistful rememberance of what might have been, but a rememberance that could be as full and complete or as empty and unfinished as she wished because she could do nothing now about Walter and about their relationship. It would only be a weakness, she told herself, to think of anything but the day to day moments of her present life that brought her the satisfaction and peace of security.

The evenings were busy ones. They went to many parties. Eddie was extremely popular among many groups at the university. Phillipa heard the term they used to describe her husband almost as soon as they had arrived: The life of the party. Not like Walter had been, not in an intellectual sense, but in a festive, friendly, humorous way. As Eddie's wife she was thrust into the laughing, drinking, back-patting center of every gatherring, and as a focal point of attention she found herself at first flattered and, after a while, enjoyably amused.

At the beginning of her second year there, in 1947, the Chairman of the Mathematics Department resigned to go to Washington to work on a special project for the government, something having to do with nuclear weapons. Eddie was appointed Chairman of the Department. Now Phillipa not only was the wife of the most popular person at many gatherings, but she assumed once again the role of hostess, as well. They moved to a larger home and soon receptions began to occupy much of her daytime planning and evening pleasures. It was a role she had not forgotten and it wasn't long before everyone in the university was talking about the parties at Eddie and Phillipa Gordon's. "Those Europeans," they would say about Phillipa, "they really have the savoir-faire for this kind of thing!" Her self-assurance as a hostess, her sophistication in decor, service, food and drink, her knowledge of the arts, her cultured behavior, her appearance of calm, commanding beauty brought her once again the personal admiration of her husband's colleagues and the envy of their wives.

She entertained not only people from the university, but visiting scholars, mathematicians and scientists who frequently came to lecture to students or meet with faculty in Eddie's department. There was a variety of talk and attitudes, much like that of the Heidelberg parties. Occasionally someone would begin a discussion of the responsibilities of the scientist in a world of potential self-annihilation and the philosophical implications of the ethical systems of thought and conduct that govern a scientist's actions. Like at Heidelberg, Phillipa would feel a sense of disturbance when attitudes became too antagonistic and political principles of action as well as thought became issues. A fear reminiscent of the past touched her whenever political involvement began to get close to her, and, as at Heidelberg, she moved herself away from such discussions. Unlike Heidelberg, however, it was somehow easier here because the political dichotomies

were not as sharp and, as she soon noted, the two major political divisions, the Democrats and Republicans, were so much
alike in all of their thinking that one could find safety in the
general uniformity and conformity that permeated American
political thinking.

As at Heidelberg, she found her greatest satisfaction in
discussions of the arts and culture and she took active part
whenever a member of the Art or Drama Departments offered
a lively analysis of the latest abstract trends in painting or of
recent Broadway openings. There was technical talk, as there
always had been when academicians gathered: Here the talk
was primarily of new techniques and procedures of math-
ematical or scientific experimentation. And there was another
kind of talk, talk which at first bored her, then amused her
and, finally, offered her, in its lack of conflict, a reinforcement of security: plantings in gardens, styles of the latest
automobiles, special achievements of certain lionized athletes,
complaints about administrative procedures at the university,
difficulties of finding domestic help, styles of clothes, food
prices—the everyday, personal undramatic material possessions and pleasures of their common community society.
These were areas of safety. These were areas that challenged
no authority, that threatened no security. More than once
she caught herself in the middle of a gathering standing in a
corner of a room, watching her guests standing, sitting, talking, munching, raising glasses to their lips with an almost
automated slowness as if they were existing in a suspension of
time and place, outside of the mainstream of the turmoil of
the rest of the world, and she felt an uneasy sense memory of
years past and an urge, almost a need, to push herself into an
activity of controversy, into a searching for and understanding of whatever forces in society were real and moving that
might in some way, some day, disturb this equilibrium, just
as her evasion of reality a decade before had been brought to

a violently abrupt end. For a fleeting moment she would feel
the experience of deja vu, that she had already been here once
and that some pattern was repeating itself, and because she
had done nothing that other time, that this time in oirder to
avoid the same continuance of circumstance, she must behave
differently.

But these moments did not last long. She had only to tell
herself that this was not the same, that she had a self-satisfaction of position and accomplishment in this university society
without the disturbances and concerns that marked even the
early years at Heidelberg. There was a freedom here, a lack of
concern, it seamed, for events of the outer world, and she had
already had enough anxiety in her lifetime. Eddie contributed
to the feeling of security. His primary interests outside of his
work were the successes and failures of the university's athletic
teams, the friendly get-togethers with friends, and a constant
brightness and good humor about almost anything and everything. He never brought home with him any of the myriad of
political and social and ethical problems that Walter, as she
thought of it now, had almost always been beset with.

She did read in the newspapers of events in other parts of
the world, but they seemed so far away from the untroubled,
pleasant, undisturbed life of this university town. She read of
the development of the Israeli state, of the fighting there, and
wondered how many of the people she had known in the concentration camp had reached that promised land. She read of
the confiscation of Palestinian homes and wondered whether
this was being done by the same people who had their homes
confiscated by the Nazis. She read of the execution of Nazi
war criminals and felt relieved inside. She wished there was
some way of telling this news to the hundreds of thousands of
faces that had passed her in Auschwitz on the way to Birkenau. She read of the acquittal of many Nazis, continuance of
others in the positions they had held under Hitler, bringing

to the United States German scientists who should be defendants in war crimes trials, and of the special efforts made to rebuild the German economy and power as a buffer to the states of Eastern Europe. And again she would feel a momentary troubling. Somehow, it was not so easy to push these matters from her consciousness as it had been fifteen years earlier. But she refused to let them disturb the tranquility of her new life and she thought about them only long enough to tell herself that her transient fears were all out of proportion to their significance. "After all," she assured herself, "this is the United States and here there is democracy and free speech that cannot be stifled. There will be no purges here, no political arrests or persecutions, no secret police, no government agents spying on ordinary citizens. People here can go about their daily lives, living their own beliefs, without fear. None of this can affect me again."

She confided her thoughts in letters to Jeanine. Partly because she felt that Jeanine, of all the persons she knew, would understand her internal need for peace and serenity after the events of the past, even though Jeanine herself had become more and more involved in active politics in France; partly because Jeanine was now the only link with the past and, through her, it sometimes seemed, there was an ethereal communication to Walter and to those to whom she might have conveyed her thoughts at another time; and partly because Jeanine was far enough away to tell things that she could not say to anyone near, for she could still not permit anyone to get close enough to share her deepest feelings and thoughts and, in that manner, see in such confidence a weakness of need that pulled her down to that other person's level. Yet, the very fact that she even wrote to Jeanine disturbed her. Why, indeed, she asked herself, did she need to tell anyone, even Jeanine, of her feelings? Always before she had no need of anyone.

"It is more than ten years late," she wrote to Jeanine one day, "but now I feel, at last, that the good life of peace and security has come. For so many years I have fought against any weakness. I have held back those inner feelings that might leave me emotionally weak, that might rob me of the strength and independence that one needs to emerge trium- phant in this world of constant battle for personal supremacy. For years I have separated myself from those thoughts, the philosophizing that leads to the tears of weak people. For years I have not permitted myself to be like the mass of self- pitying people we see everyday in every street in every city. I have fought to be above them, to survive when they could not. I can still do this. But in this country, in this new life, it seems I no longer truly have to. For I can live my life with nothing to fear. I once thought that what happened to other people was no concern of mine and, in Germany, that proved to be not entirely true. But here, in this place at least, it is true, and I can read the newspapers and set them down, and know that I am not and shall not be affected. For here each person is free. And even if I read of something happening to someone, I am not concerned because this is a democracy and justice will be done and whatever has happened cannot really affect me. Now, truly, I am free and independent. This is, indeed, the good life."

It remained the good life, as Phillipa saw it, for several years. Then, on a bright day in April in 1952, Edgar Gordon came home with some special news.

Chapter XXII

It was an early spring that year. The gardens in front of the art museum were multi-colored for the benefit of the arm in arm strollers rushing the warmth of the soon-to-be evenings of talk of love and acts of love. Inside the museum, sculpture by an instructor at the university was visited by few of the faculty and ignored, like most exhibits, by most of the students.

In the playground the children played with a baseball and bat, slid into concrete bases, forgot their bruises and concentrated on sliding heroicly into the next base. In the university stadium older children played baseball, more adriotly but no more seriously. A coach barked unsympathetically and a young man felt more dejected than if he had failed his major course. On the street corners older men spoke of the Dodgers and the Yankees as though their own futures were irredeemably dependent upon those of these business organizations hundreds or thousands of miles away. And, since this was a college town, they made brief, though not very energetic mention of the college baseball team. When they talked about college sports, it was of the new recruits for the college football team.

For most families Milton Berle and Sid Caesar were the week's most important events, arriving in living rooms on schedule through the small oblong boxes that were revered with a consistency stronger than love and which were variously called television, TV, teevee, or "the set." For some families there was a certain expectation in the announcement that a touring company of *South Pacific* would play in their city in early May. How could they know that there would be seats for only one-tenth of those who wanted to see it? For more families the new Bette Davis film at the downtown movie house was of more importance, and still others went for a second time to see what was laboriously billed as a comedy starring Martin and Lewis.

That weekend a symphony conductor from Cleveland, whose name escaped most people for the moment, was conducting Wagner in the university auditorium. Attendance was expected to be slight. The following week, announced on small placards, the university drama players would present *You Can't Take It With You.* Most people had seen the movie and attendance was expected to be slight here, too, except in the case of those students who had no money and a heavy date; there was no charge for students.

Down the street, in the little church founded by a famed evangelist, the rector prepared for the usual Sunday morning reverberation of inspired sermonizing. Across the street, in the racially segregated "University Restaurant," the town's Chamber of Commerce prepared for its weekly meeting promoting Americanism and business in the community.

In the university itself classes moved ahead as usual—painstakingly, some with boredom, some with excitement. The fraternities and sororities prepared for their year-end initiations and formal dances. The graduate students spent seemingly endless days and evenings in the library cramming for their comprehensive examinations. Freshmen badgered upper classmen for old term papers that they might use in their own courses.

Instructors discussed crowded classes and low pay. The university president made his semi-annual promise to the faculty that he would try to get raises commensurate with the rising cost of living; a few days later he made his semi-annual promise to the Board of Trustees that he would try to cut down some of the university's operating expenses, including the budget for faculty salaries, so that he could allocate more money to the recruiting of a first class football team.

It was an ordinary April in an ordinary university town. Little was ventured and not much gained. The city itself pursued its normal April pursuits, no different from dozens of other cities with a university in the center of it. The university was, however, by no means isolated in an ivory tower. Football, classes, and dating were not the only topics of discussion. Current events were important. Some Political Science classes were instructed to read the News in Review section of the Sunday *New York Times* each and every week. One instructor even gave Monday morning quizzes on this assignment. Prominent government and business heads often visited the campus for a lecture or a round-table discussion. At least once a year an enormously wealthy man was invited to give the graduating seniors advice to assist them in their forthcoming struggles in the world of action as opposed to the world of ideas. That was on graduation day when the wealthy man was given an honorary doctoral degree. He usually returned a second time, later that year, when he dedicated the cornerstone of a new industrial laboratory to be built with his generous donation and named after him. This year it was a chemical analysis building.

News events were touched on briefly or at length, depending upon the individual's interest and the particular course of study one happened to be taking. Broadway

plays, new books, the counter-revolution in a Southeast
Asian country, the election possibilities of the Labor Party
in England, the threatened war between Israel and the Arab
countries, the increased tension and increased talk between
the United States and the Soviet Union, the cry against the
United Nations throughout the country after the United
Nations did not act as expected on a United States resolution,
the hurried call by a national legislator for investigations in
the transportation industry after speculation that Russia had
exploded a bomb more powerful than any of ours and that a
man who had been a member of the Communist Party fifteen
years earlier had authoritatively revealed that hydrogen bomb
secrets had been smuggled to Russia through our transportation system.

There was some interest in the United States President's
talks to the public and some confusion concerning income
taxes, sales taxes, rising prices, civil defense, the anti-labor
Taft-Hartley Labor Act, the giving away of natural resources
to industry, and what Congress was doing about all of these
issues. There were even mutterings among some students
about racial discrimination in the university and in the town,
and vague suggestions of some pressures developing for civil
rights. It was, in fact, all in all, a very normal April in a normal university city.

In New York City, an anti-Semitic self-styled Nazi
organization grew in strength and held weekly street meetings, beating up any passers-by who disagreed with them or
looked, in their estimation, like Jews. Meanwhile, the F.B.I.
was occupied assisting a Senator Joe McCarthy of Wisconsin
obtain information on accused security risks. McCarthy's
strident voice and manner galvanized the radical right, which
supported his campaign of guilt by accusation. He cowed
politicians and the public alike. Even America's war hero,
General Dwight D. Eisenhower, running for president, caved

in to McCarthy's bidding and deleted a complimentary reference to another war hero, General George C. Marshall, in a campaign speech. Those who disagreed with McCarthy or his methods or did not subscribe to the national paranoia of a "red scare" had their loyalty questioned. Most people didn't seem to be concerned. It hadn't yet affected them.

In New York and California and Washington, Senators and Congressmen cross-examined clergymen, teachers and writers. Someone (whose name, of course, was withheld for security reasons) accused them of subversive actions (the nature of which was, of course, withheld for security reasons). Many people seemed to be interested in and enjoying the procedure. It was on television.

Among those who weren't particularly overjoyed were some members of the university faculty. They were upset because more and more educators were being called before the investigating committees. None of them was really worried, knowing that there was nothing in their classroom behavior that could be called subversive. Yet, as they watched their television sets, they noted that classroom teaching was not an issue, and many stayed awake nights searching their minds for any secret enemy who might inform the committee of some deed or statement or thought that would be attributed to them. As low as faculty salaries were, they did pay the mortgage and the rent.

This vexation had been on the minds of some for some time, several years, in fact, ever since a university in California had decreed that faculty members were no longer to be trusted, and prescribed a loyalty oath for all. Some faculty members refused to sign and were dismissed. They demanded that their loyalty be judged on classroom behavior and insisted that the First Amendment guaranteed freedom of speech and thought. But Senator McCarthy, unchallenged by the White House and almost all members of Congress,

had established his ideas as the norm and most were afraid to
contradict him. Most people didn't care one way or the other
about California, anyway. It was far away from them. And it
hadn't been on television.

A few teachers did care, for the moment and then for another moment, when teachers were fired from schools in New
York, from schools in Illinois, from schools in other parts of the
country. Most teachers publicly objected to communism in the
schools, but they were concerned that not one of the teachers
fired had been proven to be a member of the Communist Party.
However, the incidents were quickly forgotten. Why should
they become involved? Occasionally a petition on behalf of a
teacher or a school was circulated in various universities in the
country. But to most teachers California and New York and
even Illinois were miles and miles away, separated from them,
in many instances, by many state borders. How could what
happened there possibly affect them? They discussed the situation briefly at breakfast or at lunch tables and then hurried
the words out of their conversations. But somehow it became a
little bit more difficult to sleep peacefully at night.

Then, on that slow, warm April day, the miles between
California and New York were abruptly compressed. Phillipa had read about this and thought about it and it intruded
more and more upon a memory that she had increasingly put
behind her. She did not want to think about it and continued
to assure herself that it was a passing thing and would not
affect her. With the determination and strength of non-per-
sonal involvement that was her hallmark of life, she put the
thoughts from her mind.

Professor Edgar Gordon walked into the kitchen that
bright April afternoon with a half-smile, half-frown on his
face.

"Honey, I haven't had a day like this since my first day
of practice on the freshmen football squad," he complained

to her. "Calling us out of class in the middle of the morning and we've been at it all day since." He looked at his watch. "Three-thirty," he said. Phillipa waited for him to continue.

He walked to the stove, dipped a finger into a pot, withdrew it hurriedly and put it to his lips. "Hot, but good," he laughed.

Phillipa felt a tightening of her stomach, something that came from deep down and long ago.

Eddie sat on a kitchen chair, turning it backward and straddling it.

"The President called us to a special meeting this morning. With this communist scare and the investigations, the legislature and the Governor and the university administration got a little worried. So the university president got up a loyalty oath, distributed it at the meeting and asked us all to sign."

Phillipa felt the knot in her stomach beginning to grow and she sat down on a chair next to her husband.

"Some of the fellows refused to sign. They stood up and said they wouldn't sign. So the president fired them on the spot."

Phillipa got up, got a glass of water, drank it down, took another, couldn't finish it and returned to her chair, trying to gather within herself a deliberate calmness.

Eddie stood, took off his suit jacket, kicked off his shoes, reached over to the fruit bowl on the table and began to munch an apple.

"Well, all that was over by noon. But then some of the fellows called a special meeting. They hollered it out right there and then, just as the president was leaving." He laughed, then creased his brow with serious concern. "That was a scrimmage if there ever was one. There were really more than I imagined who opposed the loyalty oath. They asked the entire faculty to resign en masse if those who had been dismissed were not immediately reinstated and the oath withdrawn. First, of course, they tried to get the chairmen involved, because if we took a stand first it would be easier to draw in the rest of the faculty."

"What did you do?," Phillipa asked. Intellectually, she wanted to hear what she expected, but at the same time emotionally feared hearing it.

"Now, what do you think I did?" Eddie stood up and kissed her on the cheek. "I'm no communist. You know that." He paused a moment, understanding the implications of her question. "Of course, I don't like the idea of this arbitrary dismissal. There's no proof of anything against those who didn't sign. I signed in good conscience because I have nothing to hide. But some of those who didn't sign said they didn't because they feel this is an infringement on academic freedom. And, of course, they do have a point." He watched Phillipa's face, saw her lips tighten and lines of age creep from the edges of her mouth to her chin.

"I shouldn't have told you, Phillipa." He got up and gently stroked her hair. "I should have known how this might strike you. But, look, this is nothing like what happened in Heidelberg. This is simply a formality, a political device to get the legislature off the back of the university. You give them a sop and they're satisfied, and it'll all blow over soon. And anyway, the AAUP will make a case of it. Maybe they'll get these fellows their jobs back."

Phillipa remembered her father, how he had compromised just a little at a time, just a sop, until everything was gone.

"And you think this will not affect us, Eddie? Not at all?"

"How can it, honey? I'm clear. It'll never affect us."

"I want to believe that," Phillipa said. "I have been happy here. I must believe it."

"Well then, believe it. You're making a mountain out of a molehill. If some of those other fellows can't face up to the political realities of life and want to stand on principle at the wrong time, well, that's their decision." He waited a few moments, watching Phil1ipa's face, now deep in thought.

"Look, honey, I'm not some hard-hearted Nazi who has no sympathy for other people. And I'm not a stupid lout who doesn't see what might concern you here. But this is different. This isn't Hitler Germany. This business is just a small, temporary, political thing and won't have any real affect on hardly anyone at all."

"I can't help but think," Phillipa began very slowly, almost against her will, "that this was the way it started in Germany. Slowly, carefully, just a few at first. Just a loyalty oath. Just the communists. And then it began to spread until everyone with any non-conforming thought was suspect. It didn't happen all at once. The extremists, the fascists will take all the time they have to. What will happen ten years from now is dependent on what happens today. Hitler was elected by the people, representing a legal political party that got its foothold by just such fear and conformity. Could that happen here, Edgar?"

Eddie laughed. Then, gently: "No, it can't happen here." Then he frowned. "You know, that's what some of them said at the meeting. That this was only the beginning and if we open the door even a little it will only get worse, not better, that the more we try to appease them, the more restrictive they will become." He looked at Phil1ipa directly. "You really are concerned, aren't you?" Phillipa gave no response, but none was necessary.

"Maybe I ought to think about this a little more," Eddie thought aloud. "You know, if I do or say anything, we may as well give up the chairmanship and maybe teaching as well." He sat low in his chair now, trying to think, his eyes on hers, as if he were reaching out to her, without saying so, for support, one way or the other.

For a moment, as Phillipa looked at him, Edgar Gordon disappeared and Walter Penmann sat in the chair, his face dark and thin, his eyes hollow, asking her for help. She had not given it then. Would she be too late again? She tried to think. Perhaps it was true that to do anything would threaten their own security and would accomplish nothing. And yet to do nothing filled her with a fear that pulled her into a past that she could not seem to escape. She hesitated, started to speak, stopped, then finally knew what she had to say. But she was too late as the figure jumped out of the chair and it was Eddie again.

"Oh, hell, this is silly nonsense and I'm acting like a child who doesn't know his own mind. Your judgment means a lot to me, Phillipa, but this is one time when you're seeing ghosts and goblins where none exist. I'm a big enough and strong enough boy to know my own mind and know what to do in a case like this. You just sit back and lean on Eddie's big broad shoulders and he'll take care of everything just fine. We're just getting upset about nothing. Really, how can we judge what is right or wrong in what happened today. I'm a mathematician not . . . "—he was about to say "philosopher" and caught himself—" . . . not a statesman. When you get right down to it, we have got to realize that this is a democracy, and a damned good one, and if there is a threat to the security of our country, then that threat ought to be removed. And the F.B.I., the government authorities, the university administration know infinitely more about what the threat is and who the threateners are more than you or I do. If I can't trust their judgment, then who can I trust? We're just getting upset over nothing," he repeated. "This thing is just a passing thing to appease some politicians, and in the process maybe it is something necessary for the protection of our freedom. So maybe a few people will get hurt. No one has to. Everyone who has nothing to fear can sign. In a democracy it's the good of the whole that counts."

He slipped off his tie, unbuttoned his shirt collar. "You don't have to fear fascists here, honey," he said. "Conformity and fear and control of a political party by extremists can happen in Germany, but not here. And when you come right down to it," he laughed, "what's wrong with a little, good old-fashioned American patriotic conformity?"

He started toward the living room. "I'm going to get a drink." He stopped and turned. "Let's forget the whole business now, shall we, honey? Nothing to worry about. Certainly not for us." He called from the living room. "Some bourbon, Phillipa? Want some bourbon and soda? Phillipa? Phillipa?"

There was no answer. Phillipa ran up the stairs to the bedroom. She opened a drawer, rummaged in the back of it and pulled out the torn half of the little book by the American writer named Tom Paine. Knots continued to tighten inside of her and she put the book down. She hurriedly took her comb, combed out her hair, long and full now, and clasped it neatly at the back. She looked in the mirror, quickly rouged her cheeks, painted her mouth with lipstick. The knots refused to stop. She picked up the book again and looked at the faded pencil marks with the words, "when one is not free, then none are free," and the initials, "WP." She saw a man sitting in a living room in Heidelberg, a box-car filled with people, trucks full of ashes and charred bodies, a green hedge in Munich no longer invulnerable, and a stone wall covered with bright red roses.

She held the little book in her hands, went over to the bed, lay across it, the book pressed tightly against the knots in her stomach, and for the first time in her life she cried

Also by Robert Hilliard

Hollywood Speaks Out
Surviving the Americans
Media, Education and America's Counter-Culture Revolution
Writing for Television, Radio and New Media
The Federal Communications Commission
Television Station Operations and Management
Television and Adult Education
Radio Broadcasting
Television Broadcasting
Understanding Television
Blue Rock Land
Dirty Discourse (with Michael Keith)
The Quieted Voice (with Michael Keith)
The Broadcast Century and Beyond (with Michael Keith)
Waves of Rancor (with Michael Keith)
The Hidden Screen (with Michael Keith)
Global Broadcasting Systems (with Michael Keith)
Beyond Boundaries (with Melinda Robins)
Television and the Teacher (with Hyman Field)

Made in the USA
Lexington, KY
06 August 2010